SHARP FOCUS

The first Susie Jones investigation

DUNCAN ROBB

Dedicated to
the memory of my father
James Derek Robb
An Inspiration

Contents

PROLOGUE

Timisoara, Romania
September 2017

Consciousness returned slowly to Susie Jones, and she immediately craved the oblivion that had gone before. An intense pain throbbed in her temples and across her forehead. She squeezed her eyes shut to block it out, but the damage had been done. She blinked repeatedly, then lifted her head to take in her surroundings; her neck ached, her head felt like a lead weight and it took a supreme effort to keep her eyes open.

Darkness.

A sharp, stabbing sensation shot through her right shoulder, and she winced against it. Her legs hurt like hell. She didn't know why.

She squinted and struggled to make sense of what she could see.

A faint light spilled between the closed blades of a window blind, enough to identify the outline of desks, chairs and computer screens.

An office.

Her eyes adjusted to the gloom, and she turned her head slowly, her face screwed up against the throbbing in her head. The layout became clear as her focus returned. Her parched throat cried out for relief. She tried to swallow and lick her lips but realised with a sense of horror that something had been stuck across her mouth. It felt like tape and forced her to inhale through her nose.

A rank odour overpowered her senses. She could taste it and smell it. It reminded her of chlorine in the swimming pool, but sweeter. She felt nauseous. Her eyes watered and she blinked repeatedly to clear her vision.

She wanted more than anything to rip the tape from her mouth, but her hands had been pinned behind her back. She wriggled and pulled, twisted her hands, but a cable tie held fast and dug into her wrists. Her shoulders screamed in protest.

For a moment, panic gripped her. She wanted to gasp for air. Her breathing grew rapid as she struggled to get enough oxygen into her lungs. Her pulse raced. Her body shook, first her legs, then her arms. Beads of sweat ran down her forehead into her eyes.

An inner voice fought through the panic and forced her to take control. Long deep breaths, the voice said. It wasn't easy. She kept her eyes closed and concentrated on breathing. Little by little, she felt her heartbeat slow as her breathing relaxed.

She stared into the darkness and tried to make out shapes. She became aware of noises. She recognised the sound of computers in standby mode, fans or something. She listened, her head cocked to one side as though it would help. Another noise. At first she couldn't place it, a slow almost imperceptible inhalation, a pause, then exhalation, just as slow.

Another person.

Susie wanted to shout. She could only make an incoherent "mmmmm" noise. She couldn't even force her tongue between her lips.

The slow breathing continued, almost like snoring.

Susie turned in the direction of the noise. They had tied her to an office chair, raised to its maximum height. Her feet dangled a few inches above the ground, but she could reach one of the chair legs with her big toe and use it as a purchase to swivel round. As the chair turned, she noticed the pressure on her toe. It occurred to her that her shoes were missing. She had no memory of taking them off.

She saw more lights.

Green and red diodes, standby lights, blue charging lights, and a faint yellow glow that crept under the door from the adjacent room. She peered in the direction of the breathing noise and made out the shape of a figure slumped in another chair at the far side of the room.

Susie felt helpless. Chunks of memory slotted into place, piece by piece, a vision here, a sound there, a blurred, incoherent picture of the last few hours jumbled in her mind. She remembered talking to someone in a bar; she remembered a taxi; she remembered running after a van; she remembered a struggle. The last thing she remembered... that overpowering smell.

She struggled to think against the blinding headache.

Despite the pain, the fog lifted, and the memories began to mean something. The person in the bar, a woman, Nat something, Natalie, Natasha, Natalya. Yes, Natalya, that was her name. She was in trouble. She needed Susie's help. She had seen something bad.

Susie stared at the slumped figure. Was it Natalya? She couldn't tell.

Vague recollections, like pieces of a jigsaw puzzle, fell into place, a picture emerged, a little fuzzy at first, then sharper.

In the gloom, she made out a large packing box near the door. She recognised the logo. It explained where she was.

The conversation in the bar. The doctor, the illegal meds, the man Natalya lived in fear of. It came back to her in waves. With a sudden jolt, she thought of Nick, her husband. He was in trouble.

She had to get out of this place. She had to save Nick and get a warning to the doctor.

They had tried to stop her before, this time they were taking no chances. She'd discovered something she wasn't meant to.

So why had they left her tied up in an office at the factory? Why was she still alive? It made no sense.

She closed her eyes and shook her head. She forced herself to concentrate, evaluate, prioritise, think.

She peered around the room and began to formulate a plan.

Part One

Assignment

CHAPTER 1

THREE MONTHS EARLIER
June 2017
Newstead Press, Oxford

S usie chewed on the blunt end of a cheap biro as she typed. It hung like a forgotten cigarette from the side of her mouth and jiggled in small circles with the motion of her teeth. Her eyes, gimlet-like, focused on the monitor and followed the words as they marched across the screen. Her earbuds blotted out distractions as she replayed the notes she'd recorded. Her fingers rested at the end of a paragraph and she tapped the tablet to pause the playback.

She leant back, removed the earbuds and stretched for the ceiling. She glanced around the *Forensic Insight* office which buzzed with the urgency of a Tuesday morning. People hustled, phones trilled, keyboards clicked, conversations, greetings, chatter; the white noise of working life.

A persistent irritating icon at the bottom of the screen popped up every few seconds, determined to let her know she had mail. With equal determination she ignored it, as she had since she logged on an hour earlier. She knew what to expect and with a resigned groan, she relented.

Her shoulders slumped in sympathy with the groan.

Forty seven new messages.

Exasperated, Susie closed her eyes and shook her head.

Even with numerous filters, they still got through. Junk, spam, click bait, false promises and blatant scams. Whatever happened to GDPR and all the other regulations? Whatever happened to the promises of the email providers that this would all stop? She squinted at the screen through one half open eye in the hope that they might all disappear or that one or two of the message might be genuine. There might even be a message from someone she actually wanted to hear from.

'Chance would be a fine thing.'

'What?' The voice came from behind Susie's monitor.

'Nothing, just thinking out loud.'

'What's up?' the voice belonged to Harriet, who sat opposite Susie, their view of each other blocked by their respective monitors. She peered around her screen to check on Susie.

Susie tore her gaze away from the list of emails and met Harriet's concerned look. She nodded at her screen. 'Why do we still get all this...' She flapped her hand in search of a suitable expletive, '...this time-wasting shit.'

Harriet hadn't been at the magazine for as long as Susie and her email address hadn't been picked up by so many spiders. 'Your email is all over the place, you must get trolled and targeted all the time.'

Susie folded her arms and scowled at her screen. 'Tell me about it. How do they get away with it? Part of me doesn't want to open the mail and part of me wants a reply to messages I've sent.'

Harriet did her best to convey empathy, a nod and a considered expression, but she couldn't find the right words to respond.

'There must be people out there, vulnerable people, who fall for this shit. Some of these look genuine, banks, insurance, even HMRC. You don't have to be a genius to spot the fakes. I mean for gods sake, the typos, the bad grammar, basic spelling mistakes, dodgy or non-existent reply address' Susie continued her rant with the occasional glance at Harriet to ensure she still had an audience. Her ire directed at the list of emails as if they would wilt under the onslaught.

'Not much we can do though, is there?' Harriet shrugged.

Susie considered the remark. She studied Harriet for a moment, focused again on the emails then switched back to her captive audience. 'Maybe there is.'

Harriet cocked her head like an attentive labrador. 'Like what?'

Susie screwed up her face and peered over Harriet's shoulder at the glass walled cubicle in the corner of the open plan office. She could make out the mop of unkempt grey hair and the rounded shoulders of the editor hunched over his laptop. 'I might have an idea, if I can persuade Greg that it's got the makings of a story.'

'What? A story about spam email?'

Susie shook her head slowly. 'No. I've got a better idea. Wish me luck.' With that, she pushed her chair back, stood up and headed for the editor.

Gregor Robinson looked up from his screen at the sound of Susie's knock. The door stood open but Susie stood and waited to be asked in. 'Morning Susie, what's up?'

'Have you got a minute?'

'Sure, come in, sit down.' He indicated the low wood framed chair placed in front of his desk. The faded beige fabric had seen better days, the arms sagged outwards and one of the legs looked shorter than the other three.

'It's OK thanks.' At five feet four inches, Susie spent most of her time looking up at people. Apart from it's shabby condition and questionable stability, the chair would leave her looking up at Greg. She wanted to retain some measure of dignity even if Greg didn't play macho power games. She'd remain standing. 'I've got an idea for a story.'

Greg sat back, interested, hands clasped on his lap. 'Go on.'

'I want to do something about all the junk emails we receive.'

'Don't we all. It's...' He rolled his eyes heavenward.

Before he could say more, Susie interrupted. 'I want to trace the people behind them, make an example of them, bring them to the attention of the police.'

Greg recoiled. 'Whoa there. Before you get carried away. We're a cutting edge science magazine, we don't publish crusading exposes.'

'I get that, but what if I link it to emails that relate to the magazine.'

Greg shook his head, more in a lack of understanding than rejection of the idea. 'Not sure I follow, what's your plan?'

'I'll need to work it out, but I'm getting a load of messages promoting meds and other science related products.' Susie paused for a moment to collect her thoughts. 'Maybe some are genuine - I doubt it - but whoever's sending them out isn't just sticking two fingers up to the regs, they're pushing things that at best are unlicensed and could be potentially dangerous.'

'And how does that relate to us?'

Susie found her theme and pushed on. 'We're all about scientific development, new products, breakthroughs, research, that sort of thing. Right?'

Greg gave a single nod, his eyes narrowed. He said nothing.

'Well. People need to know about the fakes, the unlicensed, the unregulated, the dangerous.'

'I agree, but you know who the readers of *Forensic Insight* are? They're not consumers, they're not the ones falling for the stuff you're talking about.'

'You're right, but they are the ones with the production facilities, the raw materials, the knowledge, the budget and the marketing know-how.'

Greg conceded the point. 'Yeah, but what about the cowboys? What about the rogue operators? They don't care about licences and trademarks. They're off grid, they don't exist as far as the legit world is concerned. What's the point of going a rabbit hole to try and unmask them? They'll vanish into thin air and re-appear in another guise somewhere else. You'll have achieved nothing.'

Susie frowned and folded her arms tight across her chest. She let a few seconds pass before she replied.'Granted, there's some we can do nothing about, but I'm thinking specifically of the pharma stuff. They wouldn't be able to produce the meds unless they were part of a bigger operation, and that bigger operation will be regulated and be a member of at least one industry body.' She paused again to let Greg consider what she'd said, then added with a flourish. 'And they read *Forensic Insight*.'

A half smile played over Greg's face as he realised Susie had played a trump card. 'OK, OK.' He held his hands up in surrender. 'I'm not totally convinced but I can see where you're going.'

Susie wanted to return the smile. She suppressed the desire, fearing another "but" was on its way. She kept quiet and allowed Greg space to think.

Greg sat forward and tapped a key to wake his laptop. He studied the screen for a moment and spoke without looking up at Susie. 'How you getting on with that cyber security article?'

'Almost done, just a couple of loose ends to tie up.'

'Hmmmm.' Greg tugged on an earlobe while he scanned the production schedule he'd opened. 'I'm not saying yes, but come up with something a little more concrete by tomorrow. Give me an idea of time, costs, etcetera, you know the score. One side of A4, no more. I'll give you a decision then. But I want that cyber article before you do anything else.'

'Thanks boss, will do.' She turned to leave.

'Hang on, before you go.' Greg's attention returned to the production schedule. 'I've got you earmarked to research the latest graphene development.'

With her back to Greg, Susie winced at the mention of the next article she had been scheduled to start. She had a new toy and wanted to play with it. She half turned, tipped her head and looked at her editor from under her fringe.

Greg looked up and saw the reaction. He shook his head and made a shooing motion. 'Go on, I'll assign it to someone else if I like the look of your proposal.'

Susie did a mini fist pump out of Greg's sight and almost skipped out of his office.

CHAPTER 2

June 2017
Yarnton, Oxfordshire

Alone in the kitchen, with ZZ Top at full volume, Nick Cooper dipped a teaspoon into the bubbling contents of a saucepan, scooped some out, blew on it, sipped it and savoured the taste.

He didn't hear the back-door open or notice his wife had entered the room. He jumped in surprise as she gave him a playful dig in the ribs.

Susie stood just behind him and peered around to examine the source of the fabulous smell.

Nick reached over and turned the volume down. 'Hello love, didn't hear you come in.'

'There's a surprise. A herd of elephants could have stormed through the house and you wouldn't have noticed.' She struggled to remove the backpack that had become entangled with the sleeves of her cycling jacket. 'Sodding thing.' She shook her shoulders and tried to dislodge the straps.

Nick pulled the offending bag off her shoulders and almost dropped it as he took its full weight.

'What the hell have you got in here? It weighs a ton.'

'Just the usual; laptop, a few files, gym kit, you know.' She looked offended and took the bag from Nick. She changed the subject. 'Is that ready now? It smells great.'

'Whenever you are. It's veggie curry, it can simmer for a while. I was waiting for you before I put the rice on. You've got time for a shower.'

'Later.'

Nick checked his watch and realised the time. 'You're late back. Training?'

'Always. Only six weeks before the big one. Biked home the long way round.'

'I thought you went swimming this morning?'

'Yeah'

'And the gym in your lunch-break?'

'Yeah.'

'You don't think you might be overdoing it a bit?'

'Don't start. I need more miles on the bike. My running's good and swimming is okay, but I'm losing time on the bike.'

Nick squeezed his eyes shut and slowly shook his head. 'No one can accuse you of doing things by halves, love.'

'Damn right. I'm not in it to make up the numbers. Anyway, I wanted to clear my head after work.'

The remark piqued Nick's interest. 'Everything OK?'

'Yeah, I s'pose.' Susie peeled off her jacket, sat down and kicked off her shoes. 'I may have been impulsive, but I pitched an idea to Greg and he's asked me to put something together for him.' She glanced up at Nick with a mischievous grin.

Nick squinted at her bag in search of a clue. 'Come on then, tell me more.'

Susie clocked the direction of Nick's curiosity. 'I've not got much to show you, yet. I need to come up with something for him by tomorrow.'

Nick returned to the cooker and added rice to a pan of boiling water. He turned to look at Susie, one eyebrow raised. 'And?'

Susie removed the contents of her backpack and spread paperwork over the kitchen table. 'Junk email.' She spread her arms to emphasise her point. 'I got sick of all the spam and thought I could investigate where it comes from'

'Uhuh.' Nick left the curry and bent down to pick up the discarded shoes. With one hand he held them at arm's length, while theatrically holding his nose with the other. He took them out the back door and returned to the cooking without comment.

Susie appeared not have noticed Nick's actions and continued as though he'd never left the cooker. 'It's all dodgy, probably illegal and people must fall for this stuff all the time.' She gestured at the paperwork as if it would mean something.

Nick turned and took in the clutter on the table. 'I guess so, but d'you really think there's a story in it?'

'I bet there is. If I do a bit of digging. Could be interesting.'

'How you going to pitch it?'

'I'll do some research after we've eaten. Greg just wants one side of A4, so I need some facts and figures. I thought if I found something relevant to the mag I could focus on that and make an example of whoever is behind it.' She looked up at Nick and expected a reaction.

'You might upset someone.'

'I do hope so.'

Nick tipped his head back and gazed at the ceiling. 'One day you're going to get yourself into a situation...' He tailed off and lowered his gaze, a mixture of pride and disbelief on his face. He gave a resigned shake of the head.

Susie scoffed. 'Lighten up. Anyway, it'd be a shame to waste all that training.'

'Maybe. Just remember you're not Lance Corporal Jones any more, you don't have the army to back you up.' Nick changed the subject and attempted to make space on the kitchen table. 'Can I just shift this stuff for now?'

'Yeah okay, it could all come to nothing anyway, so there's no point in getting hung up about it now.'

'Great. Right now I just want to get food on the go. I'll give you a hand with it later if you want.'

Susie made a show of pouting and narrowed her eyes for a moment, then with a casual shrug, she loaded the paperwork back into her bag. 'Is it ready now? I'm famished.'

Nick wrinkled his nose in mock disgust. 'Are you staying in those sweaty clothes to eat?'

Susie sniffed the arm of her cycling shirt. 'It's OK; I showered after going to the gym.'

'You've just biked eight miles home.' Nick tried to be diplomatic 'And I know what you're like. You'd have been going for it, trying to set a new record'

'Don't be so anal. That curry will overpower anything.' She failed to make the remark sound like a compliment. 'I mean, it smells fantastic. How much longer?'

'Ten more minutes I reckon.' Nick gave the rice a stir. 'You've just got time to put this lot away and get cleaned up.'

Susie got the message and gathered the papers and files together and wandered out of the kitchen.

TWO YEARS EARLIER
April 2015
Brussels Exhibition Centre, Belgium

Sir Giles Lawrence decided he rather liked trade shows.

As he strolled up and down the aisles of the exhibition hall, he started to relish, if not bask in, the recognition. People knew who he was and they showed a certain deference that bolstered his ego. As an MEP and a member of the European Clinical Governance Council, his image appeared in the industry publications and the publicity for the event. He was expected to show his face, press the flesh, smile, shake hands and have his picture taken with exhibitors and delegates. He adopted an air of surprised modesty, though his natural hubris was never far from the surface.

It all served a purpose of some sort and, he kept telling himself, he might just possibly meet someone who could be useful to him in the future. Networking, he believed it was called. He preferred to think of it as opportunism.

'Can we have a selfie Sir Giles?' The question was asked as the phones were whipped out. He graciously agreed, adopting his best publicity face and feigning interest in whatever product they made or sold, or whatever service they provided.

He'd been at Europharm for two hours. He'd walked all the aisles and passed every stand at least once. He'd seen everything he was supposed to see and talked to a select few that had attracted his interest. He was due to be presented with an award by the Belgian Prime Minister;

it was the only reason he'd accepted the invitation to the event but he had another hour to kill before that was due to happen.

His meanderings lead him to the refreshment area in one corner of the exhibition hall. He must have passed it before, but it had somehow escaped his notice. Now he realised he needed sustenance and a chance to give his feet a rest. The place was busy, but the queue at the self service counter was short and it only took a minute to get what he wanted. He looked around for an empty seat and spotted a four-seater table with a sole occupant, a small man whose head was down as he nursed a cup of something. The man didn't look as if he was expecting company. Frank strode over and slid his tray onto the table with an look that said do you mind.

The man looked left and right as if to check there were no other seats available, then glanced up and gave Sir Giles the briefest of nods to indicate he had no objection, not that it would have made any difference either way.

Sir Giles lowered himself into the plastic chair with a groan and started to unwrap the blueberry muffin he'd been unable to resist. He caught the other man staring.

'I know,' he shrugged 'The spirit is willing but the flesh is weak.'

The man said nothing, he looked at the muffin, it was the size of a small cake, then up at Sir Giles as if unwilling to believe that such a refined gentleman would even consider such outrageous gluttony.

'They really shouldn't be allowed to tempt people with things like this.' Sir Giles spoke as he dissected the muffin with his fork and prodded the piece he'd cut off, ready for consumption. He addressed his remark to the man while he rotated the morsel in front of his face, weighing it up with eager anticipation. 'How can I stick to a diet when things like this are just sitting there, begging to be appreciated?'

The man looked at the MEP over the top of his glasses and shook his head slowly, either in disgust or pity, or awe.

'You'd think someone could come up with the equivalent of a nicotine patch for anyone wanting to lose weight, you know, something that could convince your body that you weren't hungry or that you'd had enough.' He looked at the man, expecting some sort of reaction.

The man said nothing, he continued to stare.

The lack of response bothered Sir Giles. 'I'm sorry, I'm assuming you speak English.'

'I do.' The man spoke at last.

'Ah, that's okay then.' Sir Giles popped the forkful into his mouth and closed his eyes in satisfaction. He followed the muffin with a sip of his coffee, then paused and appraised the man. 'You here as an exhibitor?' He wasn't that interested but thought he should make conversation.

The man considered the question for a moment before he replied. 'I am a visitor.'

Sir Giles nodded without making eye contact, his attention focused on the muffin as he cut off another piece. 'So, have you come across anyone making something that might help me?'

'No. I am afraid not.'

'Pity. You'd think with all the brains in this place, someone would create a magic diet pill for people with no willpower.' He chewed on another piece of muffin completely ignoring the hypocrisy of his statement. He gazed around at his fellow visitors. 'All these chemists and pharmacists, think of the money they'd make if they came up with a winner.' He stopped chewing and pursed his lips as the thought took shape in his mind. His gaze flited from person to person, wondering which one of them might have it in them to create something. Finally his attention came back to the man sitting opposite. He registered the white shirt and plain blue tie, nothing fancy but perfectly knotted. He took in the round frames of the glasses, dark grey metallic, expensive, with thin lenses. His suit jacket had a similar expensive look about it, a fine dark grey, almost black, material with a distinctly up market finish.

The man regarded Sir Giles with narrowed eyes, he appeared to be struggling with his conscience.

Sir Giles sensed the man's dilemma. 'Something on your mind?'

'Possibly.' The man spoke slowly, he considered his response. 'Something may already exist.'

Sir Giles sat forward, his interest piqued, the muffin forgotten. 'Tell me more, I'm all ears.'

The man focused on Sir Giles, his eyes drilled into him as if reading his thoughts. 'Something I've been working on.'

Sir Giles resisted the urge to respond immediately. He told himself to play it cool. 'Are you a pharmacist?' He asked, his voice muted. He glanced about, conscious that he didn't want to be overheard.

'I am a research chemist.' The man responded, his voice equally subdued, his tone expressed offence at the idea of being a mere pharmacist.

Sir Giles cocked his head, he picked up on the subtle inference of the reply and also the accent. 'German?'

'Austrian.' The immediate response made it clear his nationality meant a great deal to him.

'I see. I apologise.' Sir Giles didn't make a habit of saying sorry but felt this man had something to offer and it was worth cultivating a civil relationship. 'Would you like to tell me what this "something" is Mr...?

The man continued to lock eyes with Sir Giles. 'Schrader. Doctor Schrader.' He put particular emphasis on his title and let it sink in before he continued. 'And no, I would not like to to tell you more about anything, not here, not now.'

'Does that mean you would meet me privately?' Sir Giles suppressed an urge to be more forceful and made the question sound more like a conversational remark.

Schrader gave a barely perceptible nod and reached into his jacket. He pulled out a thin metal case from which he extracted a business card. He slid the card across the table to the man opposite. 'Call me with a time and place, but be quick, I leave the country in two days.'

Sir Giles picked up the card and read the details. 'Dr Manfred Schrader, Azllomed Pharmaceutical, Timisoara.' He looked up from the card at Schrader. 'Thank you Dr Schrader, I'll do that. Let me give you my card.' He started to move but Schrader held up a hand to stop him.

'Don't bother, I know who you are.'

Sir Giles recoiled, surprised. 'Really?'

'I make it my business to know people in this industry. I look forward to receiving your call.' With that, Schrader pushed his chair back, stood up and walked away without another word.

Sir Giles watched him go then turned his attention back to the business card. He studied it for a few seconds, deep in thought. His abandoned muffin caught his eye, he pondered it briefly then pushed it away. His mind scheming.

June 2017
Newstead Press, Oxford

Susie walked into the open-plan office a minute before eight thirty. Her skin still glowed from her bike ride. With the early sunrise of midsummer, Wednesday had become established for her early morning two-wheeled workout. If she made the effort, which she always did, she could arrive at the office in time for a shower and a rushed breakfast and still be at her desk on time, even if she hadn't cooled down completely.

She dropped her backpack onto her desk and flopped into her chair, just as Greg called from his office. 'I've been waiting, what have you got for me?'

She looked over to the cage and saw her editor beckoning. *No rest for the wicked*. 'Give me a second boss.' She dug out the contents of her bag and found what she needed.

Greg leant against the front edge of his desk as Susie's entered his office. 'Well?'

'Well,' Susie echoed, 'I spent a couple of hours last night and found a whole bunch of stuff about junk emails.' She held a single sheet of paper in her hand and she nodded at it, as though it answered all Greg's questions. Before he could say anything, she continued. 'I filtered out the fluff, and concentrated on any items with a scientific theme or subject.'

'And?'

'Then I searched for investigations into the perpetrators.' She paused and looked at Greg for some reaction. His thumbs hooked into his waistband and his attention rapt. He said nothing, but gave her a go-on signal with the index finger of one hand. 'As far as I can see, nobody has ever been exposed for sending out the sort of stuff I've been looking at. They may have been, but nothing's made the news.'

Greg nodded slowly, his lips compressed as he considered a response. 'Maybe that's because it's not considered a big enough deal to divert resources into.'

'That's possible, but there's been no incentive to investigate the source. Like you said yesterday, they just vanish and re-appear in another guise. It's not just a legal issue, it's a scientific one, a health related one and the people behind them have to have the right connections.'

'I get all that, but you'd still need to trace the senders and they hide behind layer after layer of obfuscation.'

'That's the biggest problem. I'll need a geek of some kind to help me. I can do the face-to-face stuff, but I'm not good at the cyber tech.'

Greg stood and walked around to his chair and sat down, his expression morphed from one of doubt to one of revelation, or possible revelation. 'I might have a solution to that little problem.'

Susie took a cautious step forward and placed her sheet of paper, her one page proposal, on the desk. 'I'm intrigued.'

'You know Mandy?'

'Mandy Peters, the new designer?'

'That's her. She told me her brother is one of the geeks at GCHQ, I don't know what he does, but those are the sort of guys you need.'

Susie brightened. 'Absolutely. Is it okay with you if I have a word with her?'

'Go ahead, the worst she can say is no.'

'So. Can I go ahead with this.' Susie waggled a finger at her proposal.

Greg leant forward, placed his elbows on the desk, clasped his hands and rested his chin in his knuckles. He glanced briefly at the proposal then stared up at Susie. 'I'll give a week to see what you can come up with. If it's got the makings of a story, we'll make a decision then. Sound fair?'

Susie beamed. 'Fair enough. Thanks Greg.' She felt she'd scored a minor victory and left the office.

CHAPTER 3

June 2017
Newstead Press, Oxford

A week after their last meeting, Susie tapped on the open glass door of Greg's office and walked in before she realised he had company. Lee Longmuir, the magazine's european editor, stood with his back against the side wall. He'd been hidden from her view behind a filing cabinet.

'Sorry, I didn't see you Lee, I'll come back later'

'It's okay, we're just having a quick catch up, come on in.' Greg beckoned her towards him, his eyes fixed on the buff coloured folder she held in one hand. 'You don't mind if Lee stays?'

'Of course not.' She paused, and waved the folder in one hand as if it revealed the mysteries of life. 'As requested.'

'Great, what've you got to show me.' Greg put down his pen and sat back in expectation.

Susie mopped her brow with the back of her hand in a mock display of effort. 'It's taken longer than I thought. So many dead ends and false trails.'

'I said it would n't be easy.' Greg nodded at the folder in Susie's hand. 'But, I'm guessing you've sniffed out a potential story?'

'Possibly,' Susie made a maybe - maybe not motion with her free hand. 'You were right about Will, Mandy's brother. He's been a great help. He's traced the source of some of the more interesting ones and got through various cloaking devices designed to prevent the likes of you and me from getting any further.'

'And?' Greg sat forward, his eyes wide.

'And I've focused in on three that could be of interest, including one in particular.' She opened the folder and pulled out three sheets of paper. 'All three have the potential to be of interest to us.' She placed the first one on Greg's desk. 'This one's promoting an app to measure your blood pressure.' She screwed up her nose to indicate her view on it. 'This one's trying to get people to sign up for some sort of wellness programme.' She gave Greg a sideways look and paused for effect.

'OK, OK, come on, you're saving the best till last. I can see you've dismissed these two.'

Susie smirked. 'I thought this one could be right up our street. It's promoting a weight loss drug and we've traced the source.' With a flourish, she placed the third piece of paper in front of Greg.

Greg held the paper in both hands and said nothing as he studied the message.

Susie remained silent while she waited for him to react.

'Hmmm.' Greg looked up and rubbed the underside of his chin with a crooked index finger. 'Thytomet. Never heard of it.'

'Nor has anyone else. I've done all the usual searches, but it's appeared out of the blue. No address, no manufacturer, no phone number, no email.'

'There's a website address. You've checked that out?' It was more of a statement than a question.

Susie nodded. 'Guess what? Loads of pretty pictures, glowing reviews and testimonials, links to social media, which don't go anywhere, and "buy now" buttons dotted all over it.'

'It all looks kosher.' Greg squinted at the message again. 'It's not what I had in mind, but you've got something here.' He turned his attention to Susie. 'When you say you've traced the source?'

The question hung in the air, and Susie squirmed. 'Well, not the actual sender, but the original message came from a bulk email delivery service, and we've traced that to a firm based in Slough.'

'You don't sound very confident.'

'I'm hopeful.'

'What does that mean?'

'I've tried contacting them to get the details of the sender, but they don't answer the phone or reply to emails.' She did her best to should positive, but a tone of frustration crept into her voice.

'Can Mandy's brother help?'

'Maybe. I'll have to get back to him. He's swamped with work and he's difficult to pin down, but I'll see if he can suggest a way to get them to respond.'

Greg sat back in his chair and folded his arms. 'Of course, they'll quote Data Protection all day long. There's no reason for them to give out the details of their customers.'

Susie gave a disheartened shrug and picked up the three sheets of paper from Greg's desk. She placed them back in the folder and gazed at the framed poster of an old James Bond movie hung on the wall behind Greg's desk . She remained silent for a moment, then the corner of her mouth turned up in a mischievous half smile. 'There might be a way. It could involve a little deviousness, but you said you'd back me up.'

Greg frowned. 'To a point. I didn't say I'd sanction any illegal activity.'

'Heaven forbid.' Susie's smile widened. 'I've got an idea. Slough's not that far away, I thought, if it's okay with you, I'd go there in person. They'd have to respond then.' Her eyebrows made an arch or expectation. 'If nothing comes of it, then no harm done. Leave it with me.'

Greg shook his head slowly and his eyes turned to the ceiling. 'Okay, okay, when?'

'Why hang around, I'll go tomorrow.'

'Just keep out of trouble and don't do anything that'll come back on the magazine.'

Susie winked. 'Absolutely.' She turned and left the cage on spring heels.

•●●●•

Gianfranco DeLuca tapped the speaker icon on his phone, placed it on his desk and waited for his call to be picked up.

After ten rings, a rough, accented voice answered. 'Yes.'

'It's Frank, where are you and Sergei?'

'McDonalds.'

'I mean, which town?'

'Swindon, we deliver boxes, like you said.'

'Right, listen carefully.' DeLuca checked the notes he'd made on a piece of paper. 'You need to get over to Slough tomorrow morning.'

'What for?'

'I need you to frighten someone.'

There was a momentary pause at the other end. 'How much frighten?'

'There's a journalist sticking her nose in where it's not welcome.'

'A woman?'

'Yes, rough her up a bit, make sure she's gets the message to drop it.'

'You want us break her legs?'

'Jesus Christ, no. Just scare the shit out of her.' DeLuca shook his head in exasperation. 'Take her phone, iPad, any paperwork she's got, take her purse as well, make it look like a mugging. She's going to an address in Slough in the morning, I've had a call to say she's planning to be there for eleven. I'll text you the details, just make sure you get there before she does.'

'Okay boss, we rob woman and scare shit out of her.'

'Right. And Decebal.'

'Yes boss.'

'You need to know what she looks like.'

'Yes boss.'

'I'll send a picture of her so you don't attack the wrong person.'

'Thanks boss.'

DeLuca tapped the screen to end the call then composed a text and attached the image grabbed from the *Forensic Insight* website.

He hit send and returned the phone to his pocket, satisfied he'd done what his paymaster required of him.

———————————— ••●•• ————————————

The following morning Nick left the house early; he had a job in Birmingham and went on his bike to get through the traffic quicker. Susie took their Golf and headed to the pool for a thirty-minute session before she set off for the address Will had given her. The drive to Slough took less time than she'd estimated. The email she'd sent them said she would arrive at 11.00.

They hadn't replied.

Susie rolled into the industrial estate with ten minutes to spare. She glanced at the satnav, then at the building it had directed her to. A two storey brick built office block that stretched fifty yards either side of an entrance lobby. No doubt home to many small businesses. The name Churnet House stood out in two foot high capital letters.

She parked in the visitors car park and stepped up to the door, tried it and found it locked. A number pad built into the wall caught her eye and she keyed in 44 and pressed the call button. A speaker under the buttons emitted a buzzing noise, and Susie waited. After half a minute with no response, she pressed the keys again, this time a little harder, as if it would make more noise. After another minute of silence, she spotted a CCTV camera pointed at her. She stared back at the camera and her impatience got the better of her. She leant on the call button, held it down and continued to stare defiantly at the camera.

After twenty seconds, the speaker crackled. Susie released the button and a disembodied voice spoke.

'Yes.'

'My name's Peters, I'm from GCHQ. Open the door, please?' Will had told Susie to use his name.

'What do you want?'

'I'll explain when I come up if you'd open the door.' Susie knew she would have to act with confidence, and she glared at the camera.

The sound of muted whispers, then, 'There's no-one here to see you at the moment. You'll have to come back this afternoon.'

'That isn't possible, you have to let me in now. This is official Government business.'

There was a moment's silence; it could go either way; then she heard the click as the door release activated.

•••••

Traffic in all three lanes of the Southbound M40 slowed and then ground to a halt. Decebal thumped the steering wheel with his fists and cursed as he looked ahead at the solid mass of vehicles. He sat in the outside lane and found himself trapped. He'd been on track to get to Slough well before eleven, this was the last thing he needed. He assumed it must be an accident as he had passed no signs for roadworks ahead.

He could see the motorway half a mile into the distance, nothing moved. He waited another minute and noticed drivers had opened their doors and got out of their cars. He switched the engine off and cursed again, knowing he'd have to call DeLuca.

'You there already?'

'No boss, stuck on motorway, can't move.'

'What you've broken down?'

'No, accident ahead, no cars moving.'

'Shit!' DeLuca swore, then asked. 'Where are you now?'

Decebal peered at the screen on his satnav. 'Says 36 miles to go.'

'Shit.' DeLuca repeated. 'I knew I should have sent you on the back roads.'

'Yes boss.' Decebal replied, unsure whether to agree or not.

'OK. Listen carefully.' DeLuca paused for a moment while he assessed the situation. 'Forget Slough, go straight to Reading. I know what she's after. I'll text you the address. Get there before she does and wait for her. Got that?'

'Yes boss.' Decebal clicked the phone off as a police car sped past on the hard shoulder.

•••••

Susie went through into the unmanned reception area and took the lift to the second floor. The door opened directly into an open-plan office with windows on three sides. She looked around for a moment, convinced that whoever she'd just spoken to had left via the staircase while she had ascended in the lift. There was no-one in the office.

'Hello!' she called out 'Where are you?'

From behind a low screen between two workstations came the voice that had answered the intercom. 'Here' The voice belonged to a youth in his early twenties. He had long dark hair that flopped forward and obscured half his face. His attempt to grow a beard had produced downy hair that partially hid his pale pock-marked face. He slumped down in his chair, almost hidden behind two monitors, and didn't try to get up or even make eye contact with Susie.

Susie couldn't disguise her contempt and continued with the official act, which she secretly enjoyed. 'Are you the only one here?' She'd heard whispers from the intercom and felt sure there must be at least one more person in the room. She looked around, convinced someone else would appear and her cover story would be torn to shreds.

The youth lifted his head and glanced at Susie 'Yeah, whaddya want?'

'I'm from GCHQ and I need some information.' She reached into the folder she carried and produced a piece of paper. 'I need the name and address of the account holders for these IP numbers. We've identified them as being registered with this company.'

'I'll need some ID.'

Susie had expected the request and had mocked up a card with official looking insignia and her picture, stuffed into a worn-out case that made it almost impossible to read. She passed it over, along with the email from Will that she'd printed.

The youth read the email and held up the card for examination. He made eye contact with Susie and compared the picture to the person who stood in front of him. His face twisted in a look of resignation. He tried another line of defence. 'We're not allowed to give out that information. Data Protection.'

Susie looked around the office. She felt vulnerable and guilty, conscious she could be found out at any minute. She felt sweat run down her back and hoped her face didn't give any outward signs of the way her stomach was churning.

She placed her hands on the screen between her and youth and leant over it. She gave him a look that she hoped conveyed authority and maybe just a little menace. 'Listen to me. We're investigating criminal activity here. We've phoned, we've emailed, and you have ignored us. I've had to come here in person to get the information we've requested.'

'But. Data protection.'

Susie raised her voice. 'I know all about data protection. That's my job. We're dealing with serious organised crime, trying to protect the data of innocent people. Do you want me to come back here with the Police? They'd shut this place down immediately if you don't cooperate.'

The youth recoiled and inched his chair backwards. 'I'll have to call my boss.'

'Call who you like, but make it quick. You think I've got all day to stand around here waiting?' Susie notched up the intensity of her stare and she willed herself not to blink first. She became hyper aware of other sounds in the office, she strained to hear footsteps or doors opening. Her mind played tricks on her, but she resisted an overwhelming urge to look left and right to check, or to get out while she could.

A hand reached for the phone, then hesitated. 'How many accounts?'

Susie said nothing. She glanced at the piece of paper she held in her hand as if reading it for the first time. 'Three. I need to know who they're registered to.'

The hand left the phone and turned upwards towards her, fingers outstretched.

The about-face caught Susie off guard for a beat. She handed the paper to the youth who placed it beside the keyboard, glanced briefly at it, then tapped a few numbers.

Susie tried to see what the monitor showed, but the dividing screens made it impossible. 'How long will it take?' She looked around the office again, her worry intensified with every second. She grew convinced that someone with more authority would arrive and snatch defeat from the jaws of a mild triumph.

The youth mumbled, 'A minute.' He glanced at Susie's piece of paper again and checked the details on the screen. His brow creased as he studied the screen. He tapped more keys, then shrugged. He reached for a pen and wrote on the paper that Susie had given him. 'They're all registered to the same address.' Without another word, he folded the paper and handed it back to Susie.

'Are you sure?' Susie took the paper, glanced at it briefly and placed it back into her folder.

'Sure, I'm sure.' The youth tapped the screen with the pen. 'It's all there.'

Susie gave a sage nod, as if she had always suspected that would be the case. 'That's all I need, thank you.'

She turned and headed back for the lift, convinced every door had someone hidden behind it . She hurried out of the building. Once in the open air, she relaxed and headed for her car.

CHAPTER 4

S usie examined the note the youth had given her as she returned
to her car. It took her some time to decipher the scrawled handwriting, but she eventually recognised the postcode and tapped it
into her phone. The map indicated the location was 19 miles away, a
technology park in nearby Reading.

She arrived thirty five minutes later and found a convenient multi-storey five-minutes walk from the address. The newly built Hexangle technology park featured six stylish, glass fronted buildings,
arranged symmetrically around a Hexagon shaped arboretum with an
elaborate fountain at its centre. Water gushed ten feet in the air before
it cascaded down over carefully arranged smooth black boulders.

She strolled between trees and shrubs and followed the paved path
that wound around the fountain. Each of the buildings bore the name
of one of King Arthur's knights. She checked the address again, Galahad House, and spotted the name etched into a five foot high slab of
polished grey granite near what she assumed must be the main door of
the building she wanted. The name she'd been given occupied number
44, but the sign beside the door announced it as the office of Byron
Sexton Accountancy.

Her brow furrowed; had the youth at the industrial estate given her
a fake name, or an old address, or had he just written down an incorrect
postcode?

She peered at the accountant's frontage. It looked new and up
market, not what she expected. She peered at the scrawled handwriting
again. She hadn't made a mistake. The name he'd written was Lucky

Meds, and the address, 44 Galahad House, Hexangle Technology Park.

She checked again in case she'd missed any other signs; Nothing.

What have I got to loose, she shrugged and walked up to the door. It opened without the need to press intercoms, show ID or make false claims about her identity.

———————•••••———————

Decebal felt his phone vibrate in his jacket pocket. He pulled it out and answered without looking at the screen. Nobody else knew the number. 'Yes boss.'

'Are you there yet?'

'Yes boss, we see her go in, we wait for her when she come out.'

'Good, just make sure nobody sees you, okay?'

'Okay boss.'

———————•••••———————

The woman behind the reception desk looked up as Susie entered and gave her a welcoming smile. 'Good morning, can I help you?'

'I hope so,' Susie said as she approached the desk. Should she play hard ball or go for the charm offensive? She clocked the woman's name badge and went for the second option. 'Hi Pauline, I'm looking for Lucky Meds. I've been told this was their office.' She sounded casual and returned the smile.

Pauline's expression never faltered. 'It is. This is the registered office for Lucky Meds.' By way of an answer, she pointed at the wall to her left and at what Susie thought looked like a rough imitation of an honours board.

Susie walked over to the board and studied the names that covered five columns. The names had been printed in black on thin strips of white card and slipped into grooves on the board. Gaps existed where businesses had moved on, or ceased trading. It listed them in no particular order as far as she could tell. Half way down the fourth column, she spotted Lucky Meds. She turned back to Pauline and cocked her head in the board's direction. 'Are all these companies registered here?'

Pauline nodded with enthusiasm. 'Absolutely, that's our principal business. We help people to set up companies and if they're working from home or a residential address, they can use this address. It makes them sound more professional.'

Susie gave a slow nod of her head and squeezed her eyes shut in frustration as the realisation dawned. 'I see.'

Pauline's enthusiasm blinded her from Susie's body language. She appeared genuinely pleased with the service the business offered. 'Would you like to send them a message?'

'No, I need to get in touch with them immediately.' Susie changed tack and adopted a tone that she hoped carried more authority. 'I need the contact details for the business owners.' She made it clear it was a request and not a question.

Pauline's smile faded, but she maintained eye contact with Susie. 'I'm afraid that's not possible. We guarantee our clients complete confidentiality. Even if I knew the details, I wouldn't be able to give them to you.'

Susie didn't want a confrontation. She knew a little about Registered Office Services and knew that Pauline's clients used the services of companies like Byron Sexton to avoid being tracked down by people like Susie.

'I understand, but I'm afraid this is a criminal matter.' Susie resorted to the alias she'd used at the technology park and hoped it would carry some weight.

'Where are you from?' Pauline's eyes narrowed as she studied Susie. The smile had vanished; she had pulled the drawbridge up.

'I work for the cyber-crime unit at GCHQ. We're trying to trace the people behind Lucky Meds.' It was half true, Susie thought, maybe just a little white lie.

White lie or not, the cover story had zero effect on Pauline. 'I'm not being difficult, but like I said, I don't have access to that information. Have you tried emailing them?'

Susie gave a mocking laugh. 'Thanks for the suggestion, we've sent letters, we've emailed, phoned and tried social media platforms. This is the only physical address we have for them. If we'd had a response, I wouldn't have had to drive down here today.'

Pauline understood and nodded, but the barriers remained in place. 'If you've written to them, they'll have got your letter. It's part of the service. We forward all their mail.'

Susie saw that she was getting nowhere. 'Are you telling me that if I come back with a court order to release the information I want, you couldn't find it for me?'

'I couldn't.' Pauline sat forward. Her head didn't move, but her eyes flicked right and high. She lowered her voice and put her hand up to the side of her mouth. 'I just work here, but Mr Sexton knows.'

Susie spotted the rapid eye movement and casually glanced in the same direction while she made a play of looking around the reception area for an answer. She spotted a tiny camera mounted in a corner at ceiling height. She understood. 'And where can I find Mr Sexton?' A gut feeling told her she wouldn't like the answer.

'He lives in Portugal.' Pauline said, her voice almost a whisper.

'Bloody brilliant.'

'Sorry.'

Susie slumped. She realised she could do little more. 'It's OK, thanks for putting me in the picture.' She gave Pauline a sympathetic smile, left the building, and walked back to her car.

She seethed and wanted to lash out. *Just when I think I'm getting somewhere, some evil bastard is fucking with my head.*

••●••

Susie left the technology park and headed back to the multi-story. She spotted a sign for the car-park down an alleyway that ran for around a hundred metres between two tall buildings. It made a dark, but convenient shortcut, instead of the five-minute walk if she went the long way round. She left the busy main road and turned into it. Half way along she slowed when she saw two men at the far end.

She couldn't make out their faces. The sunlight presented them in silhouette. They appeared as two black shapes, one tall and broad, the other short and squat. They filled the narrow alley and she could see no way past them.

They started to walk towards her.

Something about their gait put Susie on edge. They had a sense of menace about them.

She stopped and made a show of looking in her bag as though she had just remembered something important. She turned and headed back towards the main road.

As she turned, the two men picked up their pace.

She glanced over her shoulder and noticed the two men had sped up and closed in on her .

A satisfied smile spread across Susie's face, and she quickened again. *Come on then boys, you want a race, catch me if you can.* She wore her favourite trainers; they were never designed as serious running shoes but perfectly up to the job of a quick sprint to evade a couple of local muggers.

She took off.

She covered the 50 metres to the end of the alley in seconds. She eased off and looked back. The two men coasted to a halt. They'd given up. Susie couldn't resist giving them the finger, then headed back to her car the long way. She walked a little quicker than she had before she'd turned into the alley.

Five minutes later she arrived at the multi-storey after frequent checks behind to make sure she hadn't been followed. She headed up the stairs to where she'd left the Golf and scanned for potential threats at each landing.

An uneasy feeling gnawed at her as she pushed open the door onto level 4. She stopped with her back against the door and listened. She could hear cars manoeuvring on the floor below and heard the squeal of tyres as some negotiated the ramps between levels. She would have been grateful for some signs of life, moral support or simple reassurance, but her level remained ominously deserted.

She felt confident she could outpace most people if they chased her out in the open, but in the confines of the car park, she felt vulnerable.

She had no idea if the two men were simply opportunists or if they had targeted her. *Had they seen her park? Could they have got back to the multi-storey before her?*

A voice in her head told her to stop being ridiculous and she took a step forward. She'd parked the Golf in a bay at the far end of the level, fifty yards away opposite the ramp that descended from level 5. She stared ahead and swore she saw movement. A shadow behind a parked car. She stopped mid-stride and waited. She couldn't be sure.

She told the voice in her head to shut up, turned back to the stairs and went up to level 5. This time she didn't hesitate and jogged the length of level 5 to the ramp. She squatted down to look through the barrier at the area around the Golf. She waited a full two minutes in case she saw movement before, convinced she was safe, she clicked the remote and jogged down the ramp to the car.

She shut the door and activated the central locking. She exhaled slowly and convinced herself that she wasn't in the least bit bothered.

•••••

Susie walked into the offices of Newstead Press just before 3:00. Her mood had not lifted during the drive back from Reading. If anything, it had grown darker, and she felt convinced that forces plotted against her.

She dropped into the chair at her workstation without a word to any of her colleagues. She tapped on the keyboard to wake the computer and stared at the screen as it booted up. Her mind was elsewhere. She flip-flopped between wanting to give up, and wanting to nail the fuckers for wasting her time.

She didn't notice Greg leave the cage and walk over to her.

She flinched when he tapped her shoulder.

'What's up? You don't look best pleased.'

Susie didn't look up. She crossed her arms and pushed her bottom lip out with a petulant 'Humph.'

'Come on, fess up. Things don't always go to plan. What happened? What did you find out?'

'Fuck all Greg, that's what I found out. Fuck all.'

Greg raised an eyebrow but said nothing. He ignored the outburst and held out his hands and wiggled his fingers in a gesture that implied tell me more.

'I thought it would be simple enough once I had the name of the people sending the emails and their address, but they're devious bastards.'

Greg nodded. 'Go on.'

'I got the name behind the emails and went to the address they'd used to set up the email account, but guess what?'

'No one there?'

'Worse than that, the address is a Registered Office Service, an Accountant, and they refused to give me a name or an actual address.'

'I hate to say it, but I did say it wouldn't be easy.'

The thought of Greg claiming some sort of victory appeared to galvanise Susie. She turned and looked up at him. 'I'm not giving up. This is just a temporary setback.'

Greg knew he'd said the right thing and his expression softened. He smiled at Susie. 'You'll get there. It may take a little more effort, but you look like you're on a mission.'

Susie detected a begrudged note of pride in the way Greg's remark. It brought a hint of a smirk to her face.

Greg had a flash of inspiration. 'Have you been on the Companies House website?'

Susie recognised where Greg was going and smacked herself on the forehead. 'Of course, why didn't I think of that?'

'You'd have got there, eventually.' He watched as Susie typed in the URL for Companies House and waited while the website loaded up.

'According to the ISP, they registered the account to Lucky Meds.' Susie spoke as she typed the name into the search bar.

'And they're a Limited Company?'

'Yes, at least they were listed as a Limited Company at...' Her voice tailed off as the search came up blank.

'Try a different spelling.'

'How else can you spell Lucky Meds?' Susie glared at the screen while her fingers hovered over the keyboard waiting instructions.

Greg frowned, scanned the office, and searched for an answer. His attention returned to the screen. The results showed every company with the letters "MEDS" somewhere in its name. He rubbed the side of his face as he thought. 'Maybe they trade as Lucky Meds, but their registered name is something else?'

'Possibly, but that doesn't help much if we can't trace Lucky Meds.' Susie took out her frustration on the return key, stabbing it several times with an extended forefinger.

'Give yourself a break, step back from it and do something else.' Greg reached past Susie and rescued the keyboard. 'You're not going to do anything if you wreck that.'

Susie pushed her chair back and stood up. She ran her fingers through her hair and gave Greg a reluctant nod of acknowledgement.

Greg placed the keyboard back on her desk with exaggerated care, then checked his watch. 'Go home, go for a run or whatever you do to burn off steam. You'll not do anything productive now and inspiration might just hit you.'

●●◆●●

The inspiration she sought came after work. She arranged to meet her friend Anna Banks at the gym. They trained together two or three times a week. Susie usually went for it with vengeance; Anna not so much. Having just turned thirty, Anna felt it was time to try and get fit, while Susie obsessed over her speed, strength and stamina. Normally, never much of a talker when working out, Susie pondered how to trace the people behind Lucky Meds and mentioned it as they pedalled on adjacent stationary bikes.

Anna noticed Susie's lack of urgency as they rode to nowhere. The screen in front of her displayed time elapsed, current speed, distance covered, and calories burned. She knew Susie's normal, manic pace and could tell from the subdued effort that something bothered her.

'I take it you've tried the obvious, writing to the address you've got and asking them to get in touch?' she said, after Susie had explained the problem.

Susie tried not to look too incredulous and fought back the urge for sarcasm. 'If only it were that easy. Trouble is, they don't want to be identified. I imagine they'll go to any lengths to keep their identity and their whereabouts hidden.'

Anna wanted to help. 'Couldn't you just follow the letter and see where it gets delivered to?'

'I thought of that, but they could be anywhere.' Susie looked up at the mirror wall in front of them and saw that Anna looked confused. 'For all I know, they could have a chain of forwarding addresses. How could I follow it?'

Anna considered this for a while, then looked across at Susie, who had her head down, and pedalled half-heartedly as she watched the digital display. 'Can you not send them some sort of gadget that sends out a signal you could trace?'

Susie didn't look up immediately, but as the thought sunk in, her pedalling eased off, then stopped completely.

She turned and looked at Anna, who maintained a gentle cadence, her long dark hair pulled back in a simple plait. Her skin glowed and her brow glistened. The effect of the off-the-cuff remark had failed to register.

'Say that again'

Surprised, Anna looked at Susie. 'You know, like they do in spy films. Can't you do that in real life?'

Susie pursed her lips and gave an uncertain shake of her head. 'Why not? It must be possible. Why didn't I think of that? Anna, you may be on to something.'

'Am I?'

'You certainly are.' Susie climbed off the bike. 'Come on, Agent Banks, you've got me thinking, I need to speak to someone.'

The two of them talked about the idea as they showered and changed. The theory seemed fine, but neither of them knew how it could work in practice.

'Who did you want to speak to?' Anna asked as Susie drove them away from the gym.

'Do you remember Tim, Nick's old army mate?'

Anna's brow furrowed in concentration. 'Not sure. What's he look like.'

'Tall, black, good looking.'

'Ah yes.' Anna's wide eyed expression and knowing smile, an instant giveaway. 'He was at your party last New Year.'

Susie nodded. 'Yeah. Actually, I introduced him to Nick. Tim was in the Intelligence Corps when I was a Red Cap. We worked together on a couple of investigations. I think Nick was a little jealous.'

Anna gazed out a the passing scenery, she appeared lost in thought. 'You couldn't blame him. I can't remember speaking to Tim, but if my memory's any good, he leaves a lasting impression.'

'You've got it. And he's a really nice guy' Susie snuck a brief glance at Anna and had to smile. 'Well, his business is selling surveillance equipment, you know; mini cameras, hidden bugs, that sort of stuff.

At this, Anna's face brightened further. 'You think he'll be able to help?'

'Possibly. I'll ask Nick to have a word with him.'

••◉••

Cotswold Triathlon Club held an open water training session every Thursday evening at the nearby Chillingford lake. Along with a dozen other members, Susie spent an hour building cold water endurance under the watchful eye of their swim coach. She'd always loved wild swimming and the shallow lake was never too cold in the summer months.

Anna still ached from their time in the gym the previous evening, and it took all of Susie's persuasive powers to get her to come along. She piqued Anna's interest with the promise of good news and the additional promise that she wouldn't have to climb into a wetsuit and join her in the water.

They'd had little time to talk beforehand, and it was only after Susie had changed and they were back in the car that they caught up on the events of the last 24 hours. Anna drove and she pulled out of the car park, she spoke without looking at Susie. 'You haven't said anything about my idea. Did you talk to Nick about Tim?'

The tone of the question made Susie smile. 'I did, and guess what?'

The car swerved as Anna's attention turned to Susie, her hands involuntarily followed her gaze.

'Watch out!' Susie braced herself against the dashboard.

Anna's attention snapped forward and she steered away from the verge and back on track. 'Sorry about that.'

'Steady girl. Let's back in one piece eh.'

'Are you going to tell me then, or do I have to guess?'

Susie smirked and drew out the wait a moment longer. 'He'll be there when we get back to our place. Nick invited him round. Said he'd fire up the barbecue.'

'Did you tell him my idea?' said Anna.

'Not in any detail. I just asked him if he thought Tim might have some sort of device we could send in the post and see where it went.'

'What did he think?'

Susie pulled a face. 'He didn't say much. I don't think he understands what we're trying to do.' Susie stared out the passenger window, lost in her thoughts. 'He'd rather I went to the police and did something else. He thinks I'm going down a rabbit hole and thinks I'll end up pissed off and frustrated.'

Anna didn't respond at first. She snatched another quick glance to her left and realised Susie was miles away. 'Are you OK?'

Susie turned back from the window and looked ahead as they approached her house. 'Yeah, I'm fine, just thinking about stuff, you know; life, the universe, what's for supper, that sort of thing.'

Anna remained sceptical, but there was no more time to talk as they pulled to a stop. 'Well, let's see what Tim thinks.'

Anna followed Susie through the house to the back garden to find the two men stood over glowing charcoal as if transfixed by the flames. Each held a bottle of beer.

Nick looked up when he heard them. 'Well, if it isn't the two mermaids.' He nudged Tim, who turned to greet the new arrivals. 'Tim, this is Anna, Anna, Tim.' Satisfied he'd introduced them both, he turned to Susie and raised his bottle. 'Want one, love?'

Susie watched as Anna shook hands with Tim and didn't answer. At six feet three, Tim towered over Anna, who craned her neck to look up at him. Susie had grown used to Tim's good looks and the impact he had on the opposite sex. She was convinced he was blushing, but his coffee coloured skin made it difficult to tell. Anna appeared to have lost the power of speech and gazed into Tim's eyes, her diminutive hand limp in his over-sized paw.

Susie repeated Nick's question to Anna. 'Hello, earth to Anna, you want a drink?'

Anna nodded without looking away from Tim and withdrew her hand from his. 'Thanks, can I have what Tim's having?' The words came out in a half-hearted way, her mind elsewhere.

Susie caught the vibe and smiled. She asked Nick for a bottle of Evian and watched him duck back into the house. She pulled up a chair, sat near the barbecue and watched, intrigued by the body language between Anna and Tim.

Nick returned with the drinks, and the four of them gathered around the table.

Anna glanced at Tim whenever she thought no-one was looking.

'Did Nick tell you what we're trying to do?' Susie asked, her question directed at Tim.

'No. He just said you were working on a story and thought I might be able to help. Is that right?'

Susie looked to Nick with a questioning look, and he shrugged. She turned back to Tim and quickly outlined their idea. She explained what they hoped he could help them with.

Tim listened. He removed his shades and chewed the end of one arm. He said nothing, but he caught on quickly. 'Sure, I think I could get you something that would do the job. It transmits a signal that can be tracked anywhere in the world just using your phone.'

'How big is it? It's just that it would have to go in the post and not arouse any suspicion.'

Tim thought for a moment. 'Well, the device I was thinking about is about the size of a small box of matches, the actual transmitters are tiny, it's the batteries that take up the space. There are smaller ones, but they're not available to the public.'

Anna watched Tim, the bottle poised at her lips. She seemed to hang on his every word.

Susie glanced at her and smiled again.

Tim hadn't noticed. He closed his eyes and stroked his chin as he thought and recalled the details he needed.

'How much smaller?' Susie asked.

Tim reached into the pocket of the jacket he'd left hanging on the back of a chair and pulled out a thin, white case. He opened it and withdrew three business cards.

Susie looked at Nick and Anna, who both looked at Tim closely, unsure what he was going to do.

He took the three cards as one, folded them in half and pressed the crease to get a tight fold. He held up the folded cards between thumb and forefinger and examined the thickness with a critical eye. He looked at Susie. 'About that small.' He studied his creation with care. 'Not much to look at, but the battery life is exceptional. That's why they cost so much. Would it do for what you want?'

Susie reached over and took the folded cards from Tim. She studied them as though they were made of precious metal. 'This would be perfect. Do you sell these?'

Tim looked uncomfortable. 'I'm not supposed to. They're military spec, not on the open market, but I could get one for you.'

'I suppose they cost a small fortune?'

'They do, but as it's you, I daresay I could lend one to you on a trial basis.'

Susie looked up at Tim. She clutched the cards to her chest and twisted her nose. 'Lend? That implies you'd want it back.'

'Well, if you're going to use it to track a package, why not retrieve the little beauty as well? A little added incentive.' He smiled at Susie and glanced over at Anna, who watched his every move. 'Are you in this together?'

Susie nodded and put an arm round Anna's shoulder. 'Absolutely. It was Anna who first thought of it, so we're in it together. Right?'

'OK then,' said Tim. 'I'll have to call the supplier and persuade them to send one out. I'll let you know when I get it and you can come over to my place and pick it up.'

'Where's your place? Nick said your business was all online.'

'It is. I work from home. 'The details are on the card. Text me your number and I'll text you when I've got it.'

Susie unfolded the three cards and was about to read the top one when Anna reached over and took it. After a quick examination, she carefully slid it into the back pocket of her jeans.

The corner of Susie's mouth turned up. She saw Tim register the move out of the corner of her eye.

Part Two

Target

CHAPTER 5

A week passed before Susie received a text from Tim to let her know the package had arrived. She cycled to his place after work and arrived a few minutes after six. The double fronted detached house sat back from the treelined road with a neat, well-tended and tidy garden. A few tubs and hanging baskets added to the colour. Tim's car, a newish Audi convertible, was parked in front of the double garage, but there were no signs of life. Susie rang the doorbell and waited.

'Susie.' Tim emerged from the side door of the garage and hailed Susie, who hadn't spotted him. 'I'm over here. Come on in.'

Susie turned, surprised, and headed in his direction. She assumed the garage had been converted into an all-purpose warehouse, showroom and office.

When she entered, she stopped, struck dumb momentarily. It wasn't what she expected. The garage had been converted, one half partitioned off, the other equipped as a bright, comfortable office, insulated, carpeted and tastefully decorated to a high standard. A large picture window at the back of the garage gave a commanding view over the garden and the hills beyond. Tim's desk stood in front of the window and stretched the width of the garage. Two huge monitors sat on the desk, a wireless keyboard and mouse were the only other items, with no paperwork and no clutter. Four filing cabinets took up space along one wall with a door in the middle of them through to the other half of the garage. The opposite wall, the one with the door Susie had entered through, featured a whiteboard that took up most of the space. Tim had sealed the main garage door and the wall at that end had an old shabby Chesterfield against it, with a long, low coffee table in front of it.

Susie turned through 360 degrees as Tim watched. 'I don't get it. Where's all your stock?'

Tim smiled at Susie's puzzlement. 'What stock?'

'All the stuff you've got on your website. I couldn't resist a look.' She peered at him, seeking an answer.

'Aha, I bet you imagined some sort of shop?'

Susie jiggled her head from side to side. 'Well, more of a showroom, I suppose.'

'No need.' Tim indicated the two monitors. 'It's all online. I'm only a middleman. I know where to get things, stick them on the website and when someone places an order, I get in touch with the supplier and they ship it out to the customer. I rarely see any products.'

Susie nodded slowly as Tim explained. 'So, how do people find you? Where do you advertise?

Tim raised his eyebrows in an apologetic manner. 'Well, thankfully, I don't have to. People come to me. I've built up a bit of a reputation and it spreads by word of mouth.'

Susie shook her head slowly as she looked around her. 'You and Anna would get on famously. She loves all this sort of thing.'

At Anna's name, Tim immediately looked bashful. 'Er, did you, have you, um....'

Without another word, Susie pulled a slip of paper from her jacket pocket and gave it to Tim. 'Is that what you're after?' She winked at him and smiled at his slight embarrassment.

Tim's voice sounded disappointed, tinged with the acknowledgement that Susie had seen straight through his subtle approach. He read the details Susie had written. 'Thanks. I hadn't realised you were a mind reader.' He paused.

Susie kept quiet. She sensed he wanted to add something.

'I was just wondering.' Tim gave a helpless gesture.

Susie laughed. 'I'm no mind reader, I'd have had to be blind not to notice a certain frisson.'

Tim appeared lost for words. He shuffled his feet and studied the piece of paper Susie had given him to avoid having to make eye contact.

Susie helped him out. 'She works for the Regional Development Agency. She's away a lot on business. Her job is all about inward investment.' There was no immediate response, so she added, 'And no, she's not seeing anyone.'

He was momentarily lost for words. 'That obvious, huh?'

'Obvious?' Susie gently mocked him. 'Just a bit.'

Tim sounded almost defensive. 'Well, do you blame me? She's smart, she's interesting, and she's drop-dead gorgeous.'

'I don't blame you at all. In fact, if you ask me nicely, I might even put in a good word for you.' Susie enjoyed the game, but she was pushed for time. She looked over Tim's shoulder. 'Where is it then?'

Tim reached behind him and picked up the package from the desk and handed it to her. 'One Shackleton Mark five, GLD.'

'GLD?' Susie repeated.

'Global Location Device.' Tim explained.

Susie opened the plain white cardboard box and withdrew the contents. The dark grey metal device looked almost the exact the size and shape that Tim had demonstrated with the folded business cards. She held it in her hands and assessed the weight. 'It's light as a feather.' She looked up at Tim for a response.

'Titanium. That's another reason why it's so expensive; tough, lightweight, non-magnetic, totally waterproof and very, very cool.'

Susie examined the device closely and held it up to her eye 'There's no buttons or anything to make to it work.'

'If you look closely, you'll see a tiny little pinhole in one corner, on the edge.'

Susie turned it over in her fingers and discovered the hole.

'It's all pre-programmed, so you don't need to do anything, but if you wanted to get into it and replace the battery, you insert a pin in there and it opens up. But you don't need to know any of that. You just need to download an app to your phone, enter the code and you're up and running.'

'Amazing.' She said, temporarily lost for a more considered comment.

'Come on, I'll show you what to do, then you're ready to go.' Tim led her to his desk and explained how to set up her phone. 'You'll have to give me your passcode. I'll need it to configure the system.'

Susie tapped in a six-digit code. 'It's the same for all my devices.' She looked a little guilty.

Tim shook his head. 'Remind me to give you a lesson in online security sometime.'

'I know, Nick keeps telling me.'

It took another ten minutes while the app downloaded and Tim entered the relevant details.

Satisfied she knew what to do, she packed the tracker away and prepared to leave.

'Just remember,' said Tim, as they walked out to her bike. 'It's a pricey bit of kit and I'd like it back, so when you track down your suspect, make sure you retrieve that little baby. I called in a favour on the promise that it was a test.'

Susie nodded. 'No probs Tim, you're an absolute star.' She reached up and kissed him on the cheek. 'And I'll tell Anna she can expect a call.' She gave him another wink, swung a leg over the bike, and set off.

Tim watched her cycle away. He re-read the paper with Anna's details, then floated back to his office.

•• ● ••

Susie held the location device between the thumb and forefinger of her left hand and gazed at it in wonder. She still couldn't believe that something so small could be identified anywhere in the world. She had been so absorbed in her study that she hadn't noticed Mandy, who'd walked over to see her.

'You seem pleased.'

Surprised, Susie turned to Mandy. 'Didn't see you there.'

Mandy smiled and looked at the object of Susie's attention. 'Is that it then?'

'Yeah, isn't it amazing?'

Mandy stared at the dark metallic rectangle and tried hard to look interested. 'I guess so. I suppose it's what it does that's amazing. It's not much to look at.'

'Tim showed me how to track it. We don't even need any special equipment; you can track it just using your phone. It's all done by GPS.' Susie turned the device over a couple of times and pointed out that nothing gave it away–no buttons to press and no moving parts. 'Just feel how light it is.'

Mandy held the device in her hand as though she was guessing the weight of the cake at a village fete. 'There's nothing to it.' She handed it back to Susie.

'Tim's installed an app on my phone and it'll show me where that is anywhere in the world to within two metres.' Susie looked proud, as though she had designed the device herself. 'Clever, huh?'

'Just like tracking someone's phone.' Mandy said, almost to herself, but loud enough for Susie to hear.

Susie looked crestfallen for a moment, then brightened. 'Ah yes, but the battery in this baby will keep it going for ages. You don't need to charge it every ten minutes.'

Mandy conceded the point. 'OK. So what's your plan, then?'

Susie looked puzzled. 'What d'you mean?'

'Well, what are you planning to do? Just put that in the post and hope for the best?'

'Well.' Susie paused. 'Er, yes, we were just going to pop this in a jiffy bag and...' Her voice trailed when she saw Mandy shake her head. 'What's wrong? You don't look convinced.'

'I'm not. Think about it. If you received something in the post that you weren't expecting, you'd be suspicious, right? Especially if you had a guilty secret.'

Susie's nose wrinkled.

'I don't mean to pour cold water on the idea, but if it was me, I'd drop it in the bin without a second thought, wouldn't you? Sorry.' Mandy gave an apologetic shrug. She didn't want Susie to think badly of her.

'Hmm,' Susie considered it for a moment, then turned the problem back on Mandy. 'So what would you do? What's going to get them to keep it?'

Mandy thought as she spoke and gazed out of the window for inspiration. 'Not a lot, not if they're as clever as we think they are. They're going to be super cautious.'.

The pair remained silent for a while, as they both thought about a solution. Susie was about to speak when Mandy said, 'If we assume that whoever receives the post knows what they're expecting and will discount anything else?'

Susie nodded. 'Yes.'

'And if you think about it, from what you told me the other day, the only way you've got this far is because you traced the ISP and the accountant and they forward their mail, yes?'

Another nod in response.

'Well, if you faked a small package that looked like it had come from their ISP and made it look like it contained something important, something that couldn't be downloaded, they'd almost have to open it. Wouldn't they?'

Susie rubbed an eyebrow with the back of her hand. 'I can see where you're going, but I'm not sure, Mandy.'

'Why not?'

'When did you last hear of an ISP putting anything in the post?'

Mandy's mouth morphed from a smile to a frown. 'I'm sure they do. There must be something. What about a CD?'

Susie tipped her head at Mandy. 'Seriously? Can you even buy CDs these days?'

Mandy's shoulder's slumped, then she brightened as a thought hit her. 'Actually, they don't even need to open it.'

'How's that going to help?'

Mandy took a deep breath to buy herself time. She considered the problem, then exhaled slowly. 'You're going to use the device to locate their address, right?'

'Right.'

'So, you monitor the app, follow the package and see where it goes, then pay them a visit.'

'Hmmmm.' Susie pondered. 'For all I know, it might end up in a PO Box waiting for someone to pick it up. I could wait for days, or even weeks, and how would I know when it's arrived?'

Mandy saw the sense in what Susie said, but didn't want to give up. 'OK, granted, the plan does have a flaw, but they wouldn't have gone to the trouble of hiding their address if they weren't expecting some mail.'

'Fair point.'

'Does this thing have a motion sensor?' Mandy waved the tracker in front of her face.

'A what?'

'Well, to be more accurate, an accelerometer, a gyroscope and a magnetometer. They're in your phone, they work together with the GPS. That's how it counts your steps and how it wakes itself up when you shake it.'

Susie took the tracker from Mandy and studied it as though it would reveal the answer. 'Now you mention it. Tim said something along those lines. I must have glazed over at that point. It all got a bit too geeky, even for me.'

'Me too. I only know about it because Will's always telling us stuff like that. Some of it must have stuck.'

'Well, let's assume it does. It would make sense.'

'OK then. I'll bet there are settings in the app that will mean it goes to sleep if it's not moving and will send you a signal if it moves.'

Susie shook her head, a mixture of disbelief and amazement. 'You're a dark horse. You're wasted as a graphic designer. You should have joined MI6.'

Mandy couldn't resist a sly smile. 'Don't say that when my brother's around, he might get worried.'

'Actually.' Susie had a flash of inspiration. 'Don't give up your day job just yet. You could come up with a design for a package, make it look genuine.'

Mandy had already thought of that and added, 'I'll find a CD somewhere, even if it's just to give the package some bulk. I could easily knock up an insert for the case and design a label. I'll grab the ISP's logo off their website and come up with something that would fool anyone; at first glance, anyway.'

'Mandy, you are a star. We could stuff this thing into the padding of the jiffy bag. No one would ever know.'

'Leave it with me. I'll have something ready for you in a couple of days.' Mandy headed back to her desk.

Susie picked her mobile up and called Anna; it went straight to voicemail. 'Hi, it's me, call me when you get this message. I've got a plan.' She hung up.

••●●•

At first Susie didn't hear the 'ping'. Absorbed in a book, she had forgotten about the tracker and enjoyed a late lunch at her desk. The office noises muffled the sound, but thirty seconds later, the second ping made her jump. She dropped the book and fumbled for her phone. She gazed at the screen. A notification flashed, and the phone made a regular pinging noise every few seconds.

Three days had passed since she'd posted the package. She used the app to follow its progress from post box to sorting office and then to a small post office on the outskirts of Banbury. It hadn't moved for two days.

She called Anna. She switched the screen back to the tracking app. It showed a map view of the street and a flashing red dot that indicated the device. Anna's phone still rang out. 'For God's sake Anna, pick up!'

The flashing dot moved. She zoomed in and watched as it left the post-office and made its way along the street. She put the phone back to her ear and waited for Anna to answer, but instead her voicemail cut in.

'It's happening. I'll pick you up from your place in twenty minutes.' She ended the call and left her desk. She called across the office to Greg and told him the tracker was on the move and she was going to follow the trail. He said nothing but gave her the thumbs up.

Ever the optimist, she had come to work in the car, and parked it in the yard behind the office. She ran down two flights of stairs and sprinted to the car as though every second counted. She prayed Anna had got the message and would be waiting. It took her sixteen minutes to cover the four miles to her office.

Anna walked out the door just as Susie pulled into the car park. They spotted each other.

Susie lurched to a stop in front of Anna, leant over and pushed the passenger door open. 'Come on, get in. Someone's picked the package up.'

Anna did as instructed. Susie dropped the clutch and set off with a squeal of rubber on tarmac.

Braced against the dashboard, Anna struggled to fasten her seat belt. 'Hang on. What's the hurry?'

'We don't know where the parcel is going. We need to follow it.' Susie looked ahead. She was on a mission.

Anna settled into her seat and watched as Susie hustled through the traffic. 'Am I missing something here? Can't we just wait until it gets to where it's going and then follow along at a more sedate pace?' She flinched as Susie swerved to overtake a slow-moving van and narrowly missed an oncoming car.

'No. There's no telling what they'll do with it. They might just bin it or throw it over a hedge. We could find the parcel anywhere, but it wouldn't help us. We have to find the person who picked it up.' She shot a brief glance at Anna to make sure she understood.

Anna hung onto her seat belt, her eyes wide at Susie's driving. She nodded. 'OK, but let's try and get there in one piece.'

•••••

Twenty minutes later Susie slowed as they turned into the street indicated by the red dot that flashed on her screen.

Anna exhaled slowly and released her grip on the seat belt. 'Thank god for that. You're a bloody maniac.'

Susie ignored the jibe and focused on the screen with an occasional glance at the road ahead. She pulled into an empty space between parked cars. 'We'll park here and walk the last bit.'

'What are you planning to do?'

'Well. We've come this far. We need to make contact with our emailer.'

Anna's mouth fell open. 'But.' She flapped her hands. 'They're criminals. Who knows what they might do? Shouldn't we call someone?'

Susie made a dismissive gesture as though swatting a fly with the back of her hand. 'We'll be fine. We're just going to knock on the door.' She gave Anna a playful punch on the arm. 'C'mon partner, let's live a little.' Before Anna had a chance, Susie jumped out of the car and closed the door. She waited for Anna to join her.

Anna climbed out of the car and walked round to Susie. She wasn't convinced. She hugged herself and chewed a thumbnail. 'Just promise me you won't do anything reckless.'

Susie grinned at her. 'Reckless. Me? Never.'

One side of Anna's mouth turned up, which created a dimple in her cheek. Part of her admired Susie's attitude, another part hid behind a cushion, scared of the outcome.

Susie examined the screen again. The indicator flashed at the same point on the map as their location. 'It must be here, look.' She pointed to the screen. 'That's Nelson Street, we've just driven down, and this is Angel Way.' She looked up at the faded sign on the side of the end house. 'Whoever picked up the parcel must have gone in one of these two doors.' She looked at the cream door and alongside it a faded green one. The cream door had a black number 3 screwed to it, and the green one had no number. 'Which one do you want to try first?'

Anna looked shocked.'What? This is your call. I didn't think we were going to confront anyone.'

'Well, what did you think we were going to do? Come back tomorrow? Send them a letter?'

'I thought we just wanted to find out where they lived. I didn't think we were going to put ourselves at risk, and anyway, it's getting late and we need to be going if I'm going to be back in time.'

Susie switched off her phone and put it into the back pocket of her jeans. 'Don't worry, I haven't forgotten about your date. This'll just take a minute or two.'

Anna pinched her bottom lip between thumb and forefinger. 'But what will we say?'

'Leave it to me. I'll think of something, Susie said and did her best to sound confident. She walked over to the faded green door and knocked. There was no reply, so she knocked again.

Anna watched her and looked nervous.

'Must be the other one,' Susie said, and was about to knock on the cream door when she noticed two doorbell buttons on the door frame, one above the other. The top one had the name "Williams" written underneath it, but the other had no marking. She pressed the top one and waited. Nothing happened. She put her ear to the door and listened. Not a sound. She pressed again and held her finger on the button for ten seconds. She couldn't hear the bell ring, but caught the sound of movement from within. They heard a noise behind the door as someone approached. Susie turned to Anna. 'Fingers crossed'.

An elderly lady with a walking stick opened the door. 'Hello young ladies, what can I do you for?'

Susie recognised the lilting accent from the valleys of South Wales. It reminded her of home. The old lady had a warm, trusting face and looked surprised to see the two women standing on her doorstep. She figured the old woman didn't get many visitors. 'Hello, we're sorry to bother you, but we're trying to find a friend of ours who said they lived here. This is No 3 Angel Way, isn't it?

The old lady cupped her hand to her ear. 'You'll have to speak up, my love,' I don't hear too well.'

Susie leaned in close and repeated the question a little louder.

'Ah, you must be after the young man who lives in the flat upstairs.' The old lady helpfully pointed with her stick at the ceiling. 'He gets fewer visitors than me. He'll be pleased to see you, I'm sure.'

Someone had crudely converted the house into two flats with a common hallway. The old lady's door led to her ground-floor flat with a door at the top of the stairs for the first-floor flat.

Susie thanked the old lady, who turned and went back into her flat while she and Anna climbed the staircase. There was no bell, so Susie knocked. Anna stood behind her and waited. They heard noises from the other side of the door, and Susie knocked again.

'Who there?'

The voice sounded oriental to Susie. A young man. She had to think quickly.'Hello, my name's Evans, I'm from the council, we're doing a survey into local services. Can I come in?'

She looked at Anna, shrugged, and lowered her voice. 'Best I could think of.'

'Do you have ID?' the voice from behind the door questioned.

Susie hadn't anticipated the question, and it threw her for a moment, but Anna had a flash of inspiration.

'Show him your NUJ card. He'll never know the difference.'

Susie groped in her bag and found the rather crumpled identity card with a photo she wouldn't want to show anyone. She spoke to the door again. 'Yes, if you could open the door, it'll only take a couple of minutes.'

Noises came from the back of the door as the bolts slid back and the key turned in the lock. Then, very slowly, it opened the few inches allowed by the security chain. A hand appeared. 'ID please.'

Susie handed over her NUJ card, and the door closed again. She looked at Anna. 'Do you think he'll fall for it?'

'Depends how well he reads English,' she whispered.

The door opened again and the hand appeared with the card in it. 'You think me idiot?' The voice remained quiet and calm. 'I read English, you journalist not council person, you not come in.'

Susie took the card, but before he could close the door, she jammed her foot into the narrow gap. She grimaced as he pushed the door against her soft shoes. 'Please. We know all about Thytomet. We just want to get your side of the story before we write anything.' It was a gamble, but she felt it worth taking.

It worked. The pressure on the door eased.

The voice on the other side of the door remained unsure. 'What you talk about, I know nothing about anything, I student.'

Susie grew bold and leaned on the door. 'Can we just talk for a moment? We know you're sending out the emails, but we just want to know more about the drug.'

The door cracked. 'I know nothing about drugs. Go away. I will get big trouble.'

Susie and Anna looked at each other. It prompted Susie. 'If you don't let us in, we'll have to talk to the police and you don't want that. We can help you, we can protect you.'

The silence gathered and pressed against Susie's skin. Her heart thumped deep within her. It echoed, and then, as though she had touched a raw nerve, the door swung open.

CHAPTER 6

The young man stood in the doorway. His hoodie shadowed his face. He peered at Susie and Anna.

'What you want?'

'We just want to talk to you.' Susie stepped forward and placed her foot carefully against the bottom of the open door. 'We really can help. We can protect you.'

The man reluctantly let the door open fully. 'How you protect me? If I talk to you, I will be in big trouble. They will kill me.' He looked over Susie's shoulder and down the stairs as though he expected to see something dreadful.

Susie saw the fear in his face, his dark eyes wide against pale skin. She pressed her advantage. 'It's OK, we're on our own. We won't tell anyone if you tell us about the emails and the drug.' She smiled warmly and hoped it looked sincere. She stepped into the room and Anna followed, nervous.

The man looked back down the stairs again, then closed the door behind the two women. 'I know nothing about drugs, I just do emails.' He studied Susie and Anna intently.

'Well, that's what we want to talk to you about, Mr...?' Susie said and waited for a response.

He either didn't understand what was expected of him or wasn't prepared to give a name. He simply stared back at Susie.

Susie realised she had to be direct. 'What should we call you?'

'Name not matter.' He folded his arms and stood his ground. 'What you want to know?'

'OK then, who tells you to send the emails out?'

He frowned and dropped his gaze. He said nothing for a few moments while he considered his situation. 'If I tell you anything, they will find out and kill me.'

'If you tell us who they are, we'll make sure they're caught and can't get to you. You'll be safe with us. We just want to know who they are.'

Susie spotted the brightly coloured envelope on a table to the side of the computers. It appeared to be unopened. She didn't want to arouse suspicion. She looked around and moved casually towards it

'They bad people.' The man's eyes darted left and right. He kept his voice low, as though someone might hear him.

Anna glanced at her watch and tugged Susie's sleeve. 'We need to get going. It's almost five, and it's going to take us an hour to get back home.'

Susie felt she had made progress. She didn't need regular reminders from Anna about the time. 'Just hang on a minute. We've waited days for this and we're about to get somewhere.' She maintained eye contact with the man as she inched slowly towards the table behind her.

Anna didn't notice Susie's subtle movements. 'I know, but I said I had to be home by seven and you promised that whatever happened, you would make sure I wouldn't be late.'

'I'm sure Tim will understand. Text him and let him know I've delayed you a little.' She turned for a second to look at Anna. 'Just give me another couple of minutes.' She stepped back to the table and faced the man. She held her hands behind her back and attempted to retrieve the package.

The man understood the conversation and saw his opportunity for a reprieve. 'Come tomorrow and I speak to you then.' He wanted the two women out. 'I meet you in Starbucks, not here.'

It took a moment before Susie realised she had scored a minor breakthrough. It would stop Anna from fretting. She struggled to locate the package, and she knew she needed more time. 'How can we trust you? As soon as we've gone you could just disappear and we'd never see you again?'

He looked defiant. 'How can I trust you? How can you protect me? They will find out you come here, I need protection. You protect me if I speak to you?'

With relief, Susie felt the envelope and gripped it between two finger ends. She pulled it towards her and paused to confirm the agreement. 'Look, I promise, we can arrange a safe place for you to live and protect you from...' she nodded at the monitors as though they meant something. '...from whoever is funding all this.' The envelope snagged, it caught something on the table, and Susie's fingers fumbled as they tried to retain their grip. She grimaced, but resisted the urge to look behind.

The man gave her a quizzical look. 'What wrong with you?'

Susie felt the envelope. She had pushed it close to the edge of the table. She looked at the computers to divert his attention. 'Nothing, I'm just amazed by all the gear you've got here.'

His eyes left Susie for a second as he followed her gaze.

Susie lunged for the envelope and caught it firmly between her thumb and forefinger. She stuffed it up the back of her T-shirt and let it rest inside the waistband of her jeans. She made a show of adjusting her clothing.

The man looked back at her, suspicious. 'Just computers, nothing special.'

'Okay then, what time tomorrow?'

'Two o'clock.' He said it with certainty. 'I see you then, now you go.'

Susie took a step forward and worked herself around him so that he couldn't see her back.

Anna held the door open, her attention on her phone.

As Susie moved, the envelope slid. She hadn't tucked her T-shirt into her jeans properly. She reached behind her back and tried to catch it without attracting the man's attention. She had to keep the envelope and retrieve the tracker. It had done its job and Tim wanted it back.

Anna moved into the doorway and assumed Susie would follow. She looked back, and as the angle changed, she saw the envelope for the first time and understood Susie's behaviour. She had to distract the man. She let her phone drop out of her hands and made a show of bending down to catch it. 'Damn phone.' She looked up and caught the man's eye, then tapped the phone and sent it skidding across the floor in his direction.

The man turned to pick it up.

Susie got a firm hold of the envelope and jammed it down the back of her jeans. She smoothed her T-shirt down and side-stepped through the door.

The man handed Anna's phone to her, grabbed the door and made it clear he wanted them both to leave.

They said goodbye and confirmed their arrangement for the next day.

Anna checked her watch again. 'Come on, if we get a move on, we can be back in time.'

••●••

Susie and Anna felt as though they had scored a major victory. Anna seemed more concerned about being late for her date with Tim and urged Susie to hurry as they walked back to the car.

Susie half listened as she planned her next move. 'Are you going to come tomorrow afternoon, then?' She turned to Anna, who walked fast and looked ready to break into a jog.

'I'll let you know in the morning.' She gave an exaggerated, bashful look as they returned to the car. 'I want to keep my options open depending on how it goes tonight.'

Susie caught the look and grinned. 'Knock yourself out, lovely.' She winked at Anna as she dug the keys out of her jeans pocket.

They got in and pulled away. Anna checked her watch every few seconds. 'Are you going back to the office now?'

'Absolutely. I think I've earned some bragging rights. Can't wait to tell Greg.'

An hour later, after she had dropped Anna off, Susie walked into the offices of Newstead Press. She headed straight for the editor's office, unable to restrain her excitement, but found no one in. She looked around in the hope that she could spot him at one of the workstations. She saw no sign of him.

She walked over to her desk and noticed Harriet typing furiously, her head down. 'You seen Greg?'

Harriet paused mid sentence, looked up at Susie and couldn't help notice her bright expression. 'Oh Hi, you're looking pleased with yourself.'

'Yeah, just a bit, can't wait to tell Greg, any idea where he is?'

Harriet looked back at the editor's empty office, her features twisted as she tried to think. 'He was there a couple of minutes ago.' Her face suddenly lit up. 'That tall skinny guy...' She tapped her forehead searching for a name.

'You mean Lee?'

'That's him, I heard him call Greg over to look at something.'

'Ahh,' Susie straightened, stood on tiptoes and peered at the far side of the office. 'Thanks Harriet, can't see him, but I'll have a wander, see if I can find him.'

She weaved through the workstations and found Lee Longmuir sat at his desk with a phone held to his ear. The conversation appeared one-sided as Lee said very little other than the occasional "yes" and "okay" and "I see". Greg was nowhere to be seen.

Susie waited, she shuffled from foot to foot in restless impatience and continued to scan the office in search of Greg.

After a minute, Lee ended the call and turned to Susie. 'Hey.'

'Hi Lee, I'm looking for Greg, Harriet said he came over to see you.'

'Yeah, he did, a few minutes ago, but he had to go out. He had a meeting with someone from the council.'

'Bugger! Is he coming back?'

'No, he said it would take a couple of hours, it'll be after five when he's done.' Lee recognised that Susie had something on her mind. 'I'm joining him for a drink later, I can give him a message if you want.'

'Great. You know I've been investigating the source of some junk emails?'

'Something about diet pills, that right?'

'That's right. Can you tell Greg our little plan worked, I've tracked the guy down.'

'That's fantastic. Who was it?' Lee's expression, a mixture of surprise and shock.

'Just a young Korean lad, we're meeting him tomorrow and he's agreed to tell all in return for protection.'

Lee did a double-take. 'Protection? From what?'

'He's frightened, he's probably here illegally and whoever he's working for won't be pleased if he speaks to anyone.'

'Damn right.' Lee appeared lost in thought, he looked past Susie and gazed around the office as though checking to see who was in earshot. 'Leave this with me, I'll pass the message on to Greg later.'

'Thanks Lee.'

'No problem, nice work.'

•••••

Gianfranco DeLuca's office was not grand. Boxes surrounded him; large and small, stacked almost ceiling high against the walls and piled untidily like towers across the floor of the room.

An old desk rested against one wall, with a shabby leather captain's chair wedged under it. Paper; invoices, receipts, delivery notes, scraps with scrawled messages, leaflets and brochures for everything from vans to office supplies covered the entire desk.

DeLuca had cleared a space in one corner and leaned over the desk with a calculator. He worked his way down a list of figures and made notes in the margin of an A4 pad. He hummed a tuneless melody quietly to himself as he worked.

He paused as the incessant buzzing of a fly stopped when it landed on an adjacent piece of paper. DeLuca's eyes flickered momentarily as he registered the movement. His hand inched towards a brochure for office furniture and with exaggerated care his fingers wrapped around it. He froze for a second then struck in a blur. The desk shuddered and everything on it, jumped an inch. He turned the brochure over and with a sneer, wiped the squashed fly against the side of his desk. He returned to his work and resumed his humming.

His computer, a ten-year-old PC, did all he needed it to. Nothing fancy. He could send invoices, print off product details if he had to, and send emails if he really had to. There were no photographs on the desk or on the walls and no telephone. A single desk lamp lit his work area. His mobile phone, like his computer, did the essentials. It had a camera and did many other things Frank didn't need, but it made calls and that suited Frank just fine. He slotted a new SIM card into the handset every month to give himself a new number. As far as he was concerned, the fewer people who knew his number, the better.

When the phone rang, it surprised him–it had never rung before and at first he didn't recognise the ring tone. He couldn't remember having received an incoming call since he got the last SIM card a few weeks previously, and for a moment he was at a loss to understand what made the noise, he certainly hadn't selected the tinny melody that increased in volume with every repetition.

The noise came from under a stack of papers, and it took him a few moments to unearth the device. He looked at it with suspicion. 'Yes'

The curt greeting sounded familiar. 'Our Korean friend has been discovered.'

It took a moment before he recognised the voice and the words made sense. 'What? How the hell?'

'That bloody journalist. The one your boys couldn't catch in Reading. She's somehow managed to trace him.'

'When? I mean, how did you find out?'

'Just had a message from my mole. She's been bragging about it. Supposed to be meeting him tomorrow.'

'That can't happen.'

'No kidding!' The voice at the other end sounded blunt.

'I'll get my crew to deal with it,' Frank said.

'Apparently she's been to his place, so they'll need to sanitise it when they've dealt with him.'

'Will do.'

'And another thing. We'll need all that tech again, it cost enough. Tell your two gorillas to treat it with care and not just throw it into the back of a van.'

'I'll tell them.'

'Do it now.' The call ended.

Not for the first time, DeLuca looked at the phone, shook his head and muttered to himself about manners and pleasantries.

He tapped the keys of the phone and waited. 'Got a little job for you and Sergei.' He spoke slowly and deliberately.

He listened to the brief reply and switched the phone off.

••●••

By the time Susie had dropped Anna off and called at the office, it was just after seven before she arrived home. She found Nick pacing the kitchen floor.

'Where've you been?' He looked genuinely concerned after repeated attempts to call her.

She looked wounded by his words. 'I've been meeting our emailer. I thought I told you that's what I was doing.'

'You told me you were making some investigations. You said nothing about meeting anyone.' Nick folded his arms, but he couldn't make eye contact and turned away. He looked out the window. 'I've been trying to ring you every five minutes for the last two hours.'

Susie looked suddenly embarrassed and clasped her hand to her mouth. 'Oh shit.' She reached into her back pocket and pulled out her phone. 'It's muted. I didn't want to be disturbed when we were following the signal from the tracker. Sorry, love. Anyway, what's the problem? It's not as if I'm late or anything?'

He turned and brandished a piece of paper under Susie's nose. 'This is the problem. I told you a week or two ago, you're going to end up in trouble. Someone in seriously pissed off. They're threatening to kill you.'

Susie took the note and skimmed it.

'Stop fucking about in matters that don't concern you. We know where you live, where you work and what you do. You've been warned.'

Someone had scrawled the note in black felt tip.

She looked up at Nick. 'Where did this come from?'

Nick retrieved the note. 'It was stuck through the letterbox. I found it when I got home.'

Susie gave a little shake of her head and smiled. 'You don't need to worry, we've met the guy who's doing this, he's just a young lad. Anna reckons he's an illegal immigrant. He's not going to do anyone any harm.' She handed the note back to Nick and headed towards the door.

Nick shook the note at her. 'For God's sake, have you really got no idea?'

She stopped in the doorway and stood with her hands on her hips. She looked up at the ceiling for a moment, then looked at Nick. 'Don't lecture me. Your trouble is you over-react to anything, you have no sense of adventure or curiosity.' She pointed at the note with an accusing finger. 'That's all it takes to put you off. I'm not an idiot. I know this guy is working for someone else, but it's small beer. They've got a little business pedalling fake drugs and they don't want anyone mucking it up for them. It's hardly organised crime.'

Nick wasn't so easily placated. 'I'm not lecturing you, I'm concerned about you and I don't enjoy finding a note threatening to kill my wife. This is real life. I keep telling you, you're not a Red Cap any longer, you haven't got no back up. What do you expect me to do, laugh it off?'

'Just throw it in the bin Nick, we're meeting the guy tomorrow afternoon, and after that I'll have my story and I can go to the police. There's really nothing to worry about. I can handle myself. You know, the army taught me a thing or two.'

Nick shook his head. 'You reckon I've got no sense of adventure, eh?' He smiled ruefully. 'I sometimes wonder if you have any sense of reality. A sense of adventure is fine, but have you ever stopped to think what this little racket is worth and the measure people will take to protect their investment?'

'Seriously Nick, if you'd met the guy you'd see what I mean, he's just working for some small time petty criminal, he might put out emails but we've got no idea if they get any orders at all and even if they did, it's never going to amount to much. Keep your hair on, I know what I'm doing.' Susie considered the conversation over and left.

•••••

They came for Kang at ten in the morning.

He was still asleep when a rough hand struck him across the face; not too hard, but sharp enough to jolt him from his slumber.

Bleary-eyed, Kang looked at Sergei, who stood over him, ready to slap him again. Behind Sergei, he noticed Decebal, who lurked around the computer equipment as though checking it was all there. Kang said nothing, He had met them once before and knew he didn't want to meet them again. He lifted himself up on his elbows and blinked the sleep from his eyes.

As usual, he had gone to bed when most people were getting up and he hadn't slept well. His mind replayed the conversation he'd had with Susie the previous afternoon. He had been worried and excited in equal measure and they could land him in a whole pile of trouble with the authorities, but they could save him from DeLuca and his two assistants. Now Kang knew it wasn't a social call and his thoughts turned to survival.

Decebal looked directly at Kang. His voice brimmed with menace. 'Get dressed, you come with us.'

Kang looked around for the clothes he'd discarded before he got into bed with just his boxers and a T-shirt. He found his combat trousers crumpled on the floor and the hooded top just beside it. He pulled them on while he looked around for options.

'I need to pee.' He mumbled the words as he stuffed his feet into the baseball boots retrieved from under the bed.

'Go quick.' Decebal watched as Kang shuffled out of the room and without a word, he indicated to Sergei to follow.

Kang locked the toilet door behind him and looked around for inspiration. As he emptied his bladder, he contemplated the window above the hand basin, which was open, but small. He looked out, but there was nothing to climb down onto, just a straight drop of twelve feet to the yard below. He climbed onto the windowsill.

Sergei knocked. 'Come now.'

Kang knew he had little time. He reached up, but his elbow caught a can of deodorant and it wobbled–and in that instant his eyes shot wide as it fell into the sink and clattered.

The noise alerted Sergei. He heaved against the door.

Kang's heartbeat quickened as he pushed the window further open and wriggled half way through the gap.

The flimsy bolt snapped, and the door burst open. Sergei rushed in and grabbed Kang's leg, then his waist belt.

Caught off balance, Kang slipped and hung by one hand from the window frame.

Sergei yanked at Kang's trousers, and he crashed to the bathroom floor. His head cracked against the sink as he fell.

Decebal heard the noise and ran to the bathroom. He saw Kang sprawled unconscious.

Sergei dragged the Korean into the living room.

Decebal produced a roll of silver duct tape and jammed a length over Kang's mouth. They rolled him over and twisted his arms up behind his back. Decebal tore off more duct tape and bound Kang's wrists together, then did the same to his ankles. They half carried, half dragged him across the living room floor.

Decebal opened the door a fraction and checked no-one was around. The old lady hadn't heard them enter or Kang's attempt to escape. He grabbed Kang by the ankles and the two of them carried him down the stairs, moving as quietly as they could. They stopped again and checked the road outside. It was clear. They made the few paces to the van without attracting any unwanted attention.

They bundled Kang into the back of the van. He landed face down.

He moaned in pain as he regained consciousness.

Decebal checked Kang couldn't move, then slammed the doors shut.

Decebal and Sergei went back and forth into the flat and piece by piece brought the computer equipment down and placed it in the back of the van.

Kang struggled to move, but managed to twist onto his side as the doors opened again. His eyes wide in terror when he saw the two men.

His worst fears were realised, they had come to erase him and remove any trace that he ever existed. His insides convulsed with fear.

They loaded the monitors and servers with care, cables still attached. Desk and chairs followed until they had stripped the flat. After fifteen minutes, and panting with the effort, the work was done.

With difficulty, Kang rolled onto his back and looked up. He saw Decebal behind the wheel and Sergei in the passenger seat. Sergei looked back at Kang and sneered.

The van rocked from side to side, accelerated, braked and lurched round corners as it headed out of town. From his position on the floor of the van, Kang couldn't tell which direction they were going or where they were. He tried to break free, but the duct tape cut into his wrists., He craned to see through the windscreen once or twice, but each time the motion of the vehicle made it impossible. Unable to protect himself, he fell heavily and gave up. Some of the computer equipment fell on him and he realised it was less painful to lie still than risk further pain if more hardware became dislodged. After a while, he noticed they no longer passed any buildings and guessed they were heading out into the countryside.

After thirty minutes the van braked sharply, and Kang knew they had turned onto a track. The bumping intensified, and he bounced across the floor as Decebal barely slowed and the wheels crashed into ruts and potholes. Kang noticed trees on either side of the van and from the slight angle of the van, he knew it headed downhill on a road that twisted in different directions. The vehicle slid around corners and Decebal fought to keep it on track.

With a last slide, the van came to a stop and Decebal killed the engine.

Kang lay in the back and felt stunned and bruised by the journey. Fear crawled through his veins as the two men got out of the van and approached the back doors.

When the doors opened, Kang saw they had come to a stop close to the edge of a dark pool, and on the far side, a sheer rock face rose by almost one hundred feet. Tall pines surrounded them. All round the edge of the pool, he noticed large slabs of stone. He guessed it was a long-abandoned quarry, and terrified senses prickled.

Sergei reached into the van, grabbed Kang by the ankles, and dragged him out. He crashed to the ground and landed heavily on his shoulder. Decebal reached into one of his many pockets and pulled out a Stanley knife.

Kang, lying on his side, looked up at him. He tried to speak, but no sound came out. His eyes stared at the knife, unblinking.

Without a word, Decebal reached down and with one quick slash, he cut the tape that linked his ankles to his wrists, then the one around his ankles.

Sergei dragged him to his feet.

Kang stood warily. His legs felt numb. The two assailants blocked any escape route from the dark pool that lay beyond. His hands were still bound tightly behind his back and he knew that if he tried to run and tripped, he'd hurt himself and would struggle to get back to his feet. He had nowhere to go. Every fibre of his being wanted to scream. He looked left and right in desperation. His legs had lost the ability to move, and he remained glued to the spot, petrified. He whimpered and tried to plead with them. He saw the menace in their cold eyes. He looked around the abandoned quarry, at the trees, the wild flowers. There was no chance he couldn't get away. It was the last sight he would ever see.

Decebal opened the driver's door, got in and started the engine; for a moment Kang thought they would drive off and leave him; for a brief moment relief washed over him, but then without warning, Sergei turned away from the van and with three quick strides he crossed to Kang, grabbed him by his right arm and spun him round to face the pool.

Kang realised too late that Sergei was going to throw him in the water, and he struggled and kicked as the pool loomed. Even if his hands were free, he couldn't swim, and the water terrified him.

Sergei reached inside his jacket and withdrew a knife. Eight inches of polished, razor sharp steel, with a handle carved from ram's horn. Without a moment's hesitation, he drove the blade down hard and fast into a point slightly to the left of Kang's spine and six inches below the nape of the neck. The full length of the knife sank into Kang's flesh before he twisted it and pulled it out.

Even with duct tape over his mouth, Kang's scream was excruciating. As the blade tore through nerve endings, muscle and ligaments, his back arched and his hooded top darkened at the spot where the knife left a gaping wound and blood oozed out of it in a steady stream. His legs crumpled beneath him.

Sergei shoved him over the edge and into the pool and watched as Kang fell awkwardly. He bounced from the shale and struck his head on the corner of a protruding rock before he landed sideways in the water. Kang's inert body floated face down in the dark water. Sergei walked away without a second glance and wiped Kang's blood from the blade.

CHAPTER 7

Susie and Anna ordered coffees and found a low table in the corner with a leather sofa and matching armchair. Starbucks appeared quiet, and they had five minutes before Kang was due to arrive. Anna had talked constantly about her date with Tim the previous evening, and Susie looked forward to some respite. She did her best to sound interested, but after a dozen times, she was tired of hearing how wonderful he was, what a gentleman he was, what they had eaten, what they had talked about and how much she looked forward to seeing him again.

Susie took out her phone and checked for messages.

Anna gazed out of the window with a dreamy expression. Absent minded, she stirred her coffee. 'Did I tell you Tim was adopted?'

Susie looked up from the screen 'You might have mentioned it.' The knowledge had been firmly implanted on Susie's brain after repeated mentions. Although pleased for Anna, her patience had vanished. 'Has he told you about his accident?' The remark was a lame attempt to show interest, but it sounded heartless.

Anna scowled. 'That's a bit brutal.'

'Sorry, I didn't mean it like that.' She backtracked. 'It's just that Nick worries about him. His confidence took one hell of a knock.'

Anna softened. 'He never mentioned it at first, but I made some comment when he was coming down the stairs. He looked like he was limping and I asked if he'd hurt himself.'

Susie winced. 'How did he react?'

Anna thought for a moment. 'I think it embarrassed him at first. He wanted to make a good impression and probably didn't want me to find out until we knew each other a little better.'

Susie nodded as she spoke.

'Sounds like Tim. He's a real stoic, never lets on, never talks about it.'

'You're right. He dismissed it as a war wound, just said he was lucky to be here, and changed the subject. Do you know what happened?'

Susie made a pained expression. 'Nick told me. It was pretty horrible. They were in Afghanistan together, back in 2004. Tim was a lieutenant and had been out on patrol with his men when an IED went off. Two were killed outright and Tim was blown up. Nick thought he'd never make it, but he's made of tough stuff. They managed to save his leg, but it was pretty smashed up. They said he'd always have a limp and need a stick, but...' Susie looked at Anna for understanding. 'You've seen what he's like. He had to prove the medics wrong. Took him a couple of months, but he walked out of hospital unaided.'

Anna sat with elbows on the table, chin resting on her hands. Her head moved imperceptibly from side to side in awe. She remained silent for a while, lost in her thoughts. She looked out the window, then checked her watch. 'What do we do? Just wait here?'

'That's the plan. He's only a few minutes late. We just sit tight.'

'What are we going to do if he wants protection? The kid seemed terrified last night.'

'I hadn't thought it through really,' said Susie 'We'll have to play it by ear. I don't know what happens if we take him to the police and ask for protection. If he's an illegal immigrant, he could get deported, and he sounded just as frightened at the idea of that.'

Anna looked at her watch again 'Well it's almost ten past and he's not here. Do you still think he'll come?'

'Give him time. He knows we know where he lives and we're his only hope.'

They both gazed out the window to the street, but there was no sign of Kang. Neither of them spoke for a couple of minutes.

'We could ask in the Post Office if he's been in,' Anna suggested.

Susie didn't take her eyes off the street. 'OK, you pop over there and see what you can find out. I'll hang on here.'

Anna finished her coffee and walked down the street towards the Post Office. Susie glanced in her direction briefly, then resumed her vigil.

Another ten minutes passed before Anna returned. 'No sign of him in there. The guy said he knew who I was talking about, but he said he hasn't been in since yesterday.' She sat down. 'Should we go down to his flat and see if he's there?'

Susie pulled a face; she wasn't sure. 'I don't want to miss him in case he's gone somewhere else first.'

Anna slumped back in the sofa and folded her arms. 'We could sit here for hours and find he's changed his mind or done a runner.'

'Oh, come on then,' Susie said and gathered up the various papers she'd bought with her. 'Let's go and have a look for him.'

•• ● ••

There was no sign of Kang as they walked back to 3 Angel Way, and no reply when they rang the bell. Susie pressed the bell marked 'Williams'. She held it down again, and waited. The response was the same as the day before. It took a few minutes for the old lady to make it to the door.

'Hello again ladies.' She seemed pleased to see them. 'Lovely to see you. Are you here to see your friend?'

'Hello there,' said Susie. She nodded in case the old lady didn't hear her. 'Yes, is he in?'

'I suppose so. I have heard nothing. If it wasn't for the doorbell, I'd never know who was coming or going.'

'Can we go up?' said Susie, pointing up the stairs.

The old lady nodded, and the pair went up the stairs and knocked on the door. It had been pulled closed rather than locked and swung open when Susie knocked on it. They stepped into the room.

Susie's blood turned to ice, and the colour drained from her face, her eyes dilated as she took in the scene. Her stomach knotted, her legs felt weak and her voice fell to a whisper. 'They've got to him.' She put a hand on Anna's shoulder to steady herself.

The room was empty, the tables, the computers, the wires, all gone. They had swept the floor clean. There was no trace that the flat had been occupied twenty-four hours earlier.

'How did they find out?'

Susie walked around the room and looked for any clue that might have been left. 'I don't know, but whoever did this has been very thorough. It's like he never existed.' The realisation of what she'd said suddenly hit her and she clasped her hand to her mouth. 'Oh God Anna, what have we done?'

Anna saw Susie's reaction. 'Do you think he was right when he said they'd kill him?'

Susie nodded slowly. 'Let's get out of here, quickly. We need to call the police.'

Mrs Williams had gone back into her flat, and Susie knocked on her door. She waited, but no one answered. She knocked again, harder, and still no reaction. Anna remembered what the old lady had said and went to the front door and held her finger on the doorbell. After a few moments, Mrs Williams appeared. From her reaction, Susie realised she hadn't heard a thing.

'Are you off already?'

'He's not in, he's gone, all his stuff has gone,' Susie said, still in shock, and it came out louder and faster than she wished.

Mrs Williams looked puzzled. 'Gone you say? Not there?'

'Has anyone been since we came yesterday? Have you heard anything?' Susie raised the volume and talked slowly and deliberately. The message appeared to get through.

'No dear, there's been no-one here,' Mrs Williams said, and shook her head for emphasis.

Susie doubted she really understood what had happened. It was obvious that whatever had happened and whoever had done it, there were no witnesses. Susie had no wish to alarm the old lady by going into detail.

'He must have moved,' said Susie. 'He often does. We'll catch up with him again.'

Mrs Williams muttered, shook her head and went back into her flat.

'What are you going to tell the police?' said Anna as they walked back to the car.

Susie pulled her phone out, ready to call them. She paused and looked at Anna. 'I'm reporting a missing person.'

'Who?'

She pointed back at the flat. 'What's his name, him.'

Anna spread her arms, palms upturned in a gesture of hopelessness. 'So, you're going to tell the police that someone whose name you don't know has left his flat without telling you and done a very thorough job of tidying it?'

Susie stared at her phone, finger poised over the keypad. Her shoulders sagged. She knew Anna was right. What would, or could, the police do? They would log the call, but there was little chance of any investigation.

Anna continued. 'And anyway, for all we know, he might have gone all on his own. Took us for a couple of mugs and cleared out as soon as we left yesterday evening.'

Susie didn't like the sound of that. 'No, no, he was scared, and he wanted to talk. I just know something's happened to him.' The realisation that her investigation had come to an end dawned on her. 'Bloody typical, isn't it? We get this far and then our only lead vanishes clean off the face of the earth. What do we do now?'

Anna said nothing, but shrugged.

Susie tried to sound encouraging. 'At least we know about that drug Thytomet, we'll just have to dig deeper and find out where it comes from.'

'We? I do have a job in case you've forgotten,' Anna responded. 'I enjoy the intrigue, but I do have to show up for work now and then.'

'Sorry, but you know what I'm like when I get the bit between my teeth. There's a story here and I'm not going to let it go.' She gave Anna a mischievous wink. 'Anyway, you've got other things on your mind.'

They reached Anna's car and drove without saying a word for ten minutes as both of them gathered their thoughts. It was Anna who broke the silence and managed a positive reframe on the events of the last twenty-four hours.

'Well, you know where the emails came from and you know what they were selling. You've done well to find all that out compared to what you knew a few weeks ago. Whoever is making that stuff must be worried that you've rumbled them.'

Susie agreed, and her mood brightened by a degree. 'I guess so. I'll mull it over when I'm out on the bike in the morning and see what else I can find out when I get into the office. Thanks lovely, you've been very patient.'

••●••

Anna dropped Susie off at Newstead Press and they agreed to meet up in a couple of days. Susie wandered into the office and saw Greg on his own. She knocked on the glass wall of his office and he beckoned her in.

'What news, Ms Jones?'

Susie shook her head. 'I'm pissed off Greg. The only lead I've tracked down has vanished; promised to meet me and spill the beans and he's either got cold feet or someone didn't want him to talk and they've removed him without a trace.'

Greg's eyebrows made an animated jump. 'Bloody hell. This is getting more serious every day. I wonder what you said or did that's spooked him?'

'I don't know. I could tell he was scared of someone, but he agreed to meet us.'

'Who else knew?'

'Just you me and Anna.' Susie looked around the office, conscious that she could be overheard.

Greg gave a rueful shake of the head. 'You think someone's got to him?'

'They must've done. His place was clinically clean. No trace of him. He couldn't have done that by himself.'

'Have you told the police?'

'No. We thought about it, but what can they do? No name, no paper trail, no witnesses, no evidence.' She spread her hands in despair.

'You must have uncovered something then.' He turned his chair to face her and leaned back. 'Don't give up now. You've got this far. Sounds like the makings of a good story to me. Stick at it. What was the name of that stuff they were pushing?'

'Thytomet'

'Thytomet,' he repeated. 'We're assuming whoever's making it is behind the emails.'

Susie gave a brief nod.

'Have you ordered any?'

'At ninety quid a pop, you must be joking.'

Greg frowned and made a jiggling motion with his head as he weighed up feasible solutions. 'OK, look, if you want to take it further, place an order, put it in your name so you don't arouse any suspicion. I'll refund you, and when you get the stuff, you'll have more to go on.'

'That's if I actually receive anything. For all we know, the whole thing could be a scam.'

'Fair point, but from what you've discovered so far, they wouldn't be going to such lengths to hide if they didn't have a product.'

Susie conceded Greg could be right and gave another brief nod.

'You're going to have to delve deeper into the murky world of pharma and see what you come up with.'

'I've made a few enquiries already but got nowhere, the whole industry hides behind gate keepers and impenetrable red tape.'

Greg nodded. 'They won't make it easy for you. The system is designed to ward off the mildly curious.'

Susie set her jaw. 'If it was easy, it wouldn't be a challenge.'

October 2015
Brussels, Belgium

On a good day, Sir Giles Lawrence would admit that he enjoyed being recognised. He had never shunned publicity and as an MEP, his face appeared in the press on a regular basis. He courted the attention of the television networks whenever they were looking for an opinion or a comment. Sir Giles was never short of either.

Today was not a good day and Sir Giles did not want to be recognised. He patronised most of the better eateries in Brussels, and knew someone would spot him if he met the chemist in any one of them. He'd never been to *Chez Antoin*, but reviews on Trip Advisor assured him that the basement restaurant was dark and discreet and he could enter and leave with no one having a clue who he was.

7.00pm on a midweek evening in late October, would never be busy. Lawrence pulled the door open and stepped into the restaurant. As he expected and hoped, the place appeared deserted. He unwrapped the scarf that covered the lower half of his face and removed the fur hat he'd pulled down to eye level. He shrugged off his coat and gazed into the gloom in an effort to locate Schrader. He held his coat, waiting for someone to take it and after a moment realised that *Chez Antoin* was not that sort of place. He snorted in annoyance. He was used to better.

A waiter approached. 'You have a reservation?'

Lawrence looked around at the empty tables, then lifted his chin and looked down his nose at the man. 'Do I need one?'

The waiter frowned, unsure how to respond.

Lawrence continued before the waiter had a chance to speak. 'I'm meeting someone, a Dr Manfred.'

'Ah yes.' The waiter looked relieved. 'This way, please.' He beckoned Lawrence to follow him and headed into the main seating area before turning right through an archway into a smaller room with a low vaulted ceiling, dim wall lights, and a single table.

Manfred Schrader sat facing Lawrence. He looked up and scowled at him.

The waiter stepped aside to allow Lawrence to pass and take a seat.

Schrader waited until they were alone before he spoke. 'This is ridiculous, meeting up in places like this.' He cast a hand around the room, his tone dismissive. 'What's wrong with email?'

Lawrence checked over his shoulder to make sure no one else could hear him. 'Absolutely not. There can be no paper trail or digital signature.' He shook his head to as if to confirm his point. 'I can't take any risks. If I'm spotted anywhere people will talk, they'll make assumptions, they'll draw conclusions, this has to remain...' His hand made a circling motion beside his forehead as he searched for the right word, '... secret.' He muttered, eventually.

Schrader closed his eyes and shook his head as if unable to accept what he heard. 'I'm a respectable scientist. You're a member of the European Parliament. What does it matter?'

'It matters because of my position. If we're seen together, it would be like the gamekeeper meeting up with the poacher. I'm supposed to be detached, unbiased, objective.' He took another glance behind, then pulled out the only other chair at the table and sat opposite Schrader.

Schrader didn't comment. He studied the MEP and noticed the way his eyes flicked, left and right, up and down, unable to settle, unable to make direct contact with the man he'd arranged to meet. 'So we have to meet up like a couple of cold war spies and play this clock and dagger game?'

'Yes, I'm afraid so. Now, can we get a move on?' He checked his watch, then fixed his gaze on Schrader. 'It's been six months since we met face to face. Bring me up to speed. How did the trials go?'

Schrader reached down below the table and pulled out a buff coloured folder from the briefcase at his feet. He placed it on the table, looked up at Lawrence to ensure he had his full attention. He did. Lawrence stared at the folder, eyes wide open, his face expectant.

'Technically, the trials went better than expected.' Schrader began as he opened the folder and studied the paper it contained.

'Technically?' Lawrence squinted at the report and tipped his head as if he could read it upside down.

'Hmmm yes,' Schrader looked down at his notes. He continued without looking up. 'The formula worked as predicted, but...' He tapped a highlighted section towards the bottom of the page and paused.

'But what?'

Schrader's face screwed in discomfort. 'There were side effects.' He said simply.

Lawrence's eyes narrowed, and he leaned forward without speaking. The waiter returned with menus. Lawrence grabbed them and dismissed the man with a peremptory wave of his hand. His eyes never left Schrader. 'Go on.'

'Some of the test subjects became ill.'

'So. That's only to be expected, isn't it?'

Schrader gave a couple of nods. 'Some were seriously ill, critically ill.' He braced himself before delivering the news he knew would cause Lawrence to react. 'Word got out and reached Archer.'

Lawrence squeezed his eyes shut and tipped his head back, his fists clenched on the table. 'Fucking Archer. How the hell did he find out?'

'I don't know. I have my suspicions, but I can't be certain.'

'Bloody fucking brilliant, Manfred. You assured me your operation was secure.'

'It was. I mean is, it is secure. I vetted all those working on the project. They were sworn to secrecy.' Schrader stuttered. He resented the accusation.

Lawrence opened his eyes and stared at the ceiling. 'Don't tell me. He got all high and mighty and told you to stop?' He ground the words out.

Schrader shook his head slowly. 'Not just stop. He told me to destroy all stocks of the formula and all the paperwork and research I'd done. I've never seen him so riled about anything.'

Lawrence's jaw dropped. 'Idiot man, doesn't he realise what it could be worth?'

'He's not interested in the money. He went on and on about ethics.'

'Ethics!' Lawrence snorted. 'Fucking ethics.'

Schrader held up a hand to calm the man opposite. 'I'm not stupid. I made a show of shredding a load of paperwork and burning a pile of samples. No one checked, all the staff believed I'd done as Archer asked.'

Lawrence exhaled, his shoulder slumped and his mouth curled in a slow smile. 'Good man. So where are we now?'

'We?' Schrader's eyebrows rose.

'OK, where are you now?'

Schrader nodded briefly to acknowledge the correction, then continued. 'I've been building stocks ever since. Working evenings and weekends, no one else knows. There's over three thousand boxes, labeled and ready to go.'

'Have you changed the formula as a result of the trials?'

Schrader looked down at his notes and rubbed his hand over his mouth as he spoke. 'There's been some adjustment.' He mumbled.

Lawrence paused, his eyes narrowed, and he turned his head to look sideways at Schrader. He studied the scientist for a moment, deciding whether or not to pursue the point. He relented and continued. 'What have you done about the packaging?'

'There's nothing to trace it back to the factory, all fake numbers and contact details.'

Lawrence liked what he heard and gave an appreciative nod. 'Excellent. I've got my man ready in the UK. You can start to ship them with the official stuff, just number the boxes as we agreed and he'll pull the ones we want to one side.'

'Is he going to manage the order fulfilment as well?'

'Absolutely, all set up.'

Schrader consulted the report again and turned a page. He tapped a handwritten note in a margin with his finger. 'Is this the same man that's handling the marketing?'

'Indirectly. He's found a computer geek, a Korean, who's hacked into some of the big online retailers. He's been harvesting email addresses for the last few weeks. I set him up with all the hardware he asked for and he's got over two hundred thousand names already.' Lawrence sat back and puffed himself up as if he had personally achieved the feat.

Schrader had his head down and missed the display of undeserved self congratulation. He had taken out a pen and wrote additional remarks in the margin of the notes. 'I still have a problem with Archer though.' He spoke as he wrote, without looking up.

Lawrence caught the change in tone of the scientist's voice, a mixture of hate and resentment. 'What sort of problem?'

'As long as he runs the company, he gets all the glory, all the awards, the accolades, the magazine articles. And.' Schrader stopped writing and looked directly at the man opposite. 'He prevents me from making progress, he's banned me from doing any research outside his own narrow ethical remit.' Schrader's fists clenched tight on the table, his knuckles white as he ground out the last three words.

Taken aback by the venom, Lawrence frowned. 'So, why not leave? He'd be up shit creek without you.'

Schrader snorted at the idea. 'And do what? Start again from scratch? I've got a whole factory at my disposal. When he's not there, I can do what I want, I can produce what I want.' His fists started to pound slowly on the table and the colour rose in his face. 'I'd receive the recognition I deserve. I'm the brains behind Azllomed, not Archer.'

'Steady on, Manfred.' Lawrence looked around, worried that the raised voice and the thumping on the table might have attracted unwanted attention. A thought occurred to him. 'What would happen if Archer wasn't there?'

'He's not there, most of the time, he only comes to the factory four or five times a year.'

'No.' Lawrence lowered his voice and leaned forward. 'What would happen if Archer was no more?'

The remark caused Schrader to jerk back, his eyes bore into Lawrence. 'What are you suggesting?'

'Accidents happen Manfred.' Lawrence gave a casual shrug, 'If Archer had an accident, who would take over at Azllomed?'

'I'd have to, I'm a director of the company and the plant manager.' As he spoke Schrader's eyes scanned the arched ceiling of the small dining room while he contemplated a scenario he'd never considered before. Then his face tightened again as a new reality hit him. 'There'd be a problem with the CGC, they have a seat on the Board and they don't like me.'

'Maybe. But you'd be the obvious choice to take over.'

'They'd put someone else in to replace Archer and control me.'

'We could work around that.'

'How?'

'Manfred, have you forgotten, I'm a member of the CGC. I could make sure I was appointed as some sort of caretaker CEO. You'd be free to do whatever we wanted.'

Schrader considered this. He sat back with arms folded tight across his chest. He scrutinised Lawrence through narrowed eyes. 'It's an attractive proposition, but...'

'But how do we arrange for Archer to have an accident. Is that what you're thinking?'

'Hmm, yes. But I want him to suffer.'

Lawrence recoiled at the sudden vindictive attitude, but realised that Schrader's mind had moved forward a pace. 'That's up to you Manfred. You're the research chemist, if you can't come up with something to make someone suffer, then nobody can.'

———————— ••●•• ————————

Susie cycled back from work and arrived home around six. As she dismounted she realised something was missing, the Golf. It took her a moment before she remembered Nick was working at a conference in Manchester and he'd taken the car. He'd told her he'd be back by seven. She seized the opportunity for a quick change from cyclist to runner, not quite at the transition speed she'd aim for in a race, and headed out for an easy three-mile run.

She rounded the corner into their road twenty-five minutes later, and expected to see the Golf parked in the driveway. No car.

She assumed Nick must have been held up in traffic and knew he'd be cursing that he didn't go on his bike. While she cooled down, she made a start in the kitchen and got to work preparing salad ingredients.

Half an hour later, showered and dressed, she sat at the kitchen table, engrossed in her triathlon magazine, when she heard the car pull up.

Nick walked in with bags slung over his shoulders. He looked exhausted. 'Hello love, missed me?' He carefully placed his camera bag on the table before he leaned over and planted a smacker on Susie's cheek.

She patted his face. 'Of course I missed you.' She glanced up at the kitchen clock. 'I'm guessing you got stuck in traffic?'

'I hate the bloody M6.' Nick rolled his eyes in despair. 'Thirty miles of roadworks and a fifty limit all the way.'

Susie tutted in response. 'I bet you wish you'd gone on the BM.'

'Just a bit. I'd have been back two hours ago.' He took his camera gear to his office and returned to the kitchen. He picked up one of the salad servers and gave Susie's creation a curious prod. 'This looks great. I'm starving.'

'Well, sit yourself down. I'll dish up and you can tell me about your day.' Susie got up and loaded two large bowls. She placed one in front of Nick. She picked a couple of forks from a nearby drawer and retrieved a bottle of dressing from the fridge. She sat down opposite Nick and looked expectantly at him.

'You'll never guess who I've been taking pictures of today?' he said.

Susie looked up with her head cocked.

'Only our glorious leader,' Nick said.

Susie appeared genuinely impressed. 'You mean Theresa May? Did you not know she was going to be there?'

'Well, the organisers knew, but they weren't allowed to tell anyone, bit of a surprise.'

'What was she doing?'

'That's the best bit,' Nick said with a flourish. 'She was there to present some awards and one of them was to an MEP who's been campaigning about all the junk email and email scams. I thought you might be interested.'

Susie raised an eyebrow. 'Who was he?'

'Some guy called Lawrence, never heard of him. I mean, who knows who their MEP is, or was? They're all going to be out of a job soon anyway.'

Nick placed a forkful of salad in his mouth and chewed on a piece of grilled haloumi.

'This guy Lawrence. Did you get any more info on him?'

Nick still chewed his food and couldn't speak for a moment. He placed his hand in front of his mouth. 'No, I'm just the humble snapper. It'll all be online though.'

Susie shrugged. 'Did he say anything? Did anyone say anything about him?'

Nick finished his mouthful and swallowed before he answered. 'He didn't, but they had someone from local TV acting as MC. She said a bit about him leading the fight against unsolicited email and his drive for tighter regulation around personal data.'

Susie twirled her fork in the air. 'Could be interesting.' She reached for her phone. 'What was his name?'

'Lawrence, Sir Giles Lawrence.'

She tapped the screen a few times and within seconds, her face lit up. 'Aha, here he is.'

Nick struggled to see her screen.

She turned the phone to show him. 'That him?'

Nick nodded.

Susie scowled at the image. 'Hmm, looks like he's had one too many corporate lunches to me.'

'Naturally. What else d'you think MEPs do?'

'It says here he has a logistics business, GPL, that's basically trucking isn't it?'

Nick didn't look up from his salad. 'Something like that, distribution and storage.' He spoke through a mouthful of food.

'Hmm. He could be interesting. I'll make a note to get in touch with him.' She put her phone down and resumed her meal.

CHAPTER 8

Gianfranco DeLuca held out his hand as the bookie counted out his winnings in crisp twenty-pound notes.

'That's three hundred and forty.' The bookie paused and pulled a handful of coins from his pocket. He counted out four pound coins and dropped them into the waiting hand. 'And four makes three, forty-four.'

Frank nodded and stuffed the notes into his wallet.

His racing buddy, a round-faced man with a florid complexion, stood next to him. He shook his head in disbelief. 'Lucky by name, lucky by nature. Who else would put fifty quid on the nose of a complete outsider?'

DeLuca smiled and tapped the side of his nose. 'Not a complete outsider, but decent odds. I had a hunch it would win.' They both turned and headed for the bar.

He'd only gone a few steps when he felt his phone vibrating. He pulled it out and glanced at the screen. 'Bloody hell.'

His companion hadn't heard the phone, but heard the reaction. 'What's up?'

'I need to take this. Get the drinks in, my round.' He pulled one of the twenties from his wallet and handed it over. 'I'll be back in a minute.'

The phone continued to vibrate on silent and DeLuca waited until he'd reached a quiet spot near the parade ring before he answered. 'Yes.'

'Where the hell are you? What took you so long to answer?'

'And a very good evening to you, too.'

'Never mind that, we've got trouble...' The public address system burst into life to announce the next race. '... where the hell are you?'

'Stratford racecourse, evening meeting. Why, what's the problem?'

The curt voice at the other end didn't actually care where DeLuca was. 'That bloody woman has been in touch.'

Caught off guard, and not sure who *"that bloody woman"* was, DeLuca could only respond with. 'I see.'

The voice continued. 'She actually called me for help. Can you believe it?'

DeLuca's brain whirred and puzzle pieces slotted together. 'Why wouldn't she? You're the man of the moment. Like you've said, the perfect cover.'

'Maybe so, but she's a great deal smarter than we've given her credit for. She's asked if I'd be prepared to go public and get the media to run negative stories about the product. Kill it dead.'

'Bloody hell.' DeLuca looked around to check nobody could hear him.

'Exactly. I've told her to do nothing for a couple of days, but she's impulsive and I can't rely on her keeping her word.'

'Uh huh.' DeLuca remained noncommittal. He suspected what was coming next. 'So what d'you want to do?'

'We can't risk her finding anything else out. There's too much at stake.'

DeLuca took the phone from his ear and stared at it. He knew what he was being asked to do. He didn't get involved in what some called "wet work" but he recognised when necessity dictated it. He returned the phone to his ear. 'So you want my boys to deal with her?'

'Precisely.'

'Like they did with our Korean friend?'

'Yes, not like they did when they tried to stop her in Reading. I've had a better idea. They don't even need to get their hands dirty.'

DeLuca glanced about. Spectators returned to the parade ring. He walked across to a small wooden building that offered a wall to lean on. He cradled his phone between neck and shoulder and withdrew pen and a small notebook from the breast pocket of his jacket. 'OK, go ahead.'

He listened intently as the disembodied voice detailed the plan. He wrote down place names and times and clicked the ballpoint repeatedly as he listened.

'Can you trust your "*boys*" to do that?' the voice asked when finished.

'It sounds simple enough. You're sure about the times and the route?'

'I've got a picture of her route, I'll send it to you.'

DeLuca nodded at this. 'Leave it with me. You'll have no more trouble from her.'

'That's what I wanted to hear.' The phone clicked off.

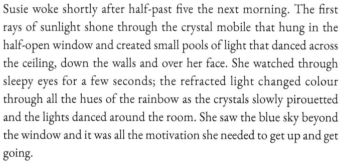

Susie woke shortly after half-past five the next morning. The first rays of sunlight shone through the crystal mobile that hung in the half-open window and created small pools of light that danced across the ceiling, down the walls and over her face. She watched through sleepy eyes for a few seconds; the refracted light changed colour through all the hues of the rainbow as the crystals slowly pirouetted and the lights danced around the room. She saw the blue sky beyond the window and it was all the motivation she needed to get up and get going.

She looked forward to her Wednesday morning bike ride. The thirty-mile route combined quiet country lanes with a challenging climb and a long, fast descent back through the woods. She loved it. She had a map of the route pinned up beside her computer at work and at various key points, she'd written times, distances and average speeds. Her exploits were the subject of many water-cooler conversations and she delighted in sharing the footage from her helmet mounted GoPro that Nick had bought her for her last birthday. Maybe today she could break her record and get under ninety minutes for the trip.

She looked over at Nick; sprawled out on his chest, his breathing slow and shallow, with the duvet that barely covered him. The lights danced across his naked back. She smiled and shook her head. Dead to the world; she wished she could sleep so deeply.

She silently rolled out of bed, made for the bathroom, then into the spare room where she'd left her cycling gear laid out ready. She dressed quickly and quietly, headed down to the kitchen for a glass of water, then into the garage for her bike.

She checked her watch, clipped her iPhone into the bracket on the handlebars and made sure it picked up the signal from her heartbeat monitor and the bike mounted sensors. Once out of the garage, she swung a leg over the crossbar and stood poised and ready. She activated the GoPro, clipped her helmet in place and hit go on the Strava app. She pushed off down the lane and her cycling shoes clicked into the pedal binding with a reassuring snap.

A hundred yards ahead, she swerved to avoid a white transit van parked on the roadside, its engine running.

••◉••

Decebal dozed in the driver's seat and jerked awake when Sergei shook him. He looked to see what has caused his passenger to act and saw the cyclist they had been waiting for.

He knew which way she was going, he was in no hurry. He waited until she had rounded the corner and was out of sight, before he pulled out and followed.

••◉••

Susie relished the early morning, the quiet roads, the late July sun and the way nature came alive all around her. She headed west and aimed for the hills with the sun on her back. She sucked in the cool clean air, her muscles warmed to the task and legs pumped up and down as she pedalled, her cadence smooth and strong. She stuck to the back roads where the landscape undulated gently, and she rarely needed to change gear. She stretched forward, and rested her elbows on the bar pads. Her hands gripped the extended bar ends in the classic racing tuck of the downhill skier.

She checked her watch again and made a quick mental calculation; she needed to be back home by eight. She had plenty of time. She felt good. If she really went for it, she would smash ninety minutes. The thought spurred her on; she shifted position, moved her hands to the normal, wide handlebar grips, stood up in the saddle, and through gritted teeth, she pushed, faster and faster, harder and harder. She flicked the gear lever; the chain whirred onto the smallest cog on the back wheel, top gear, and she pushed harder again. Her heartbeat rose, beads of perspiration formed on her brow, and her breath became more laboured.

When she could pedal no faster, with the bike up to speed, she sat back down and assumed her aerodynamic tuck, and forced her legs to maintain the same cadence. The screen on her phone indicated twenty three mph as she passed Nook Farm and headed along Quillow Lane. The road flattened out. The gentle breeze was on her back. Susie glanced down at the screen and between breaths managed an encouraging, 'Come on!' to herself. She felt the lactic acid building up in her legs with the effort and as the road turned left and started to climb slightly, she eased up on the pedals, changed down a couple of gears and continued at a more sustainable pace.

After thirty minutes and nine more miles, she came to the village of Upper Fromston and joined the main road that ran north towards Craneborough.

The van followed two hundred yards behind her.

At the small roundabout, two miles beyond Upper Fromston, she turned left and again headed West towards the hills. The road climbed gradually, then steeper as it made its way towards the gap between Yewtree Hill and Linley Down and the ridge beyond.

••●••

Decebal pulled into a gateway and checked the picture that DeLuca had sent to his phone. He didn't want to get too close and watched as Susie started her climb. After a while he moved off again.

●●◆●●

The climb became more acute, and it forced Susie to change down through the gears. She stood up on the pedals and rocked the bike from side to side to maintain her smooth progress. The road narrowed, gave up its direct assault on the slope, and headed up the wooded hillside in a series of hairpin bends. The trees on either side created the illusion of a tunnel with shafts of dazzling light that lanced across the road. The light picked out tiny airborne bugs and added a vibrancy to the vivid colours of the broadleaved branches that reached out and down and caressed passing vehicles, or cyclists too close to the verge.

The road climbed, and Susie's breath became more strained. She got out of the saddle and pushed hard for fifty revolutions, then sat down again and ground out another fifty before repeating the process. She rasped hard, but she was beating the hill and she loved it. The road levelled out as she reached the top of the escarpment and between two rows of sycamore trees and she headed north. She sat back in the saddle and stretched out on the aero bars, to minimise her profile and maximise her aerodynamic efficiency. She clicked the gears up a cog and settled again into a steady rhythm. Her breathing eased and a bead a sweat dropped from her brow onto the phone. The screen read twenty-four mph.

A quarter of a mile behind her, the transit still followed her, but Susie hadn't noticed.

The sun climbed, and the shadows cast by the sycamores became shorter. Susie continued along the ridge, gradually heading more West than North. It was approaching six-thirty. She knew that from there it took her another forty-five minutes to complete the loop back home. The best bit was yet to come. The highlight of the route for Susie had always been the drop off the ridge, and she loved the thrill of the descent and the speed she could manage as the road dropped through the trees in a series of fast open curves she could take without touching the brakes. She bragged to Nick, and anyone else who would listen, that she could top forty mph plunging down Linley hill. Nick worried about her and cautioned her about the limited traction offered by the skinny tyres and the complete absence of any suspension to soak up the bumps of a road badly in need of resurfacing. Susie would have none of it.

The road fell away. Susie passed the 'steep hill' sign, clicked the gears to select the highest possible of the twenty-four ratios. She stood up in the saddle and pushed the bike as fast as she could down the hill.

The transit started closing on her, but Susie's attention remained riveted on the road ahead; with the occasional glance down at the screen to see if she could top forty.

The narrow road swooped down, the gradient sometimes steep, sometimes gentle, but always down. Trees crowded on both sides, with no footpath and no verge. Susie stretched out on the bike, sat as far back on the saddle as she could, her elbows on the padded rests and her hands gripped the ends of the bars.

The road levelled for a few hundred yards before its final descent to the valley below. A blind bend to the right over a crest led to a sharp drop before a fast, open left, then it dipped and turned right again as it crossed a bridge over a small stream. Susie braced herself as she went over the brow - she knew the road was bumpy and was ready as the bike bounced and shook. She relaxed her grip on the bars and let the gyroscopic effect help the wheel stay on track. The fast left approached, and she swung out wide to the right and then swept over to the left, her knee hanging out motorcycle style, as she leaned the bike over and raced through the bend. She risked a brief glance at the screen–forty-four mph - she was approaching the bottom of the hill. Faster, faster, she told herself. She tucked in, her chin almost on the bars, her elbows braced, and she willed the bike to go faster. For once, she wished she was heavier.

She didn't see the white van until it was alongside her.

The van gave her no room - what was the driver doing?

The bend was almost upon her; she needed all the road.

At that speed, she couldn't slow down in time.

The van moved closer and pushed her towards the verge. A hand reached out from the open passenger window.

Susie screamed; an incoherent yell, a combination of terrified realisation and total outrage.

The fingers of the hand were splayed, four fingers, no thumb and a tattoo.

Images flashed through her mind. The bridge rushed at her. She could see a gap between the van and the stone parapet. Maybe she could make it.

The van nudged to the left and the extended hand pushed against Susie's shoulder.

In desperation, she grabbed both brakes with all her strength but hit the low stone parapet. The front wheel buckled immediately.

The impact catapulted the bike through the air. Susie's feet remained clipped into the pedals. She hung onto the handlebars and gripped the brakes instinctively, as she flipped upside down. The world made no sense. A blur of colour, shapes and images flashed past at impossible speed, a rush of wind, but no other noise. She flew inverted and back to front. Her mouth remained open, but no sound came out. She could see the ground below her, green and brown and unforgiving. She didn't see the tree that stopped her flight. The Scot's Pine just happened to be in the wrong place.

The impact was sudden and brutal.

She hit it first with her right shoulder, then the side of her head. Her helmet cracked with the impact. An intense pain shot through her arm and neck. It felt as though she had been stabbed. The bright morning sunlight faded in an instant, and the world went black.

She was unconscious before she came to rest at the bottom of the tree, and landed in a thick patch of nettles. The bike ended up on top of her.

From the road, a keen-eyed observer might have spotted the wheel of a bike lying at the bottom of the embankment beside the bridge, but it was unlikely.

The transit didn't slow down or stop; it continued on its way.

Part Three

Revelation

CHAPTER 9

Nick strolled into the organiser's office adjacent to Hall 3 of the National Exhibition Centre, made his way to where he'd left his gear, and placed his camera with deliberate care alongside his laptop.

He pulled his phone from the depths of his camera bag and thrust it into the back pocket of his black jeans without looking at the screen, and went in search of refreshment. The clock on the wall read 10.55. He'd been busy for almost two hours and needed a break. Thankfully, the organisers, always keen to get rave reviews from the press, had supplied a tempting selection of Danish pastries to accompany the freshly brewed coffee. Nick poured himself a mug, no milk or sugar, and grabbed a cinnamon whirl before returning to the spot he'd claimed.

He sat down, picked up the camera, popped the card out, and slotted it into the laptop. As he waited for the images to download, he blew on the coffee and took a hesitant sip. He pulled his phone from his pocket and placed it alongside the laptop without paying it much attention. The movement brought the screen to life, and he noticed a text message and a notification of a missed call. They were both from the same number. He didn't recognise it. The text asked him to call back as a matter of urgency.

Bloody sales calls, he thought, another scam. He swiped the message to delete it and was about to do the same to the notification, when the phone rang again, same number. He stared at the screen and let the phone ring, reluctant to answer it. His natural wariness told him not to, but curiosity and an uneasy sixth sense won out. He tapped the green button.

'Hello.' He kept his tone neutral.

'Is that Nick Cooper?' a female voice asked.

'Who wants to know?' It came out a little more aggressive than Nick meant.

'My name is Elizabeth Gardiner. I'm a doctor at Whitney Hospital.'

Nick sat up, curiosity replaced by concern. 'Err yes, I'm Nick Cooper. Is something wrong?' He didn't like the sound or the feel of it, and the seconds dragged by before the voice continued.

'We've had a lady brought in who has your number listed as her emergency contact on her phone. She has no other ID on her.'

His pulse raced. He felt sweat on his brow and uncertainty in the pit of his stomach. For a moment he thought he was going to be sick - his stomach knotted, and colour drained from his face. 'Oh my God, that's my wife, is she, is she...'

The voice was calm, reassuring, and professional. 'She's unconscious Mr Cooper. It appears she's been in an accident. Are you able to get to the hospital?'

Nick found it hard to think straight. 'Err, yes, I'm at the NEC at the moment. It'll take me a while to get there. Is she all right?'

'The doctors are with her now, Mr Cooper. What's your wife's name?'

There was panic in Nick's voice. 'It's Susie, Susie Cooper. What happened? Can't you tell me anything?' Nick got to his feet and held the back of the chair for support.

'We don't know what happened. She was brought in about thirty minutes ago. We're running tests at the moment. We'll know more by the time you get here.' She paused. 'Are you all right to drive?'

'Yeah, sure, I'm on my way. Tell her I'm on my way.' Nick ended the call and looked around the room, momentarily rooted to the spot. Tears threatened. His heart pounded and made him breathe hard; he felt as though his legs would give way. He wanted to sit down, but needed to move. He turned left and right and left again. He moved for the door, then returned to his gear, then headed for the door again. He couldn't make a decision. In an instant, his world had turned upside down, and nothing else mattered other than Susie. He stopped, closed his eyes, and took a deep breath to calm himself. He exhaled and opened his eyes.

Clarity.

He crammed his equipment into its bag, grabbed his jacket, and headed out the door.

—————————— ••●•• ——————————

Lights emerged from the darkness; bright, swirling, and out of focus. Indistinct, muffled sounds seeped into her world as consciousness returned. She became aware of the smell; clinical, antiseptic, chemical and her nose wrinkled against it. Her mouth tasted metallic, her lips dry, her tongue parched. Confusion filled her head, which throbbed with a dull ache.

Susie squeezed her eyes shut and re-opened them. She squinted against the light and focused on her surroundings. She slowly turned her head to her right and a sharp pain shot through her shoulder.

She cried out. 'Holly fuck!'

She heard people beyond the confines of her room. 'Hello!' She called out, her voice a painful croak.

She stared at the ceiling and waited for a reaction. An intense sensation gripped her arms and legs. They felt as though they were on fire. She rubbed her left forearm with her right hand, but the movement caused the pain in her shoulder to stab through her entire body and she screamed again.

The noise alerted a nearby nurse, who immediately called for the doctor before approaching Susie..She placed a gentle, restraining hand on Susie's good shoulder and carefully took her right hand and placed it over her chest. 'Shh, keep still. You've got a fractured clavicle. Jumping around like that isn't going to help.'

Susie stared wide-eyed at the nurse and tried to sit up. The pain was too much; she cried out and slumped back down. 'Where am I? What's happened?'

The nurse smiled down 'You're in safe hands. That's where you are. We were hoping you might tell us what happened. It's Susie, isn't it?'.

Susie's vision cleared slowly, and she took in her surroundings and her situation. She noticed they had wired her up to a monitor that pinged rapidly with her exertions. The ward had one other bed, vacant, and expensive looking machines that surrounded her. The door stood ajar and hinted at activity beyond - lights, noises and people.

Susie peered at the nurse's badge. *NHS Whitney Hospital*, it announced her name was Muriel. Susie nodded, 'Uh-uh, Susie, how d'you know?'

'Your husband told us, he's on his way here.' Muriel took her hand away from Susie's shoulder. 'Now keep still, you'll just hurt yourself more if you move.'

They were interrupted by the arrival of the doctor, a tall slim woman in her late 20s, dressed in green scrubs with the obligatory stethoscope, which hung around her neck. 'Thanks for call Muriel, how's the patient?'

'The patient is hurting like hell and extremely pissed off.' Susie spoke before Muriel had a chance to reply.

The doctor looked at Muriel, who responded with a helpless shrug. 'Susie, this is Doctor Gardiner. She's the one who spoke to your husband.'

Susie's eyes narrowed, and she glowered at the doctor. 'What's happened to me? Why are my arms and legs burning up? It's agony.'

'According to the paramedics, they found you in a nettle patch at the bottom of a tree with a bicycle on top of you. You've been stung all over. We're all wondering how you ended up there.'

Susie gave an uncomprehending look, as though the doctor should know the answer. 'I was riding down the long hill from the ridge through the woods.' Her eyes flicked from side to side, as she searched for recollection. 'There was a white van.' She paused, her brow furrowed in concentration. 'I can't remember…'

The doctor looked puzzled. 'Are you saying the van ran you off the road?'

Susie screwed up her face, one eye closed. 'It's all a bit of a blur. I was flat out; the bike was bouncing about all over the place; I remember that.'

'Did the van come towards you or from behind?'

'It appeared out of nowhere. I just remember it appeared suddenly alongside me.' Susie shuddered as a picture formed in her mind.

The doctor exchanged glances with Muriel. They both stared, open-mouthed, at Susie. 'That sounds very deliberate.'

Susie cocked her head to one side and winced in pain at the movement. 'I don't know, it's a narrow road.'

'Don't you think it's strange it didn't stop?' the doctor said.

'Hmmmm.' Susie considered the idea and remained quiet for a moment as she processed her thoughts. She changed the subject to avoid further interrogation. 'Can you give me something for the nettle stings? It feels like I'm burning up.'

The doctor nodded at Muriel, who slipped out of the ward. 'We'll get you some cream for that. Muriel must have mentioned your fractured clavicle?'

Susie closed her eyes and dipped her chin a fraction in response.

'It's a clean break, but it'll take a few weeks to mend. There's not a lot we can do with it.'

'Can't you pin it or plate it or something?'

'It's an option, but that would require surgery and there's always the risk of infection. It's best to let it mend on its own.'

Susie grimaced and opened her mouth to reply when she heard a familiar voice from beyond the ward.

'Susie!' Nick's tone a mixture of panic and desperation. 'Susie, where are you?'

Before Susie could call out, the doctor went to the door and saw a man at the reception desk. He appeared agitated as he looked around and turned in circles. The doctor caught his attention and beckoned him over.

'Is she all right?' He was breathless and flushed. 'Can I speak to her?' He tried to push past, but the doctor laid a calm hand on his shoulder.

'Your wife is in a lot of pain, so don't go hugging her.' She kept the hand on his shoulder and restrained him until she was sure he understood. 'She's broken her collarbone, but she'll be OK. She's very fragile, so...'

Nick brushed the doctor aside before she had finished and went straight to Susie.

She recoiled in terror with wide, frightened eyes. 'Don't touch me.' She held her left hand up to reinforce her message as Nick, arms outstretched, moved towards her.

Nick checked himself and went no closer. 'Don't worry, I've got the message.' He studied his wife for a couple of seconds and looked for signs of injury. He shook his head and gently reached for Susie's hand. 'What have you done? How did this happen?'

Susie said nothing for a few moments and instead composed herself. She bit her lip and withdrew her hand from Nick's grasp. She covered her eyes from the glare of the lights. Her voice faltered and became faint. 'I don't know exactly. I must have crashed or something. I can't really remember anything.'

The doctor stood next to the bed and looked puzzled. 'I thought you said a van pushed you off the road?'

Nick turned. 'What?' He looked back at Susie, who still had her hand over her eyes.

She shook her head slowly. 'I've got a splitting headache; I can't really remember anything properly. I think my brain is playing tricks on me.'

'What's the last thing you can remember?' Nick noticed the rash on Susie's forearms. 'What the hell happened to your arms?'

'They found her in a bed of nettles.' The doctor looked at Susie, unable to understand why she had changed her story in less than a minute.

Nick smiled at the doctor and noticed her name badge. 'Sorry Doctor, it was you that called me, wasn't it?'

The doctor nodded.

'Sorry for barging in like that. This is all a bit of a shock.'

'No need to apologise. Anxious relatives are all part of the job.'

Muriel returned with a tube of ointment. She held it up to show Susie. 'Some topical antihistamine cream to relieve the itching.'

Nick backed off towards the door, inclined his head at the doctor, and mouthed. 'Can I have a word?'

She got the message and followed him out to the reception area while Muriel applied the ointment.

'What is it?'

Nick looked back at Susie to make sure they were out of earshot. 'I just wanted to thank you for all you've done and find out a bit more about what's happened to her.'

'No problem. What do you want to know?'

'When was she brought in? How is she? What state is she in?'

The doctor had Susie's notes in her hand and consulted them. 'They admitted her at 10.26 this morning.'

'Bloody hell, she left the house at stupid o'clock this morning, same every Wednesday. She has a regular route out in the country, normally takes her less than two hours.' He gazed over at Susie's bed. 'She could have been out of it for hours.'

'We have no way of knowing, but we're always a little wary when someone's brought in unconscious.' She pointed to Susie's notes as though it meant something to Nick. 'An unconscious patient is category one. That's why she's in the ICU.' She read from the notes without looking at Nick. 'She's been x-rayed and we've taken blood tests. We'd routinely intubate, but we assessed her and felt her breathing was normal and all her vital signs were within range. She had a GCS score of 12.'

Nick interrupted. 'Is that good or bad?'

'It's a scale of 3 to 15, so 12 is good. The x-ray revealed the fractured clavicle, but there's not a lot we can do about that, other than morphine for pain relief. The only other thing that concerned us was her heartbeat.'

Nick looked worried. 'What's wrong with it?'

'We couldn't believe it at first. We thought there must have been a technical fault with the machine.'

A smile spread across Nick's face, and he nodded. He understood. 'Too low?'

'It was less than 40 beats per minute. A normal pulse is around 72.'

The nodding turned to a resigned shake of the head. 'She's obsessed with her heartbeat monitor and her resting pulse. A couple of mornings ago, she took great delight in telling me it was 39.'

The doctor returned the smile. 'Your wife must be very fit.'

'Something like that. She's trains like a maniac every day. It's an obsession.'

'What for?'

'Triathlon, she races regularly, got a big one coming up in a couple of months.' Nick glanced back at Susie's bed with a look of pride.

'Well, I'm afraid she's going to have to make other plans.' The doctor studied the notes and gave a rueful smile. 'I doubt she'll be able to do much more than walk for at least a month.'

Nick's face fell. 'Oh God, she'll be impossible.'

'Let's just get her better first. She needs peace and quiet and lots of rest.'

'She can't sit still for two minutes. Trying to get her to rest will be a challenge.' Nick responded as he gazed into the middle distance and contemplated Susie's reaction to the news. A thought hit him and he turned to the doctor. 'Do you know where they found her?'

'Hang on.' The doctor reached for the folder that held the admissions forms. She found Susie's. 'It says here she was on the side of Kingsmoor road, near a bridge. The woman who found her was riding her horse through the woods.'

'I don't suppose they got the woman's name?'

The doctor checked and raised her eyebrows in surprise. 'Would you believe it? They did; name, address and phone number. Wonders never cease.'

Nick peered over her shoulder at the form. He slipped his phone from his back pocket, turned on the camera and snapped the note before the doctor realised what he was doing.

'You can't do that, Mr Cooper. These notes are confidential.' The doctor closed the folder and scowled at Nick.

Nick winked at her. 'Don't worry, nobody will ever know.'

The scowl turned to a frown, then one corner of her mouth turned up. 'Any other liberties you want to take?'

Nick looked around. 'Are the paramedics who brought her in still here?'

'I doubt it. Once they've brought a casualty in, they're usually back out on another job. I could ask for you?'

'Would they have brought her bike as well?'

'It's unlikely there's not much space in the ambulance.'

Nick shrugged, then had another thought. 'What about her crash helmet and her phone?'

The doctor consulted the notes. She turned the page and looked for any reference to personal effects. 'They found her phone, that's how we could call you, but there's nothing here about a crash helmet. I guess they must have left it where they found her.'

Nick scratched the top of his head, his focus miles away.

The doctor's eyes narrowed as she looked at Nick. 'Is it important?'

'Well, the bike certainly is. It's a carbon fibre thing, cost a small fortune, god knows what state it's in. No, it's the helmet I'd like to get back. I think it might have a story to tell.'

CHAPTER 10

It took Susie a few days to recover from the nettle stings and for the rash to disappear from her face, arms, and legs.

The broken collar bone presented a more serious problem and her impatience to return to training only made it more frustrating. She tried some gentle jogging, but the broken bones grated with every step she took, and no amount of paracetamol could numb the agony she felt.

With her best bike smashed beyond repair, she fixed her old one to the turbo trainer in the hope of some form of workout, but even that proved too much as her shoulder protested the moment she leant forward and took her weight through her arms. After just a couple of minutes, she gave up.

She had attempted and abandoned swimming. Whatever stroke she tried involved the rotation of the shoulder joint. The connecting tissues pulled and pushed the broken pieces of collar bone. She couldn't manage a single length and had Climbed out of the pool, exasperated and annoyed. She'd snapped at everyone who had approached her.

Nick had made his views clear about the whole incident. He had pleaded with her to forget her investigation and had pointed out that she was dealing with people prepared to go to extreme lengths to stop her. The police couldn't track down the white van that had run her off the road and despite several phone calls from Susie and her Editor, they were not prepared to investigate the matter any further, and claimed they lacked the necessary resources, much as Mandy's brother had intimated.

She had been officially signed off work with instructions to rest. She found it impossible to sit and do nothing. She relished being busy and felt powerless to do anything active.

It had been four weeks since she had ordered a box of Thytomet and with all the drama around tracing the source of the emails, tracking the man behind them, being run off the road and then recovering, she had given up waiting. She assumed that Greg had been right when he suggested the whole thing was a scam. So when she heard a package drop through the letterbox on a rainy Wednesday morning, it mystified her. She hadn't done any online shopping for at least a week.

She ripped open the package and extracted a white box about the size of a cigarette packet. It had the word Thytomet printed in bright green, front, back and sides against a pale yellow background. Additional small print covered most of the box. Susie noted that the small print was too small to read without the aid of a magnifying glass.

She opened the box and found two blister packs, each containing 16 orange pills in four rows of four. Each pill completely spherical and the size of a garden pea. The pills had no letters or logo stamped into them. Susie turned the blister pack over and saw the brand name printed repeatedly across the backing foil. She shook the box and something fell out and landed on the floor. A piece of paper folded multiple times. She reached down to retrieve it and winced as the movement aggravated her fracture.

She straightened up and unfolded the paper. She spread it out over the kitchen table and peered at it. Unlike the writing on the outside of the box, the font was large enough to be read. Apart from a few gushing paragraphs of marketing spiel, it gave the usual warnings about seeking medical advice before starting any course of treatment. It listed every possible side-effect or symptom that might be experienced as a result of taking the medication.

Susie dismissed it as a load of legalese designed the cover all and every eventuality in case of litigation. She searched for something that named the manufacturer or gave some indication of official licensing, a certificate number or reference to national or international regulations.

There was nothing.

Having not thought about Thytomet since being run off the road, it all flooded back into the centre of her consciousness and she sat at the kitchen table with the box in one hand while the other flipped the paperwork over and over, hoping she might spot something she'd missed at first sight.

Her initial impression had been correct. Whoever had sent out the stuff did not want anyone to know where it had come from. How was it possible, she thought, to bypass all the clinical governance and sell something on the open market with no recourse?

She had resolved to spend the day cleaning out all the kitchen cupboards. The task was well overdue and was the last thing she wanted to do, but she told herself in hopeless desperation; it needed doing, and she'd exhausted all valid excuses. Now, to her enormous relief, she had an excuse. She pulled out her laptop.

Her enforced sick leave gave her the time she needed to research medical regulation and clinical governance, and she quickly became absorbed in the dubious world of counterfeit and fake pharmaceuticals.

She spent the rest of the day scouring the internet for information about Thytomet. She tried every social media platform or group she could think of. She tried weight loss and diet forums and wasted hours down several rabbit holes, chasing what she hoped would be some sort of lead. Simple Google searches revealed nothing.

When she heard Nick arrive home at six, she quickly shut the laptop and hid all evidence of the package. She couldn't face another confrontation and with guilty realisation, she remembered it was her turn to produce the evening meal.

Nick left at nine the next morning, and Susie picked up where she had left off. The work was tedious, but having got that far, she found she had a burning desire to see the assignment through to the end. Even if it wasn't exactly the assignment Greg had given her.

Having examined and dismissed what she saw as the end users, the consumers of the drug, she decided to go to the regulatory authorities, hoping someone could help.

She started in the UK and found a contact number for the Medicines and Healthcare Products Regulatory Agency (MHRA). They passed her from one office to the next. None could provide her with any clues at all. The name Thytomet didn't ring a bell with any of them. Two of the divisions claimed they could only help her if she emailed a request to them or provided a court order. She spent another fruitless day trawling through a long list of UK based pharma companies and grew increasingly frustrated at the brick walls she came up against. Simply getting past the gatekeepers proved almost impossible, and when she managed it, she met suspicion and sometimes outright hostility. She quickly got the message that her enquiries were not welcome, either that, or they were paranoid about security and industrial secrets.

The next day was a Saturday, which meant she couldn't make any phone calls. She would normally have been at the local parkrun at 9.00am. She contemplated going along as a volunteer but couldn't find the motivation. She knew the sight of the other runners would do nothing to lighten her mood. The weekend dragged. The weather, unusually cold and damp for the end of July, added to her dark mood, and she looked forward to getting back on the case on Monday morning.

Her next stop was the European Medicines Agency (EMA). It took her a couple of hours of detective work to find a contact number for the organisation and when she eventually got through to a human being; a softly spoken young male voice greeted her in perfect English with just a trace of a Dutch accent. After a brief explanation of her enquiry, he put her through to the licensing department where an administrator, an equally friendly woman, listened carefully as Susie ran through her well-worn script about Thytomet.

For once, she didn't get dismissed out of hand. She heard the woman tapping keys.

'Can you spell the product name for me?' the woman said.

Susie did so and heard more tapping.

'Ah, I think I might have found something.'

●●●●●

Thirty minutes later, Susie couldn't wait to call Anna. 'Fancy going to Romania with me?' She blurted out the question as soon as soon as Anna answered the phone.

It took Anna by surprise.'Er, what? Hello, why? What on earth are you up to? Sorry Susie, you've caught me on the hop. I'm trying to finish a report into that last trade mission. They want it for first thing in the morning. What's on your mind?'

'Well, you know that stuff being advertised in the emails we were tracking?'

'Thyro something.'

'Thytomet,' Susie corrected. 'Well, I've got news.'

Anna remained quiet for a second or two. 'Don't tell me you're still chasing a story?'

'Yes, I am still chasing the story.' Susie's tone was defensive, bordering on hurt. 'Someone tried to have me killed or at least scare me off.'

'Hey, I know, I did visit you in hospital remember. But, I thought you'd given up when the guy we tracked down went missing?'

'I had, sort of. But I'd forgot I ordered some of the stuff. It arrived out of the blue last week.'

'So it does actually exist?' Anna sounded dubious.

'Wonders never cease. But here's the thing. There was nothing on the box or in the box to say who made it or where it came from.'

'So it's illegal,' Anna stated, 'and untraceable.'

'Yes...' Susie replied, with a pause for effect, then continued with relish.'... and no.'

'You mean you've found something out?'

'Eventually. It took a few days and a few dozen phone calls, but yes, I think I've got something.'

'But.' Anna's voice sounded plaintive. 'But... what can you do about it? I mean, if the police won't investigate, what do you think you can do?'

'The police haven't got the time or the inclination to do anything about it and the regulating bodies have got so many cases to investigate it would take them years to get around to this stuff.' Susie waited for a response from Anna and took her silence as a signal to continue. 'All we did was track down the person sending the emails and he's disappeared. We know what the product is called and I've found out who makes it.'

'What are they called?'

'Azllomed,' said Susie

Anna followed Susie's track. 'And they're based in Romania?'

'Actually no. Their HQ is here in the UK, but when I rang them, they denied any knowledge of Thytomet. They claimed they had never heard of it. I've checked on their website and there's no mention of it. According to the regulators, there's no such medication. As far as they're concerned, it doesn't exist.'

Anna sounded confused. 'So why Romania?'

'Ah well,' Susie's tone sounded almost triumphant. 'I spoke to the European regulators and got through to someone helpful. They searched for the name and it turns out an aborted application was submitted by a Dr Schrader with an address in Romania.'

'Not a company?'

'No, that's the thing. This Schrader submitted an application for a licence in his own name, but before it could go through the approval process, he withdrew the application. That's why it took so long to find it.'

'Uh huh,' Anna murmured as she digested the information.

'Anyway, I did some digging to find Dr Manfred Schrader, and it turns out he's the production manager and chief research scientist for Azllomed.'

'I'm confused.'

'So was I initially. It turns out Azllomed's registered office is in Swindon, but their production facility is in Romania, a place called Timisoara.'

'You're joking!' Anna's voice jumped an octave.

Susie sounded surprised by Anna's response. 'No; Timisoara. Why, what's the problem?'

'That's where I was born. At least I was told I was born there. I know that's where I came from.'

Susie paused, surprised. 'Really? I knew you were from Romania but you've never mentioned Timisoara. Small world eh?' She continued. 'Well, we'll have to go then. We can track down the factory and do some digging to find your roots.'

Anna wasn't convinced. 'I'm not sure Susie. I don't know if I want to know. I have a good life here. I've been to Bucharest twice for work, but never Timisoara, there's no one there I know.'

'You speak the language though, don't you?' Susie asked

'Well, not really. I know a few words, yes, no, please, thank you; that sort of thing. I'm hardly fluent. I just do the usual Brit abroad thing and expect everyone else to speak English.'

'Well, if you've never been to Timisoara, this is your perfect opportunity,' Susie replied. 'What's the worst that could happen? How many orphanages can there be in Timisoara? I'm sure they keep records. You could find out who your parents were, you might find a long-lost relative. It could be fun.'

Despite Susie's encouragement and positivity, Anna remained sceptical. 'My family has been so good to me. Mum and Dad have always treated me just the same as Jenny and Mark, and we've never really talked about my life before they adopted me. I was only a month or two old at the time.'

'You're a lucky girl, Anna. There must have been so many children in those orphanages who never had the chance you did. Wouldn't you like to know how you came to the UK? I'm sure your folks would understand.'

Anna pondered. 'Maybe. I'll give Mum a ring when I get home, have a quiet word, see what she thinks. I'd hate to hurt her feelings.'

'Well, I'm doing nothing at the moment, just sitting here and vegetating. If you want some moral support, just let me know and I'll come over.'

●●●●

The idea of a trip to Romania had taken a firm hold in Susie's mind. She spent over an hour online, checked airline schedules and discovered more about Timisoara on YouTube. Even if the Azllomed factory turned out to be a dead end, the city sounded interesting and if she persuaded Anna to go, then the trip was on. She printed out the information and covered the kitchen table with paperwork as she discovered more.

Nick returned from a busy day running a photography workshop and walked into the kitchen a moment after Susie had left the room. He flopped into a chair, lent back, stretched his arms out wide and gazed at the ceiling. His gaze fell to the table, and he surveyed the paperwork. He didn't have to be a genius to realise that she was up to something.

Susie hadn't heard Nick return, and his shadow in the kitchen startled her. She found him studying a printout of flight times and prices.

'Oh, hello; I wasn't expecting you back so soon.' Her expression looked a mixture of guilt and annoyance.

Nick didn't look up and instead he poked a finger at the piece of paper in his hand. 'So it would seem.'

'How did the workshop go?'

'What? Oh that, it was… I'm not stupid, love.' Nick waved the sheet of paper at her and gave her an accusing look. 'What are you up to now?'

Susie became defensive. 'I'm not up to anything.' She snatched the sheet of paper out of Nick's hand and gathered the rest of the paperwork together without making eye contact with him. 'I'm signed off work. I've had to stop training. I'm bored and pissed off and I suggested to Anna that we go to Romania for a few days and see if we can trace her family roots.'

Nick dipped his chin and studied her through narrow eyes. 'So, this is nothing to do with the people behind those emails, the ones you upset, the ones who tried to kill you?'

Susie turned away. She couldn't tell a bare-faced lie. 'You know that's where she came from. She's always wanted to find out more about her birth family. She's never had a chance before and had no one to go with. It's a perfect opportunity.' She hadn't answered his question, but she hadn't lied.

'Hmmmm.' Nick knew how stubborn Susie could be. He tried to read her body language. There was something she was hiding. 'You're up to something. I know what you're like.'

'Look, I'm sitting round, kicking my heels. I can't do anything useful. Anna can take some time off. She speaks enough of the language to get by. It'll be a bit of a mini break.'

'Did it ever occur to you that I might be prepared to take some time off and go away with you?'

Susie turned to look directly at Nick. 'Maybe I don't want to go away with you.'

The remark struck hard, and he reeled. 'What's that supposed to mean?'

Susie realised she'd stepped over a line. She could apologise, bottle up her feelings, forget the whole thing, or say how she really felt. She went for the latter. 'Oh, come on, you know perfectly well. We've hardly been close lately. You've done nothing to support me. In fact, you've gone out of your way to prevent me making any progress.'

Nick raised his voice. 'Hold on a minute. I tried to stop you from getting into a whole lot of trouble. I warned you about what you were doing and it's sheer good fortune they didn't kill you. If you see it as me standing in your way...' He looked at the ceiling and spread his hands in desperation. 'Then maybe you do need some time away.'

'Don't play the burning martyr. You've made it clear all along that you'd rather I dropped the investigation. I like the excitement. I enjoy ruffling feathers. It's what I want to do. It's given me a sense of purpose.'

Nick lowered his voice and tried to reason with her. 'You're so bloody obsessive, you go at things without thinking of the consequences. I'm just trying to protect you from yourself.'

'And you're so...' Susie closed her eyes, clenched her fists and searched for the right word. 'So bloody unadventurous.'

'If that's really what you think, then be my guest. You and Anna, go to Romania. See how you get on if you're after excitement and a sense of purpose. In fact, why not move in with Anna? Then you don't have to put up with my boring ways.' He meant it as an ultimatum.

Susie stood in the doorway and folded her arms, her lips compressed into a tight line as she considered it. She turned as though to walk out of the room, then stopped and turned back. 'You know, that's the most sensible thing you've said since you walked in the door. In fact, it's the best idea you've had for a long time.' She turned again and left the room.

'Where are you going now?'

'Just following your instructions, darling. I'm off to pack my bags.'

CHAPTER 11

Ten days later, Nick worked in the garage. He had removed the
tank and seat of the BMW, which had enabled him to get at the
machine's inner workings. With an oily rag in one hand and a screw-
driver in the other, he tinkered around and felt content. He treasured
the bike, and he wished he had more time to make adjustments, fiddle
with settings, and simply clean it. The local main dealers managed
the more technical stuff that required plugging it into their diagnostic
computer. Thankfully, that was only once a year.

He'd set his phone on the workbench, connected to a Bluetooth
speaker with his favourite playlist blasting out a selection of 70s and
80s road trip rock classics. The music was more than background.
It absorbed him and he hummed along, occasionally breaking into
muted, out-of-tune singing. He was in the process of increasing the
rebound rate of the rear damper when the music suddenly stopped to
be replaced by his ring tone. Initially, he thought the track was on the
playlist, then realised it was his phone.

He ignored it, but curiosity got the better of him and he got up
and peered at the screen. He didn't recognise the number and debated
whether to answer. He relented and stabbed the green button, then
hit the speaker icon without picking the handset up.

'Hello.' He said as he gave the phone a wary look.

'Is that Nick?'

'Who's calling? He was still unsure and remained guarded.

'It's Gregor Robinson, Newstead Press, Susie's boss. Is that you
Nick?'

Cogs in his brain whirred and clicked into place. Nick relaxed 'Oh, Hi Greg, sorry, I'm getting too old and cynical. How are you? Haven't heard from you for ages.'

'Fine thanks. Listen Nick, bit of a long shot, but would you be interested in covering a conference for me in Montreux?'

Nick stood up straight and studied his phone for a second. He'd supplied Greg with pictures at several events over the years, but they had always been in the UK. 'You mean Montreux in Switzerland?'

'If there's another Montreux, I've never heard of it,' Greg replied. 'It's a European Pharma Conference, big event, all the major players under one roof. Great opportunity to get shots of all the top people. On top of that, the head man of one of the UK companies is being presented with an award and we need pictures of that, if nothing else. It'll be a big feature in the magazine and I could do with a bunch of up-to-date pictures to go with it.'

Nick warmed rapidly to the idea. 'Sure Greg, sounds great, and yes, I'm interested. When is it?'

Greg passed on a few more details. 'I'll email all the info to you. I just wanted to see if you'd be prepared to go.'

Nick had a flash of inspiration. 'Tell you what Greg, I'll save you the cost of the plane tickets. If you'll pay me mileage, I'll go on the bike.' He stood back and appraised the BMW.

'Seriously?' Greg sounded incredulous. 'You'd go all the way there on a motorbike?'

'Absolutely, why not? I've toured Europe before and I've got a little more time on my hands these days. I could do with the diversion.'

Greg picked up on what he meant. 'Ah yes. How is your good lady?'

Nick snorted. 'Good lady? She's over at her mate's place, been there for almost a fortnight. Apparently, I'm a boring old fart and I'm at fault for not being supportive enough. Can you believe it?'

Greg sounded apologetic. 'I hope you don't blame me Nick, you know how stubborn she is. I had no idea that they had warned her off. I'd have told her to drop it if I knew.'

'Not at all Greg, she's her own worst enemy, obsessive and blind to any argument. She's determined to get to the bottom of it and come out of it with a story, whatever it takes.'

Greg measured his words carefully and didn't want to offend. 'You're right. She's hugely capable but, well, she's not afraid of taking risks in pursuit of the big scoop.'

Nick laughed. 'Nicely put, but what you mean is, she's bloody reckless.'

'You said it. Anyway, I hope she gets better soon and things work out for you both. I'll get these details over to you and confirm the job and a mileage rate for you. And thanks again, Nick.'

'My pleasure Greg, thanks for the call.' Nick hung up and went back to work on the bike with renewed enthusiasm.

••●••

In Anna's apartment, they completed their plans for the trip; they had booked flights and made a hotel reservation for a hotel in the centre of Timisoara.

'I think we're about done,' said Susie.

Anna tapped the details into her phone. 'And you're sure the man you want to speak to is going to be there?'

'That's what his office said. Why would they tell me any different?'

'Well, I hope you're right, but being there is one thing, agreeing to see you is another.'

'I have a plan.' Susie tapped the side of her nose in a conspiratorial manner. 'He'll see me.'

Anna shook her head. 'I'm not going to ask. I just have to hope I have some luck with these orph..., I mean, children's centres. She waved a piece of paper at Susie. 'I've got a list of ten possible ones here and no way of contacting any of them. They're all in the right area, but they've changed the names and who knows what records they've kept.'

'Did they not have to keep records?' Susie asked.

'They did at one time, but they were so overwhelmed and so disorganised. Records were either lost, destroyed or inaccurate.'

Susie showed genuine interest. 'Have you never tried searching for your parents before?'

'It's over thirty years ago. You were right when you said I was one of the lucky ones, rescued before any damage was done. I was only a couple of months old when the world found out about all the kids. I'd only been in there for a few weeks.' Anna looked thoughtful and gazed at the picture on the opposite wall, a watercolour print of an English rural scene 'This is my home. This is all I know. My parents love me and I love them. I was told my birth parents both died in the revolution and that's why I was in the orphanage. I've never wanted to dig up the past before now. I've been curious, but never curious enough to do anything about it.'

Susie looked at her friend. 'You poor thing, I've never really thought about it. I suppose I just take my past for granted. My Dad was always banging on about it: grandparents, uncles, aunts, cousins, great-grandparents, who did what, who's related to who, all the usual family stuff; it drove me round the bend. I can't imagine what it would be like not to know.'

Anna turned back to Susie. 'You can't choose your family; they might drive you nuts at times, but when you realise what it would be like not to have a family at all, you are a little more forgiving.'

Susie was still contemplating the idea of not having a background. 'What happened to all the other children, the one's that didn't get rescued?'

Anna shuddered. 'You don't want to know. Some children were in those places for years; unloved, un-stimulated, dreadful conditions, lack of any human contact. They've grown up with all sorts of problems; mental health issues, attachment issues, drugs, prostitution, crime, suicide. There's the odd one who's made it, but they're rare. The system couldn't cope. It still can't.'

'You mean it's still going on now?'

Anna nodded slowly 'It's not as bad as it was before the revolution, but it's still an embarrassment to the government. They say they're doing something about it, but there's so much poverty it will take decades, or a miracle.'

Ever the journalist, Susie couldn't help but probe. 'How did it all happen in the first place?'

'Really Susie, it was headline news at the time. Surely, as a journalist, you'd be all over it.'

Susie held a finger to her bottom lip and shook her head.

'Ceausescu's children? Never heard the expression? The bastard decreed that every mother should have at least five children and the state would do a better job of bringing them up than their parents would, hence all the orphanages and over a hundred thousand children being subjected to their regime.'

Susie continued to shake her head in disbelief and said nothing for almost a minute. 'And here I am, complaining about my family. At least I have a family. Dad and I haven't spoken in years, all over some stupid disagreement, when Mum died. My brother's an idiot and never calls. I occasionally hear from various cousins, Christmas cards from aunts and uncles, that sort of thing, but we're not close. Still, they're there and I know where I've come from. Do you really know nothing about your background?'

'How could I?' Anna shrugged. 'When the Western NGOs swooped in, there was no one keeping track of all the comings and goings. They smuggled babies out with no paperwork. I was one of them.'

'No birth certificate?'

'That's all I've got.' Anna tugged her earlobe and screwed up her nose. It looked to Susie as if an invisible wire ran from ear to nose. 'Just a name, a birth date and names of mother and father, nothing else.'

'Surely that'll be a start.' Susie encouraged her. 'Keep positive. If I've got time, I'll come with you. Between the two of us, we'll find out where you've come from and who your family are.'

'Were.' Anna corrected.

'You never know; you may still have relatives out there.' She hugged Anna. 'Come on, I need some sleep.'

January 2016
International Convention Centre
Birmingham

Sir Giles Lawrence sat in the main conference hall and did his best to look interested in the man on stage and what he said. In truth he was bored to distraction, but given his position, he couldn't be seen to look at his phone, fall asleep or look as bored as he felt. As an invited guest he'd been given VIP front row seating and he knew any lapse in attention would be seen, photographed, shared on social media and generate unwanted comments. He smiled at the speaker's attempt at brevity and looked sage and serious at other times.

He found himself distracted by the event photographers and watched them with interest. The gap between the front row of seats and the stage appeared to be their hunting ground. He saw they had free rein of the venue.

While he suffered the ignominy of having his bag searched, he'd seen them, laden down with equipment, by-pass all but the most cursory security checks. He seen them come and go as they pleased with unfettered access to all areas of the building.

He watched how they worked, how they positioned themselves at the edge of the stage to get close up shots of the speakers. They were only a few feet from CEOs and Government Ministers.

He saw a solution to a problem that had bugged him for the last three months.

It gave him an idea and he couldn't wait to make a call.

The session broke up and delegates filed out for lunch. Lawrence skirted around the queue for the buffet and went outside. He found a quiet corner overlooking the canal basin and pulled out his phone.

It took four rings before Manfred Schrader answered. 'Hello.'

'Manfred, I think I've solved the problem.'

'What problem is that?'

Lawrence sighed, frustrated that the other man was unable to read his mind. 'What we talked about.' He paused and looked around to make sure nobody was near him. 'The problem of removing the obstacle to our joint venture.'

Schrader made a small noise of acknowledgement.

Lawrence continued. 'I remember you saying that *"the obstacle"* was a regular speaker at industry events.'

'I don't need reminding, if he's not giving a presentation, he's getting an award. It makes me sick. Why are you telling me this?'

'This might seem like an odd question Manfred, but is it possible to produce a small quantity of poison gas?'

Schrader coughed. 'What?'

'I don't know what you call it, but something that could be concealed in a telephoto lens.'

A note of suspicion crept into Schrader's tone. 'I don't understand. Where are you going with this?'

'I'm at the Clinical Excellence conference in Birmingham. I've been watching the photographers, they get up close and personal to their subjects and their long lenses would be a perfect way to deliver...something.'

Schrader remained silent for a moment then cleared his throat. 'I see, and you think I could produce this...something?'

'Well can't you? You told me you had a background in chemical research.' Lawrence had researched Schrader's background and played to his ego.

'That's true, my Grandfather was an eminent research chemist back in the 1930's.' Pride replaced the suspicion in Schrader's tone.

'Really,' said Lawrence, 'What did he do?'

'You've heard of Sarin?'

'Vaguely,' said Lawrence, 'Does he have some connection to it?'

'He's the S in Sarin.'

'I'm stunned Manfred, that's some legacy.' Lawrence winced, he hoped his sarcastic remark had gone over Schrader's head.

'It is, and I have all his papers, he was a brilliant man.'

Lawrence realised he'd found the weakness in Schrader's frosty make up. 'So is it possible to produce a small amount of sarin?'

'It's totally illegal, it's the most lethal nerve agent ever created.'

'I'm sure it is, but could you make some?'

Schrader couldn't refuse the challenge. 'Of course.'

'Well there's our answer. You get onto it and I'll order the camera equipment and get it shipped over. You can work out a way to conceal it.'

'We'll need to look ahead and see when and where *"he"* is going to be speaking.' Said Schrader.

'Leave that with me, my nephew's the european editor for one of the scientific magazines, he's always happy to give me the latest gossip in return for whatever news I can give him.'

'Okay, and in the meantime, I'll press ahead with Thytomet.'

Lawrence ended the call and looked around with a sly smile.

————————••●••————————

Three weeks had passed since being run off the road. The broken collarbone still ached but frustration got the better of her and Susie felt able to have another attempt at swimming, even if it meant "legs only" up and down the pool, wearing fins and pushing a float. She tried a few gentle strokes but recognised the damage it did to her recovery and with ill concealed reluctance resumed kicking her way from end to end, and back again.

The forced hiatus in her normal routine allowed her to dwell on what Anna had told her and her normal obsession with counting lengths drifted off as she reflected on her own family and how little contact she had with them.

Her stubbornness refused to let her apologise to her father. As far as she was concerned, he was in the wrong and she had nothing to apologise for. He'd done everything in his power to stop her joining the police. He'd spent his career in the Met and didn't want his daughter to have to deal with some of the events and people who had left indelible scars on his memory.

She abandoned the journalism degree course to come home and look after her mother when she became ill and after she died, Susie felt rudderless. She'd passed the army recruitment centre in town many times, but a poster in the window caught her eye one day and on impulse she went in.

She smiled to herself as she remembered coming home and telling her father she had signed up. Ever the rebel, she had taken great delight in presenting a fait de'accompli. She still had to go through basic training and she didn't let on at the time, she'd set her heart on joining the Military Police. That bombshell, as he saw it, was the final straw and they hadn't spoken since.

She told herself she didn't care what he thought but deep down she knew she wanted his approval. If not his approval, then at least she wanted him to admit that she'd done the right thing.

She climbed out of the pool with renewed determination to show him what she could do. He'd been a detective, an investigator, and from what she'd heard, he'd been a good one. As she showered and changed, she resolved this trip to Timisoara and what she uncovered there, would make him proud.

CHAPTER 12

The Airbus 320 touched down at Timişoara Traian Vuia International airport shortly after 2pm local time. The bright, early September sun reflected off the puddles left by an earlier shower and created rainbows in the spray as the tyres kissed the tarmac.

Susie and Anna emerged from the arrivals hall forty-five minutes later. Both looked bleary-eyed and a little lost. They'd been up since 4am to catch the four-hour budget airline flight from Luton, and had only slept fitfully after some hasty packing the previous evening.

Susie examined the multitude of signs in English and Romanian and looked for directions for the bus into the City Centre. Anna went in search of an ATM to get some local currency. It only took a few minutes before Susie found herself accosted by would-be escorts, drivers and guides, eager to show her around.

Anna returned. She smiled at Susie's attempts to fend them off.

'Thank God you're back.' She grabbed Anna by the elbow and propelled her towards the exit. 'I thought I'd be abducted by force if you'd been any longer. Talk about persistent, they don't take no for an answer round here.'

'They're harmless enough,' Anna said. 'Just looking for a rich tourist to make a bit of ready cash. Have you spotted the bus?'

Susie pointed at a door at the far end of the building. 'Out that way and turn left, according to the signs.' She hurried towards the exit. Anna had to break into a jog to keep up.

The bus for the City Centre looked half full when the two women climbed aboard and made their way to the back and sat down. When it looked like no one else would board, the door slid shut with a hiss, the air suspension lifted the bus to travelling height, the revs rose and they pulled out for the ten-mile journey to Timisoara City.

Susie sat at the window and took it all in. 'It's more modern than I was expecting.' She turned to Anna for a response.

'What did you expect, horse-drawn wagons and peasants pushing hand carts?'

'Well, not exactly, but I didn't expect all this.' She waved a hand at the newly built road complete with landscaped borders, the high-tech bus, the cars, advertising hoardings and all the usual accoutrements of Western civilisation. 'I'm impressed; I hadn't realised there was quite so much wealth.'

'Don't scratch too deep,' Anna cautioned. 'Once you get out into the sticks, it's nothing like this. This is all for visitors. Smoke and mirrors.' She looked serious and shook her head. 'There are a few making money, but wages are so low you wouldn't believe. Those guys hassling you back at the airport would make more from acting as your guide for a few hours than they could working in a factory for a week.'

Susie let that sink in for a moment. 'So where's the money made?'

'The usual; crime, drugs, sex, gambling, dodgy dealing, you name it, they're all at it. Wait till we get into the city. You can play spot the supercar all day long.'

Susie looked troubled. 'But surely there must be some legitimate business?'

'Sure, there's some clever people who've set up some big companies; textiles, furniture and, of course, pharmaceuticals, lots of them.'

Susie's inquisitive mind worked overtime. 'Why pharma, what is it about here that attracts the medical companies?'

Anna's brow furrowed as she looked at her friend. 'You really should have done your homework. Didn't you read all that stuff I dropped off with you last week? There was a DTi report into the Romanian Pharmaceutical Industry that explained it all; loads of statistics, graphs and pretty pictures.'

Susie looked abashed. 'I glanced at it but thought I'd wait till we got here and you could give me the abbreviated version; the edited highlights.'

Anna sighed. 'Talk about a busman's holiday.' For the rest of the half hour journey, she explained to Susie how the education system produced bright minds and the employment system kept the wages low, which made it an ideal recruiting ground for young ambitious locals. With the information she had discovered at work, Anna also explained that companies built factories in the country with offers of subsidised land prices and rent-free holidays.

Susie listened and quizzed Anna about the incentives persuading Western companies to invest in the country and the control exercised over them.

Susie nodded as she took it all in and gazed out the window as the bus passed through the outer suburbs. The road became busier and their speed slowed. The greenery of the city surprised her, as did the parks and the floral displays on the central reservations, verges, and roundabouts.

The bus pulled up outside the Centre Hotel,

Anna had booked a twin room for their three-night stay. 'We're on the third floor.' She handed Susie her keycard after checking in for them both. 'If we drop the bags off, we've got time for a quick look around town.'

'OK, let's go. I might need your help to make a phone call now we're here, then we can go wandering.'

———— ••◉•• ————

They unpacked, freshened up, and took the lift back to the lobby ten minutes later. Anna picked up on Susie's earlier remark. 'Who did you want to ring?'

The question caught Susie unaware, and she had to think. She had lost her train of thought as she took in the surroundings. 'Oh, I've got a number for the Azllomed factory. They gave it to me in England when I called them. They said the boss was over here and he was the only one who could answer my questions. I might need your help with the language.'

Anna smiled. 'They'll speak English, they have to. You don't need me for that. Anyway, I'm going to be struggling when I start poking around orphanage records. I'll bet their English won't be quite so good.'

'Is it worth calling them now? It's after five already.' Susie looked at Anna for guidance. 'I want to see if this Doctor Archer will grant me an interview.'

'What are you going to tell him? You've found some fake medication and you want to expose his company?'

Susie put a finger to her lips and made shushing noises. She took Anna's elbow and led her out of the hotel into the evening sunlight. 'Keep your voice down. You don't know who's listening. Of course not. I'm not going to arouse his suspicions. I want to wait until I've got the entire story, the marketing, the sales, the distribution. I want to know who is behind it all. For all I know, he may know nothing about it and if I make him wary, he might do something that would scupper the whole thing.'

Anna turned and looked at Susie, her forehead creased. 'So, what's more important, stopping the sale of unlicensed medication, or you getting your scoop?'

Susie's head jerked back an inch at the jibe. 'They're both important. Of course I want my story, but I need the whole can of worms. When the story comes out, there's no way they will be able to sell the stuff.'

'Why not just go to the police?'

'Has Nick been bending your ear?'

'No.'

'You know why; they'll do nothing, they haven't got the manpower to investigate something like this.' She pointed to the park. 'Come on. We can ring from over there.'

Susie relaxed her grip on Anna's elbow. They headed into the park and found a bench.

Anna remained unconvinced and rubbed her hand over her mouth as Susie found the saved number and pressed the call button. 'So, what are you going to tell them?'

Susie held up her hand for silence as a voice answered.

'Buna ziua, Azllomed.'

Susie looked flummoxed for a second before she responded. 'Hello, do you speak English?' She felt ashamed that she had made no attempt to learn even the most basic of expressions before calling.

The female voice at the other end switched immediately into English with only the slightest trace of an accent. 'Of course. How can I help you?'

Susie composed herself before she launched into the story she had rehearsed. 'My name's Karen Green. I'm writing an article about British business interests in Romania for The Guardian and I wanted to interview Doctor Archer. I called his office in England a few days ago and they said he was here for a few days.' She looked up at Anna, whose hand had frozen over her mouth in disbelief.

The voice sounded friendly. 'One moment, please.'

Susie waited.

Anna mouthed at her. 'Karen Green?'

Susie shrugged her shoulders and held the phone to her chest.

'They're not going to check, are they? Who would come all the way out here unless they were genuine?' She put the phone back to her ear and waited.

After a minute, a man's voice broke the silence. 'Hello, is that Karen?'

The voice took Susie by surprise and she almost blurted out her own name, but she quickly assumed the role of her new persona. 'Yes, Karen Green.'

'Karen, I'm Julian Archer. Natalya tells me you want to come and see me.'

Susie had not expected to get through to the man himself and was all set for a battle of wills with the receptionist. It wasn't in the script and she had to think quickly. 'I was hoping you might spare me an hour, Dr Archer. I want to ask you about why your business is based here and what advantages and disadvantages you've found.'

'Well, I'd love to help Karen but I'm off to a conference tomorrow and planned to spend time finalising my presentation.'

'Oh. When will you be back?' Susie's shoulders fell.

'Not for some time, I'm afraid - I'm catching a train tomorrow evening and I'm going back to England when the conference is over. I'd be happy to see you when I'm back.'

Susie had no option. 'I'm sorry to be so pushy. I was hoping to put the story to bed over the next couple of days. Could you spare me a little time tomorrow? I know it's short notice, but I'd really appreciate it.'

There was a pause at the other end. 'Let me have a word with Natalya.'

Susie glanced at Anna, fingers crossed. She waited. Silence for a minute. Then he was back.

'I don't want to let you down. I'll always try to help when I can, but I've got a very full day tomorrow.'

Here we go, thought Susie, the big brush off. He doesn't want to speak to me. He's got something to hide and wants to let me down gently.

'Tell you what, if you can get here at about three thirty tomorrow afternoon, I'll get Natalya to give you the grand tour of the facility and I'll see you after that. It'll have to be a flying visit, though. Can you squeeze your questions into thirty minutes?'

Susie gave a little victory fist pump. 'Thank you Doctor Archer, that's very kind, I won't keep you any longer than half an hour.'

'Fine. That's sorted then. I look forward to meeting you tomorrow.' The phone clicked off.

Susie tried to high-five Anna, who hadn't expected the jubilant slap of the hand. In the excitement, she completely forgot about her recovering collarbone and winced in pain at the sudden movement. She clutched her left hand over her right shoulder. 'Shit, bloody shoulder.'

'Now what?' Anna asked, her expression a combination of horror and admiration; 'You've got a nerve, haven't you? Are you going to come clean when you see him?'

Susie jumped up. 'Of course not. Come on, a little celebration is in order. We've got a night out on the town to enjoy.' She put her arm round Anna's shoulder and steered her across the park towards a promising-looking bar on the far side.

—————————— ••●•• ——————————

Susie didn't know what to expect as she approached the Azllomed factory. The company website featured bright, colourful images that depicted health and wellbeing. She noticed paragraphs of marketing hyperbole about the various medications they produced, official licence numbers, and EU standards. There were no pictures of the factory, and the only people featured were obviously models. She assumed the factory would be a modern purpose-built plant, lots of polished concrete, glass, chrome, and expensive fittings.

She was wrong.

The Uber wound its way through the industrial quarter to the South-East of Timisoara and turned down a road lined with what appeared to be a row of derelict warehouses. The driver slowed and looked at the address on the piece of paper Susie had given him. He continued towards the end of the road and stopped. He turned to Susie and with a wave of his right hand he indicated the last building on the right.

'Here is.'

Susie followed his gaze at the eight-foot high rusted iron fence with rolls of barbed wire strung along the top. Fifty feet beyond the fence, a dull grey-walled building loomed, with dark opaque windows, and others that had been boarded up. A large roller-shutter marked what had to be a loading bay, with a small access door built into it. There was no sign of life, no sign of any kind.

Susie stared and turned back to the driver. 'Is this it?'

The driver's English was basic, but the tone of Susie's question was clear. He held up the paper and pointed to the address Susie had written on it, then pointed at a small sign that hung at an angle on a fencepost with the number '85' in barely legible figures.

'See.'

Susie looked at the address again and back at the sign and made a decision. She gave a resigned shrug and climbed out. She was on the point of asking the driver to come back in two hours, but before she could open her mouth, he'd dropped the clutch and set off without looking back. She watched as he turned right at the T-junction and disappeared out of sight. 'Thanks, pal.' She gazed about her and couldn't see another soul. She heard little noise other than the traffic from the roads around the industrial zone, but nothing moved on her road.

She looked again at the foreboding fence and walked back down the way she'd come. After fifty yards, she came to what she assumed must be the main gate. It stood open, but the red and white barrier just inside the gate blocked the way. The unmanned gate office appeared abandoned and Susie gazed around, looking for cameras. She spotted what she assumed must be some sort of CCTV system mounted on the corner of the building, but it looked old and rusted. If there were any other cameras, they weren't obvious.

She took a deep breath and slipped around the end of the barrier and walked back towards the door she had spotted where she had been dropped off. She looked for an intercom or bell, but could see nothing. She tried the door built into the roller-shutter, but found it locked. In frustration, she banged on it and the metallic noise reverberated. They can't miss that, she thought.

A minute passed, and nothing happened. Susie was about the bang on the door again when the latch unlocked and the door opened inwards. Susie peered into the building.

A dark-haired woman greeted her, dressed in a long white coat and white lab boots. She appeared about the same height as a Susie. She gave a polite smile. 'Can I help you?'

Susie stepped back in surprise, momentarily lost for words 'Er, I'm here to see Dr Archer'

'Karen Green?'

Susie gave a curt nod.

'Dr Archer is expecting you, please follow me.' She turned and headed through the gloom of the loading bay into the main factory, with Susie on her heels.

The main factory looked more like what Susie had expected - brightly lit and spotlessly clean, but much smaller than she expected.

She followed her guide past a range of machines, packing bays and sorting desks. Staff in white coats went about their work and didn't look up or acknowledge her.

They went through another door at the far end of the factory and turned left into a windowless corridor with doors off to the right every twenty feet. Susie asked a question, but the woman held up her hand for silence.

They stopped at the fifth door; the woman opened it. 'Please wait in here'. She ushered Susie into the room, closed the door, and left.

The room, like the rest of the factory, had white walls and a white resin floor, a white suspended ceiling with four light panels and an air-conditioning outlet built into it. There were no windows, but pictures - abstract art - on all four walls. A water cooler stood in one corner of the room and four modern easy chairs had been arranged around the low coffee table in the middle. A clock ticked on the wall above the door. It was 3.25pm. Susie had turned up a few minutes early. She sat down and pulled the iPad from her shoulder bag. She scanned through the list of questions she had prepared for the interview. The door opened, and Dr Archer walked in.

'Karen, hello, I'm Julian. How are you?' He smiled warmly and extended his hand. 'Sorry to keep you cooped up in this box. We don't have many visitors, so this is the best we can do for a waiting room.'

Immediately taken with the man; she shook hands and mumbled something about the waiting room and it not being a problem.

He glowed with health and vitality. Bright grey eyes set off a clean-shaven face that looked tanned from an active outdoor life rather than hours lying in the sun. 'Slight change of plan, Karen.' Archer explained. 'I need to be away sooner than expected, so Natalya's going to give you the tour after you've asked your questions. Is that OK?'

'Absolutely, whatever works for you,' she gushed.

'We'll go to my office. It's a little more comfortable. Would you like to come this way?'

She felt guilty at the ruse she perpetrated. He was so open and direct that she wanted to confess the truth and tell him her real name and the reason for her visit, but she resisted the urge and followed him meekly out of the room and back down the corridor to his office.

She estimated he must have close to six feet tall and he moved with a long legged stride that ate up the yards. He wore cream chinos, tan shoes, a pale blue shirt, no tie, no jacket. Casual, but businesslike. She approved.

Archer apologised for the basic office and indicated a seat for Susie. 'I don't come here very often myself, so I'm afraid we're a little lacking in creature comforts.' He waved a disparaging hand around the room. 'It does the job, I suppose.'

Susie smiled back. 'That's OK, it's you I've come to see, not the office.' She met his gaze.

Stay professional Jones, don't let him distract you, she told herself

She reverted to her plan. 'I appreciate you taking the time to see me, Dr Archer.'

'Julian, please,'

'Thank you, Julian, I don't want to appear rude but as you're rushed, can we make a start?'

'That suits me Karen, fire away. Natalya will be ready for you when we're done. That's who met you at the door.'

'Ah yes, you don't go in for bright lights and neon signs. I'd never have guessed from outside that this was the Azllomed factory.'

Archer nodded and looked serious. 'We don't advertise our presence. We try to keep as low key as possible. The more nondescript the better. People assume that pharma companies must have something worth stealing; drugs, secret formulas, that sort of thing, so security has to be tight.'

Susie looked intrigued. 'But I didn't see any security. There was no one on the gate and no one challenged me when I came through the barrier.'

'Believe me, we watched you from the moment the taxi dropped you off. The security team let me know you were here and Natalya went off to greet you. You'll see now why it took so long for the door to be answered.' Archer paused. 'You were expected, after all. If we weren't expecting you, you would have been waiting for a very long time at the door.'

'But the people who work here, how do they come and go without arousing any suspicion?'

'I shouldn't really tell you this, but there is another entrance from the road at the back of the factory. All the cars are parked under cover in another old warehouse so you'd never know, even from the odd cheeky drone.' He sat back, steepled his hands, and rested his chin on his forefingers. 'Now, what would you like to ask me?'

Susie turned to her iPad and worked through the questions she'd prepared, which maintained the cover of writing an article about British companies setting up manufacturing plants in Romania and the benefits and drawbacks that they had found. Archer listened carefully and answered as honestly and directly as he could. He'd been working in the country for over thirty years and had seen it change and develop for the better.

Susie kept away from specifics and didn't ask about any of the brands Azllomed produced. She wanted to see if Archer volunteered anything or even if he was aware of the email marketing that had alerted her to his company.

She slipped in a question as he talked about research. 'Are you developing any new medications at the moment, Julian?'

'We have an excellent team of research chemists led by Dr Manfred Schrader. He's the Plant Manager here.' He paused and gazed out the solitary window in the office. He looked troubled for a moment before he returned his attention to Susie. 'They're always looking at new formulas and coming up with drugs to treat different symptoms and different conditions.'

Susie nodded and tapped a few notes. 'Anything revolutionary?' She made the question sound conversational rather than inquisitive.

'No, nothing worth getting excited about at this stage.' He smiled back. 'I'm sure you know, it can take years, several years, to get new medication to market. The testing, approval and licensing is so tightly controlled. You wouldn't believe the regulations we have to go through before we can bring a new treatment to market.'

He stood up and went to a cupboard against one wall of the office and pulled out three A4 sized manuals, each an inch thick, and dropped them on his desk. The desk shook under the impact. 'Those three are just the start; they're the EU regs detailing the specification of anti-inflammatory medicines. There's another set for every other category of medication and then a whole cupboard full of regulations for the U.S. It goes on and on, different regulations in different continents and new ones being introduced every month. I have a staff of twelve back in England whose sole job is making sure we comply with all this.' He nodded at the manuals and the cupboard in an almost helpless gesture.

Susie couldn't help but ask, 'What about the black market, the online selling and the counterfeit drugs? How do you deal with the criminal side of it all?'

Archer contemplated the question, his lips pressed into a fine line. He frowned and shook his head. 'There will always be a criminal element looking to make a fast buck. It's the nature of the beast. The temptation is too much for some. All we can do is make sure we're squeaky clean and that we distribute our products through the proper channels, there's not a lot we can do about fakes and copies except keep an ear to the ground and report anything that comes to our attention.' He looked up and noticed the time; it was 4.30pm. 'Karen, I hate to appear rude, but we've overrun our schedule and I really need to get on.'

Susie glanced at the clock. 'Of course, I'm sorry to have delayed you. Did you say you were off to a conference tomorrow?'

'Yes, I'm catching the train to Vienna later this evening and then flying to Geneva tomorrow afternoon. I've even allowed myself a little treat. I'm catching up with some old friends in the morning, which is always a pleasure.'

Susie looked puzzled. 'Is there no quicker way to Geneva? If you don't mind me asking?'

'They have asked me to give the keynote address on the opening day, and I wanted some time to complete my presentation; a sleeper car and no distractions.'

Susie's curiosity got the better of her. 'What's the conference?'

Archer looked a little embarrassed. 'It's the Conference of the European Clinical Governance Council, the ECGC. It only meets once every five years and for my sins I'm on the Executive Committee.'

Susie stood up and shook Archer's hand. 'Well, thank you again for your time. I do appreciate it. Have a pleasant journey and good luck with the presentation.'

'Thank you, Karen.' Archer opened the door and called for Natalya, who appeared from an adjoining office. 'Natalya will show you round the factory; she can answer any questions you have.'

Natalya nodded in response.

'I hope you get all you need for your article and enjoy your visit to Timisoara.'

With that, he ushered the two women out of office and closed the door.

Part Four

Capture

CHAPTER 13

S usie turned to Natalya and held out her hand. 'How do you do Natalya, I'm Karen. We haven't said hello properly.'

Hesitant at first, Natalya took the hand and held it for a little longer than custom dictated. She looked at Susie through a fringe of dark hair.

Susie thought she looked nervous, as if being watched.

Without saying a word, Natalya headed off down the corridor and beckoned Susie to follow. She stopped at the main office, where she asked Susie to remove her shoes and replace them with a pair of white lab boots. She then gave her a white coat and an elasticated white hat to complete the look.

The factory tour took a pre-determined route, and followed the process of drug manufacture, from synthesising and blending, to pill production, bottling and packaging. Natalya didn't divulge any trade secrets, and she answered Susie's questions with polite, factual answers.

Susie felt her guide was operating to an agreed text, and several times tried to divert her with a comment or remark unrelated to the tour, but Natalya remained non-committal and quickly returned to her script. She noticed how Natalya spoke in guarded tones, how she repeatedly looked over her shoulder as though someone watched her every move. She appeared unwilling to make eye contact almost as though she feared her guest would read something into it. Susie had the distinct impression that Natalya lived in fear of somebody or something. It made her uncomfortable.

After the tour, they returned the protective garments. The two women headed for the exit door and almost collided with Manfred Schrader, who stepped out of an office.

He glared at Natalya, then at Susie. He demanded to know who the stranger was. 'Cine este aceasta?'

Natalya visibly recoiled and shrank away from him. Her voice trembled as she explained that Susie was a guest. 'Dr Schrader, ea este Karen Green, oaspetele doctorului Archer.'

Schrader looked slightly shorter than Natalya, but he puffed his chest out and drew himself up to his full height. He positioned himself inches from her face. His voice threatened as he asked what Natalya had told Susie. 'Ce i-ai spus?'

His aggression surprised Susie. He made no attempt to hide his anger in front of a stranger. She felt her hackles rise. She wanted to do something, but knew she couldn't intervene. The reason for Natalya's fear stood in front of her.

Natalya's voice sounded timid. 'Nimic, doctore Schrader. nu i-am spus nimic.'

Susie didn't understand what Schrader had said, but she could tell from his sharp tone and Natalya's stiff body language that she feared him, and instantly a sensation of loathing and contempt for the bespectacled little man flooded Susie's body and turned her stomach.

She tried to come to Natalya's defence. 'Natalya has been a professional and courteous guide.' She guessed Schrader would speak or at least understand English.

Schrader gave Susie a brief withering glance, ignored her, and turned to Natalya again. His shadow crept around them like toxic vapour. His voice lowered. 'Voi vorbi mai târziu.' Without another word, he pushed past the two women and headed down the corridor.

Susie looked at Natalya, who bit her bottom lip in a determined effort not to show any emotion. She wanted to hug her or at least show some empathy. 'Are you all right, Natalya?'

Natalya nodded and closed her eyes as though to shut out the memory of the encounter. 'It's OK, I'm used to it, don't worry.' Her eyes swam, and she glanced up at Susie.

'Do you want to talk about it? Is there something I can help with?'

Natalya looked over her shoulder to make sure there was no one in sight. Her eyes dropped to the floor. 'Not here, not now. He watches me every minute.'

Susie reached into her bag and took out a small notepad and a pen. She wrote quickly, then tore off the sheet, folded it in half and thrust it into Natalya's hand. She came closer and lowered her voice to a whisper. 'That's my number. If you want to meet up later and have a chat, call me.'

Natalya gave a furtive glance left and right as she slipped the folded piece of paper into the pocket of her lab coat. She grabbed Susie's hand firmly, made eye contact, and held her gaze. 'Thank you, thank you so much.'

Susie smiled and nodded. 'I mean it, I'd like to help if I can.'

Natalya stepped forward and opened the door that led to the undercover parking area at the back of the factory. 'We've ordered a car for you. It should be waiting on the other side of the gate.' She pointed to the exit at the far end of the warehouse.

Susie was about to speak when Natalya held her finger up to her lips. Her eyes flicked up and left, indicating the camera mounted below the eaves and just above the doorway. Susie got the message and shook Natalya's hand in what she hoped looked like a genuine parting.

'Thank you again for showing me round. Goodbye.' She headed for the exit and the waiting car.

Natalya closed the door and headed back into the plant to face Schrader.

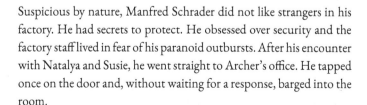

Suspicious by nature, Manfred Schrader did not like strangers in his factory. He had secrets to protect. He obsessed over security and the factory staff lived in fear of his paranoid outbursts. After his encounter with Natalya and Susie, he went straight to Archer's office. He tapped once on the door and, without waiting for a response, barged into the room.

Archer glanced up, expecting Natalya, and looked surprised to see his plant manager.

'Hello Manfred, you look a little ruffled. What's up?'

Schrader's normally pallid features had coloured with anger. His fingers curled and clenched tight. His fiery expression burned through Archer's cool demeanour. 'I've just found Natalya giving a strange woman a tour of the factory. Did you know about this?'

Archer studied Schrader for a moment. He remained calm and inhaled slowly. 'Of course I knew about it. She came to interview me, and I asked Natalya to show her around.'

Schrader's voice rose in both pitch and volume. 'Why wasn't I told?'

'Manfred, you do a first-class job as my plant manager and I appreciate how conscientious you are about security, but please credit me with a little respect. I'm quite capable of making my own decisions about who I talk to and who gets to look around the plant. I'm sure you have quite enough on your plate without getting involved in my business as well.' Archer hoped he'd struck the right level of authority.

Schrader looked unimpressed and took the statement as a personal rebuke. 'I insist on knowing who is in the plant. You should have asked me before making any arrangements.'

Archer pressed his lips together and his eyes narrowed. He planted both palms on his desk, pushed his chair back, and stood up. He leaned forward and glared down at Schrader. 'It takes a great deal to make me lose my cool, Manfred, but there are times when you come very close.'

Schrader's left eye twitched, although he didn't shrink beneath Archer's shadow.

'Can I just remind you who works for whom around here, and suggest you wind your neck in.' Archer leaned close to emphasise the point; the colloquialism seemed lost on Schrader.

Schrader gave a dismissive, haughty shrug, and turned from Archer. He stopped in the doorway. 'Natalya said the woman was called Karen Green. Where was she from?'

Archer sat down before he answered. He ignored Schrader and made a point of shuffling a pile of papers on his desk. Without looking up and in a tone that bordered on contempt, he eventually responded.

'She was from the Guardian, not that it's any of your business. Now close the door on your way out.'

Schrader closed the door a little more firmly than necessary and headed back to his office. His distrust stifled any logic. He had a bad feeling about Dr Archer's visitor. It took him less than five minutes online to discover, much to his surprise, that there was indeed a journalist called Karen Green who listed her credits as having written articles for the Guardian. But doubt still nagged at the back of his mind and he searched social media for a picture. He had paid little attention to the woman with Natalya when he bumped into her in the corridor. She was a little taller than Natalya, blonde hair tied back to reveal a narrow face and a slightly pointed chin. From memory, she looked similar to the woman in the picture he'd found. He had a flash of inspiration. He headed for the security office, hoping the CCTV system would have picked her up.

He tapped a couple of buttons and brought up the feed from the camera at the back door. He rewound the recording to the time he'd seen the two women about to leave. He scrolled forwards and backwards until he had a clear view of the woman claiming to be Karen Green. He pressed pause, zoomed in and took a screenshot. Within a couple of seconds, he had a print in his hand, black and white, a little grainy but sharp enough to make out her features with enough clarity. He scuttled back to his office and compared the print to the image on his monitor. The two pictures could be of the same person. It was hard to tell. It did nothing to quell his suspicions.

The doubts gnawed at him as he walked to the meeting room to prepare for his visitors.

●●●●●

Julian Archer quickly forgot Schrader's outburst. He had more important matters on his mind. He replaced the files he had pulled out to show Susie and carefully sorted the paperwork he had selected for his journey.

It took him a few minutes to pack everything he needed into his bag, and he stood to appraise his desk before he decided he was good to go. He collected his roller bag from where it stood beside the door and stepped out into the corridor.

He looked around, and half expected to see Schrader waiting for him. The corridor was deserted. He walked a few paces to the office next to his own, knocked, and pushed the door open.

No sign of Natalya.

Her office was little more than a cupboard. There was nowhere she could be concealed. Archer frowned, *most unlike her*, he thought. She usually fussed about him and checked he had remembered everything she had prepared for him. She'd gone through the itinerary she'd prepared for him earlier in the day, so there was no need for her to see him off.

Archer thought of going to look for her to say goodbye but a quick time-check made him change his mind. He shrugged and headed for the back door and the taxi Natalya had ordered to take him back to his hotel.

••●••

Manfred Schrader slammed the meeting room door shut behind him. His anger had not abated, and the walls reverberated with the impact.

He threw the two pictures onto the table in the centre of the room and glared at them. His eyes flitted from one to the other and back again. Was it the same woman, or were they two different people? Something about Archer's explanation didn't ring true. Why would a Guardian journalist want to interview him? The last thing Schrader wanted was an unexpected visitor snooping around the factory. He stood with his arms tightly folded across his chest, his body rigid and his face contorted in a furious scowl as he stared at the picture he'd printed off from the camera.

Who are you? The question repeated in his mind, over and over. Who the hell are you?

A quiet knock on the door shook him, and he jumped in surprise. He turned to see Natalya nervously open the door.

'What?' He spat the words.

'Dr Schrader, the men you're expecting are here.' She spoke without making eye contact.

Schrader ignored her, but he made a dismissive signal with his hand to indicate she should show them in and then leave.

Natalya held the door while two men walked in. Neither acknowledged her presence. She closed the door and left.

••●••

The car dropped Susie off at the hotel just after 5.15pm. The drive back from the Azllomed factory had been less than three miles, but the rush-hour traffic had slowed progress and it had taken over forty-five minutes. Susie couldn't help but think that on a good day, she would have run the distance in half the time.

She made her first call to Anna, but there was no response. She left a message. 'Hi, it's me, I'm back at the Hotel. Let me know when you're back.' She ended the call and noticed she'd had a missed call from Nick. She stared at the screen for a moment; did she want to hear from him? Did she want to speak to him? Did she want to return his call? She decided the answer to all three questions was no. He'd just want to give her a lecture about her investigations, and right now, that was the last thing she wanted.

She stuffed the phone into a pocket and looked around. She saw nothing of interest to distract her. It was a pleasant evening and there was no way of knowing when Anna would get back. She could wait around and kick her heels or she could go for a run. She'd brought her running kit as she always did and firmly believed there was no better way to discover a city than to run in it.

Mind made up, she shunned the lift, jogged up the stairs and continued at pace along the corridor to her room. The exercise invigorated her. The prospect of a run dispelled any lingering worries about Anna. She changed quickly into T-shirt and shorts, strapped on the heartbeat monitor and pulled on her running shoes. She headed for the door and reached for her phone as she went. As she picked it up, it buzzed into life.

She assumed it was Anna and answered without looking at the screen. 'Hi, how you getting on?' She didn't expect the response.

'Is that Karen?' The voice at the other end sounded hesitant and quiet.

It took Susie a few seconds to recognise the voice. 'Is that Natalya?'

'Yes, you said I could call you.' She sounded tearful. 'Is it OK?'

'Of course it is. Are you all right? You sound upset.' Susie felt concerned; she had worried about Natalya since she left Azllomed.

'Could we meet up for a chat like you said? After you left, something happened and I'm worried. I don't know what to do. I need to speak to someone and I think you would understand.'

Susie stopped before reaching the door. She turned and walked back to look out the window. She tried to sound encouraging. 'Absolutely. When would suit you?'

Natalya was almost pleading. 'Is it possible to meet tonight?'

Susie checked the time again. Half five, and still no word from Anna. 'Sure, Natalya, I'm staying at the Centre Hotel. Do you know it?'

Natalya's voice sounded hesitant. 'I know it, but can we meet somewhere else, somewhere quiet?'

'It's your city, you name the place; I'll get an Uber.'

Natalya must have given it some thought before she called. 'There's a bar called The Amber Lounge close to you. It's nice and quiet. It's my favourite. You can walk there, it's on the other side of the park opposite the hotel, down Strada Patriarh Miron Cristea, then first right onto Mihai Eminescu Boulevard. You'll see it on the left about fifty metres along. I'll be there in twenty minutes.'

Susie wavered for a moment, she was psyched up for a run but sensed Natalya was in trouble. She reminded herself that she had offered to help. Besides, she might have information that would help her story. She repeated the directions to make sure she understood. 'I'll see you soon, Natalya.'

Susie peeled off her running kit and freshened up before pulling on an old pair of combats, a clean T-shirt and her favourite trainers. She tried Anna one more time and left another voice message to bring her up to date. She picked up a lightweight leather jacket and grabbed a few essential which she stuffed into various pockets, then headed out of the hotel and across the park.

CHAPTER 14

I t took Susie only ten minutes to find The Amber Lounge. It took a while for her eyes to adjust to the light inside as she searched for Natalya.

It was Natalya who spotted Susie and gave her a little wave, only a raised hand in acknowledgement. Susie wouldn't have recognised Natalya without her lab coat and with her dark hair loose around her shoulders, she looked so different, yet somehow familiar. Susie ignored the polite extended hand and hugged Natalya when she stood to greet her. She stepped back and held her the shoulders. She gazed directly into her eyes. 'Let me get you a drink then we can talk, OK?'

Natalya nodded. 'Just an orange juice for me, thank you.'

Susie returned with the drinks after a minute and sat opposite Natalya. 'Thanks for ringing me. I was hoping you would. When I left, I was worried about you. I got the distinct feeling there's something going on and you couldn't say anything.'

Natalya picked up her drink and stared into it as though to seek an answer. 'I've never been able to talk to anyone before. I'm really worried about Dr Archer. There's something going on with Schrader. There are things happening at the factory that make little sense.' She looked up at Susie. 'I don't know where to start.'

Susie watched Natalya closely. 'Take your time, start from the beginning and tell me what you do at Azllomed.'

Over the next half hour Natalya explained her role, how long she'd worked at the factory, her worries about Schrader and fears for the safety of her boss.

Susie listened, she empathised, she probed and prodded. She asked Natalya to expand on key points and describe people and events in more detail. A story emerged of a frightened staff, an unsuspecting boss, and outside influences and contacts that left no trace. Two or three times tears welled up in Natalya's eyes and Susie had to console her with a comforting hand and reassurances she could help.

Natalya excused herself for a minute and Susie checked her phone, puzzled by the lack of any news from Anna. What Natalya had revealed disturbed her, and she wanted to share the information. The human story took priority over the real reason she came to Timisoara. She called Anna again, but it went straight to voicemail. She left another message.

"Me again. Where are you? You're not going to believe what Natalya's told me. It's nothing like what I expected. Call me."

She had to think fast about what to do with Natalya.

Natalya returned and sat down. She said nothing for a long time as she stared into her drink. Finally, she looked at Susie. 'What do you think Karen, what do you think I should do?'

Susie couldn't maintain the pretence any longer. 'Natalya, I need to be honest with you. I told Dr Archer a little white lie. My name's not Karen and I don't work for the Guardian.'

'What do you mean?' Natalya looked confused. 'I don't understand.'

'My name's Susan Jones. I am a journalist. I work for a scientific magazine called *Forensic Insight* and I'm investigating a drug called Thytomet. It's being marketed online and according to my investigations it's made here by Azllomed. That's why I came to interview Dr Archer.'

Natalya gave Susie a puzzled look. Her head tipped to one side and her eyes squinted as she tried to make sense of the news. Then, as the fog of confusion lifted and realisation dawned on her, she made a short involuntary gasp and held both hands to her mouth. 'Thytomet.' She said the word as though discovering something that had been hidden for an eternity. 'I remember the name now. Schrader came up with a list of brand names for a weight loss drug he was working on; that was one of them. It's so long ago I can't even remember the chemical name. There was a trial, a year or two ago. It proved too unstable, the side effects were horrendous. It would never have passed clinical governance.' She balled her hands into fists and gazed intently at Susie while the full impact of the revelation sunk in. The news about Susie's true identity hardly registered.

'So you know about Thytomet?'

'Not really. I'd forgotten the name until you mentioned it, but I couldn't forget what happened. It was going to be the best weight loss drug ever made and Schrader was raving about it. It was all his R and D, he developed the formula. If I remember right, it boosted metabolism and raised thyroid levels, something like that. He was pushing to get it to market, but Dr Archer was sceptical. Actually, he was more than sceptical. He was dead set against it.'

Susie wanted to understand. 'Why? Surely it would make millions for Azllomed.'

'Sure, it would make a lot of money, but it was the ethics of it that Dr Archer disagreed with. He wants to develop medications that help people with what he considers life-threatening issues, and in his opinion, being overweight isn't one of them. He's a very ethical man.'

It intrigued Susie. 'You said there were side effects?'

Natalya shook her head slowly as she recounted events and gazed past Susie into the middle distance. 'We did an RCT.' She caught Susie's puzzled expression 'Sorry, randomised controlled trial, just small in-house clinical trials with about a hundred volunteers, all of them a few kilos overweight. Half of them took the pills, Thytomet, for ten weeks, the other half took a placebo. We weighed them every Monday morning.' She stopped and dropped her head into her hands.

Susie saw that the memory troubled her. 'What is it, Natalya?'

'It was terrible; of the fifty taking Thytomet, ten stopped after a week, they couldn't cope. They couldn't sleep, they were buzzing, their metabolism had gone off the scale. Those that stuck with it were losing kilos at an alarming rate but suffered the same symptoms; insomnia, hyperactivity, complete loss of appetite, they were ill, some were developing traits of schizophrenia. They kept dropping out of the trial. By week eight, we only had six people left. Everybody involved was worried and wanted to call it off, but Schrader insisted the trial continued to the end. He's so cold, he doesn't care about anybody.'

Susie's jaw dropped, and she sat forward to catch Natalya's words. She sensed the worst was yet to come. 'What happened in the end?'

'Two of them died,' Natalya said, her voice barely audible. 'They died because of taking one of our products.'

They sat for a full minute without saying a word. Susie took in the truth about the drug she had been investigating. Natalya stared at the floor as she re-lived the events of eighteen months previously.

Susie broke the silence. 'What did Dr Archer do?'

'That's just it, Schrader never told him. He said that two of the volunteers had developed complications because of their weight and in his report concluded that the formula for the drug needed modification before being submitted for approval.'

'Did he accept that?'

Natalya bridled at the suggestion. 'Absolutely not, he told Schrader in no uncertain terms that the project was terminated. To cancel all further development and destroy all existing stocks. He made it quite clear that Azllomed would not be going into the diet pill business.'

'I can't imagine your dear friend Dr Schrader liked that very much.'

'He went ballistic. He ranted on about Archer being awarded for all his good deeds, while he was ignored by the industry and never got any recognition. He's got a real chip on his shoulder about it. Until five minutes ago, the name Thytomet has never been uttered again. He reported that he'd done as instructed.'

Susie sat back, folded her arms, and pondered. She wanted a story, but hadn't expected to uncover a rogue chemist who had produced dangerous drugs under the cover of a legitimate company. She looked at Natalya, her head still bowed. She noticed that her hands trembled. 'Bloody hell, it's no wonder the little man is so wound up. He must be paranoid about somebody blowing the whistle.'

'I wanted to tell Dr Archer, but Schrader threatened me.' Natalya glanced up at Susie, her eyes glassy with tears. 'Two or three times he's physically assaulted me, pinned me against a wall or pushed me. He's never actually hit me, but he's raised his hand as if he's going to. I was told if I ever said anything that I would regret it. He knows where I live, how I live, what I do. I don't trust him, but I have no choice. He said Dr Archer didn't need to know, but if I'd known he was still producing it, I'd have said something. Schrader has a vicious temper. He watches me all the time, he checks my emails, he reads my phone messages and Dr Archer isn't here very often.'

'So what happened after I left this afternoon?'

'Two men arrived to meet Schrader. He told me to meet them. I'd never seen them before, a big guy and a shorter fat one. They both looked rough'

Susie frowned and leaned in, curious. 'They sound familiar. What did they do?'

'I showed them straight to the meeting room.'

Susie saw from Natalya's face that something concerned her. 'Don't tell me you listened at the door?'

Natalya shook her head. 'Not initially. I went back to the security office. I often work in there. The controls for the CCTV are in there.'

Susie caught on immediately. 'So you listened in?'

'No, I watched them. There's no sound. But it's what I saw that made me call you.'

Susie looked around, then drew herself closer to Natalya. 'Come on then, what did you see?'

Natalya recounted the scene she had witnessed; an expensive camera, a long zoom lens and a silver blue cylinder that she'd seen inserted into the empty lens. 'They designate those cylinders for poison gas. I don't know what they are planning, but it's got nothing to do with taking pictures.'

'What did you do?'

'I got my stuff to go, but I couldn't resist stopping by their door to see if I could hear anything.'

'And?'

Natalya held her clenched hands in front of her face as though in prayer. She nibbled a thumbnail and turned to meet Susie's intense gaze. 'I heard the words Montreux and conference several times. Schrader did all the talking, like he was giving orders.'

'Jeez, Natalya, this gets worse by the minute. Is that when you called me?'

Natalya nodded, slowly. Her eyes watered. 'I didn't know what to do or who to call.'

Susie laid a reassuring hand on Natalya's. 'This ends now. You have my word.' She checked her watch. 'It's twenty past seven, we need to get hold of Dr Archer. What time does his train leave?'

'Not for an hour. I made his reservation. The train for Arad leaves at 8.46pm.'

'OK, so we've got time. Can you ring him?'

Natalya shook her head. 'I could try, but he won't answer.'

Susie gave her an expression that cried out *why the hell not?*

'He switches his phone off when he's travelling. He hates being disturbed.'

'Great.' Susie gazed out at the gathering dusk. 'Do you know where he stays when he's here?'

'He stays at a little hotel on the way out to the airport, but he said he was going out for a meal before he got the train and he didn't tell me where.' Natalya shrugged in apology.

Susie drummed her fingers on the tabletop and rubbed her forehead while she searched for an answer. 'We know what time he's going to be at the station.' She looked at Natalya, who nodded in agreement. 'How far away is your place?'

'Ten minutes in a taxi. But why...'

Susie held up a hand to stop her. 'Have you got a passport?'

'Yes, why?'

'Just in case we miss him at the station, you may need it.'

Natalya's expression shifted from confused to worried. 'What are you thinking?'

'He's going to Vienna, right?'

'Uhuh.'

'That's two border crossings. Best be prepared.'

'But.' Natalya stopped, unable to comprehend Susie's train of thought. 'But, we'll catch him at the station, won't we.'

'We should, but things don't always go to plan.'

'What could go wrong?'

Susie stood and picked up her bag. 'Hopefully, nothing, but sod's law dictates otherwise. Let's try and cover all bases.'

Natalya's frown intensified, but she followed Susie's lead and got to her feet. 'OK, if you're sure.'

'I am. We need to get going. If we get a move on, we've got time to pick up your passport and get to the station in time to meet him.'

'I just hope we catch him. I can't go back to Schrader after what you've told me.'

———————————••●••———————————

Decebal and Sergei left Schrader, thirty minutes after they had arrived. They carried three plain cardboard boxes and had explicit instructions about where to go and when to be there.

Schrader stood at the meeting room door and watched as they made their way down the corridor to the rear exit of the factory. As soon as they had disappeared from view, he turned sharply and walked back to the security office, expecting to find Natalya.

There was no sign of her.

He called out, 'Natalya.'

A silence met him, broken only by the quiet hum of computers left on standby and server fans that whirred in the background. He looked around, and waited for a response, and in the process, he noticed the glow of light from the screens that faced away from him. Puzzled, he walked round to see the bank of eight CCTV monitors. Black-and-white images showed various rooms and corridors in the factory. He noticed one had been switched to show an empty meeting room.

At first, it made no sense. Schrader glanced at the other monitors. They were all focused on what he considered to be important areas; labs and critical access points. Why would anyone select the meeting room?

A sudden thought hit him and his blood ran cold. He checked the timer at the bottom of the screen, it indicated how long the camera had been active. Forty minutes.

He cursed and banged his fist on the table as he stared at the active monitor.

'Natalya.' He screamed her name so loud that it seemed to slice the air, and he spun around in search of something to vent his frustration. He picked up a wastepaper bin and flung it at the wall. The bin crashed to the floor with a deafening metallic din and scattered its contents as it rolled to a stop.

Schrader glared at the mess, and back at the monitor. His face darkened, and his fist clenched.

His phone rang. He ignored it for several rings before he pulled it out of his jacket pocket and glanced at the screen.

Gianfranco DeLuca. The last person he wanted to speak to. The phone continued its incessant noise and Schrader closed his eyes in frustration. He knew he had to answer.

'Yes.'

'Manfred?'

'Yes.'

'Can you talk?'

'Yes.'

'Have my boys been?'

'Yes.'

'And have they left?'

'Yes.'

'What's up Manfred, you sound angry.'

Schrader exhaled slowly and said nothing.

'Speak to me, man.' DeLuca's limited patience wore thin.

'Natalya.' Schrader spat the word out.

'Archer's assistant?'

'Yes.'

'What about her?'

'It looks like she saw my meeting with them.'

'Not sure I follow you. How?'

'I've just found the meeting room camera was active at the time I was in there with them.'

'Jesus Manfred, what could she have seen?' DeLuca's voice rose.

'Depends on how long she watched for, but I demonstrated the mechanism for them and made the one who's going to use it...'

'Sergei.'

'Yes, Sergei, I made him strip it down and rebuild it so he knew how it worked.'

'Bloody hell, where's Natalya now?'

'Gone. No sign of her.'

'She's no fool. She'll be trying to get to Archer to warn him.' DeLuca paused to think. 'Where is he now?'

'I don't know. She makes his arrangements for him, but I know he's impossible to get hold of. He switches his phone off when he doesn't want to be disturbed.'

'At least the bloody woman has got no one else to turn to for help.'

Schrader nodded in agreement as if DeLuca could see him, then he froze as a thought hit him.

'Manfred, you've gone quiet on me again. What's wrong?'

Schrader cursed again and squeezed his eyes shut in anticipation of how DeLuca would react to what he had to say. 'I found her showing a journalist round the factory earlier. There was something about her that made me suspicious.'

'What?' It was DeLuca's turn to shout. 'Have you checked her out?'

'Of course.'

'Well then, why are you suspicious?'

'There was something about her that didn't add up. I checked her out, but I have my doubts.'

DeLuca spoke slowly, his voice calm and his tone measured. 'Have you got a picture of her?'

'Yes, I took a screen grab from the CCTV. It's quite clear.'

'Ping it over now, let me see.'

Schrader grimaced and retrieved the print from where he'd left it by the door. He hated the fact that DeLuca had taken control.

'You know how to send me a picture, Manfred?' DeLuca's mocking tone did nothing to make Schrader's job any easier.

Schrader fumbled with his phone, placed the print under a desk light and snapped a picture. He ground his teeth but refrained from rising to the bait. He studied the result of his photography and tapped the screen to send it. His voice brimmed with resentment. 'On its way.'

The phone remained silent for ten seconds and Schrader looked at the screen again to make sure the connection hadn't dropped out. 'Have you got it?'

He heard a sharp intake of breath at the other end, then an explosive outburst. 'I don't fucking believe it. You have to be fucking joking.'

Schrader jumped back as if hit by the force of the statement. 'Wh - wh, what is it?'

'It's that fucking Jones woman, the one who's been causing us all the problems over here. Didn't you recognise her?'

'How would I know? You've never sent me a picture of her. She said her name was Karen Green, and she worked for the Guardian.'

'For fuck's sake, Manfred, how the hell did she get through your security? I told you not to allow anyone into the place unless you checked them out first and let me know.'

'She bypassed me and went direct to Archer. I didn't know she was here until I saw her leave with Natalya. And I object to you telling me how to run my factory.' Schrader did his best to regain some sense of authority.

'I don't give a fuck about you and your factory, Manfred.' DeLuca's fury simmered. 'But we've invested too much time and money in this project, and I'm not letting her fuck it up. She's a loose cannon and a sodding liability. I thought we'd got rid of her or at least scared her off.'

'Well, you've obviously failed.' Schrader took some solace in being able to score a point. 'You can't blame me if you don't share what you know.'

DeLuca was in no mood to concede, but his mind moved on. 'You have to stop her getting to Archer or Jones.'

'I have to get to her?' Schrader put the emphasis on the first person pronoun. 'Exactly how am I meant to get to her?'

'You know where she lives, I presume. Get one of your security people to sort her out.'

'In case you hadn't noticed, security comprises one man sitting behind a desk. When he can be bothered to turn up,' Schrader said, as he looked around the empty office. 'And when he does turn up, I can't send him out and leave the factory unguarded.'

DeLuca groaned in exasperation. 'For the love of God, text me her address. I'll send Decebal and Sergei to go and get her. They won't have gone far.'

'What are going to tell them to do with her?'

'She's got to be eliminated. Why, do you care?'

'Not really, but I want nothing coming back on me.'

'She's your responsibility Manfred, I'll get them to bring her back to you.'

'Oh great, what about the other woman, Jones?'

'I suspect if they find one, they'll find the other. You can deal with them both.'

'What do you expect me to do with them?'

DeLuca snorted. 'You've been looking for a couple of guinea pigs to test your potion on. Do whatever you want to find out if they've warned Archer, then get rid of them.'

The idea appealed to Schrader, and his mood visibly brightened. 'I've got a small supply left back at my apartment, I can't keep it here. I've ordered a taxi, so I'll leave now. Tell your boys to bring those two women back here then come and pick me up.'

'Okay, just make absolutely sure they haven't got to Archer. If they have, we'll have to cancel the whole bloody plan.'

Schrader ended the call and squeezed his hands together in anticipation.

••●••

A sense of renewed urgency gripped Susie as she and Natalya emerged from the Amber Lounge. Susie reached for her phone. 'I'll order an Uber.'

Natalya nodded in the hotel's direction. 'Don't bother, there's a taxi rank over there. They wait by the park.'

Susie shrugged and put the phone away. 'Old school, eh? Come on, we need to hurry.' She broke into a jog.

Natalya followed. 'Slow down, I'm no runner.'

They reached the taxi rank, a row of cream Mercedes, and jumped into the first in line. The driver looked up from his mobile and glanced at his passengers in the rear-view mirror. He paused his game and waited for instructions. Natalya rattled off her address, and he set off without acknowledgement.

Susie grasped Natalya's hand and fixed her gaze. 'Are you sure about this? I don't want you to lose your job because of me.'

Natalya gave a brief nod and answered without delay. 'I've never been more sure. I can't believe what Schrader has done; is doing. I've always been wary of him, but I had no idea just how far he had gone.'

'Good.' Susie said. 'In that case, we'll get everything you need from your apartment, so you don't have to stay there tonight.'

Natalya met Susie's eyes. 'What do you mean?'

'Call me suspicious, but from what you've told me about those people you saw and what you heard, they're up to something. I don't know what it is, but if you heard them mention Montreux and conference, we can only connect it with what Dr Archer is doing. It can't be a coincidence.'

'You think he's in danger?'

Susie rubbed her chin with her thumb and gazed out at the passing traffic. 'I do. And I think you're in danger as well.'

'Me?'

'Absolutely. Who else knows Archer's itinerary and who else knows what Schrader's been up to behind his back?'

'But,' Natalya began, but then she paused and considered what Susie had said. 'He doesn't know that you and I have talked about Thytomet. Why would he see me as a threat?'

'It's not the Thytomet. From what you've said, he sees you as Archer's spy in the camp. If anything happens to Archer.' Susie caught Natalya's worried look. 'You'll be the only one who knows what's going on. He couldn't take the risk of you telling anyone.'

Natalya sat in silence. She knotted her fingers as she absorbed Susie's words.

Susie could see the worry on Natalya's face and reached for her hand again and gave it a reassuring squeeze. 'Don't worry. We'll stick together. We need to get to Dr Archer and put him in the picture.'

Natalya gave a half smile. 'Sounds like a plan.'

The taxi slowed and turned off the main road, down a minor road and into a residential area. The driver slowed as he searched for the address Natalya had given him.

Natalya pointed out her building and asked the driver to wait. She turned to Susie. 'I'll be a couple of minutes. A few essentials and a quick change.'

'Quick as you can. And if you got any cash, grab it. Do you want me to come with you?'

'No, wait here. Stop him driving off.'

Susie agreed, then added. 'Don't forget your passport.'

'Okay. Hang on.' She headed for the doorway of the apartment building.

Susie took out her phone and composed a text to Anna.

"With Natalya going after Archer, something going on. Call you later x."

She looked out at the apartment building. Natalya had disappeared inside. She pressed send, then checked her emails; nothing that couldn't wait. She took in the surrounding scene. The setting sun cast a warm orange glow over the grey concrete of the buildings, and brightened what she was sure would have been an otherwise dull neighbourhood. She took in the few parked cars and noticed a total absence of any people, no kids playing in the street, no-one walking the dog or out for an evening stroll. She assumed the rush-hour must have passed and everyone had settled down for the evening. Apart from the distant rumble of traffic from the main road, the area seemed peaceful. She returned her attention to her phone, surprised to find she had a decent 4G signal. She checked the news while she waited.

CHAPTER 15

Decebal checked the address he'd scribbled on the piece of paper against the name on the apartment building. Sergei followed him through the back entrance into the lobby. Decebal turned to Sergei and held an extended forefinger in front of his mouth, then pointed to the sign beside the lift. He tapped on the sign to point out level three, top floor, and lifted his chin in the staircase's direction.

Sergei's shoulders fell. He got the message, shook his head in resignation, and started the climb.

Decebal tapped the button to summon the lift and waited.

••●••

Natalya emerged from the lift. The door closed behind her and she heard it descend. She checked the corridor to her left, then turned right and headed for number 309. As she hurried along the corridor, she pulled the keys from her bag. She glanced back over her shoulder. After what Susie had said, her anxiety levels had escalated. A door to one of the apartments on her left opened suddenly. She stopped, frozen mid-stride, and held her breath.

An elderly man came out. He walked with a stick. He turned and noticed Natalya. He smiled, nodded, and hobbled past her towards the lift.

The tension released, Natalya slumped with relief and she scolded herself for being so edgy. As she reached her apartment and inserted the key in the lock, she heard the ping of the lift door opening. In the corner of her eye, she caught a brief glimpse of the elderly man as he stepped in. The corridor looked quiet and empty. She pushed open her door, walked in, and switched the light on.

•••••

Decebal stood in the lift as it stopped at the third floor. The door opened, and he saw an old man waiting to enter. He placed a boot in the door's path to prevent it from closing and beckoned to the old man to come in.

He waited a few more seconds and kept his boot in place. The mechanism detected the obstruction and banged against it, backwards and forwards in small frustrated increments. The old man looked up at Decebal and raised his stick slightly to point out the problem. Decebal ignored him and leaned out of the lift to check the corridor. Satisfied, he stepped out and let the door close behind him. Opposite the lift, the doorway to the staircase stood ajar and he heard laboured footsteps as Sergei approached. Without waiting, he turned to his right and hurried down the corridor. He passed number 309 and kept going until he reached a small recess in the wall where he flattened himself out of sight. He looked back and saw Sergei stick his head out from the doorway. Decebal motioned for him to stay hidden. Sergei ducked back into the stairwell, hidden from view.

•••••

Natalya knew what she wanted and where to find it. She kept the apartment as though she expected an impromptu inspection from an overbearing landlord. She had only moved in a few weeks beforehand and had little in the way of furniture or furnishings. She promised herself that in time she would decorate and make it more homely, but for now the apartment served a purpose; a place to sleep and eat. She'd developed a bit of a sentimental attachment to it. It took her a little over five minutes to change out of her work clothes into a pair of black skinny jeans, a sweatshirt and a lightweight jacket and collect the items she needed. She grabbed her passport from a drawer in her bedside cabinet, stuffed it into her bag with everything else, and headed for the door.

Before she turned off the lights, she took a last look at the room. She felt a sense of foreboding and thought she may never see it again. She shook her head and told herself not to be so ridiculous and stepped out into the corridor.

Her phone buzzed, and she pulled it from the back pocket of her jeans and stared down at the screen as she headed for the lift. She had saved Susie's number in the name of Karen Green and for a moment; it meant nothing. The subterfuge already forgotten. She answered.

'Hello'

'Hi Natalya. Are you OK?'

'Yes, why?'

'You've been ages. I thought you were just going to dive in and pick a few things up.'

Natalya glanced at her watch. 'Sorry. I thought I'd only been a couple of minutes. I'm on my way.'

'OK, but hurry, the driver's getting impatient.'

Natalya's attention focused on the lift. Ahead of her on the left, she didn't look behind her or notice the door to the stairwell on her right. 'I'm getting to the lift now.' She pressed the down button. The lift was already at the third floor and the door slid open. She stepped inside and turned to see a large man in black clothing enter the lift behind her.

He turned his back to her and faced the door.

'Susie,' Natalya whispered.

She never heard the reply.

———————— ••●●• ————————

Anna felt tired; beyond tired–she felt totally exhausted. She had been on the go constantly for almost ten hours and it approached 7.30pm. The day had been harrowing but fruitful. She had some exciting news to tell Susie. The orphanages she'd visited had not been helpful, but the last one, the eleventh or twelfth - she'd lost count - made up for all the rest.

The taxi dropped her outside the Hotel and she made her way in. Her phone had died on her just after lunch. Its search for a signal proved too much for the battery. She was keen to get back to the room and get it charged. She also wanted to see Susie. They hadn't spoken since they parted company just after an early breakfast. She was sure Susie would have tried to get in touch and she looked forward to hearing her news. Then there was Tim. She'd called him earlier in the day for a quick chat, and she couldn't wait to tell him what she had discovered.

She took the lift to the third floor, weaved her way along the corridor, drunk with tiredness, to number 375. She expected to find Susie, but she found the room in darkness; no one at home.

She fell through the door and collapsed on the bed. She wanted to sleep. She knew if she closed her eyes, she'd go out like a light. She resisted the temptation and decided on a shower to revive her aching muscles and wash away the mental grime of the day. She put the phone on charge, staggered wearily into the bathroom, and shed her clothes as she went.

———— ••●●• ————

Decebal followed Natalya along the corridor a few metres behind her. He measured his footsteps to keep time with hers and made no noise. He let her enter the lift, waited a second, then walked in a moment before the door slid shut. He acted as though he hadn't seen her and turned to face the door.

As soon as the lift started to descend, Decebal moved. He turned quickly, grabbed the hand that held the phone, and twisted it behind her back.

Natalya screamed in shock and pain.

Decebal prised the phone from her hand, killed the call and pulled a gauze rag from a jacket pocket. He forced the rag over Natalya's face and pinned her arms to her side. She dropped her bag, kicked and writhed and fought for breath. Decebal held tight. The lift arrived at the ground floor and Natalya's struggles faded, then stopped.

The door slid open.

Decebal looked out into the deserted lobby. He dropped Natalya's phone into her bag and bent down to pick up her limp body.

Sergei arrived, out of breath. He grumbled about climbing two flights of stairs for no obvious reason.

Decebal ignored the remark and looked up at him. 'Carry her.'

Sergei flipped Natalya over his shoulder as though she weighed little more than a child. Decebal held the door open for him and the pair headed outside and made for their van, parked at the back of the apartment building.

As they approached the vehicle, they heard a shout and turned to see someone running towards them.

Decebal growled at Sergei. 'Quick, put her in.'

He headed for the driver's door while Sergei opened the back door of the van and, without ceremony, dropped Natalya into it.

••●••

Susie looked up at the apartment building and saw an old man with a walking stick emerge from the front door. The taxi driver had resumed his game and paid no attention to her. She had to do something. She grabbed her bag and opened the door. The driver turned, concerned that she was about to run off without paying.

Susie handed him some cash, more than enough for the fare. 'Wait here.' She held up two fingers. 'Two minutes.'

The driver nodded. 'Thank you.'

Susie repeated the message. 'You wait, yes?'

The driver nodded again. 'Wait, yes.'

Satisfied, but not convinced he understood, Susie climbed out and headed towards the main entrance of the apartment. She slung her bag over her shoulder and hurried. An uneasy feeling crawled up her spine.

She stopped at the glass door and peered into the lobby. It looked deserted. She stepped inside, checked left and right, and pressed the button to summon the lift. It was still on the ground floor and the door slid open immediately.

The lift stood empty apart from a shoe on the floor. Susie recognised the gold-coloured buckle Natalya had been wearing earlier. She stepped back, suddenly on edge, and spotted the back door. It stood ajar. A narrow gap remained where the closing mechanism had paused before shutting the last few inches.

She rushed at the door and pushed it open. She could see two men thirty metres in front of her. The taller of them approached the driver's door while the other opened the back door. He had a shape over his shoulder. She saw arms hanging loosely down the man's back. It had to be Natalya.

She ran towards them and shouted. 'Stay where you are.'

The men moved quickly. She saw them dump Natalya into the back of the van. The one beside the driver's door jumped in and started the engine. The other slammed the back door and ran to the passenger side as the van started to roll forward. He jumped into the moving vehicle and pulled the door closed as they gathered speed.

Susie caught up with the van, reached out, and grabbed the driver's door handle. She hung on and managed to pull the door open, then let go of the door and snapped at the driver's jacket collar and pulled. She sprinted alongside and, with her left hand, swung her bag at the driver.

He held an arm out to ward off the blow and caught the bag. He accelerated and pulled Susie with him.

Susie hung on; she had no choice. She'd wound the strap of the bag around her wrist. but the driver held the bag tight and used it to drag her off her feet.

She could go no faster, but couldn't let go of the bag. Something had to give.

She screamed in frustration and fury, and fell. Her free hand windmilled in a vain effort to hold on to something. She hit the side of the van and kept moving, dragged by the strap. She slipped backwards as the rough surface of the road ripped into her clothing, her feet inches from the rear wheels.

The speed increased, every lump, bump and sharp-edged imperfection in the road gouged into her. The driver veered to the left and aimed at a parked car to scrape her off. She rolled onto her side to save her knees and tugged at the strap with all her strength. There would be no space between the van and parked car, she would be smashed against it. The driver released his grip on the steering wheel for a moment and slammed the door shut. He missed the end of her fingers by inches, but the impact severed the strap.

Released from the arm-wrenching drag and stretched full-length, she continued to slide, then the momentum turned into a fast roll and she disappeared under the parked car. She stopped abruptly with her head wedged between the rear tyre and the road, her cheek pressed firmly into the still-warm tread.

She lay still, unable to move, and panted with shock and exertion. She winced as pain washed over her. She lay wedged on her side with one arm pinned beneath her body and the other trapped against the underside of the car. The heat from the exhaust pipe felt hot against her hip. She tried to wriggle out. She could move her lower legs, and she pushed with her toes and twisted her body to roll onto her back. Her hands felt numb and at first she couldn't feel the cuts and grazes in her palms and knuckles. The feeling returned, and she winced again.

She didn't see anything. The sound of her breathing; harsh, rapid gasps, were the only noise. Whatever the car had recently driven through overwhelmed her sense of smell. Her heart pumped against her ribcage.

Inch by inch, she pushed back with her feet and gingerly took a little weight on her hands to shuffle between shoulders and backside.

With a final gasp, she emerged from the darkness, turned her head and looked up. She didn't like what she saw.

●●●●●

Anna emerged from the bathroom wrapped in a white bath towel. She rubbed her hair dry with a hand towel and glowed from the effects of twenty minutes under a hot, powerful shower.

Still no sign of her roommate. She reached for her phone and found it had bounced back to life. She had three voicemails and one text, all from Susie.

'Hi, it's me, I'm back at the Hotel. Let me know when you're back.'

Anna checked the time: 8.02pm, Susie had left the message at 5.2 3pm. She sat on the edge of the bed and tapped on the next message.

"Me again. Where are you? I'm meeting up with Natalya for a drink. We met at the factory earlier. Call me when you get this and I'll give you directions."

Sent just after 5.42pm.

The last of the messages had been left almost an hour later.

"Me again. Where are you? You will not believe what Natalya's told me. It's nothing like what I expected. Call me."

She tapped the text icon.

"With Natalya, going after Archer, something going on. Call you later x."

Sent at 7.37pm. Anna frowned, an uneasy sensation gripped her.

She wasted no time and called Susie. She listened. A brief pause, a click and then the ring tone. Once, twice, three times. She waited and counted. After five rings, the voicemail kicked in. 'You've reached Susan Jones. Leave a message. I'll call you back.'

Anna slumped. 'Bloody brilliant.'

She ended the call and stared at her phone. She pinched her nose between thumb and forefinger, as though seeking inspiration.

Tim.

She sprung up, galvanised by the notion; he'd know what to do and anyway, it was a good excuse to ring him.

He answered on the second ring. 'Hi Anna, just been thinking about you. How've you got on today?'

'Hi babe, got loads to tell, but you'll have to wait.'

'You tease. What's more important?'

'Could be something, could be nothing, but I've got back to the hotel and there's no sign of Susie. She's left a bunch of weird messages and I can't get hold of her. It sounds like she's on to something.' The words tumbled out in a breathless rush.

'OK, OK, take your time. Deep breath, tell me what's happened.'

Anna paused and did as instructed. She paced back and forth as she recounted the events of the last ten minutes and read out the messages that Susie had left. 'What d'you think?'

Tim remained calm and decisive, his voice reassured her. 'This has to be related to that drug she was on about. Maybe the people who ran her off the road haven't given up, and if she's opened a can of worms, they're going to ramp things up.' He paused. A thought occurred to him. 'This Natalya she's mentioned. Was she someone she met at the factory today?'

Anna held the phone tight to her ear, her nose twisted. She nodded. 'I suppose so. She's never mentioned her before.'

'Look.' Tim paused, 'What's the time over there, 8.10? It's not late, we might be overreacting. You told me your phone had died. Who's to say hers hasn't died too, and she's out on the town with this Natalya?'

'Possibly,' Anna said, without conviction. 'If that's the case, how do you explain the text about something going on?'

'Hmmmm. There may a perfectly innocent explanation. I'd give her another hour, keep trying her phone just in case. If she's not back by 8.30, call me and we'll go to Plan B.'

'What's Plan B?'

'Give me a break, it'll take me a minute or two to think of one.'

'You could talk to me for the next half hour.'

'I'd love to, sweetheart, but I've got a courier coming to collect a couple of special orders. I need to get busy.'

Anna pouted at the phone. 'Shame I didn't FaceTime you. I might have been able to distract you from your work. I've just got out the shower.'

'Wicked girl. How am I meant to concentrate now?'

'You'll manage. I'll go and put some clothes on and head down to the bar to wait for Susie.'

'OK, but no talking to strangers and call me back, either way.'

———————— ••●●•• ————————

Decebal checked his wing mirror as he brushed past the parked car. He couldn't see the woman who had tried to stop them. He slammed the brakes on and the van slewed to a stop.

He pushed the door open and looked back down the road. He could see no sign of her.

He got out and looked again. Nothing.

Curiosity got the better of him, and he walked back to the parked car. As he got closer, he saw hair, blonde hair wedged under the back of the rear wheel. His lips twisted in a half-smile.

Sergei opened the passenger door and got out of the van.

Decebal signalled to him to stay where he was and moved to the back of the parked car without making a noise.

He looked down at the woman as she struggled to free herself from the underside of the car. He could see she lay on her back with her head twisted to one side, unable to see him.

He waited.

The woman inched her way out, then turned her head and blinked. Decebal stood over her, silhouetted by a streetlight behind him. He reached into his jacket pocket and pulled out the gauze rag he had used to overcome Natalya.

The woman must have caught the smell. She reacted with a speed that took him by surprise.

She twisted onto her side and lashed out with her upper leg, an un-aimed kick that caught him on the back of the knee. His leg buckled, and he staggered back a pace. His arms flailed to maintain his balance. The rag fell from his hand.

She twisted again onto all fours and sprang to her feet. She ducked under his outstretched arm and charged into him, head down. She drove her elbow into his unprotected lower ribs.

He tried to turn away from the impact, but she hit him with such force, it caused him to gasp, more in shock than pain. He steadied himself and caught hold of her upper arm.

She may have been small and light, but he hadn't anticipated her strength. She spun away from him and he lost his grip.

He expected her to run, but she turned and came at him again, fast and low. He crouched to meet her, low and wide, arms outstretched and feet planted. Would she go left or right?

A few feet short from him she jumped, and her arms pumped together to give her height. Her feet rushed towards his face, but he dodged to his left and grasped for her leg and missed, but the outside edge of her shoe smacked into the side of his face.

He reeled from the impact, momentarily stunned. He cursed, sure she would get away from him this time, but her flying leap had ended badly. He turned to find her sprawled on the ground behind him. She gasped for breath and held her shoulder; her face a mask of pain.

He recovered the gauze rag and pounced on her. He flipped her onto her front and straddled her, his knees pinned her arms to the ground. She squirmed like an eel and screamed at him, but her strength could not overcome his weight. He grabbed a handful of her hair with one hand to hold her steady and jammed the rag over her mouth with the other.

She struggled for a full minute, lashing out with her legs to try and dislodge him, but second by second the fight in her faded and eventually she became still.

Decebal took a long, deep breath and climbed to his feet. He rubbed the side of his face with the back of his hand and snarled at the inert body on the ground.

He glanced up and down the street. It remained quiet. No-one appeared to have been disturbed by the noise. He bent down and picked the woman up with one arm around her waist and carried her back to the van.

Sergei had done as instructed and remained in the van. He jumped out when he saw Decebal return with the woman and opened the rear doors. They bundled her in without speaking, closed the doors, and continued their journey.

Decebal regained his composure as he drove and passed the bag she had tried to hit him with to Sergei. 'See what's in this? It's heavy.'

Sergei opened the bag and peered in. He pulled out an iPad, a pair of shoes, a purse, a change of underwear, a lipstick and a hotel card key. He held the last item up to examine it in more detail and nudged Decebal with his elbow. He pointed to the hotel name.

Decebal nodded slowly, his mouth curled up at one side. He held the steering wheel with one hand and pulled his phone from a jacket pocket. He tapped it with his thumb and waited.

DeLuca answered after two rings 'Have you got her?'

'Got both.'

'Both?'

'The other woman with her.'

DeLuca remained silent for a moment, as he digested the information. 'Where are they now?'

'Back of van.'

'OK. Take them back to the plant and secure them in the security office with Igor.'

'Boss.'

'What?'

'We have woman's hotel card. She stays at Centre Hotel.'

Another silence, this time longer.

'You there boss?'

'Yes. I'm thinking.'

Decebal looked at the phone as though it had a fault. He continued to drive with one hand. A junction forced him to slow down. He jammed the phone between his thighs while he changed gear.

DeLuca's voice returned. 'Has the hotel card got her room number on it?'

Decebal took the card that Sergei still held and checked both sides. 'No, nothing, just magnetic strip.'

'Bugger.'

Sergei tugged at Decebal's sleeve and held up a small folder the card had been in. Someone had written the number 375 on the back of it.

'Hang on boss.'

'What is it?'

'The card was in folder, the folder has 375 on it.'

'Bingo.'

'Bingo?'

'Doesn't matter. That has to be the room number. Make sure Igor keeps them safe. Go to the hotel and search her room. Pick up anything that looks important, anything she might have used to make notes.'

'You want me pick Dr Schrader up first?'

'No, get him after you've been to the hotel. Understand?'

'Yes boss.'

CHAPTER 16

Anna sat by herself at a table in a quiet corner in the hotel bar. She'd chosen the spot so she could watch the foyer and see Susie when she arrived. She sipped a long chilled glass of fizzy water, and studied every new arrival. She resisted the urge to pick up her phone, text Tim or surf the net and willed the minutes away to 8.30..

The pendulum of a large wall-mounted clock swung back and forth, the intrusive tick-tock a frustrating reminder to Anna of how long she had sat there. She forced herself to wait until the minute hand clicked the final increment and hit the bottom of the hour. She drained her glass and stood up. Susie had still not arrived.

She weaved her way through the people in the foyer and made for the lifts. She waited a moment for one of the three doors to open, stepped aside to let two women out, then jumped in before the door closed. She pressed the button for the third floor. The door slid shut and Anna pulled out her phone to ring Tim. Twenty seconds later, the door slid open.

Two men stood waiting for the lift, dressed in black fatigues with black caps pulled down low over their faces. Each carried a canvas bag. Anna had to push past them. She recoiled at the smell of stale sweat and tobacco smoke. They did not make way for her. She turned and watched them enter the lift. They appeared out of the place in the hotel, especially at that time of night.

She shook off her concerns and headed for room 375. She tapped on Tim's name and held the phone to her ear while she reached into her other pocket for the room keycard, ready to open the door.

Tim answered before the phone had rung once. 'Bang on time, darling.'

'Absolutely, you can rely on me.'

'Well?' Tim asked, straight to the point.

'No sign of her.' Anna spoke slowly and with little enthusiasm. 'Hang on.'

'What is it?'

Anna reached the door to room 375 with the keycard held out, ready to insert into the lock. The door stood ajar. 'The door's open and the lights are on. I made sure I locked it before I went down to the bar.'

'You sure?'

'Positive.' Anna pushed the door open wider with her foot and peered into the room without entering. 'I switched the lights off and locked the door. I'm a bit OCD about things like that.'

'Maybe Susie's back. You missed her, and she's gone looking for you?'

'Maybe. But why leave the door open and not switch the lights off?'

'Granted, that's a bit strange. She could be in the shower.'

Anna pushed the door fully open and stepped cautiously into the room. She froze. 'Oh my God!'

'What?' Tim's voice shot up two octaves.

'We've been robbed. Someone has trashed the place.' Anna took in the scene. All the drawers had been pulled out and upturned, the meagre contents of the wardrobe and been scattered on the floor. Both their travel bags had been upended and the both beds had been stripped bare. 'Jesus, Tim, someone's been in here while I was down in the bar. They've wrecked the place.'

'Any sign of Susie?' Tim's voice dropped to his usual calming tone.

Anna picked her way through the debris of their possessions and peered into the bathroom. 'No, nothing. She's not here.'

'OK, well, that's something, at least.'

'Guess so. I wouldn't like to have walked in on whoever's done this.'

'My thoughts exactly.' Anna had a sudden thought. 'When I got out of the lift just now there were a couple of rough looking guys waiting to get in. They looked out of place.'

'You think they were ones who'd turned over the room?'

'I don't want to jump to conclusions...' Anna's whisper trailed off as she stood in the middle of the room and looked around, and her eyes settled on the door. She cocked her head to one side as another thought hit her. 'How did they get in?'

'I assume they just kicked the door in'

Anna stooped to examine the door frame in more detail. 'That's just it, there's no damage, they must have had a passkey.'

Tim had an alternative idea, and he didn't like it. 'It's too much of a coincidence, and I don't believe in coincidences. Susie goes missing, and your room gets trashed. Maybe they had her key?'

'Oh God.' Anna slumped onto the end of one of the beds. 'I wish you hadn't said that. The thought hadn't occurred to me.'

'Sorry,' Tim said. 'I don't see how else they could have got in so easily.'

Anna agreed and came to a decision. 'I need to ring the police.'

'Just call reception babe, they can call the police.'

'OK, and I can report Susie missing at the same time.'

'You can mention it. I doubt they'll do anything about it. She's not missing, she's just late getting back in.'

'Will the hotel be able to tell if it was her key that opened the door?'

Tim thought for a moment. 'I doubt it, it's unlikely their system is that sophisticated. You could ask if housekeeping has lost any passkeys.'

Anna stood up and walked to the door. She reached out to close it and stopped. 'I don't dare touch anything. It's a crime scene.' She withdrew her hand and clutched it to her chest. She held the phone tight against her ear and stared at the mess of the room, her eyes wide, her shoulders hunched. 'I can't sleep in here tonight.' Her voice sounded little more than a whisper.

'No, you can't. Even if you wanted to, the police won't let you.' Tim did his best to reassure her. 'The hotel will find you another room.'

'But what about Susie?'

'When she gets back, the hotel will send her to the new room.'

'If she gets back.' Anna's voice trembled.

Tim sensed her fear. 'How about I come over there and help you find Susie?'

His words had an immediate effect on Anna. She jumped to her feet, instantly galvanised. 'Really?'

'Sure, I'll get a flight first thing in the morning. I can take a few days off.'

'Oh Tim, you absolute superstar.'

'Anything to help my girl. Call reception and get them to move you. I'll sort out a flight and text you the details.' Tim considered his next move. 'Keep trying Susie, just in case, but check out in the morning, make sure you've got all your valuables and meet me at the airport. OK?'

Anna visibly brightened. 'That's more than OK, that's fantastic, thank you, you gorgeous man.'

••●••

Susie forced herself to remain calm, ignore the pain, breathe slowly, and think.

A thick wire or rope, she couldn't tell what it was, held her in place, and coiled around her waist and the back of the chair. A cable tie bound her wrists behind her back and the duct tape over her mouth effectively silenced her.

Her feet were free, her toes could touch the legs of the chair to turn her, but the floor was a tantalising inch or two out of reach. Her fingers were free, but she could do little more than wiggle them.

She tried to force her lips apart and open her mouth. The tape stuck fast and pulled on her cheeks. She twisted her jaw from side to side, but it had little effect. She looked around for a sharp edge, something she could scrape the tape against and work it loose. She pushed and pulled with her toes, she swivelled the chair through 360 degrees and studied the office in more detail. There had to be something.

The effort of turning intensified the pain. The cable tie dug deeper into her wrists and her shoulders screamed at her to stop. She winced and took a couple of deep breaths through her nose, then started a second revolution, more determined this time. It occurred to her that finding something was only half the problem, the difficulty would be getting to it.

She had turned halfway around when her eyes caught the reflection of one of the red LEDs. She stopped and peered into the gloom. At first she couldn't make out what had reflected the light, but the more she stared, the shape began to reveal itself. The second drawer down of a four-drawer filing cabinet had not been closed fully, or something had jammed, which prevented a flush finish. The top corner of the drawer front had bent slightly out of shape. She could make out the rough metal corner. It had possibilities.

She threw her weight forward in the chair; the casters turned and clunked, and she moved forward an inch. She thrust forward again, this time she kicked her legs at the same time. The rear casters lifted and tapped back down with a dull thump. The added impetus propelled her three inches closer to her goal. She kept going, a few inches at a time. She developed a rhythm; *kick roll tap, kick roll tap*, and after a minute, she had covered over three feet. The effort raised her pulse, and unable to breathe through her mouth, she stopped to recover. Whatever held her to the chair bit into her waist with each jerk. She fought against the pain and pushed on; only two more feet to go.

She had moved another foot when the office door suddenly opened. Light flooded in.

Susie froze.

The silhouetted figure of a bulky man dressed in black combat clothing filled the doorway.

Susie feigned unconsciousness, slumped in her chair, and her head flopped forward.

The man said nothing. He gazed at Susie, cocked his head to one side and scratched the side of his nose. She wasn't where he had left her; he felt sure. He took another couple of steps into the office and grabbed the back of the chair with Susie in it. He dragged it back to where he had originally tied her up. He bent down to check his knot and made sure she was still out cold. He prodded her cheek with an extended finger and got no reaction. Satisfied, he straightened up and walked out of the office.

Susie heard the lock engage and lifted her head to stare at the door. She tried to curse but could only manage a mumbled grunt.

She took a long, slow and resigned breath, turned back to face the filing cabinet and started the process again, *kick roll tap, kick roll tap.* This time, she paused after each kick and sat back slowly to avoid making any noise. Her actions seemed more deliberate, more focussed and more determined.

It took her five minutes to cover the distance. Her shoulders heaved with the effort as she examined the corner of the drawer front. At close range, it wasn't as sharp as she first thought, but it would have to do.

She pressed her cheek against it and slid it along until she could feel the end of the duct tape catch on the corner. She pushed her cheek harder against the metal and twisted her head to catch the tape on the corner. She felt it pull. She repeated the action, and the tape stuck to the corner of the metal and pulled against her skin. She kept her cheek tight to the drawer front and inched it along the line of the tape. More peeled back and stuck to the metal and, with a final flourish, it came away from her mouth.

She pulled away and took several huge, welcome lungfuls of air, then listened for any noise from the other side of the door.

No reaction.

She propelled herself back the way she had come, little by little, as silently as she could, until she reached Natalya. Still no sign of life.

Natalya faced away from her and Susie turned so they were back to back and their hands could touch. She grabbed Natalya's fingers and squeezed. She whispered over her shoulder. 'Natalya, wake up.'

Natalya groaned in response, curled her fingers and withdrew them hurriedly, an instinctive reaction to danger or threat.

Susie tried again, 'Natalya, it's Susie, wake up.' This time she reached higher and tugged on the sleeve of Natalya's jacket.

Natalya jerked awake. Her eyes opened and her head lifted. She blinked at the darkness and moaned at the pain.

'Shhhh,' Susie hissed at her. 'Keep quiet.'

Natalya moaned again, unable to speak. More duct tape.

Susie kept her voice low. 'Turn around and lean forward. I'll pull the tape off your mouth.'

Natalya got the message and tried to move. Her toes could only just reach the feet of the chair, and she struggled to rotate.

Unable to see behind her, Susie waited. 'Can you see my hands?'

Natalya made an incoherent noise of acknowledgement as she turned to face Susie's back.

Susie reached behind her, wrists bound but fingers groped for Natalya's face. 'Bend forward. I can't stretch any further.'

Natalya strained against the ties that held her, and her chin made contact with Susie's fingertips.

Susie jerked her chair back another inch and felt Natalya's face. 'Turn to one side. I can't feel the end of the tape.'

Natalya twisted her head to one side.

Susie's fingers traced the duct tape as it ran over Natalya's mouth until she reached the end. She pushed back as far as she could, pinched the end between thumb and forefinger and pulled.

At the same time Natalya sat back, and with a noise like tearing card, the tape came away. Natalya inhaled with relief.

Susie turned to face her, her voice hushed. 'You OK?' .

Natalya squinted at Susie, her head to one side. 'What are you doing here?'

'What do you mean?'

'They wanted me. How come you're here?'

'I saw them take you. You think I'd let them?'

Natalya shook her head slowly as she tried to make sense of it. 'You didn't need to do that.'

'Of course I did. I got you into this. I'm responsible, and besides, you're a mate.'

Natalya bowed her head and looked at the floor. 'Thank you.'

'No need. Are you OK?' Susie repeated the question.

Natalya's shoulders heaved as she filled her lungs. She nodded. 'Give me a moment. My head hurts so much, I can't think straight.'

'Any idea where we are?'

Natalya looked around, and peered into the dark. She gave a resigned snort. 'I don't believe it.'

'What is it?'

'I know exactly where we are.' She looked sideways at Susie and gave her a knowing half smile. 'We're in the security office.'

Susie shrugged, 'So?'

'I work in here sometimes. There should be some scissors in the top drawer of that desk behind you.' Natalya pointed with her chin. 'Can you reach it?'

Susie looked over her shoulder and reversed herself back to the desk in a series of backward thrusts. Her hands were a little too low to grab the handle of the drawer and she had to sit as high as she could and reach back. The cable dug tighter into her waist and she turned her elbows out against the pull of the tie that bound her wrists. She slid a finger into the handle and pulled. The drawer slid open with a jerk and squeaked on worn runners. The noise filled the office.

She stopped mid pull, held her breath and gazed at the office door. She waited.

Nothing happened.

Satisfied the noise had gone unheard, she pulled the drawer open a little further.

Natalya craned her neck, unable to do any more to help. 'Can you reach into it?'

Susie pulled and pushed. Her heartbeat sounded loud and fast in her head and she breathed deep, but the fear of making a noise held her back.

Natalya encouraged her in hushed tones. 'They should be on the top.'

'Got them.' She held them in one hand, manoeuvred towards Natalya and presented her bound wrists to be cut free.

Natalya worked blindly and felt for Susie's wrists. She held the tape in her left hand and snipped with her right. She caught Susie's skin twice and caused some hushed cursing, but eventually cut the cable tie.

Susie rubbed her wrists with relief, took the scissors and cut through the tape that bound Natalya's wrists. With her arms free, Susie lowered the chair and sat down. They massaged the circulation back into their wrists for a few moments before they turned their attention to the cables that were wrapped repeatedly round them and knotted tight across their laps.

'Whoever tied this was never in the boy scouts,' Susie muttered as she struggled to release the knots. 'And it's been pulled so tight. I can't find a way to undo it.'

Natalya suffered similar problems. 'We need a sharp knife.'

'Try those scissors again, see if they'll cut through it.'

Natalya worked the point of one of the scissor blades into the knot, twisted it, then tried to close the other blade.

'No, use it like a knife, saw at it.'

The technique worked, and the blade cut through the thick outer casing. Then one by one, each of the inner wires. The last copper wire snapped apart, and the knot fell open. Natalya caught the cable before it fell and passed the scissors back to Susie.

In a few seconds, she'd freed herself and took stock. 'Now what? Even if our friend wasn't waiting outside, this door's locked, and it's the only way out. Isn't it?'

Natalya nodded, then slowly her expression changed from one of concern to one of inner satisfaction. She took in her surroundings and realisation gradually dawned on her. 'I can get us out of here.' She grinned at Susie. 'They've locked us in the wrong room, or I should say, they've locked me in the wrong room.'

Susie didn't understand. She shook her head and looked at Natalya for explanation.

Natalya reached across to the desk in front of her and opened the third drawer down. She pulled out a block of blank plastic credit card-sized passes. They had the Azllomed logo printed on one side and a magnetic stripe on the other.

Susie remembered that everyone who worked in the factory had a pass that hung around their neck on a lanyard or clipped to the pocket of their lab coat. Each door had a sensor built into the lock and when the swipe card was in close enough proximity to the lock, the light on the lock turned from red to green and the lock clicked open. Natalya had explained the system to Susie during the course of the factory tour earlier in the day. Susie nodded slowly and tried to understand Natalya's apparent joy.

'I thought you told me the cards all had to be programmed to open specific doors?'

'They do, and guess who does the programming?'

Susie realised. She pointed a finger at Natalya. 'You?'

'Right here.' Natalya pointed to the monitor on the desk and Susie guessed the small square device alongside it had to be the printer for the card.

'And that prints the cards?'

'It prints the user's name if required. What it really does is code the card depending on the access level of the user. Senior staff, every door, lab staff, the lab doors, office staff, office doors; you understand?

A smile of satisfaction played across Susie's face.

'Every time someone opens a door, it's recorded here. No one can enter or leave without the system knowing. I can even set it up so that someone can go through a door one way, but not the other.'

Susie made calm down signals with her hand and held a finger to her lips for Natalya to keep her voice down. 'That solves the small matter of getting out of here, but we've still got our friend to deal with.' She glanced back at the door and half expected it to burst open. 'If we can get out of this room, can you print a card that will get us out of the building?'

Without saying another word, Natalya tapped the keyboard; the monitor flickered into life and a blue glow lit the room. She took one of the blank cards and placed it in the printer. Susie watched as she typed quickly and set up the card to open any door in the factory. With a flourish, she pressed the print option. The card printer hummed quietly for a few seconds, then with a click, it ejected the card via a slot in the front. Natalya held it up in triumph. 'Our ticket out of here'

Susie thought about their guard and how to get past him. 'Can you make adjustments to an existing card on there?'

Natalya caught on quickly. 'I don't adjust the card, but I can go into the settings menu and adjust the permissions for any card.'

Susie stabbed a thumb in the man's direction. 'Do you know who he is?'

'Igor Malinescu. He's one of the security team. I doubt he has a clue who I am. Those guys don't come in here much.'

'Can you programme his card to let him come in but not get out?'

Natalya smiled as she realised what Susie had in mind. 'It'll take me a couple of seconds.' She turned back to the monitor and, in less than a minute, hit the enter key with an exaggerated stab of her forefinger. 'Done.'

'Right. I've got a plan.' Susie slid her chair nearer to Natalya and whispered in her ear, 'You must need the loo by now?'

Natalya gave Susie a quizzical look. 'What do you mean?'

'The loo, the toilet. You need to go.'

Natalya shook her head. 'No, I'm OK.' She paused a moment, then she understood. 'I... Oh, I see.'

Susie looked around the room for something that could help them. 'When I'm ready, start shouting and telling Igor that you're bursting for a pee. I doubt he'll be bothered, but keep shouting. I just want him to come through the door.'

'What have you got in mind?'

'I need something heavy; that guy's built like a tank, he's not going to go down without a fight. Can you think of anything in here that would do the job?'

Natalya peered into the gloom 'What about that?' She pointed at a white box about four inches square and four feet long that rested against the far wall.

Susie followed her gaze 'What is it?'

'It's a replacement part for one of the tablet presses. It was just delivered today. It's a steel roller. It weighs a ton.'

Susie's eyes lit up. 'Sounds ideal.' She inched herself off the chair and crouched low as she crept over to the box. She reached and pulled it away from the wall into an upright position. She put a hand under the box and tried to lift it up. 'Bloody hell, you weren't joking.' She gave up on lifting the box and quietly opened it to withdraw the contents. The solid steel roller - contained in moulded polystyrene - was less than two inches in diameter, with a narrow section at each end where it fitted into the mechanism. Susie picked it up with difficulty, held it by one end, and swung it slowly. 'This is perfect.' She crept back to her chair. 'Put the cable over you so it looks like you're still tied up, then keep your hands behind your back. Keep shouting to keep him distracted, try not to let him notice me.'

Natalya took two or three deep breaths and composed herself. 'Are you ready?'

Susie gave a curt nod and braced herself.

Part Five

Escape

CHAPTER 17

The white Azllomed van raced down the wide Boulevard towards the Industrial Zone of the city. Schrader urged Decebal to go faster.

They had already committed every possible traffic violation and each set of red lights raised his anxiety levels another notch. He braced himself with one hand on the door handle and the other against the dashboard. Decebal revelled in the freedom to drive like a maniac without fear of losing his job. He took risks, cut corners and jumped stop lights and he'd swerved several times to avoid other cars that had right of way. He ignored the furious blaring or car horns, the shouts of abuse and the creative hand gestures. He pushed hard towards the factory.

Schrader had a rudimentary knowledge of Timisoara. He travelled by taxi and never took much notice of which roads the driver took. He checked his watch: 8.36pm. They had locked Natalya and the other woman in the security office over an hour ago. The plans developed over the previous months would come to nothing if either of them talked. He would make sure they didn't.

He didn't look at the Decebal. 'How much further?'

'Two minutes' came the terse response, as the tyres squealed, and the van lurched sharply to the left down an empty street.

True to Decebal's word, they braked to a standstill outside the factory a couple of minutes later. Schrader climbed out, while Decebal opened the back doors for Sergei. The three men headed for the main door.

Schrader went to the door and held his keycard out for the reader to register. The red light remained on. The door remained locked. He tried again, but held the card closer to the reader, then turned it over and tried again. Still nothing.

Schrader rubbed the back of the card against the sleeve of his jacket to clean the magnetic strip and waved it under the reader for a third time. The light remained stubbornly red.

'Sheisse' Schrader held the card up to the light and examined it in case he could identify some visual imperfection. He turned and kicked the door with the heel of his shoe in frustration.

Decebal and Sergei stood and watched. They glanced at each other, but neither dared to speak.

Schrader turned again and stood back, hands on hips. He looked up at the building, hoping to spot a solution. His gaze tracked left to a gap in the roofline, and he followed it down to ground level and recognised the narrow alley than led to the rear parking area. He set off at a fast walk and called back over his shoulder to the Decebal and Sergei. 'Don't just stand there. Come with me.'

He arrived at the rear door to the factory, wheezing, and tried the card again with the same fruitless result. His shoulders fell and in exasperation, he hammered on the metal door to vent his fury. The noise reverberated around the yard.

He knew the door had been designed to resist determined efforts to break in. The locking mechanism comprised steel bolts, and a frame set into reinforced concrete. He knew, because he had designed it. He turned to the two men and pointed an accusing finger at the door. 'Break the fucking door down and hurry.' His mind ran through other options and discarded one after the other.

Decebal looked around for a suitable battering ram while Sergei stood and looked back along the alley, his head cocked to one side He turned to Schrader and held his hand up with a finger extended like a small boy asking teacher for permission to leave the room.

'What?' Schrader muttered, irritated by the man's interruption to his train of thought.

Sergei pointed back down the alleyway. 'Toilet.'

Schrader suppressed the urge to hit him. 'If you need a piss, just go for God's sake.'

'No, not go toilet. Window,' he said, and made hand movements that depicted a window opening. 'Come.' He headed off into the darkness of the narrow alleyway and the other two slowly followed, wondering if they were doing the right thing.

Sergei led them thirty metres into the alleyway, then stopped. He searched for something and scanned left and right, up and down. 'There.'

Schrader followed his directions and made out a small window about eight feet above ground with no bars over it. The window appeared shut but looked big enough for a man to climb through, if he could get up to it.

Having run out of options, Schrader conceded it might work. 'OK, you go up, get Decebal to give you a boost. Smash the glass, open the window and climb in.' He didn't look at either of his two men. He knew they'd come up with excuses. 'Once you're in, find your way back to that door.' He pointed to the second one they had tried. 'I'll tell you what to do once you're there.'

Decebal translated.

Sergei understood and was about the protest, but thought better of it. He instructed Decebal to back up to the wall, interlace his fingers and create a step. He placed a boot in the foothold and heaved himself up.

Decebal grunted with the effort and lifted.

Sergei held the adjacent down-pipe and got his other foot onto Decebal's shoulder. With one more push, Sergei made it and stood with one foot on either side of Decebal's head. He levelled with the window and without waiting, raised his right fist, loosely wrapped in his jacket and punched clean through the window with one blow.

●●●●●

Natalya closed her eyes for a moment, calmed her frantic heartbeat, then opened her eyes. 'Salut. Esti acolo? Am nevoie la toaleta.' There was no response, so she tried again. 'Te rog, chiar sa plec.' For added effect, Natalya started kicking the side of the desk in front of her.

Susie waited; she had arranged the cables over her lap and held the roller behind her with one end that rested on the floor. She tensed herself, ready for the door to open.

Nothing happened.

Natalya turned the volume up and shouted even louder. 'Te rog, am nevoie de o pipi.'

There was a noise from the other side of the door; footsteps. 'Liniste, sau te voi impusca.'

Susie leaned closer to Natalya and whispered. 'What did he say?'

He told me to be quiet, or he'd shoot me.'

He's obviously not realised we've got rid of the tape over our mouths. 'Go on, keep shouting, don't stop!'

'Nu pot fi linistit, trebuie sa plec sunt disperat, te rog, da-mi voie sa plec.'

They heard more noises. The small light on the door lock changed from red to green. The door flew open. Igor didn't enter the room, but he stood in the doorway with a pistol raised in his right hand and pointed at Natalya. 'Ultima avertizare, fii linistita.'

Natalya remained calm and pleaded. 'Trebuie sa plec, trebuie sa plec.'

Susie watched, impressed by Natalya's ability to draw Igor into the room.

Igor glanced briefly at Susie to his left, then took two steps into the room to come closer to Natalya, who continued to plead with him.

Susie knew she only had a few seconds to act. She willed Igor forward. The muscles in her arms and shoulders ached. She needed Igor to move, to give her space. He stood too close, and she needed room to swing the roller.

Natalya's eyes held Igor's attention. She realised Susie's predicament and pushed her chair as though backing away from the pistol.

Igor stepped forward.

Susie measured the distance, and in a single motion, she stood and swung the roller. She put everything into it, and aimed for the man's head.

Igor heard Susie's chair fall backwards and turned. In his peripheral vision he saw a blur of movement, but his reactions were too slow and the dull sound of metal against bone filled the room. His head snapped forward and his legs buckled like crumbling masonary.

Natalya winced at the sound.

Igor stumbled forward and almost landed on Natalya. The pistol slipped from his grip and he hit the floor close to her feet.

Natalya jumped clear.

Susie gasped with pain and clutched her shoulder. The impact of the blow had sent shock-waves through her collarbone and she dropped the roller. She stood with her eyes screwed shut. She gasped for breath and grimaced.

Igor lay still.

Susie forced herself to move. She bent down and picked up the pistol, a Beretta. She checked the safety was on and pulled the slide back a fraction. The chamber was empty. She cycled the action to load a round, but didn't hear the distinct click that would indicate she'd succeeded.

With her right thumb, she hit the button to release the magazine and caught it as it dropped.

Empty.

She replaced the magazine and cycled the action again to check.

Natalya watched her, openmouthed. 'Where did you learn to do that?'

Susie, still breathing hard, frowned at the empty weapon. She glanced at Natalya. 'Army.'

'You were in the army?'

'I'll tell you when we've got more time.'

'I thought you were a journalist?'

'It's a long story. Right now, we need to get out of here.' Susie jammed the pistol into the waistband of her combats, grabbed Natalya and made for the door. 'Which way?'

'What about our shoes and everything they took from us?'

The thought hadn't occurred to Susie. She felt in her back pocket for her phone. 'Shit, they've taken my phone.'

'And mine.' Natalya looked around the room for any sign of their belongings.

'Where would they put things?' Susie made her way from the security office into the outer office and hunted through the contents of the desks. 'I've got nothing on me at all.' She suddenly felt vulnerable and violated. 'Someone's been through my pockets, my cards have gone and the cash and my bag.'

'Is that it?' Natalya pointed to a black holdall under the desk where Igor had been sitting.

Susie grabbed it and tipped out the contents. 'My passport and notepad.' She held the items. 'I left these in the hotel. The bastards must have broken in and taken them.' Realisation hit her. 'I had the hotel keycard in my bag. They could just walk straight in.'

Natalya reached into the contents of the bag and pulled out her passport 'At least that's still here, but there no sign of any phones. And they've taken the cash and my cards.'

'We're not going to get far without money or any way of paying for anything.' Susie looked round the office as she spoke. 'Is there a supply of petty cash anywhere?'

Natalya looked shocked. 'Well, yes, but we can't go into that. It's stealing.'

Susie paused and did her best to restrain herself. 'Natalya, we're in deep shit. Whatever else is going on here, the theft of a little petty cash is the least of our worries.'

Natalya looked worried. 'But what will Dr Archer say? He trusts me.'

Susie levelled with Natalya. 'Just a hunch, but I've got a bad feeling that if we don't get a move on, Dr Archer won't be around to say anything. Come on Natalya, think. Where's the petty cash? We've got to get going. They wouldn't have tied us up if they didn't want to talk to us. I'll bet someone's on their way and I doubt they're planning a cosy chat.' She needed Natalya to get a grip.

Natalya bit her bottom lip. She turned and went back into the security office, opened the second drawer of one of the desks, and pulled out a red metal box. She handed it to Susie. 'There should be some money in here.'

'Please tell me you know where the key is?'

Natalya nodded again and reached into the top drawer. 'It's in here somewhere.' She rummaged around for a moment. 'Found it.' She turned back to Susie and held a small key.

Susie opened the box and tipped the contents out. There were a few coins and a bunch of notes. She fanned them out. 'How much is there?'

Natalya quickly counted the cash. 'There's a couple of hundred dollars, the same in euros and over a thousand Leu.'

'Is that a lot?' Susie hadn't got her head around Romanian currency.

Natalya did a quick mental conversion. 'It's just over two hundred pounds.'

'It's better than nothing. Come on, you take the money. I'll get that bag and all our gear.' She headed for the door and transferred the pistol from her waistband into the bag.

'How far are we going without shoes?'

Susie was used to spending hours without shoes, and it hadn't dawned on her she was barefoot. 'Hell. I suppose you're right.' She looked around the office for inspiration. 'I don't suppose there's a cupboard with a selection of spare shoes. A pair of size four Nikes would do nicely?'

Natalya's eyes lit up. 'Lab shoes.' She dashed to the far side of the office and returned with two pairs of white flat-heeled ankle boots. 'These are what we give visitors who are going into the labs.'

Susie looked unimpressed. 'I know. You made me wear them earlier, remember? Not exactly Jimmy Choo, are they?'

Natalya shrugged. 'Not much choice, it's these or black rubber boots.'

Susie shrugged, took a pair, and slipped them on. 'One size fits all, eh?'

'Something like that, there's only small, medium and large.'

'Come on then, we're in no position to be fussy, let's get a move on.' Susie stepped from foot to foot and tried out the shoes. 'For all we know, whoever's coming to see us could be on the other side of that door.'

'If they are, they won't get in.' Natalya slipped her boots on, picked up the cash and headed for the door. 'I made a couple more adjustments to the system. This card will open any door in the building, but I've programmed it to prevent anyone from getting in, no matter what card they have.'

Susie shook her head, amazed. 'I'm glad we're on the same team.'

'Can you drive?' Natalya asked as an idea developed.

'Of course, why?'

'We'll need transport, won't we? The keys to the vans are here, but I can't drive.' She pulled a key from a desk drawer and opened a small wall cabinet that revealed bunches of keys that hung on numbered hooks. She selected one of them and tossed them to Susie. 'Come on, follow me.'

Natalya took the lead with Susie on her heels.

They'd gone through two doors when they heard the distant sound of breaking glass, followed by the thump of something, or someone heavy, landing on the ground.

Natalya froze. 'What was that?'

Susie urged her on. 'I don't want to know. Keep going, how much further?'

••●••

None of them cared about the noise - there was no-one around to hear it. Before the last shard had tinkled to the floor, Sergei reached in, unfastened the lock and swung the window wide open. He grasped the inside edge of the window frame and pulled himself up. His boots swung and caught Decebal in the face and made him swear.

Sergei had got in.

Schrader stared up into the darkness and tried to make out what was happening. He heard Sergei drop to the floor with a crash, followed by more cursing, then a light came on as he got to his feet and found the switch. 'Get back along to the door. There should be a keypad beside the lock.'

Schrader and Decebal headed back to the door and waited. They saw lights come on as Sergei made his way down the corridor, then a faint glow appeared under the door as he reached the exit lobby.

Sergei's silhouette appeared at a window, and he shouted.

Decebal translated for Schrader. 'He wants to know the code?'

Schrader had expected the question. He closed his eyes, head bowed in concentration as he thought back to the security system and the codes he had set up. He thumped his fist against his temple as though divining the information from long forgotten recesses. The six-digit code was his date of birth, but he struggled to recall the rest of the button sequence. He opened his eyes suddenly and looked up, hit by a moment of clarity. 'Try this. Press the star key twice, then 171063, then the hash key.'

Decebal translated and Sergei repeated the instruction then disappeared. Silence hung in the air for a moment, then a click, and the light on the lock turned green and the door swung open.

———————— ••●•• ————————

Driven by a growing sense of urgency, Natalya and Susie rushed through the building. The swipe card turned red lights to green as they went. Natalya ran with a confident stride; she walked the corridors every day and could have done it blindfold. They emerged into the covered parking area where five small white vans stood in a row. Natalya clicked a button on the key fob. Lights blinked on the van second from the end and in the yard's silence, she heard the doors unlock.

Susie headed for the right-hand door and found herself tangled with Natalya as she headed in the same direction. She realised her mistake. 'Left-hand drive, sorry.'

They climbed in and Susie turned the key. The dashboard lit up, and the engine fired.

Natalya looked across. 'How much fuel?'

'Just over half full.' Susie acclimatised to sitting in the left-hand seat. 'This is weird; I've never driven on the wrong side of the road before.'

'Great time to learn.'

Susie engaged first gear and moved towards the gate. 'Which way then?'

'Through the gate and turn right. Where are we going?'

'You're asking me?' Susie didn't take her eyes off the road. 'We need to get to Dr Archer. Where's he going to be?'

Natalya looked blank for a couple of seconds while she thought. She looked at the dashboard lights. 'What time is it?'

Susie glanced at the digital clock 'I don't believe it. It's 8.41pm. We must have been out of it for over an hour. It's no wonder my head's splitting.'

'His train leaves at 8.46pm. That takes him to Arad, where he picks up the sleeper. He said he was going to get an early night. If we hurry, we might get to the station in time.'

They approached the junction at the end of the road. Natalya gave Susie directions; left here, next right, keep going.

Susie obeyed without question, and with little traffic, they made quick progress,

They headed towards the city centre and the main railway station.

·····•●●●●··· ─────────

Sergei stood in the doorway and grinned.

Schrader pushed past him without a word and headed for the next door. His swipe card worked on all the doors that led to the security office. Natalya's rushed re-programming only applied to the outer doors, but it had delayed him. By the time they arrived at the security office, it was almost 9pm.

Schrader burst into the security office, angry, out of breath and out of patience. He'd had enough of Susan Jones; she had caused him too many problems. He'd make sure she would be no more trouble to him ever again. He looked around for Igor but he'd vanished; just a half drunk mug of coffee on the desk. He checked the doorway to the inner office, but it had been locked. He looked through the window. There was no sign of the women.

'Get this door open.' He glared at Decebal. 'Now.'

Decebal nodded and without a further prompt, he charged at it, and turned his right shoulder to the door at the last minute. The door remained locked, but the entire frame ripped away from the surrounding wall and it gave way to 220 pounds of determined aggression. Decebal lost his balance as his feet became tangled in the splintered woodwork and he sprawled headlong into the inner office.

Schrader walked in as Decebal got to his feet and saw Igor lying motionless on the floor behind a desk. The security guard opened one eye and groaned. Schrader looked at Decebal and, behind him, Sergei. For a moment, his heart sank. His plans had fallen apart.

He wanted to scream; he wanted to blame someone. Instead, he shook his head, and cursed.

CHAPTER 18

D riving at night, in a foreign city, in a strange left-hand drive vehicle on the wrong side of the road and in a desperate hurry, felt bad enough, but with a head that ached from the effect of whatever had knocked her out, a shoulder that throbbed as a result of clubbing Igor and all the cuts and bruises from being dragged along the road, Susie felt far from happy as she followed Natalya's instructions.

She didn't dare take her eyes off the road. 'Time?'

Natalya looked at the digital display in the centre of the dashboard. 'Eight forty three, we're almost there. The station is just ahead on the left, after these lights.'

The lights changed to green as they approached, and the traffic seemed quiet as the van raced into the station concourse a few seconds later. Susie didn't park, and instead she came to a stop in the drop-off zone, pulled the keys from the ignition, jumped out, and ran for the main entrance.

'Which way?' she called back to Natalya a few feet behind her.

Natalya pointed ahead as she tried to keep up with Susie. 'Platform 1. All the Arad trains go from Platform 1, straight through that archway.'

They emerged onto the platform, out of breath. They paused and read the numbers on the side of the carriages. All the doors had been closed and a uniformed station official scanned the length of the train and looked out for any last-minute passengers.

He saw the two women rush onto the platform with no luggage and head for the train. He stepped forward quickly. 'Prea târziu, uşile închise .' He held up his left hand in a "halt" signal and shook his head at the same time.

Susie pulled up and pleaded with him.

'Please. We need to talk to one of the passengers. It's an emergency.'

The official either didn't understand or didn't care and repeated, 'Ușile închise.'

Right on cue, the platform clock clicked to 8.46pm, and the train moved. Susie ducked around the official, but he put his hand out and stopped her. 'Prea tarziu.'

The train quickly gathered pace, and Susie and Natalya watched as it pulled out of the station. Natalya silently counted the coach numbers and hoped to catch sight of Julian Archer. Number 17 approached just as the station official walked in front of them both and shepherded them off the platform. Natalya attempted to duck under the outstretched arm, but he was a big man and he caught her arm and turned her back.

The train disappeared from the platform into the gathering gloom on its way to Arad.

Susie and Natalya shook off the official and walked in frustrated circles.

'What now?' Susie didn't expect a reply; she thought out load.

Natalya grabbed Susie by the wrist. 'Quick, back to the van before it gets taken away.'

'Why? Where are we going to go now?'

'Doesn't matter, we need transport. Come on.'

Susie took a last look up the track in case, by some miracle, the train headed back. It didn't.

They reached the van and found another uniformed official, who they assumed was police. He studied the van and reached for his radio just as Natalya got to him.

She indicated to Susie to get in the van. 'Start it up and move away. I'll jump in in a second.'

Susie started the van and manoeuvred away from the kerb. Natalya climbed in a couple of seconds later and looked pleased with herself. Susie said nothing, but gave Natalya an expectant look.

'Told him we were delivering medical emergencies. Just go, get out of here.'

They pulled forward and re-joined the main road.

Susie thought out loud and tried to remain positive. 'OK, so what do we do now? No phone, no credit cards,'

'What about your friend, Anna? She could help us,' Natalya offered.

'Good thinking, which way to the hotel?'

Natalya quickly took stock. 'Keep going up this road, then turn right; the hotel is less than a kilometre away.'

It took them three minutes to get to the Centre Hotel. They neared the portico, but Susie spotted the rhythmic flash of blue lights across the entrance, then spotted the police car outside. She sped up again without saying a word.

Natalya looked puzzled. 'What are you doing? I thought you wanted to find Anna?'

'They'll be looking for us.' Susie seemed agitated, unsure what to do. 'That man I hit, someone must have reported it. They'll have gone through all the stuff they took off us and found out this is where I'm staying.'

Natalya understood, but didn't agree. 'Why not tell the police what happened, and that we were attacked and tied up? We've done nothing wrong.'

'Apart from club a man to death. You really think they'd believe us?' Susie's tone mocked. 'By the time we've been arrested, questioned and told them our side of the story, Dr Archer will be halfway to Montreux. They could lock us up in a police cell for days before anyone believed us–that's if we're not charged with murder.'

'What about Anna?'

Susie watched the scene behind her in the wing mirror as she drove slowly from the Hotel. Could she risk going back to find Anna? She made a decision. 'No, it's no good. If we go in there, any chance we have of stopping whatever it is they are planning in Montreux will disappear.'

'So, what about Anna?' Natalya repeated.

'Anna's no fool. She'll tell them she hasn't seen me since this morning. We just need to get a message to her and arrange to meet up.'

'OK, but how? They've taken all our stuff.'

Susie pondered. 'There's no point in going back to your place. For all we know, they might be waiting for us.'

The thought saddened Natalya. 'I only moved in a month ago. I really liked it.' It occurred to her she might never see it again.

Susie took a last look at the flashing blue lights outside the hotel and reached a decision. 'How long will it take to drive to Arad?'

Her eyes narrowed as she tried to follow Susie's thinking. 'Why?'

'Can we get there before Dr Archer gets his sleeper train to Vienna?'

Natalya glanced at the clock, which read 8.52pm. 'His train arrives at 10.45pm and the Vienna train leaves at 10.59pm.' She didn't drive, she didn't know the road, and she didn't know if they could make it, but it was the only option they had. 'Let's go. That way.' She pointed to her right.

Susie wasted no time. She floored the throttle and dropped the clutch. The tyres squealed as the van lurched away. 'Just read the signs, hang on tight and keep me on the right road.'

———————————••●●•———————————

The road from Timisoara to Arad, a new, almost straight, dual carriageway, was, for the first ten kilometres, well lit. Susie and Natalya made swift progress. They had to. They chased a train and had less than forty-five minutes to intercept Julian Archer.

'D'you think we can make it?' Susie didn't take her eyes off the road. She had grown used to driving on the right, but the strain of the day affected her.

'If it stays as quiet as this, we should make it.' Natalya turned to Susie and saw the concentration on her face. 'It's just over 50k.'

Susie did some quick mental maths. 'Is that all? How come the train takes so long?'

'It's just one of the regional ones, stops a few times on the way.'

Susie squinted against the oncoming headlights. 'Does the sleeper train start in Arad?'

'No.' Natalya closed her eyes and tried to remember the details. 'There was something about changing platforms onto the main intercity line. I had to book his compartment all the way from Bucharest. It was the only way they'd accept the booking.' She stared ahead, worried. 'What are we going to do when we see him?'

'I hope it's when, and not if,' Susie said. 'We'll have to tell him everything we know; he obviously knows nothing about what Schrader's up to. At least he'll be able to help us. I mean, we've got nothing. If we don't see him, we're really screwed.'

Natalya nodded and remained in silent concentration for a moment. 'Just keep driving.' She stared and watched the road and the traffic, deep in thought. Suddenly, she smacked her hands to her head. 'Oh no, I've just remembered!'

'What?' Susie took her eyes off the road for a second and glanced at Natalya. 'What is it?'

'They'll be following us.'

'Who?' Susie looked puzzled.

'The van has a tracker built in. They all do. It's a security thing, so we know where the drivers are at any time. I'd forgotten all about it.' Natalya's face fell. She shook her head.

'How do they follow the vans?'

'On the computer in the security office. It's one of the jobs I've done in the past.'

Susie understood immediately, 'OK, OK, but who is going to know we've taken one of the vans?'

Natalya knew Susie had a point. 'You're right, but it won't take them long to realise one van is missing and put two and two together.'

'OK, so they could follow us if someone knew what to do, but we've got a head start and so long as we can get to Arad before they figure it out, there's nothing they can do.'

Natalya sounded despondent. 'What if we don't?'

'Keep positive Natalya, just keep me right with directions. I'll get us there in time.'

After thirty minutes, they turned off the dual carriageway and headed into Arad. The road surface deteriorated and Susie weaved the van between potholes. The traffic had remained light and Susie pressed on, her right hand glued to the gear stick. She kept her foot wedged to the floor and extracted every morsel of horsepower.

The traffic increased as they approached the outskirts of the city, and Susie grew impatient. She raced through red lights and jinked between lanes. 'How long have we got?'

Natalya instinctively glanced at her wrist and forgot that her watch had been taken. 'I can't believe my watch has gone.' She sounded bitter.

'Your friend Igor must have taken it when he tied you up.' She glanced at the clock on the dashboard. 'This says 10.51pm if that's any help?'

Natalya glanced out of the window, her features lined with despair. 'We've got eight minutes before the sleeper leaves.'

Susie's driving became erratic. The van sped over junctions, ignored signals, road signs and furious horn blasts from cut up drivers. 'How much farther?'

'The station's at the end of this road. It's less than a kilometre away.' Natalya braced herself. She looked worried and bit her bottom lip and hardly dared to look ahead as Susie kept her right foot pinned to the floor.

They approached a major intersection, and the traffic ahead slowed to a crawl. There appeared no way through, and Susie screamed in frustration. She saw the station a hundred metres beyond the junction, but had become hemmed in on both sides. She slammed on the brakes and veered to the right. The van skidded to a standstill with its front wheels on the pavement.

'Come on, get out. We'll have to leg it.' She threw open the door and leapt out.

It took Natalya a second or two before she realised what was happening. 'I've just got these lab shoes, they weren't meant for running.'

'Just do your best.' Susie picked up her bag, ran around to the passenger side, grabbed Natalya's hand and pulled her out of the van.

They headed towards the station and ignored the cacophony of noise and chaos they'd left behind.

Natalya took one last backward glance at the Azllomed van and resigned herself to running along the pavement in strange white boots. Despite the late hour, the place looked busy, but no one looked twice at the two women that sprinted between them.

Susie ignored the lights at the junction, dodged between cars, and dragged Natalya with her.

They reached the station in less than a minute. The ornamental clock over the entrance read 10.59pm. They raced in and took in their surroundings.

Susie turned to Natalya. 'Which way? What's the destination of the train?'

Natalya scanned down the departures board. 'There, Vienna, Platform 7.'

Susie nodded and searched for direction signs. 'That way, up the escalator.'

The pair rushed up the escalator and followed the signs to the right that led to Platform 7. As they ran over the bridge; they saw the sleeper carriages of the Vienna bound train at the platform. Stairs dropped to the platform on either side of the bridge. Susie pulled Natalya to the left.

They were halfway down the stairs when the train moved.

'Come on,' yelled Susie. She made a last-minute dash to the train and reached the door as it picked up speed. The automatic locks had cut in as soon as the train moved, and she banged on the door in a futile and frustrated attempt to gain access. She gave up and bent over, hands on her knees as she gasped for breath. She cursed as she watched the red rear lights of a train disappear into the darkness for the second time in an hour. She looked around and caught Natalya with her head in her hands. She wheezed. 'Are you OK?'

Natalya peered at Susie through her fingers and shook her head. 'What now?' She looked close to tears. She looked down at her boots and in a faint, resigned voice added, 'And these shoes.'

Susie stood up and went over to Natalya. She took her by the shoulders and forced her to look up and make eye contact. 'We've got no choice.' She studied Natalya intently and sought agreement. 'We have to follow Dr Archer. We can't go back. The police will probably be looking for us and the Azllomed people will track us down.'

She looked around. The platform and station appeared deserted. The digital indicator board had turned blank. 'Come on, we need to get out of sight before someone starts asking questions.' She led Natalya to a bench in the bridge's shadow. She hoped to take Natalya's mind off their current predicament. 'How long is the good doctor in Vienna for?'

Natalya's brow furrowed as she tried to understand the question, and it took a moment before the fog cleared. She screwed her eyes shut and tried to remember the details of the timetable. 'He gets into Vienna just before 9am in the morning, I think.' She nodded to herself as if in confirmation. 'He's allowed four hours for his meeting, then he gets the shuttle train to the airport and the Geneva plane leaves at 2.15pm.' She looked up at Susie, baffled. 'Why?'

Susie thought quickly. 'We need another train. Somehow, we have to get to Vienna before one o'clock tomorrow.'

'But...'

'I know, I know, we've not got much money, yaddah, yaddah, yaddah. We're going to have to be a little creative, Natalya.' Susie did her best to lift their spirits. 'Is this the main line from Bucharest to Budapest?'

Natalya nodded.

'So, there's got to be another train coming along soon. Any train. How much cash did you say we had?'

Natalya didn't need to check. 'Dollars, euros and Leu, a few hundred pounds.'

'And how much is a ticket to Vienna?'

'I don't know, we could ask.' Natalya looked across the platforms to the ticket office and noticed the light on.

The ticket office was officially closed, but Susie spotted a female member of staff in the back office when she peered round the side of the blind drawn down over the window. She tapped on the glass and attracted the woman's attention.

'Can you help us? Please.'

The woman looked up and made signs. The office had closed and she shook a pointed finger at Susie.

Susie turned to Natalya. 'See if you can persuade her. I don't know what to say.'

Natalya smiled at the woman. She adopted a little girl lost look.

The woman came over to the window and opened the blind - 'Am inchis.' *We're closed*. She didn't wait for a response and closed the blind. She returned to the back of the office.

Natalya banged on the window. She leaned closer and called through the mesh at its base. 'Te rog ajută-ne'

Susie could only guess what Natalya said, but she saw the woman look back at them and shake her head.

Natalya produced some of the currency and waved it at the woman. 'Te rog, suntem disperați.'

The woman turned again and scowled, then she saw the notes. She looked left and right as though to check there were no witnesses and returned to the window.

Natalya smiled at her. She held the notes like a peace offering and spoke quickly and quietly. The woman's demeanour softened.

Susie stood alongside Natalya and watched the performance. She couldn't understand a word, but for the second time that night, found herself impressed at Natalya's acting skills.

The woman, explained something to Natalya, her eyes never leaving the preferred notes.

Natalya responded with, Mulțumesc, mulțumesc.' and handed over the cash.

'What's happening?' Susie asked, her voice low.

'She's going to write us out a couple of tickets. We're supposed to pay by card, but I told her we'd been mugged and only had a little cash.' Natalya watched as the woman turned away and wrote on an official-looking pad.

'How much have you agreed with her?'

'We've agreed on four hundred Leu for two tickets to Budapest on the next train. Don't know what the fare should be, but it sounds like a bargain to me.'

The woman returned to the window and handed over the slip of paper without another word. She closed the blind and disappeared from view.

'Amazing job, Natalya. If all else fails you could get an acting job. Somehow, I don't think that cash will ever be recorded, do you?'

Natalya just shook her head. 'There's a train to Budapest due in twenty minutes. We need to get back to the platform.'

Susie headed over the bridge back to where they'd missed the previous train. 'You can tell me more when I know we're safe.'

Natalya spoke as she jogged alongside Susie. 'She said the train is a sort of goods train, no buffet car, no refreshments, just seats. It's not going to be very comfortable and we'll have to find another train when we get to Budapest.'

They got to the platform and waited.

Half an hour passed before they heard a train. It approached slowly. It emerged from the dark, old and tired, a faithful retainer given a thankless task. It pulled a ragtag assortment of carriages, trucks, vans and flatbeds. No doubt it stopped at every minor station between Arad and Budapest. It jerked to a halt and a uniformed guard jumped down from one of the carriages.

Susie and Natalya climbed aboard. The interior looked as old and tired as the loco; frayed fabric on the seats, the smell of stale sweat, and decades of smoke ingrained into the walls and ceiling. There was only one other person in the carriage, an old man who rested against the window, fast asleep. Susie and Natalya sat down opposite each other and looked for spots where the bumps and lumps in the upholstery were at least bearable. They heard noises farther down the platform; something heavy being loaded or unloaded, a door that slid shut, and then a whistle. The loco shuddered and jerked, couplings clanged, and they pulled away from the platform.

The guard appeared.

'Biletele vă rog' He looked at the two women with suspicion and held out a hand in the expectation of something.

Natalya handed him the piece of paper the woman had written out for them.

The guard looked at the note, lines appeared on his forehead as he studied it. He looked at Susie and Natalya and back at the note and then scribbled his initials on it. He handed it back and thanked them. 'Mulţumesc.' With that, he left.

Susie didn't speak until the guard had left the carriage. 'What does it say on there?'

Natalya held the ticket and read it. 'Arad to Budapest, one way for two people.' She looked up to see Susie's reaction and continued. 'Ticket price four hundred Leu each, total eight hundred Leu and it's been endorsed with her official stamp.'

'I thought you paid her four hundred?'

Natalya smirked. 'I did, but like you said, who's going to know?' She folded the piece of paper and placed it in her bag.

Susie let out a long sigh and relaxed as the train gathered speed. She felt a little safer. It was going to be a long, uncomfortable night. She squirmed in her seat and tried to get comfortable. 'What did I say about sod's law?'

CHAPTER 19

The squeal of brakes and the juddering of the carriage woke Susie as the train rolled into the station. She rubbed her eyes and peered out into the darkness.

Without a watch or her phone, she didn't know the time, but it had to be sometime close to sunrise, judging by the purple glow on the eastern horizon. The station appeared deserted and their train had been directed to one of the minor platforms away from what little light there was.

She nudged Natalya, who lay across two seats, her head propped against the window cushioned on her folded jacket. Natalya groaned and opened her eyes. It took her a few seconds to take in her surroundings and remember where she was.

'Stopping again?' She rubbed her neck and blinked repeatedly in an effort to focus.

'End of the line.' Said Susie.

'Budapest?'

Susie nodded. 'We just passed a sign. We're going to have to abandon our lovely beds.'

Natalya groaned again and sat up. Her hair had adopted a life of its own and stuck out at strange angles. Her cheeks bore crease marks from where she had been resting on her jacket.

'You look as rough as I feel.' Said Susie with a resigned smile.

Natalya glanced at Susie's dishevelled appearance and returned the compliment. 'Ditto.'

They both stared out at the empty platform as the train shuddered to a stop. After who knew how many stops since they had boarded the train in Arad, they had grown used to the sounds and sensations. Every time it had woken them from a fitful sleep, but each time they had somehow nodded off again. This time, they had to get off and face the world.

'Come on then, we need to get going.' Susie stood and stretched. She ached all over and she grimaced as the pain from her shoulder made its presence felt.

The two women climbed down from the train and looked around to get their bearings. Susie made for the lights and what she assumed was the main entrance to the station.

'What's your plan?' Natalya asked.

'I wish I had one.' Susie replied, 'We're just going to wing it.'

Natalya caught sight of the digital indicator board. 'There's a train to Vienna in eight minutes.'

Susie nodded but said nothing, her eyes focused ahead. She spotted a phone booth. She tapped Natalya on the arm and pointed. 'I've had an idea.'

'Who're you going to call?'

'I suppose I'd better call Nick. He's been trying to call me. He won't mind me waking him.' She picked up the phone and poised a finger over the numbers. She hesitated and bit her bottom lip as she stared.

'What's wrong?'

'Er, don't laugh.'

'Why?'

'I can't remember his number.' Susie looked at Natalya as if she would know.

Natalya frowned. 'How come?'

'I just ring Nick. The phone knows his number.' Susie squirmed as she realised how ridiculous it sounded.

'Can't you guess?'

'I don't have a clue, I know it starts with 07 but that's the same for all mobile numbers, so it's no help.'

Natalya focused on the station clock. 'We haven't got much time and we need to get tickets. We'll try again when we get to Vienna.'

Susie replaced the handset. 'Sorry, you must think I'm hopeless.'

'Anything but. Nobody remembers numbers these days.'

'Guess so. Come on then partner, onwards and upwards.' She put an arm around Natalya's shoulders and went to buy more tickets.

•••••

Anna waited at the arrivals gate, nerves on edge. She shuffled from foot to foot, unable to settle. Tim's text said he'd got a seat on the early flight and he'd be with her by breakfast time. The hotel had moved her to a new room, but she hadn't slept well despite her tiredness. As predicted, the police and the hotel staff reassured her and promised to get back to her with any news. There wasn't any.

Anxiety over Susie gnawed at her and her appetite had disappeared; she'd made herself a couple of cups of herbal tea but they didn't help. She couldn't wait for Tim to arrive; she needed him. Part of her, she was ashamed to admit, felt thrilled that he was flying in to help.

She checked her watch for the umpteenth time, then the indicator board. Tim's flight status had changed from "landed" to "baggage reclaim," and she wondered how much longer he would be. She peered into the bowels of the arrivals hall for an early glimpse of those approaching. Taxi drivers and chauffeurs jostled her for position and held up cards with names scrawled on them, looking bored, as they waited. She looked down at her phone to see if there were any messages, and when she looked up, Tim appeared in front of her.

'Hi.'

Anna stood on tiptoe and threw her arms around his neck. The chrome barrier between them hardly mattered.

Tim reached round with a free hand and held her.

'Oh Tim, thank you, thank you, thank you.' She hugged him as though her life depended on it.

Tim put down his shoulder bag. He took her arms and gently peeled Anna off his chest. 'Hey, steady on sweetheart, I'm here now. We'll sort this out.' He kissed her quickly and took in the surrounding crowd. 'Come on, let's get out of here.' He picked up his bag and walked to the end of the barrier with her.

Anna dabbed her eyes and squeezed Tim's hand. 'We can get a coffee over there.' She pointed to an unremarkable-looking café at the far end of the arrivals hall. It catered for the taxi drivers, chauffeurs, and waiting loved ones. The seats and tables looked quiet. It would do the job.

She had so much she wanted to talk to Tim about. She tugged his hand. 'Come on, let's grab a seat.'

Tim waited at the counter while the barista poured their coffees.

Anna spotted a table for two near the back of the cafe and took a seat. She struggled to contain herself but waited for Tim to arrive with the coffees before she explained what had happened in the last twenty-four hours. It came out in a rush.

Tim held up a hand. 'Slowly, slowly, take your time.' He reached out and took Anna's hand and held her gaze with a steady smile. 'From the beginning, tell me what you know.'

Anna took a deep breath and started from when she and Susie had arrived in Timisoara. She told Tim about the phone call to the Azllomed factory, the false name Susie had used, and the meeting planned for the next day with Dr Archer.

Tim listened carefully, prompted her for more details and confirmed times and places as her story unfolded. 'So, when did you last actually speak to her?'

Anna stopped and thought. 'Yesterday morning, I suppose.' She nodded to herself. 'Before I left the hotel.'

'You didn't talk to her during the day?'

'No, I was busy going from orphanage to orphanage. The signal was rubbish, and I was frightened the battery was going to die.'

'What about texts or voicemail?'

'Oh yeah, there's three voicemails and a text message.'

Tim's brow creased. 'Can I listen to the voicemails?'

'Sure.' She handed her phone to him.

He tapped it twice, held it an inch away from his ear and leaned over the table, so Anna could hear the messages, their faces only inches apart.

Tim listened to the three messages. His expression changed from interested to curious to concerned. He looked at Anna. 'You mentioned someone called Natalya last night?'

Anna nodded.

Tim tapped the message icon.

"With Natalya going after Archer, something going on. Call you later x.'

He stared at the message. 'What's she on about?'

'It's all to do with the emails she's been chasing and the Thytomet stuff I was telling you about. She was convinced it was coming from here. She must have found some evidence.'

Tim leaned even closer. 'This Natalya. She must have met Susie after work, right?'

Anna nodded.

'Just a guess, but what if Natalya told Susie something crucial, something to do with the Thyto whatever.'

she didn't know when she left the factory, right?'

'That makes sense.'

'The guy she was meeting, Dr Archer. What did she know about him?' Tim asked.

'Not much, but he sounded very genuine and friendly when she called. He was leaving for a conference in Switzerland last night and he made time to see Susie before he left.'

'A conference in Switzerland.' He repeated the words; they rang a bell.

Anna was curious. 'That's what he said. Is it relevant?'

'Maybe, maybe not.' Why did that mean something? He rubbed his the side of his head as though the thinking process hurt his brain. Wheels whirred, conversations recalled, references made, who, when, what. 'It'll come to me when I'm firing on all cylinders.'

'Anyway, I've been trying to ring ever since I got back to the hotel. She never answers. It just goes through to her voicemail,' she said, and her voice trailed off.

Tim gave her hand a comforting squeeze. 'Keep positive. We'll sort this out and find her. Susie's one tough cookie, she'll be OK.'

Anna twisted her fingers together. 'Maybe Nick was right. He's been trying to get her to forget it ever since she started. Even more so since they nearly killed her. But she's really fired up about it, she sure she's on to something.'

Tim agreed, in part. 'You can understand Nick's concern, can't you? He's told me how determined she is, but he's worried she's putting herself in danger in search of the breakthrough story.' Tim rested his chin in his hand, his eyes focused on Anna. 'You've got to admire her tenacity. Nick's told me stories about her. She's a terrier, she won't let go and the more anyone tries to stop her, the stronger she'll fight.'

Anna nodded slowly. 'I know you're right, but that's not going to help us find her.'

Tim shifted position. He sat up and placed his palms on the table. 'When did you last try calling her?'

'About an hour ago. Same thing, voicemail.'

'You'll get voicemail even if the phone has died. It's a new iPhone, right?'

Anna nodded slowly, again.

'So, maybe the battery has still got some life in it. If I log in to the "find my" app, as Susie, we'll know one way or the other and we might even find out where it is.'

'How can you do that? You'd need her username and password.'

Tim had his phone out and checked his notes. He smiled at Anna. 'Got it. She gave them to me when I installed the tracker.'

Anna watched as he logged out and then logged in as Susie. She stood up and came to sit next to him. She snuggled up closer to get a better look. A map appeared on the screen, then two identical small thumbnail pictures three inches apart. 'That's Susie's profile image. Why are there two of them?'

Tim zoomed in on the first image. 'Ah, that's her iPad.' He zoomed closer. 'What the hell?'

'What is it?'

'She's in Vienna.'

'Is she?'

Tim squinted at the screen. 'Well, her iPad is.'

'If she's in Vienna, what's the other picture?' Anna squeezed closer to Tim, and their cheeks almost touched.

Tim zoomed out, then scrolled down to the second thumbnail image and zoomed in on it. His brow furrowed, and he stared at the screen for a few seconds without speaking.

'Well?'

'Well,' He paused and tapped the image to refresh the screen in case his eyes deceived him. 'This is her phone, and it's close to us.'

'How close?'

Tim dragged the image left and right, up and down, then zoomed in and out a couple of time. 'We're here.' He tapped the screen. 'At the airport.'

Anna saw the runways and airport buildings clearly marked on the map. She nodded.

'And Susie's iPhone is here.' He pointed at the thumbnail image. 'Looks like a residential area. It can only be a mile or two away.'

Anna sat up, shocked. 'We need to find her.'

Tim laid a hand on Anna's arm. 'If that is her.' He injected a note of caution. 'That's her phone, but we've no way of knowing if it's Susie. Someone might have stolen it.'

Anna considered the idea. 'Well, she must have had it when she sent that last text at half eight.' She peered at Tim as though she'd find the answer in his eyes. 'If it was stolen, why hasn't she found a way to get in touch with me?'

'Hmmm. If her phone is working and she hasn't called, then...' He paused and ran a hand over his jaw while he processed what they knew. 'We're going to have to accept that something must have happened to her.'

Anna held her cappuccino in both hands and studied the design the barista had created. A leaf of some description. It seemed a shame to disturb it. She bit her bottom lip and raised her eyes to look at Tim. 'What are you saying?'

'I'm saying nothing, but from what you've said about the mess in your room in, I'd say someone was either trying to find Susie or something she's got.' Tim paused and weighed up the options. 'It's too much of a coincidence for the two things not to be connected. We know where her phone is, and we have to assume that she can't get to it.' He paused and looked at Anna.

She nodded.

'The question is,' Tim said, but then fell silent for a moment as he studied the screen, and sought more information. 'How do we know if she's with her phone or her iPad?'

Anna gave a helpless shrug. 'What? In Vienna?'

Tim tipped his chin and gave her a questioning look without saying a word.

'You know what I mean; why would she travel there overnight?' Anna shrugged again.

Tim considered the question. 'Could be anything, it's an international city, world headquarters, UN offices, big pharma, big business, conferences. That's without all the tourist stuff, which I'm assuming we're ruling out.'

Anna gave a brief nod. Her brain ticked. 'Just a thought; conferences and big pharma, could be a connection?'

Tim concurred. 'I thought you said this Archer guy was going to a conference in Switzerland?'

'Like I said, just a thought.' Anna slumped, her hands fell to her lap, and she turned and gazed at the digital departures board on the wall behind them. Her eyes lit up suddenly. 'There's a flight to Vienna in a couple of hours.'

Tim turned to follow her gaze. He spotted what she had seen. He turned back and smiled at her. 'OK. Here's a thought. Why don't we get a taxi and go to where this thing is telling us her iPhone is.' He tipped his head at his own phone. 'If she's there, great. If not, we get back here and see if we can get a flight to Vienna.'

Anna jumped to her feet. 'Come on then, we'd better get a wriggle on.'

'OK, OK, just let me throw this down my neck.' Tim gulped the rest of his coffee and got to his feet. Anna abandoned hers.

●●◉●●

The taxi driver understood enough English to follow their directions to the location the app indicated. It took less than ten minutes to arrive at the residential street with apartment buildings on both sides and parked cars at irregular intervals.

Anna asked the driver to wait while she and Tim searched for Susie.

Tim held the phone and peered at the screen as he walked along the footpath. Anna walked alongside, one hand wrapped around the crook of his elbow.

They stopped and turned back. 'It's got to be here somewhere.' Tim scanned the vicinity. 'There're no buildings anywhere near enough. We're right on top of where the phone should be.'

Anna's attention swivelled left and right. She studied the parked cars and looked for clues.

They walked over to a row of green wheelie bins, each filled to capacity. Rubbish overflowed to leave them standing in a sea of discarded glass bottles, aluminium cans and plastic packaging. Tim prodded two or three shiny objects with his foot in case Susie's phone was hidden among them.

'She could have dropped it.' Anna peered at the ground, then let go of Tim's arm and squatted down.

Tim watched her. 'See anything?'

Something caught Anna's eye, and she crouched lower, her head almost at ground level. 'I'm not sure. There's something shiny under there.' She pointed at the parked car they had stopped next to.

Tim bent over and followed her gaze. 'I can't see anything.'

'Behind the wheel.' Anna shuffled closer and reached into the darkness. 'Got it. Oh.' She stood up and held the small battered metal case she'd retrieved. Whatever it had been, before being run over, it had never been a phone. 'Bugger. I thought I had it.' Her shoulders sagged and she walked over to the wheelie bins and placed the scrap metal on top of one of the piles. She glowered at the rubbish, crossed her arms and exhaled loudly, .

Tim returned to her side. 'I don't want to sound like a broken record but it has to be here.'

'We've looked everywhere.' A dejected note crept into Anna's voice.

'You were on the right track looking under that car. I can't think of where else to look.' He gave her a gentle squeeze to encourage her. 'Come on, I'll go along this side of the road, you do that side. There's only a dozen cars it won't take long.'

With exaggerated reluctance Anna left Tim's side again and crossed the road. She started at the rearmost vehicle and walked around it, bent double to check each wheel in turn. She crouched down and peered under the centre of the car. No sign of a phone.

She stood up and saw Tim mirror her actions with the same result.

On to the next car. And the next.

By the time they had investigated the underneath of ten cars between them, their spirits flagged. The last two cars, both on Anna's side of the road, were more than 100 metres from the location indicated by the app.

Tim studied his phone then appraised the two cars. 'We must have missed something, those last two are too far away.'

A dispirited Anna wanted to agree, but she didn't want to be the one who gave up. 'We've come this far, I might as well go and inspect them.' She walked up to the eleventh car and got down on all fours.

Tim watched her with a mixture of pride and begrudged tolerance, not sure if he'd have had the same willingness to continue.

Then he heard a muted squeal of excitement.

'I think this is it.' She wriggled on her belly and stretched under the rear of the car.

Tim ambled over as Anna reversed back out.

She got to her feet and held the phone in her hand as though it were made of fine china. She turned the phone over in her hands. 'It's Susie's. It's a bit scraped, but it looks OK.' She tapped the screen and the locked screen lit up.

Tim shook his head in admiration. 'Eagle eyes.' He hugged Anna.. 'And it's still working by the look of things.'

'What's her passcode?' Anna asked, her finger poised over the screen.

Tim told her without a moment's pause, the numbers somehow etched into his memory.

'It's alive.' Anna beamed. 'And still got some life left in it.'

'Brilliant.' Tim scanned the area again. 'Doesn't tell us a whole lot, though. Susie's obviously not here.'

'Let's get back to the airport. We can do some digging on the way, see what this can tell us.' Anna took Tim's arm and led him back to the taxi.

—————— ••●●• ——————

Ten minutes later, they were back at the airport. Tim investigated the flight situation and to their relief found the Vienna flight was only half full. He bought two tickets, one-way. They checked in and made their way through security.

Anna had packed Susie's bag as well as her own. Tim only had his shoulder bag, so he took Susie's to avoid having to check anything into the hold.

'It's on time.' Anna announced, after checking the departures board. 'Should be boarding soon.'

Tim flopped into one of the plastic seats. 'Your gut instinct was right then.'

Anna gave him a smug smile. 'That last message, the one she didn't send; it's a bit of a no-brianer.'

Tim frowned. 'She only said she was going there. Anything could have happened. We don't know why she never sent the message.'

'You know what it's like. We've all done it, typed out a message and think we've sent it.' She sat down next to Tim and turned to him, eyebrows raised as she waited for a response.

'You're pretty convinced Susie's in Vienna? She could be in a hospital here in Timisoara, or in a police cell, or anywhere within five hundred miles of her. Or...' His face twisted at the thought. 'She could be injured, or worse, and we'd have no way of knowing.'

'Possibly, but call it gut feeling, whatever; she tried to tell me something, she must have been rushed.'

Tim studied her. 'You think we'll find her in Vienna?'

'You got a better idea, big boy?' Anna gave him a cheeky wink.

Tim lent back in his chair, folded his arms and gave a resigned shrug. 'I might regret this...'

'You won't. It's the only option that makes sense.'

Tim looked up and nodded at the departures board. 'Come on, that's us, they're boarding.' His visit to Timisoara had lasted a little over two hours.

CHAPTER 20

It had taken Schrader ten minutes to calm down after they had found Igor in the security office. Consumed with rage, he was convinced their plans had gone up in smoke and the two women would get to Archer and warn him. He had to speak to DeLuca. He took a deep breath and dialled.

As predicted, DeLuca fumed and blamed Schrader for not simply killing the two women when they had the chance. He ranted for a minute before they both agreed they had to act, and act fast.

Initially they didn't have a clue where Susie and Natalya had got to. They needed to know Archer's itinerary but the man hadn't consulted Schrader. It took DeLuca's determined persistence for Schrader to consider Natalya's computer. He had access to it and he knew she organised his diary.

DeLuca waited while Schrader logged in and found his way to the information they needed. 'He's on his way to Vienna, he's got a meeting at the Franz Joseph hotel at 9.00am.'

'How far it that from you?'

Schrader didn't drive and had no knowledge of the road network. 'How do you expect me to know that?'

'Hang on.'

There was silence, other than the sound of tapping on a keyboard.

'It's about 350 miles, 550 kilometres, give or take.'

'What are you suggesting?'

'My two men can drive there. It's a fast road all the way. If they set off now and drive through the night, they'll be there well before 9.00am, even if they have a couple of short breaks.'

'They're supposed to be driving to Montreux.'

'It's not too much of a diversion. They don't have to be there until Thursday morning. They've got plenty of time.'

'We allowed plenty of time to make sure everything goes to plan. If anything goes wrong...'

'Nothing will go wrong. We've been through this. The whole point of going by road is to remain in control. Well, that and the fact that the equipment wouldn't get through security.'

'Hmmm.'

'Don't worry about it Manfred. They can get to Vienna, take care of business and be on their way to Montreux with time to spare.'

'What are they going to do when they get to Vienna?'

'They make sure the two women don't got to Archer. If they show up, they're dead.'

This appeared to satisfy Schrader and he passed the phone to Decebal who listened while DeLuca gave him detailed instructions.

———————•••••———————

The express train from Budapest to Vienna took than three hours. Susie wished they'd had enough cash to travel by it and not the early morning commuter. It stopped at every village and town on the way and, as a result, took over four hours to cover the 100 mile journey.

After an uncomfortable, long night on two slow, noisy trains, complete with lumpy seats in cold carriages, Susie and Natalya felt relieved when they eventually rolled to a stop in Vienna. The absence of any on-board refreshments left them hungry and thirsty, and tired. As soon as they hit the platform, the search for food and drink became the number one priority. The digital indicator boards clicked 11.26am as they reached the central concourse and looked for something quick and simple that wouldn't use up too much of their dwindling supply of cash. The bureau de change swapped their dollars and Romanian currency for euros at a rate well below the market value. They were in no position to argue or go elsewhere, but at least they had funds.

Susie walked as quickly as she could without spilling her coffee and spoke with a mouthful of pannini. 'How far is it to this hotel?'

Natalya struggled with lab boots that were too big for her. 'It's just a couple of hundred metres.' She nodded in the hotel's direction. 'Really close to the station.'

Without a watch, Susie felt anxious. 'How much time have we got?'

Natalya pointed to a clock on the wall of an office building. 'He said he'd be three hours, so we've got about half an hour before he has to leave. We'll be OK.'

'I see it.' Susie saw the sign for the Franz Joseph hotel and in her excitement grabbed Natalya's arm, which caused her to spill her drink. 'I just hope they let us in looking like this.' She caught a glimpse of herself in a shop window. 'God, we look rough.'

Natalya agreed and made a brief, if unsuccessful, attempt to straighten her hair and smooth down her creased shirt. 'Anyone would think we'd slept in our clothes.'

Susie pulled a face halfway between a grimace and a smile. 'I bet we don't smell too great, either.'

They reached the once grand entrance, where the concierge looked distracted by two Japanese tourists that emerged from a taxi. They slipped through the doors and entered the foyer, but no one took any notice of their appearance. For a moment, they stood still, took in their surroundings, and got their bearings.

Natalya stood on tiptoe and looked for her boss. A crowd of conference delegates emerged from one of the function rooms and filled the foyer, which made it difficult to identify anybody.

Susie spotted the main staircase and tugged on Natalya's sleeve. 'We'll see better if we get a little higher.' Their appearance raised a few eyebrows as they made their way through the crowd and up the wide, sweeping stairs. Half way up, Susie stopped and looked back at the foyer. She focused her tired eyes and surveyed the people sitting at the tables, and hoped to identify Archer.

Natalya did the same, and scanned left and right, front to back. She spotted him first. 'There he is. Come on.' She pointed to four men hunched over a corner table and pulled Susie down the stairs.

Susie quickly glanced in the direction Natalya indicated. Something else distracted her. Two faces in the crowd looked familiar, but she couldn't place them. Where had she seen them before? She held back.

'I thought we needed to get to him as quickly as possible?' Natalya said.

Susie didn't look at her; the two faces in the crowd preoccupied her. 'Yeah but...'

'What is it?' Natalya followed Susie's gaze. 'What are you looking at?'

Susie ducked down behind the banister and pulled Natalya down alongside her. 'The two men who attacked us last night.'

'What? Where?'

'Down there. I caught a quick glimpse of them.' Natalya moved to stand, but Susie grabbed her. 'Keep down. Don't let them see you. I think they're looking for us.'

'What? Who knows, we're here. How could anyone be looking for us?'

Susie screwed her eyes tight shut and beat her fist against her forehead. 'What the hell are they doing here? We're in deep shit.'

••●●•

It was Sergei who spotted Natalya; he recognised the logo on her sweatshirt before he saw her face. He tugged Decebal's sleeve and headed through the throng towards her.

Decebal followed the direction of his gaze and picked out Susie and Natalya, halfway up the staircase.

They made eye contact.

••●●•

With no baggage to collect, Tim and Anna negotiated passport control and customs at Vienna airport and boarded the shuttle train into the city. They arrived as the lunchtime crowds thinned out. Tim's thought processes worked overtime. His speciality, if he had one, was the analysis of data and making judgements based on available facts.

His Intelligence training had been based on assumptions, likely scenarios and possible outcomes, all backed up by the evidence at hand. He and Anna had mulled over what they knew, the messages that Susie had sent, and their own understanding of what she had tried to achieve.

He had to admit; they had little to go on. Susie's iPad still worked, and it showed that it was still in Vienna. In fact, it hadn't moved for a couple of hours. The accuracy of the built-in app wasn't as precise as the expensive tracker he had lent to her, but it indicated a location only a few hundred yards from the station, and that would be their first stop.

He couldn't be sure that Susie had made it to Vienna, but Anna remained convinced. The trail of missed calls and text messages showed she had been active three hours after her meeting. As far as Anna was concerned, the evidence indicated she had acquired information in that time and Vienna had to be the most obvious place to look.

Tim occasionally checked on his phone to make sure they headed in the right direction. They joined the bustle on Wiedner Gurtel, and the pulsing image - Susie's iPad - lay ahead. He stopped and studied the screen carefully. 'According to this, Susie's iPad is just in front of us.' He drew Anna close to show her.

'This feels very familiar. It's only a couple of hours since you had me doing the same thing to find her phone. Anna peered at the vehicles in front of her. 'How accurate is that thing?'

'Stay here.' Tim walked on a little farther, then turned and walked back to Anna. He looked puzzled. 'If this thing, as you call it, is right, then Susie's iPad is in here.' He pointed to a white van parked on the roadside.

Anna walked up to the passenger side window and peered in. 'No sign of life.' She banged on the side of the van with her fist and went to the back doors. 'No rear windows.' For good measure, she repeated her actions from earlier that day and peered under the vehicle. She shook her head.

'See if it's open,' Tim said.

Anna paused for a moment, considered the implications of her actions, then looked around to see if anyone was watching them and then grabbed the handle. To her surprise, it turned. She hesitated for a moment and dreaded what could be inside. Images shot through her head–what might have happened to Susie, and it made her shudder.

Tim joined her, placed his hand on hers and together they pulled the door open.

⸺ •●●●• ⸺

'Those two men who attacked us last night.' Susie pulled Natalya closer and whispered in her ear. 'I'm pretty sure they are the same two that ran me off the road.' She risked a quick peek above the heads of those on the staircase below her.

Natalya stood to look, but Susie pulled her back. 'Can we get to Dr Archer?' She looked to Susie for a decision.

Susie struggled. Her mind flip-flopped between the need to attract Archer's attention and the need to dodge the two men. They'd have to negotiate the stairs and the crowd and avoid being seen. She only had seconds to decide. There was something about being in a crowd that offered a degree of security. 'Come on.' She tugged Natalya's sleeve. 'We've got to have a go; they can't do anything with all these people about.'

Natalya didn't argue. 'OK, you lead, I'll follow, make some noise and try to attract his attention. If he sees us, he'll stop and see what we want.'

Susie crouched down low and kept close to the banisters as she descended the stairs. Natalya followed, anxious not to lose contact in the crowd.

Susie risked another peek at Archer. He had risen to his feet and gathered up the papers on the table. 'Quick, they're getting up to leave.' Susie scanned the foyer for the two men she had spotted. One of them stood head and shoulders above the crowd. 'Oh shit.'

Natalya turned and saw the tall man. He held back. The shorter, squat man came forward and was only a couple of metres away, but two hotel porters, each with a stack of conference chairs, blocked his path.

Memories of the previous evening rushed into her head and for a moment she remained rooted to the spot, unable to move, unable to decide what to do. Her hands trembled, and she clung to one of the staircase rails, more to steady herself than for support. She felt her stomach lurch and thought she would throw up.

The two stacks of chairs acted like a barrier, and Natalya cowered out of sight.

Archer headed for the door.

The hubbub of noise in the foyer grew as more people emerged from the function room.

Susie panicked and shouted, 'Dr Archer!' She looked back for Natalya and saw her frozen in place, saw her eyes wide, mouth clamped tight and her knuckles white.

She reached back and grabbed Natalya by the wrist and shook her. 'Natalya, move, now!' She pulled her away from the rails.

Natalya shook herself, tore her eyes away from the men who had attacked them, and turned back to Susie. She followed Susie's gaze and got the message. She screamed above people's heads, 'Dr Julian, it's me, Natalya.'

Archer turned and looked in the direction of the commotion unaware of his name being called. He appeared to look worried and continued out of the hotel.

Sergei lunged at the stacks of chairs, pushed them out of the hands of the two porters, and grabbed for Susie. The chairs crashed to the ground and fell against the banister, metal against metal. The noise drowned out all other sounds in the foyer and all eyes turned to look at the source of the disturbance. Guests and delegates screamed and shouted.

Susie thought she had escaped from the two men. She ducked down behind one of the porters, who tried to catch as many chairs as he could and prevent them from hitting hotel guests at the bottom of the stairs. She was almost on all fours and near the bottom of the staircase when she felt a hand seize her right foot. She froze for a second, suddenly terrified of her assailant when she saw the tattoos on his arm and realised it was the same man who had run her off the road.

Anger overcame fear, and she kicked with all her strength, held onto the banister for support and stamped on the man's hand with her left leg.

He grunted in pain as her boot slammed down and across his knuckles. The blow raked his skin and drew blood, but he held tight and grasped for her other foot.

One chair had toppled from the stack and Susie reacted instinctively and caught it by a leg. She heaved it, swung it sideways and slammed it into the man's skull. He recoiled, let go of her leg, and dropped to his knees.

Without hesitation, Susie scrambled clear and looked for Natalya. She noticed her, caught in the melee, as she picked her way through the fallen chairs and people.

Natalya looked beyond Susie to the hotel exit, where the taller of the two men had retreated to cut off their escape route. She yelled at Susie. 'Behind you, the other one is still there.'

Blood and noise pumped in Susie's ears. She had no idea what Natalya shouted. She caught movement to her right.

The man who'd grabbed her stumbled to his feet. He stared at the floor and shook his head to clear his vision.

Susie didn't hesitate and swung the chair again, hard, driven by a sense of revenge.

The man had no time to react. The solid steel frame of the chair back slammed against his head with a dull thwack. He staggered, his eyes rolled, his legs gave way, and he went down.

Breathless, Susie stared down at the man, her teeth gritted, her eyes ablaze. She twisted the chair to one side to give it extra momentum, then with all the force she could muster, aimed it at the blood that oozed from the wound she had created, and hammered it into his head.

This time, the man stayed down.

People nearby backed away, no-one, staff or guests showed any enthusiasm to intervene.

'Come on, Natalya,, jump.' Susie screamed.

Natalya landed at the bottom of the stairs. She looked up and realised the tall man still guarded the doorway. They would have to get past him if they planned to escape.

Susie grabbed her and propelled her towards the door.

'No, he's still there.' Natalya held back and pulled Susie in the opposite direction.

'Who?'

'The other one, he's standing by the door to cut us off.' She didn't look at the door; instead, she searched for another way out.

Susie looked towards the exit and peered between the crowd of people, none of whom took much notice of the commotion. She noticed the tall man edge towards them. She understood immediately what Natalya was trying to do. She kept low and headed for the back of the hotel. They made for the function room, recently vacated by the delegates. Staff were busy cleaning up after the morning session.

'Keep going, there must be a back entrance where they bring the equipment in.' Susie glanced back and saw the tall man help the other one to his feet. The squat man looked unsteady. Blood flowed from the side of his head.

•●●••

A senior member of the staff argued with the two men about the mess and the blood and pointed to the exit. He wanted them out.

The tall man brushed him aside and half carried and half dragged his colleague. He followed Susie and Natalya into the function room. He made slow progress.

Natalya spotted an access door to the left of the stage at the back of the room. Someone had propped it open and she saw daylight beyond it. 'You're right, there's a way out over there.' She tugged Susie's arm and the two of them rushed past stacked chairs, folded tables and transit cases for the AV equipment.

The doorway led into a small lobby, then out into the service yard, which was large enough for a dozen vehicles, mostly for supply deliveries, all parked haphazardly as drivers unpacked the contents and disappeared into the bowels of the hotel.

Susie had an idea. 'Let's see if any of these vans have got keys in the ignition.'

'Why?'

'In case anyone needs to move them,' Susie said.

Natalya stopped for a second. She tried to follow Susie's train of thought. Then she smiled. 'I think you like driving vans as much as you enjoy hitting people over the head with heavy things.'

'Well, it's that and keep running in these ridiculous boots or get caught by those two.' She made for the vehicle nearest the exit, a dark blue Mercedes Sprinter with the name *Wien Wäscherei* emblazoned in large white letters on both sides. The driver had left the sliding side door open and bundles of fresh sheets and towels awaited collection after the driver had gone inside to collect the day's dirty laundry.

Susie glanced back. Their pursuers emerged into the yard.

She tried the driver's door, and it came open. To her relief, the driver had left the keys in the ignition. 'Quick, Natalya, jump in the back.'

Natalya needed no further encouragement and rolled into the back of the van, then slid the door shut with a hard slam as Susie fired up the motor.

Behind them, the tall man made a last desperate attempt to catch the van, released his hold on the other man, and ran after it.

With complete disregard for any vehicles around her. Susie launched the van through the gate.

The tall man gave up, bent double, and gasped for air. He took his anger out on his partner, who, still concussed, lay on the floor and held a blood-soaked rag to the side of his head

Susie turned sharply right and accelerated hard down the narrow street.

Natalya clung to the back of the passenger seat for support before she climbed forward and dropped into place. She fastened her seatbelt. 'Here we go again.' She hung onto the grab handle and braced herself against the dashboard. She shook her head slowly and gave Susie a sardonic smile. 'Never a dull a moment with you.'

Susie's pulse raced. She focused on the road, the traffic, and the vehicle controls. 'If we can get around to the front of the hotel, we should be able to catch Dr Archer before he gets the train to the airport.'

Natalaya clung on. She said nothing but mumbled her assent.

At the end of the narrow street, Susie wanted to turn right and head towards the station, but the exit onto the main road had been blocked and she found herself forced to turn left down a narrow alleyway. 'Hell, we're not going to catch him. I don't think delivery vans are meant to go this way.' She had to negotiate commercial waste bins and squeeze between gaps just wide enough for the van. The alleyway continued for two hundred metres and by the time they emerged onto a main road, their chances of getting to the station had disappeared.

Susie scanned road signs and looked for direction. 'How far to the airport?'

'The airport?'

'We'll have missed him at the station by the time we get there. We need to get to the airpot before he boards.'

Part Six

Cornered

CHAPTER 21

Decebal stood hands on hips and watched the laundry van disappear from view. He scowled at Sergei.

Sergei lay on his side and groaned. Blood poured from a deep gash above his left ear.

Decebal resisted the urge to kick him. How could he fail to catch the women, again. He blamed Sergei, but felt humiliated and dreaded having to report to DeLuca. He knew the reaction would be explosive.

He dragged Sergei to his feet with a hand under each arm. He barked at him to move faster and pulled him across the yard and back into the hotel. He'd prevented the two women from getting to Archer at the hotel, but he knew the man would be on his way to the airport. He had to get there before they did.

When they re-entered the reception area, the staff assigned to clean up the mess looked up with a mixture of horror and surprise. They stopped what they were doing. Decebal spotted an industrial sized roll of paper towels on a service trolley and tore off several sheets. He passed them to Sergei to staunch the blood from the head wound. He brushed off the protests of one smartly dressed man who appeared to be in charge and pushed his way through to the front door and out onto Wiedner Gurtel.

Sergei held the paper towels to the side of his head and struggled to keep up with Decebal, who hurried back to their van.

Decebal had left the van parked illegally on a side street 200 yards away from the hotel. It had been there for almost three hours.

⎯⎯⎯⎯⎯●●●●●⎯⎯⎯⎯⎯

It was dark in the back of the van. It took a few seconds for Anna's eyes to adjust to the gloom. There was nothing apart from a couple of boxes and a small rucksack piled up against the front bulkhead. 'No sign of Susie, but that's her bag.' Anna couldn't decide if she was more relieved Susie wasn't there, or disappointed they hadn't found her.

Tim glanced round at the people in the street, then dived into the back of the van and grabbed the rucksack. He climbed out, shut the doors and nodded to Anna. He pointed to a bench twenty yards away. 'Let's see what's in here. Come on.'

They sat side by side on the bench, and Tim reached into the bag. 'Bingo.' He pulled out Susie's iPad. 'The system works.' He entered Susie's passcode and the iPad lit up. 'Just in time. There's only just enough juice left to keep it alive.' He showed Anna.

'What else is in there?' Anna reached across and pulled out a mobile phone she didn't recognise. 'The iPad could be useful. She uses the voice recorder for interviews and writes any notes on it. She always has it with her.'

'Anything else?'

Anna reached into the rucksack again and pulled out one Converse trainer, then another. 'Those are Susie's. They're her favourites.' She looked worried. 'Why would anyone take her shoes?'

Tim thought about it. 'It wouldn't stop them running away, but it's a hell of a deterrent. That's what I'd do.'

Anna's concern grew, and she bit on the knuckle of her thumb. 'Where can she be? Don't tell me we've come all this way, and she's not here.'

Tim took the iPad. 'For once, I hope my words fell on deaf ears.'

Anna peered at him, perplexed for a moment, then remembered Tim knew her passcode.

He tapped in the same code he'd used for the phone. It worked. He shook his head. 'I really must talk to her about security.'

Anna's tone was slightly more upbeat. 'Where's the voice memo app?'

Tim scrolled through the screens, tapped the app icon, and clicked the latest recording. They heard Susie's voice stating the time, date and location before launching into her questions.

Anna leaned in closer to Tim and listened.

After a few minutes of general chitchat, Susie switched to the questions she prepared, and Tim and Anna heard Archer's answers, clear, unambiguous and open. Tim spotted the recording length. 'This goes on for almost 45 minutes.'

'Scrub it forward and see if he says anything nearer the end.' Anna knew how Susie operated.

'What was that?' Anna said when she heard a reference to Vienna.

They paused the recording and rolled back to play it again. They heard Archer talk about meeting friends in Vienna and making a keynote speech in Montreux.

Tim looked at Anna and his expression changed as he made the connection between the conference in Switzerland and what Anna had said earlier.

He smacked his palm against his forehead. 'That's it! It has to be the conference that Nick was talking about. He mentioned something about taking pictures of some bigwig being presented with an award.'

Anna concurred, and for a moment, neither said anything.

Tim studied the van parked twenty yards away. 'I'm guessing that at some point Susie was in that van.' He paused and looked sideways at Anna.

Anna nodded.

Tim continued and thought out loud. 'She wouldn't have left her stuff in there by accident. Someone must have taken it from her, and knowing Susie, that would have required some force. Agreed?'

Anna continued to nod slowly as Tim spoke.

'Trouble is, we have no way of knowing if she's even alive or not.' He rubbed his fingers over the stubble on his chin, his focus shifting from the van to the iPad and back. 'If she is alive, we haven't got a clue where she is or who she's with. If anyone.'

Anna held up the second mobile phone. 'It looks like she's not on her own.'

'That would figure.' Tim agreed. He pulled Susie's phone from his pocket and looked at the list of recent calls. 'She tried to call you five times but there's a number here that's not recognised. Someone called her at 5.30pm last night. Does that mean anything to you?' He pointed out the number.

Anna shook her head. 'Try ringing it.'

He indicated the phone that Anna held. 'Is that on?'

She nodded.

Tim pressed the call button, and after a couple of seconds, the second phone chimed into life. 'So, whoever owns that phone called Susie at 5.30pm. When did she call you?'

'Just after that, she said she was meeting this Natalya woman for a drink.'

'If that was just after she got back from the factory, then it has to be her. That would make sense.' He looked at Anna for confirmation.

Anna pursed her lips. 'I'm sure she said something like "you'll like her" which means it wasn't Dr Archer.'

'Fair point.' Out of curiosity, he rummaged in the rucksack again for anything that might give them a clue. 'Aha, what have we here?' He pulled out a pair of plain grey sling-backs, folded in half, and smaller than Susie's trainers. 'Susie's new friend has tiny feet. I think you're right, it wasn't Dr Archer.'

Anna gazed forlornly at the busy street, the tourists, office workers on their lunch, commuters, locals, and dozens of people. 'How can we even begin to start looking?'

Tim sat forward, elbows on knees, and he searched for an answer. He stared at the ground and weighed up options when Anna grabbed his arm.

'Don't move,' she whispered. 'Two men are getting into the van.'

Tim slowly looked up and saw a tall, lean man who supported a shorter, stocky one at the passenger door. Blood covered the side of the shorter man's face. He looked unwell and struggled to stand. The big man opened the door and bundled his injured companion into the van, slammed the door shut, walked round to the driver's door and climbed in. The engine fired up, and without indicating, the van lunged into the traffic and was gone.

Tim and Anna watched, motionless and silent, and dared not to breathe. As the van vanished, they both exhaled and relaxed.

'Those two look like trouble, especially the big one.'

Anna held her hand to her mouth. 'I've seen them before.'

Tim's brows furrowed. 'Go on.'

'Last night, when I came back to the room. I was about to ring you when I got out of the lift. I'm sure they were waiting to get in.'

'You think they were the ones who trashed your room?'

'It never occurred to me at the time. It would make sense, though.'

'Well, at least we know they haven't got Susie with them.' Tim wanted to sound positive. 'And it looks like one of them has had a bit of an accident.'

Anna sounded dispirited. 'And how are we going to find her?' As an afterthought she added, 'It's just a shame she hasn't got that tracking device you lent her.'

Tim sat up at the remark and turned to Anna. 'Whatever happened to it? She said she'd give it back to me after you tracked down the guy sending the emails.'

'I know she picked it up when we went to his flat. The last thing I saw was her sticking it in the pages of her notepad. I don't have a clue what she did with it after that.'

Tim reached into his own bag and pulled out a laptop and flipped it open. 'I should still be able to trace it.'

Anna looked doubtful. 'That was over a month ago, won't it have died by now?'

'Possibly, possibly not; the reason those things are so expensive is because of the battery, in the right conditions they can last for six months without recharge. It's worth a try.' The screen on Tim's laptop lit up, and he tapped a few keys to bring up his dashboard for the tracker. 'I'll send a re-boot code and see if I can wake it up.'

Anna watched as Tim went to work. A map of the world appeared and then a red dot flashed in the centre of the screen. 'What's that?'

'It's acquired a signal. The thing is still working. It'll take a few seconds to locate itself.' As they watched, the image of the world zoomed in towards Europe and then closer, panned right and centred on Austria, then zoomed again on Vienna.

Anna squealed in excitement. 'It's here in Vienna. She must have it with her.'

Tim watched as the screen focused on the red dot. The resolution sharpened. Tim brought up the map overlay and the red dot appeared on a road travelling West. 'She's moving by the look of things. Must be in a vehicle, not going fast. She could be driving or a passenger, no way of knowing, but if she's got this far, she must be on a mission.' The magnification of the map emphasised the speed as the red dot headed out of Vienna on the A1.

Anna watched, fascinated. 'Where's she going?'

'I'd guess she was heading towards Montreux. That's the only other place she's mentioned. There's obviously some connection with the conference the Doctor is going to. And if that's the same conference that Nick is going to be at, then she has more than one reason to go there.'

'Except she doesn't know Nick is going to be there. He asked you not to tell her, remember?'

Tim rolled his eyes. 'And you've said nothing?'

'No, I didn't think it was important.'

'Not until now.'

Anna tapped the flashing red dot as if trying to communicate with it. 'I wish we had a way of getting in touch with her.'

'Hmmm, if only. These things transmit but don't receive; there's not much we can do but at least we know now where she is. That's if the tracker is with her.'

'I remember her putting into her little note pad. She was wearing her combats at the time, it's probably still there. It's so thin she's probably forgotten it.'

Tim agreed and considered their options. 'We need to catch up with Susie and find out what's going on. There's no point in us going to Montreux if we don't know what she's doing. We might track her down, but she has no way of contacting us or anyone else.'

'What are you suggesting, another plane ride or the train?'

Tim folded away his laptop and stood up. He shook his head, 'No point, we need to chase after her. We can't do that in a plane or on a train.' he took hold of Anna's hand 'Neither. Come on my girl, we need to hire a fast car.'

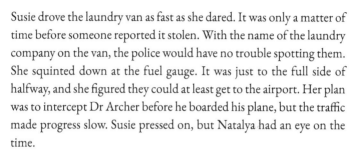

Susie drove the laundry van as fast as she dared. It was only a matter of time before someone reported it stolen. With the name of the laundry company on the van, the police would have no trouble spotting them. She squinted down at the fuel gauge. It was just to the full side of halfway, and she figured they could at least get to the airport. Her plan was to intercept Dr Archer before he boarded his plane, but the traffic made progress slow. Susie pressed on, but Natalya had an eye on the time.

'He'll be checked in and through security before we get there, there's no way we'll be able to get to him.'

Susie didn't want to give up, but reluctantly acknowledged the facts. The airport was only ten kilometres away, but it would take them at least another fifteen minutes. If they got there and abandoned the van, they would have no way of going anywhere else. She slowed, pulled to the side of the road, and stopped. She turned to Natalya. 'OK then, where do we go?'

'We've got to get to Montreux.' Natalya gave a helpless shrug. 'You said it yourself. We have no option.'

Susie looked around the van. 'Why the hell is there no sat nav? See if there's a map anywhere, an A to Z or something like that.'

Natalya opened the glove compartment and the door pockets. Fast food packaging and empty soft drink cans littered the floor.

Susie reached behind the passenger seat, but found nothing, then behind the driver's seat, where she found a street map of Vienna and surrounding area. She checked the road signs ahead and quickly established their location. 'We're here.' She pointed to a spot on the map. 'We need to get on the ring-road and head for the A1, should be signposted Salzburg.'

Natalya didn't argue. She'd never learned to drive and couldn't offer any local knowledge. 'Go for it, sorry I can't help.'

'You can read a map?'

Natalya nodded.

'OK, just keep an eye on the signs and keep me right.' Susie pulled out into the traffic and accelerated little more gently, conscious of saving fuel. 'I don't know how far we'll get before the tank runs dry, or we get pulled by the police, but I can't see what else we can do.'

'We can always buy more fuel.' Natalya offered. 'But there's not much we can do about the police.'

Susie focused on the road ahead, checked each overhead sign for directions, and watched her mirrors for blue flashing lights. She turned onto the outer ring road that took them South of the city and then West. As they merged on to the A1, the roadside sign informed them that Salzburg was 292 kilometres away.

'Make yourself comfortable Natalya, we've got a long way to go.' She took a long, deep breath and settled back into the driver's seat, and kept the van at a sedate pace and under the speed limit in the hope it would make the fuel last longer and avoid any unwanted attention.

•••••

Consumed with anger and frustration, Decebal cut through the Viennese traffic with little regard for road manners, other drivers or speed limits. Ten kilometres stood between the airport and the city centre, but his need to find a clear route eluded him. He had to get there before the two women could get to Archer. All he had to do was make sure the good doctor made it to his plane. At least then he could report back that he'd followed instructions.

In the passenger seat, Sergei drifted in and out of consciousness. He blinked against the pain, moaned and mumbled, as he held the paper towels against the side of his head to staunch the blood. The wound needed stitches. It would have to wait.

They approached an intersection. Red lights made Decebal brake hard and Sergei lurched forward against his seat belt. The movement caused him to curse, and he dropped the towels as he braced himself against the dashboard.

Decebal ignored him and blasted the horn when the car in front didn't move off the split second the lights turned to green. He swerved past it and floored the accelerator. He glanced at the overhead gantry, Flughaven 6.

In the light mid-afternoon traffic, he sat forward in his seat, hunched over the steering wheel with his right foot planted. He looked ahead and spotted a blue van in the slow lane. It looked familiar.

He slowed as he got closer and saw the sign on the back and sides: Wien Wäscherei. He pulled alongside, glanced quickly at the driver, and saw a flash of blonde hair. He needed no further encouragement.

He sped up again to move half a length ahead of the van, then steered to his right and closed the gap between the two vehicles. The laundry van slowed as both vans almost touched. Decebal veered right and crowded his quarry towards the meagre hard shoulder. The laundry van braked suddenly, Decebal continued forward and, for a brief moment, an escape route opened to the left of the laundry van. Decebal realised what could happen and stood on the brakes. He swerved in front of the other van and left no room for it to get away. With no other option, the laundry van skidded to a stop. Decebal jammed his van into reverse and rushed backwards until he collided with the front of the laundry van. His rear bumper crumpled with the impact. The other vehicle stalled as a result of the sudden stop.

Decebal jumped out and rushed back to rip open the laundry van driver's door before it could drive away. Distracted by passing traffic, he didn't look up at the driver. He had her this time and she wouldn't get away again. His hand shot out and grabbed the ignition keys. He ripped them from the lock and flung them over his shoulder into the path of passing traffic. He braced himself ready to attack the driver, then noticed the shoes. Not white lab boots, but a pair of trainers.

For an instant he thought the woman must have found new footwear, then he looked up and met her face.

His shoulders slumped. He screwed his eyes shut, threw his head back, and yelled obscenities. The driver, a woman in her early thirties with shoulder-length blonde hair, sat rigid as both hands gripped the steering wheel. She looked terrified and stared wide-eyed at the large angry man who'd almost caused her to crash.

Decebal slammed the door shut and stomped back to his van. His passenger opened one eye and peered at him in search of an explanation. Decebal said nothing. He dropped into his seat, crashed the gear lever into first, and dropped the clutch. The van set off with the front wheels scrabbling for grip on the loose gravel surface.

CHAPTER 22

S till smarting from his encounter with the laundry van and thirty
minutes after they staggered away from the Franz Joseph Hotel,
Decebal turned off the Autobahn for the airport and drove for the
departure drop-off point. Numerous signs warned they would tow
away vehicles if left, but he took the risk. He left Sergei to guard the
van and forced his way through the other travellers that headed for the
check-in desks. A quick glance at the indicator board for the Geneva
flight told him what he needed to know and, without attracting unwanted attention, he hurried to desk 25.

The queue was short, maybe 10 individuals. Decebal stopped and
did his best to look casual and leaned against the counter of a car rental
agency while he watched. No sign of Archer. He looked around at the
throng of people who arrived and departed from different directions.
A lift door opened to Decebal's right and a group of six emerged.
The woman on the Avis desk tapped Decebal on the shoulder to gain
his attention, but he brushed her aside, his attention focused on the
group.

He was there.

Julian Archer stood out in the crowd; he walked with the confidence of a man in control, who knew where he was going, and without
a glance, he headed straight to the check-in desk.

Decebal casually walked away from the counter and monitored
the queue. He needed to confirm that Archer made it through into
Departures and after that, he could continue his journey. As the only
person on the concourse not doing anything or going anywhere, it

made the frustration of the wait much worse, but he would not leave until he was sure.

He anxiously watched new arrivals, and half expected the two women who had escaped him to burst in at any moment and intercept Archer in the queue. One by one, the passengers showed the required paperwork, checked in their luggage and made their way airside. With no luggage to check-in, Archer only needed to present his passport, and he was through.

He breathed an audible sigh of relief, then headed back..

Decebal jogged back to his parked van and, from fifty metres away, saw two airport police in confrontation with Sergei. He'd emerged from the van and stood holding onto the open door as if he would fall if he let go. The blood stained clothing and the obvious head wound appeared to give the officials concern and he noticed they viewed Sergei with a mixture of fear and suspicion.

Unaware of Decebal's approach, Sergei pointed a stubby finger of one hand at the departures door, and with the other, indicated the driver's seat of the van. Hampered by non-existent linguistic skills, his naïve sign language appeared to confuse the two uniformed men.

Not wanting to get into a protracted discussion or risk any troublesome questions, Decebal took the diplomatic approach and ushered Sergei back into the passenger seat while indicating to the police that his companion was not right in the head. The police appeared to either understand, or seemed reluctant to initiate several hours of tedious form filling. They conferred with each other for a moment and ordered Decebal to remain where he stood. One of them appeared to want to take details and investigate further. The other, who looked the senior of the two, shook his head and pointed to his watch. They reached a decision, took a step back and indicated to Decebal he could go.

With a sense of relief, Decebal climbed into the van, closed the door and started the engine. He moved off and ignored Sergei's grumbles about officials. Within a few minutes, his wounded passenger had lapsed back into a semi-comatose state. Decebal threaded his way through the traffic, conscious of the time and the long journey ahead, and that he'd been on the go for thirty-eight hours without a break. He had to keep going; sleep would have to wait.

He had to get to Montreux before tomorrow morning. He also had to ring DeLuca and tell him the two women had evaded him, but that they hadn't got to Archer. That was what he had asked him to do. He could report that Archer was on his way to Geneva. Sergei groaned from the passenger seat and even though the head wound had stopped bleeding, he looked a mess. He had a thick skull and as far as Decebal was concerned, not much inside was at risk of damage. He'd live. He would have to stop and clean him up before the morning and hopefully Schrader would have something suitable for him to change into when they met him.

By the time he merged onto the A1 headed West, Decebal had drained the contents of another energy drink and convinced himself he could drive all day and all night. It's what he did. He kept the throttle nailed; the revs stayed high, and the speedo hovered around the one fifty mark. The road followed the Danube valley and weaved between lush green fields, forested hillsides and pretty villages. But Decebal had no time for the scenery.

•●●●•

Nick hadn't enjoyed himself so much for ages. The road surface of the Grimsel Pass was new, smooth and gravel free with a blue sky and dry, warm air. The BMW engine growled, then roared, then howled as the revs rose and fell. It powered up the wide sinewy tarmac as it swooped, turned, and twisted towards the top. The occasional car, bus or truck, passed with a flick of the throttle. Nick's progress felt smooth, effortless, and rapid. He felt in the zone, at one with the machine, as he flicked up and down the gears almost subconsciously. He changed direction in fluid movements, braked late into the hairpins and the front forks compressed as the weight shifted forward, then he wound the throttle open and the rear tyre would squirm under the power. As the valley floor dropped behind him, he climbed higher and higher.

His face creased with concentration. Inwardly, he grinned from ear to ear.

After his conversation with Tim the previous evening, he hadn't slept well. The hotel had been comfortable enough, but his concern for Susie and her whereabouts kept him awake.In the end, at something like three in the morning, tiredness caught up with him and he drifted off for a few hours. He woke, bleary-eyed, later than he intended, grabbed a quick breakfast and then resumed his journey.

Nick couldn't wait to get into the mountains and wasted no time once on the move. He stopped only once for fuel before he turned off the autoroute and took to the hills. He crossed the border into Switzerland at Basel and headed south towards Berne and Interlaken. The countryside became greener, the mountains higher and the road more inviting with every passing mile.

He could have taken a shorter, more direct route, but the website he'd found rated the Grimsel as one of the more exciting roads. The website had been right. He loved it. He checked distances and times and estimated an overnight stay at the Grimsel hotel put him within a comfortable ninety-minute ride to Montreux in the morning.

The road levelled off at the top of the pass where a gift shop and café overlooked the Totensee and tempted passing travellers to stop and take in the spectacular scenery. Even in early September, the place looked packed with motorcycles. The road had a reputation and Nick wasn't the only one who'd been testing his skills.

He pulled into the parking area. The engine pinged and popped as it cooled in the late afternoon sunshine. He removed his crash helmet and gloves and sat a little longer and soaked in the view. After a minute or two, he climbed stiffly off the bike, unzipped the jacket of his leathers and let the mountain air cool him, too. He placed his hand on the wide rear tyre and quickly wished he hadn't. It was almost too hot to touch. He smiled inwardly, satisfied that he hadn't lost his touch. He headed for some refreshment.

●●◉●●

The Mercedes E class was the only fast car the rental company had available at immediate notice. It was that, or a VW Polo, and Tim didn't fancy crossing half of Europe in what he considered a shopping trolley. The Merc was ideal and seemed right at home in the fast lane of the autobahn.

Anna sat in the passenger seat with the laptop and watched their progress on the screen. The software provided regular updates to keep Tim informed.

'She's still on the A1, hasn't turned off or stopped.' She scrolled left and right to gauge the distance between them. 'She's not going very fast; we should be able to catch her up before too long.'

Tim didn't take his eyes off the road. He scanned ahead and checked his mirrors and knew they were well over the speed limit. He didn't want to get stopped. 'She'll have to stop eventually, for fuel or the loo or just a rest.' He risked a quick glance at Anna. 'Judging by her speed, she's either on an economy drive or she's in no hurry.'

Anna looked over at Tim. She felt safe with him. He looked calm and confident; he knew what he was doing. For the first time in what felt like many years, she relaxed. She had someone who cared for her, someone she could trust. She watched him, laid-back but in control, one hand on the wheel, while the other rested on his thigh. His small eye movements took in everything. She reached over and squeezed his free hand. He squeezed back. 'Thank you for coming to my rescue.'

He didn't take his eyes off the road. 'Funny, I thought we were rescuing Susie.'

Anna smiled. 'We are rescuing Susie. But you are rescuing me. I haven't felt this content for... forever.' She sat back and basked in the sensation.

He smiled and squeezed her hand a little tighter.

Neither spoke for a while. They approached some road works and the traffic ahead slowed. Tim glanced down at the laptop. 'How's it looking?'

Anna studied the screen. 'We're closing on them really fast. How do I tell what the distance is on this?'

'There should be a scale at the bottom right of the screen. Can you see it?'

Anna squinted against the low sunlight. 'Ah yes, got it.' She studied the screen and compared the distance between the two dots with the scale. 'If I'm reading this right, we're only twenty kilometres behind her.'

Tim thought for a moment. 'When we get back up to speed, we'll catch her in less than half an hour.'

————————••●••————————

Twenty kilometres in front of Tim and Anna, Susie's attention alternated between the road ahead and the fuel gauge. 'This thing must be faulty,' she muttered as she tapped the gauge in the vain hope that it would make a difference.

Natalya caught the remark. 'I thought you said the tank was almost full?'

'It was when we started, but it hasn't budged.' She stared at the gauge and her brow creased. 'I know I've been taking it steady, but we've been going for three hours. We must have covered over 150 miles.' She pondered for a moment and did some quick calculations. 'Even if this thing did thirty miles per gallon, which I doubt, that would mean we'd have used 5 gallons and I doubt the tank holds any more than 12 gallons.' She stopped and glanced at Natalya. 'We could go on for another couple of hundred miles or grind to a stop at any minute.'

Natalya pushed her bottom lip out as she considered their dilemma. 'If we pull in at the next services, can we check?'

'I guess so.' Susie eased up on the accelerator and the van slowed. 'If I go any slower, we're going to cause an accident, but if I go faster, we could run out before we can check.' She took a long look in her wing mirror. 'That's provided we don't get pulled over first. I can't believe nobody has reported the van stolen.'

The right-hand wing mirror had cracked, and Natalya squinted at the distorted view behind. 'I'll keep a lookout for flashing blue lights. Just keep going.' They passed a sign for the next restplatz. 'Only ten K to go. Can we make it that far?'

Susie shrugged. 'There's only one way to find out.' She held the speed at a steady 90kph and hugged the inside lane of the autobahn. The other traffic had to swerve to avoid it. Cars honked in protest as they sped past. Susie focused on the road and didn't dare turn to meet the gaze of the drivers. The kilometres rolled slowly by. The two women willed the van on, and both held their breath as though it would help.

●●●●●

The road climbed steadily as it left the flat valley floor, and forested hills pressed in on both sides. Susie felt the engine note change with the uphill effort and she had to change down a gear to keep it from stalling. Their speed dropped again and Susie squirmed as pushed gently on the throttle. 'C'mon, c'mon,' she whispered.

She felt a judder in the transmission, then heard the engine miss a beat. Susie stamped on the throttle and it picked up again. She held her breath and changed down another gear. The engine coughed again, but this time it missed a few beats.

'No, don't do this. Just keep going!' Susie screamed. She pumped the throttle pedal and pleaded. 'Just keep going, please lovely van.' She flicked the steering wheel sharply left and right to rock the van side to side, hoping to find the last few drops of precious fuel. The engine caught and missed and caught again. It kept running, just.

The road continued to climb and she could see nowhere to pull in. She changed down another gear, their speed little more than walking pace. She checked her mirror, nothing coming behind. She hit the hazard warning lights and bounced up and down in her seat. Natalya did the same. It made no difference, not that they expected it would, but desperation had taken over.

There was nothing they could do. They ground to a standstill. The engine died.

Natalya sat in silence and stared ahead. She didn't dare look at Susie.

Susie collapsed over the steering wheel, shook her head in frustration, and cursed. She turned the key in the ignition. The starter whirred. She flattened the accelerator. The engine coughed and spluttered as the dregs found their way down the fuel lines, but there wasn't enough to keep it running, and after thirty seconds of trying, Susie gave up and released the key. 'Shit.'

Natalya turned to look and Susie. She opened her mouth to speak, but the look on Susie's face made her think twice. She took the wise option and remained quiet.

Susie continued to stare at the road ahead. 'How much further to the services?'

'We just passed a sign. I think it said three kilometres.'

She sat back in the seat and gazed through the fly splattered windscreen. So near and yet so far. Her eyes narrowed, and her stare intensified and from deep down inside, her determination re-surfaced. She shook her head as though clearing the sleep from her eyes; the move regained her focus. She looked over at Natalya, who waited for a response. 'We can't sit here. We need to get out and walk.'

Natalya slumped, said nothing, but nodded in agreement.

CHAPTER 23

Decebal passed Salzburg and rewarded himself with another swig from the can of energy drink that he'd stuck in the cup holder. The chemicals in the liquid had the desired effect. He felt alert, his body buzzed. The early evening traffic had thinned and his speed increased.

Sergei stirred in the passenger seat, opened his eyes, and took in the passing scenery. He mumbled something about his injury and reached up to touch the raw gash on the side of his head. He squeezed his eyes shut and winced with the pain. Decebal took his eyes off the road for a second to glance over at him. Blood had congealed in Sergei's short cropped hair to emphasise the wound and it had dried in streaks down his neck and around the collar of his shirt. He looked a mess.

Decebal's attention returned to the road, his mental state a mixture of anger and frustration. Anger that the two women had got away from him, again, and frustration that he could no longer rely on Sergei for help, if and when he needed it. He took a long, slow breath and set his jaw in a determined snarl. He pushed his foot to the floor and pulled out to pass a line of slower moving trucks.

The road climbed and Decebal could see it winding its way ahead through the undulating landscape in a series of long sweeping curves. Green fields sloped down to the valley floor on the left and the forest rose to the right. In the distance, he spotted a van stopped on the side of the road. It had a familiar look to it and he eased up on the throttle pedal, his interest piqued. The van's hazard lights flashed, but there was no other sign of life. Decebal indicated and slowed as he approached the van. Suddenly excited, he recognised the colour and the sign on the back, the laundry van; he switched his own hazards on as he came to a stop behind it.

He told Sergei to wait, jumped out, and ran to the van. He yanked the door open and peered inside. After slamming it shut, he ran back and climbed back in. Sergei gave him an enquiring look.

Decebal shook his head, crunched into gear, and pulled out. He drove slowly and looked ahead, but not at the road, at the embankment to his right. The setting sun blinded him and he squinted against it. His speed increased to keep up with the traffic and he concentrated on staying between the white lines.

He almost missed them, but as he passed a sign for the services ahead, he glimpsed the blue and white striped top that he recognised from earlier. He stood on the brakes and swerved onto the verge. It was them, the two women.

They walked along the top of the embankment. To their right, a tall chain-link fence hemmed them in. It had been erected it to keep wildlife and vehicles apart, but to Decebal's eyes it was the perfect net to catch his prey.

He jumped out. This time he had them and they wouldn't get away again.

——————— ••●•• ———————

'Good job we've got wellies.' Susie attempted to find something positive about their situation.

Natalya shrugged but said nothing. She walked behind Susie through long grass wet from a recent shower. The embankment dropped away to her left and the chain-link fence crowded in on her right. There was no path and no other way to go, short of walking alongside the road, and they both agreed it was the safer option. She trudged on, tired and miserable.

A sports car with a loud exhaust raced past and caused Susie to turn to what it was. She saw the van.

She gasped involuntarily. 'Oh, fuck.'

Natalya followed her gaze. Lost for words, she reached for Susie's shoulder as she saw the man climb up the embankment.

Susie grabbed Natalya's hand and dragged her along the path. 'Run Natalya.'

The white lab boots had never been designed for running and both the women had little left in the tank for a late evening run, but fear and adrenalin took over and the pair sprinted for their lives.

Susie looked ahead. She searched for a way through the fence. It was too high to climb over and too well maintained for any gaps to have formed. She glanced back over her shoulder to see the big man who she'd fought with the previous evening. He had reached the top of the embankment and looked out of breath, bent over with his hands on his knees. He looked up and shouted something. Susie ignored him and encouraged Natalya. 'Come on, keep going. He can't keep up with us.'

'Easy for you to say.' Natalya gasped as she ran behind Susie.

Susie knew Natalya was right, and she dropped back to coax her onwards. 'He's dead on his feet. We just need to keep jogging till we get to the services.'

The dense trees on the other side of the chain-link fence appeared to strain against it, and Susie could see no way through. A hundred metres ahead of them, she saw what she assumed must be a mobile phone mast next to the fence.

She had an idea, and it spurred her on.

An access ladder ran up the side of the mast within touching distance of the fence. 'Quick, Natalya, climb up there and drop over the other side.' She made it sound so simple.

Natalya breathed heavily but did not have the resolve to protest and realised they had little choice. She climbed until she was level with the top of the fence and looked down at Susie, who stood on the ladder just below her. 'Now what?' She stared at the thick mass of branches and saw nowhere to go.

'Just throw yourself over, the branches will cushion your fall.' Susie looked back down the path to see the big man pick up his speed when he saw the two women on the ladder. 'Make it quick. He's gaining on us.'

Natalya gave a slow shake of the head, unable to believe what she was about to do. She put one foot on the top of the fence, then launched herself into the trees. She fell through the extended boughs of the pine trees and, much to her surprise, landed feet first without injury. She moved clear in time to hear the snap of branches and mild curses as her new friend followed.

Susie landed face down and even more dishevelled. She had caught her foot in one of the thicker branches and her face had picked up some angry scratches on the way down, but otherwise she was in one piece.

The branches were thinner at ground level and for two or three feet above. If they crouched down as they ran, they could move through the trees without too much obstruction.

Susie pushed against sharp needles, thankful that she was small enough to duck below the bigger, stronger branches. She held her hands in front of her to protect herself from the lower branches that whipped into her face.

Natalya kept her head down and followed Susie's footsteps.

Behind them, they heard their pursuer as he battled his way through the trees. They could no longer see him, but could hear him grunting and cursing. He sounded closer.

In the gloom of the trees, Susie lost all sense of direction. The gentle incline gave her a clue, and she figured if they just kept going uphill, they must be travelling in a straight line. But for how long?

Susie saw light in front of them and she pushed on until they emerged onto a track, some sort of access route for forestry workers and just wide enough for a vehicle. The track ran level along the contours of the hill. Susie looked left and right. With its overhanging canopy of branches, the track reminded her of a tunnel, but there was no light at either end.

She made a snap decision, a sixth sense made her turn left. 'This has got to lead somewhere and the service station was that way.' She pointed towards the fading sunlight.

Natalya gave a resigned nod and followed.

They jogged up the track, aware that the man following could spot them, but equally aware that they had no choice. Susie risked a glance back over her shoulder and saw the big man emerge from the trees two hundred yards behind them.

'Keep going Nat, we're getting away from him.'

The track levelled off and turned right. The forest thinned out and then gave way to a small lake, surrounded by trees with a narrow rocky margin that ran down to the waters's edge. The two women slowed as they took in the change of scenery. Out of sight to their left, they heard what they assumed must be a waterfall.

'This track has to go somewhere.' Susie cast about as they approached the edge of the lake.

Natalya stopped, and gasped for breath. She pointed. 'Over there.'

Susie followed the direction of Natalya's outstretched finger and made out a chalet virtually hidden among the trees on the far side of the lake. 'Bloody hell, I didn't see it, it's proper Hansel and Gretel.'

The track continued all the way round the lake to the chalet. The two women jogged and reached the cabin which they thought would provide some sort of sanctuary. The shutters were closed, there were no vehicles in sight, and no sign of life.

They continued at a slow jog and circled the chalet, hoping to find a way in, but the owners had taken steps to ensure that wouldn't be possible.

'Bugger,' Susie cursed as she returned to the front door and rattled it again.

Natalya interrupted her frustration. She grabbed her and pulled her back behind a wall of the chalet.

'He's there.' Natalya nodded in the track's direction.

Susie peered out from behind the wall and watched as the big man lumbered along the track. He'd seen them. She looked in the opposite direction. A path of sorts ran along the water's edge. She squinted into the fading light and made out a shape. 'That looks like a boat.'

Natalya had crouched out of sight and stood up to see what Susie had seen. Her mouth fell open. 'Don't tell me.'

Susie didn't respond. She set off with renewed purpose. Natalya took a deep breath and followed.

Someone had pulled the small rowing boat out of the water and left it partially hidden among bushes. Susie assumed the chalet owners must have used it for fishing, but it looked as if it hadn't been in the water for some time. It had a bench seat that spanned the middle, and a single oar.

'Come on Natalya, if we're out in the middle of the lake he can't get us,' Susie said, and pulled on the boat which slid, bow first, into the lake. She stood ankle deep in the water and beckoned Natalya.

Natalya stood, arms folded, chin tucked into her chest, reluctant to follow.

'Come on, he's coming.' Susie implored her.

Natalya shook her head slowly.

'What's wrong? Come on, he's getting closer.'

Natalya couldn't meet Susie's gaze. 'I can't swim.'

Susie did a quick double-take, unsure that she'd heard correctly. 'For god's sake, Natalya, you don't have to swim. We just wait till he gives up, then we come back.'

Natalya stood her ground.

Frustrated, Susie reached up and took her hand. 'Come on, I'll make sure you're safe.'

Natalya looked back to see the big man only thirty yards away. The fear of being caught by him outweighed her fear of water, and she allowed herself to be led into the boat. She sat down in the middle of the bench seat and gripped the sides.

Susie jumped aboard and pushed them out into the lake, using the oar to punt them away from the shore.

———————••●••————————

Anna's brow creased as she stared intently at the screen. 'This makes little sense.'

'Tell me more.' Tim shot a quick glance at the screen but couldn't tell what had caused Anna to look so alarmed.

'If the little red dot is Susie, then she's gone off road.'

Tim slowed in response and raised an eyebrow as he looked at Anna for some clarity.

'I've zoomed right in, and you can see the road, but the red dot has gone off at an angle and there's no road marked on the map.' She turned the laptop to show Tim the screen.

Tim pondered, his attention switched between the road and screen. 'Try refreshing the screen in case there's a glitch.'

Anna did as instructed. The screen darkened and after a few seconds, came back to life. 'Same thing, the red dot is moving, but not on a marked road.'

'Switch it to terrain mode.' He reached over with his right hand and pointed at an icon in the top left corner of the screen.

'Got it.' The screen changed from map to satellite view. 'It looks as if she's in a forest.'

'Any buildings?'

'No, but there's a faint track.' Anna paused while she studied the screen. 'Hang on.' She moved the laptop to reduce the glare from the car's dashboard. 'It looks like the track goes to a lake and there's something there. It could be a building, but it's surrounded by trees. It's hard to tell.'

'Zoom out and see if there's a way we can get to it from the autobahn.' Tim picked up speed and looked ahead.

•●●●•

Decebal reached the water's edge a moment after the rowing boat punted out of reach.

One of the women, the one he had picked up in the lift the previous evening, sat in the middle of the boat, and hung on to the sides as though her life depended on it. The other stood at the back and used an oar to propel them towards the middle of the lake.

He considered wading out to catch them, but they had pulled away too fast.

He had chased them for ten minutes and had climbed through dense forest, and his chest heaved. He took deep breaths and cursed through gritted teeth. He wished for a gun, but only had a knife. His orders were to stop them, but he also had orders to be in Montreux by eight the following morning. He was torn.

He looked left and right in search of a solution. He saw nothing but trees and stones. His eyes fell to his feet. Stones. Nice round stones, the size of his fist. His frown transformed into a cunning snarl.

He reached down and picked up two pale grey stones, weighed them in his hands and looked out at the rowing boat that had reached the middle of the little lake. The woman at the back of the boat, the one who had put up a fight and left him with a livid bruise on the side of his face, stood at the back of the boat and looked back at him in defiance.

They were about thirty metres away, Decebal estimated, easily within range. He steadied himself, took aim, and threw the first stone. The direction was right, but it fell a few metres short and splashed the two women. The side of his mouth curled. He had them now. The next one wouldn't miss.

————————————••●••————————————

Susie brushed the water from her face as the ripples from the first stone subsided. She watched the second stone as it flew towards them and held the oar like a baseball bat to defend herself. She adjusted her footing and turned sideways to reduce the chances of being hit. As she moved, the little boat rocked and Natalya shrieked in alarm.

The stone glanced off the side of the boat, only just missing Natalya's fingers.

'Stop jumping around. You'll tip the boat over,' Natalya implored. She watched the man on the bank as he looked around for more ammunition.

'Don't worry, we'll be OK. Just keep your head down.' Susie didn't look back at Natalya, her concentration focused on the next round of incoming stones.

The man had got his eye in both direction and distance, and the next two stones both hit the boat. Susie jumped to one side to avoid what would have been a direct hit then the boat tipped and its sides dipped below the water's surface for a moment.

Natalya threw herself in the opposite direction to right the boat and shouted at Susie again. 'Keep still. I told you I can't swim.'

'I wish I could, but if I don't move, I'll get hit.' Susie squatted down at the back of the boat, unwittingly exposing Natalya.

As the next volley headed their way, Susie adjusted her grip on the oar and intercepted one of the stones. The impact smashed the dry, brittle wood and left her holding a useless stump. She ducked as the other stone headed straight for her head and she lost her footing. She fell back into the belly of the boat and landed on her back. She looked up and saw Natalya flinch as the stone passed within millimetres of her.

'Get down'

Natalya took little persuasion and released her limpet like hold on the sides of the boat and dropped face down. She felt around her. 'Where's all this water come from?'

Susie turned to see what Natalya meant. She assumed the water inside the boat had come from the rocking motion, but she spotted the problem and groaned. 'Oh shit.'

'What?' Natalya hadn't seen what had caught Susie's eye.

'Now I know why they'd left this thing hidden in the trees.'

Natalya followed Susie's gaze and recognised the steady ingress of water between the overlapping boards that formed up the hull of the little boat. 'If we don't stop it, we'll sink.' She looked at Susie with panic in her eyes.

'We must have made it worse by jumping around.' She peered at Natalya, who didn't look convinced. 'OK, I made it worse by jumping around.' This time, Natalya gave a barely perceptible nod.

Susie raised her head to see where their attacker had gone. The boat had drifted further from the shore and turned sideways to it, giving the man a bigger target. Without an oar, she could do little to manoeuvre other than put a hand over the side and paddle.

The boat turned slowly, the water level in it kept rising.

———————— ••◆•• ————————

Decebal had moved around the shore of the lake to reduce the distance between himself and his target. The stones started flying again. This time, he lobbed them higher, so they dropped into the boat. He guessed their predicament as he watched them, and decided to try and destroy the little boat instead of hit them.

He grew increasingly frustrated. He paced along the shoreline like a caged tiger. He kept the boat and the two women within range. He'd left Sergei sitting in the van on the side of the Autobahn and he knew he had to get back to him and continue the journey. But he couldn't bring himself to walk away and leave the two women now that he had them in his sights.

Whenever he saw a suitable stone, he bent down, picked it up, took aim, and hurled it high in the air. Each one fell within feet of his target. Some hit the sides of the boat, and some made a satisfying crack as they landed in the boat's bottom. He got a perverse kick as he watched the two women dodge the falling rocks. He jeered at them.

He found two stones side by side, grey, round, a little larger than his previous projectiles. He picked them up. One in each hand. Rather than throw them overhand, he lobbed them underhand. Both at the same time. They sailed up and out and arced towards the little boat. As their trajectory altered and they began to fall, he watched with mounting malevolence as the two women jostled each other to avoid being hit. He could see the dilemma they faced. They might avoid one stone, only to be hit by the other.

The woman at the back of the boat held the stump of the oar as if it would give her some protection. She watched both the stones and Decebal saw her flinch to one side and avoid them both. The other woman had lain down flat in the boat's belly. Decebal couldn't see her, but he saw both stones drop out of sight. He noticed that water splashed from inside the boat and heard a muted splintering noise, followed by a scream.

CHAPTER 24

The second stone had struck Natalya on the temple. She had turned her head to one side, and the stone had impacted with full force. Blood seeped from a cut and marched across her pale skin. Natalya didn't move.

Susie dropped to her knees and screamed. 'Natalya.' She pulled the inert, unresponsive figure clear of the rapidly rising water. Susie popped her head up to check for any incoming stones and saw the man talking on his phone. She looked around and realised the boat was sinking. Water poured through the hole made by the stone, and the sides of the boat were less than an inch above the water.

Within seconds, the boat was little more than an empty hull floating just below the water's surface. The natural buoyancy of the dry wood kept it from sinking completely. The two women floated out. Susie swam with one arm, while she supported Natalya under the chin with the other.

Grateful for the regular open water swim training she'd done during the summer, she could cope with the cold water. Her concern was for Natalya. She had to get to the shore as soon as possible. She saw the man on the shoreline watching her as he paced back and forth and talked on the phone.

Susie looked behind her and sculled one-handed towards the opposite shore. Trees grew close to the water's edge and branches hung over the surface. She could see they provided some cover, and she made for them. She glanced back and watched as the man gesticulated wildly. He appeared to be arguing with whoever he was speaking to on the phone.

While she may have swum many miles in open water, she had never had to do it fully clothed, or while under aerial bombardment, or while supporting an unconscious victim. She struggled and, with an effort, kicked the lab boots free. The tree lined shore was still twenty metres away and her progress was slow. In what she considered normal circumstances; unencumbered, a wetsuit and a pair of goggles, she'd have covered the distance in a few seconds. She turned and swapped hands, checked that Natalya hadn't swallowed any water. With renewed determination, she pressed on towards the shelter of the trees.

When she felt her foot touch something, she realised the shore on this side of the lake had a more gentle gradient and the water was only a couple of feet deep. She stopped swimming and allowed her feet to sink until she could stand. She planted both feet but remained in a crouch; her face just above the surface of the water. She searched for the man on the far side of the lake. He had disappeared.

She scanned around the shore in both directions, suddenly fearful that he could have snuck through the trees, waiting for her just a few yards away.

Despite her exertions and the adrenaline that coursed through her veins, Susie felt the cold, and she shivered. She put her ear close to Natalya's face, close enough to detect faint breathing. She knew she had to get her new friend to safety and moved through the overhanging branches, every sense on heightened alert.

She strained to hear anything above the sound of the waterfall; the crunch of footsteps on the stones, the snap of a branch, the laboured breathing of her pursuer, or the sound of his voice talking on the phone. Nothing, only the steady flow of ice-cold glacial meltwater, somewhere out of sight.

She moved closer to dry land, the water only inches deep, and peered through the branches. The gathering gloom cast long shadows and made it impossible to identify anything that might be vaguely human. She held Natalya with one arm under her shoulders and pulled her out of the water. She kept low and looked around. Satisfied they were both safe for the moment, she turned her attention to Natalya.

The cut on side on the side of her face bled freely, although the water had washed the wound clean. Susie recalled her basic training and knew she had to staunch the bleeding, but with nothing suitable she would have to improvise. She peeled off her waterlogged jacket, then pulled her T-shirt off. She intended to rip it into strips to make a bandage, but it proved tougher than she imagined. She cast around for something to cut it with and spotted the jagged end of a broken branch. She dropped the T-shirt over the branch and heaved on it. It came apart easily and once started; she found she could tear it with her fingers. She bundled a section of the cloth into a pad and laid it against the cut.

The pressure made Natalya stir. She moaned quietly and pulled away from the pad.

'Keep still Natalya.' Susie cradled her head and whispered into her ear as she fastened two strips together and tied them to hold the pad in place.

Natalya's eyes flashed open, and she gasped in pain and shock. 'My head, what's happened?' Her hands reached for her head, but Susie caught them.

'Shh, you're OK, we're safe. You got hit with one of the stones, and the guy who was throwing them has disappeared.'

'I'm so cold.' Natalya shook herself free from Susie's grip and wrapped her arms around her shoulders. She shivered uncontrollably and her teeth chattered.

Susie recognised the signs of trauma. Natalya's body had rerouted blood supply to her main organs because of the injury and the cold water. She needed to be warm and dry. Dressed only in her combats and the crop top she had on under her T-shirt, Susie had nothing she could use. She reached for the waterlogged jacket she'd removed, but quickly discounted it as any form of warmth. It was ruined.

She remembered the chalet on the other side of the lake. 'Natalya, can you stand up?'

Natalya squeezed her eyes tight shut, her jaw clenched, she shook violently and didn't reply.

Susie gripped Natalya by the shoulders and pulled her into a sitting position. 'Come on, we've got to move. If we stay here, you'll die of hypothermia.'

'I can't move. I'm too cold.' The words emerged one at a time between blue lips.

Susie had other ideas. She moved behind Natalya and lifted her to her feet. 'You'll feel better once you move.' Natalya's knees buckled when Susie released her and she almost fell before Susie caught her and put one of her arms over her own shoulder and half carried, half dragged her through the trees and around the shoreline.

Susie was still on the lookout for the man who had caused them so much trouble and she scanned ahead into the darkness. No sign, no sound.

Then she saw light moving in the trees ahead, approaching headlights. She heard the noise of tyres crunching along the track, then the sound of an engine.

'Oh shit.' Susie stopped in her tracks, cold, tired, and desperate.

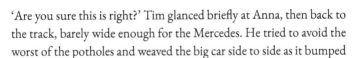

'Are you sure this is right?' Tim glanced briefly at Anna, then back to the track, barely wide enough for the Mercedes. He tried to avoid the worst of the potholes and weaved the big car side to side as it bumped along at walking pace between the trees.

'Keep going. Not much further, it's showing as just ahead.' Anna didn't look up from the screen, the red dot almost at its centre.

The car's powerful xenon main beams lit up the track as though it was daylight. They rounded a corner and saw the chalet 100 yards ahead of them. The track opened up into a turning area in front of the building. Tim let the car roll to a stop when they reached it. They could go no further.

He and Anna opened their doors and climbed out. The headlights cast long shadows across the water and through the trees. They both stood silent and still, and peered into the darkness beyond the reach of the lights.

'Susie!' Anna called out, her voice clear and unnaturally loud in the forest's quiet.

She waited a few seconds for a response, then raised her hands to her mouth, ready to shout louder. She heard the snap of a branch. Tim tugged her sleeve and pointed.

'Over there.'

She followed his gaze and saw movement. 'Susie, is that you?'

'Don't just stand there, we could with some help.' The disembodied female voice came from the shadows. She sounded strained and out of breath.

Anna started forward towards the source of the voice. 'I can't see you. Keep talking.'

'This way, over here. There's a footpath along the shoreline, just keep going.'

A couple of steps behind Anna, Tim called to Susie. 'Are you all right? Can't you move?'

'Not really. You'll soon see.'

As she walked forward with the headlights shining behind her, her shadow fell on her path and Anna almost tripped over unseen branches. The shoreline curved to her left. Her shadow moved out of her line of sight, and she saw Susie for the first time.

Not just Susie, she had someone with her.

Anna rushed to close the gap between them and made to hug Susie before she saw the state she was in. She pulled up short. 'What the hell happened to you?' Susie, dressed in combat trousers and crop top, looked wet, bedraggled and frozen. The person she held up looked much worse.

'We need to get inside and warm up.' Susie's teeth chattered as she spoke.

'Who's this?' Tim asked, as he reached to take the limp figure from Susie. He lifted Susie's companion bodily, ignoring the soaked clothing. He turned back to the chalet without waiting for an answer.

Susie hugged herself as she walked and followed in Tim's footsteps. 'That's Natalya. We met at the factory yesterday.'

Anna stepped up beside Susie. 'So, what the hell are you doing out here in the middle of nowhere?'

Susie couldn't find the strength for a coherent reply and, in response, she pointed to the chalet. 'We need to break in to that place.'

'Don't tell me you haven't got a key?' Tim joked as he negotiated the rocky path while he carried Natalya, one arm under her legs, the other supporting her shoulders. Her head rested against him. He made it look effortless.

'Right now, I'll break the bloody door down with anything I can lay my hands on. I just hope they have some form of heating in there.' Susie, barefoot, walked gingerly and became more animated as they approached the building.

Tim reached the steps that led up to the front door and gently lowered Natalya to the ground. He removed his jacket and wrapped her in it.

Susie continued past Tim, walked straight to up to the door, turned her good left shoulder to it and hit it with as much force as she could manage. The door shook but refused to open. She bounced off it and cursed as she regained her footing 'Shit. We need something heavier.'

'Let me have a go.' Tim stepped up beside Susie and rattled the door to assess the position of the lock. The narrow step gave no room for a run up, so he turned his back to the door, braced himself against the uprights of the storm porch, kicked back and struck the door with his heel, just below the handle.

The door was solid and remained in one piece, but the frame proved to be the weaker link and Susie heard it splinter and saw the door move. Without waiting for Tim to lash out again, she threw herself at the door and this time, accompanied by a pained rending noise from the frame, it gave and swung open.

She peered into the gloom, unable to make out anything, until Tim brought out his phone and activated the torch. The door opened directly into a simple, sparsely furnished room with an open fireplace. 'Can you see if there're any lights?' She stood still in the middle of the room and shuddered against the cold.

'In your dreams. You seriously think they'll have any electric in the middle of the woods?' Tim scanned around the room using the light on his phone.

'What's in there?' Anna's voice called from outside. 'Your friend needs help.'

'Hang on, I'll carry her in, come inside and see what you can find.' Tim went outside to bring Natalya in.

Anna entered the room with her phone lit up. She spotted Susie and held her elbow. 'Come on, we need to find light and heat.'

Susie mumbled in agreement and let Anna guide her as the two of them explored the rest of the chalet.

They discovered what they assumed must be the kitchen. Anna's torch lit up the chalet wall opposite the door and they saw a sink and a gas hob. Susie made Anna wait while she turned one of the controls. She listened for the sound of gas and sniffed the air, hoping to detect it. There was neither sound nor smell.

'There must be a master valve somewhere.' Susie announced as she reached for Anna's hand and directed her to shine the light around the kitchen area. 'It'll be bottle gas. It could be outside.'

Anna didn't respond to Susie. She'd spotted some wall mounted cupboards and opened them in search of supplies. 'Matches.' She said with a note of triumph.

Tim called from the fireplace. 'Throw them over here, I can get a fire started, there's a stack of logs and plenty of kindling.'

Anna left Susie in the dark and took the box of matches over to Tim. She returned to find Susie groping through the cupboards. 'What you trying to find?'

'There's got to be some candles here somewhere.' Susie said, 'Stands to reason, either that or a decent torch. We can't rely on your phone lights for too long.'

Anna played the light over the cupboards and within a couple of seconds, Susie gave a satisfied 'Yes!' She turned to face Anna and held a box full of long, white candles. She pulled two out and headed over to Tim, who had lit crumpled pieces of newspaper and was in the process of feeding the flames with thin strips of dried kindling.

'You got those matches handy?' She held out her hand and Tim passed her the box.

Part Seven

Fightback

CHAPTER 25

W ithin a minute, Susie had lit ten candles and placed them around the chalet. They had light, and the fire threw out heat as it picked up with Tim's encouragement. Anna went outside and returned a short while later. 'I found the gas cylinder and turned the valve on the top. It made a hissing noise, so I'm guessing it must be on.'

Susie returned to the hob with the matches and turned the control knob. This time, there was no doubt. She held a match to the ring and blue flames popped into life. She held her hands over the ring, then rubbed them together as something approaching normal circulation returned.

Tim found a couple of picnic blankets folded neatly on one of the chairs near the fireplace and wrapped Natalya in them. She needed little encouragement to come and sit in front of the fire. She huddled close to the warmth with one blanket over her head like a cowl and the other over her shoulders and back. She still shivered, but colour gradually returned to her features.

Anna and Susie searched around the inside of the chalet. They figured there had to be a store of some sort. They discounted the idea of finding anything fresh and assumed that without electricity, there wouldn't be anything frozen. But there had to be a supply of essentials.

Susie found it. A tall cupboard built into the wall. The door had been painted the same pale yellow colour as the walls and they'd missed it at first. The handle gave it away. Susie caught her shoulder on it as she brushed past, and it took her a moment before she realised what it concealed. She pulled the door open and in the gloom could make out tins, jars and packets stacked on shelves that ran from floor to ceiling.

'Anna, over here, look what I've found.'

Anna joined her and shone the light into the cupboard. Her face broke into a broad smile as she saw enough supplies to keep the four of them fed for a week or more. She played the beam up and down the shelves, taking in the range and quantity of provisions. 'Whoever owns this place is either planning a long stay or they know something about the future that we don't.'

Susie reached up and grabbed a couple of tins of minestrone soup. 'Whatever their reasons, they're my new best friends.'

'I doubt they'll be sending you a Christmas card when they see what you've done to their front door.' Anna said, as she retrieved a pack of dried pasta. 'I'll cook this. It'll go with the soup.'

The pair had already found some pans, and within minutes they warmed some soup and boiled some pasta.

The heat from the fire became so intense that Natalya had to move back and remove the blanket. She still sat in her soaking clothes, which steamed as she dried out. The makeshift bandage on her head wound remained in place. She looked numb, unable to do much more than stare at the flames.

Anna turned from the cooker and saw Natalya's discomfort. She left Susie to manage the food and went to her aid. 'Hi, I'm Anna.' She said formally, aware that they'd never spoken and Susie hadn't introduced her.

Natalya nodded without turning to look at Anna. She managed a simple 'Hi.'

'We need to get you out of those wet things and fix up that bandage.' Ever practical, Anna saw what needed to be done. She looked around for Tim and saw him stagger through the front door with an armful of logs. 'Tim, can you be a superhero and get my bag out of the car?'

Weighed down by the logs, Tim grunted some sort of acknowledgement, continued to the fire and dropped his burden into a wicker basket. He stood up and stretched, then gave Anna a confused look. 'What d'you want your bag for? Planning to stay the night?'

'Not for me.' Anna said and tipped her head to indicate Natalya.

Tim nodded. He went back outside and returned in under a minute. 'Here you go.'

Anna took her bag and looked around the chalet for somewhere private. 'There must by another room? Where do people sleep?'

'There's a bedroom and bathroom through there.' Tim said and pointed to the back wall of the chalet. 'It's not obvious. You could miss it easily.'

Anna encouraged Natalya to her feet. 'Come on, you look about the same size as me. There'll be something in here to fit you.' She tapped her bag, took one of the candles, and headed for the door. Natalya followed.

'Hang on, Natalya.' Susie called from the cooker. 'There's a first aid kit here. See if Anna can do a better job than I did on your head.' She passed the green plastic box to Natalya, who took it and stepped into the bedroom behind Anna.

'Are you going to tell us how you ended up here?' Tim asked as soon as the door closed.

'There's time enough for that. More to the point, how the hell did you find us?' Susie turned from stirring the soup to peer at Tim, eyes narrowed.

Tim's face broke into a broad smile. 'Remember that expensive bit of kit I lent to you some time ago?'

Susie frowned. She squinted at Tim, comprehension eluding her.

'Remember, I told you how good it was?'

Susie's mouth opened and her eyes widened as her tired mind started to make sense of his words. 'You mean the tracker?'

Tim's smile never faltered. He gave Susie a theatrical wink.

'But.' Susie appeared lost for words. She shook her head. 'How come? I don't even know where it is.' She held her arms out, palms up, as if to demonstrate she wasn't concealing the device.

'Anna said you stuck it in a little notepad and she reckons the notepad is in one of the pockets on your combats.'

Susie looked incredulous. Her combats were wet but no longer soaking. She patted the pockets front and rear and pulled out a few coins and some waterlogged notes. She looked at Tim and shook her head.

He smiled back, said nothing, but dipped his head to indicate she should continue.

Susie remembered the large thigh pockets, checked them and came up empty-handed. 'There's nothing Tim, I'd have remembered.'

'Keep looking' He dropped his gaze to Susie's bare feet.

Susie looked down and saw what Tim had seen. A small additional pocket positioned on the outside of each leg below the knee. Each pocket had a zip fastening. 'They're just detailing. They're not real pockets.' She looked up at Tim briefly. He continued his gaze.

Susie shrugged and reached for the zip on her left leg. The zip refused to move at first. It confirmed Susie's belief that it was just there for show. She gave it a sharp tug, and it suddenly opened. Her eyebrows jumped in surprise and she prodded the inside of the pocket with a couple of fingers. Nothing.

She tried the right leg. It opened immediately. She felt something in it. Something small, thin and wet. She picked it out between thumb and forefinger. The notepad.

Tim clenched his fist in triumph.

Susie held the little notepad by its spine and shook it. She held her other hand under it, waiting for something to fall out. The soaked pages stuck together. She shook it harder and without a sound, Tim's tracker dropped into her waiting hand.

She held it in awe, unable to believe what she was seeing. 'It's been there all this time.' She looked up at Tim. 'It must have been through the washing machine at least three times.'

'Told you it was tough.'

'And it's still working?'

'That's how we found you.' Tim reached out and retrieved the tracker while he had the chance. He held it up and kissed it. 'You little beauty.'

The door to the bedroom opened. Susie turned and stared into the half light. She made out a figure wearing an oversized blue and white striped rugby shirt. Tim had given it to Anna, and it had become her favourite. 'How's Natalya?'

'I'm feeling a little better now.'

Susie peered closer and realised she was looking at Natalya. She had a clean gauze pad over the wound on her temple, held in place with a broad crepe bandage wrapped several times around her head. Her hair had been dried and pulled back into a neat ponytail. She wore a pair of patterned compression tights that Susie recognised and a pair of Anna's trainers. 'That's great. You couldn't have looked much worse. How's the head?'

Anna appeared as Natalya was about to respond. 'I've cleaned it up. It's not as bad as it looked, but she's going to have a real shiner by tomorrow.'

Natalya looked puzzled. 'What's a shiner?'

Susie answered. 'She means you'll have a one hell of a bruise.'

Natalya nodded and reached up to touch the gauze pad with an outstretched forefinger. She winced. 'What's happening?"

Susie gave her a hug. 'Tim's looking for the number for the conference centre in Montreux, so we can warn them about Schrader and alert the organisers.'

Anna asked Natalya. 'Have you been in touch with your family to let them know you're safe?'

Natalya felt touched. 'It's OK, I don't think anyone is going to miss me.'

Susie intervened. 'You and Natalya have something in common.' She let the remark hang while it registered with Anna.

Anna's brow furrowed as she tried to work out what Susie was talking about.

'This is hopeless.' Tim interrupted. He looked up from his phone. 'I'm going outside to see if I can get a signal'

Susie watched him go, then turned back to the two women. She waited for a reaction. 'The orphanages?'

Anna sat up. 'Yes. I spent all day yesterday visiting orphanages in Timisoara. I came from one of them and I was trying to find out something about my family. It was traumatic.'

Natalya noticed Anna's expression She and Susie had talked briefly over the previous twenty-four hours, and she knew Anna could relate to her own early years. She reached for Anna's free hand. 'You don't need to say any more. I know.'

Anna looked closely at Natalya; her expression darkened. 'You mean you were in an orphanage, too?'

'Hmph.' Natalya rolled her eyes. 'They like to call them Children's Centres. They think it sounds better,' For a moment, she couldn't look Anna in the eye and stared at the floor. 'I spent the first five years of my life in one of them.' The memory made her shudder as though someone had dropped ice cubes down the back of her shirt.

Susie put a comforting arm round Natalya. 'I didn't want to say anything, but I knew you two had a little shared history.'

Anna was about to speak when Tim returned.

'Bloody hopeless.' He looked at his phone and shook his head. 'I've wandered around out there, trying to find a signal, but there's nothing, not even a hint.' He looked up at the three faces who'd turned towards him and felt as though he had interrupted something. 'What?'

'We've just discovered that Anna and Natalya both spent the start of their lives in an orphanage,' Susie said. 'Well, you knew Anna did. Natalya went through the same hell.'

Tim looked from Susie to the other two, uncertain what he was meant to say. 'Hmm. Right.' He paused and studied Anna and Natalya as if for the first time. 'Were there many orphanages?' he asked in all innocence. 'Which ones were you at?'

'Anna hasn't told us what she found out yesterday.' Susie said.

They all turned to Anna. After a few moments, she leaned forward over the table. 'I had a rough day, going from orphanage to orphanage, sorry *"children's centres".*' She mocked the last two words with air quotes. 'I think I must have gone to eleven or twelve. To be honest, I lost count. Some were still operating; more than half had closed.'

'They were all shocking.' She shook her head at the memory.

Tim sat down next to her and squeezed her hand.

'None of them were much help, too far in the past.'

Natalya nodded to herself as she listened and continued to stare at the floor.

Susie hung on every word. She felt responsible for persuading Anna to travel to Romania. She prayed for a positive outcome. 'So, what did you do?'

'One of the staff at the last place I went to was a little more helpful than the others. She spoke better English and told me they had taken all the records to the Sala Civica, the Civic Hall, and were being digitised into a central database.' Anna paused, drew breath, and studied the burning logs in the fire. The light and heat appeared to give her renewed strength. 'So that's where I went. It was my last resort. I just wish I'd found out earlier. It could have saved me hours.'

'And?' Susie leaned in and bit her bottom lip. 'Cut the suspense. What did you find out?'

'Well...' She paused again for effect. 'I found my records. Knowing my date of birth helped. I'd always assumed my adopted parents named me Anna, but I was in the records as Ana, with one n, Sofia Orban, born 5th November 1989, my parents...'

Natalya gasped. She looked up from the floor stared at Anna. 'Did you say *Orban* O.R.B.A.N?'

Anna nodded 'Yes, you know, like the president of Hungary. Why? Does that mean something to you?'

Natalya said nothing. She sat in silence and gazed at Anna for a long moment. She reached into her bag pulled out her passport. She opened it at the information page and passed it to Anna.

Anna looked at the photograph and read the details. She saw the name and inhaled slowly. It was the only sound. Without taking her eyes off the page, she showed Tim.

He scanned the information. 'What's the chances, you've got the same surname. You might even be related.'

Anna read from the passport before Natalya had a chance to reply. 'Natalya Daniela Orban, born 23rd April 1988. That's just too spooky' She looked up. 'Do you know who your parents were?'

Natalya answered without hesitation. 'Of course I do. That bit wasn't so difficult. They were Ioan and Daniela Orban.'

Anna recoiled as though hit with an electric shock. She stared at Natalya with renewed intensity and shook her head slowly. 'Those are the names of my parents.' She clutched both hands to her chest and goose-bumps appeared on her forearms. She shivered. Her hands moved up to cup her cheeks.

Susie and Tim exchanged glances.

Natalya held one hand to her mouth.

Anna continued to stare.

Natalya finally spoke. 'I was told I had a baby sister. I've spent so much time trying to find her. I gave up long ago when I discovered that some officials from the Western aid agencies took babies away to be adopted.'

Anna appeared to have lost the ability to talk. Her mouth opened and closed, but no sound came out. She pointed at Natalya. 'You're my big sister.' She said at last.

Natalya nodded.

'I can't believe it. All this time... I had no idea.' Anna reached for Natalya and pulled her into a tight embrace. 'I have a sister...'

Susie gawped wide-eyed and shook her head in tiny increments. 'Unbelievable, totally unbelievable.' She tore her gaze away and glanced at Tim, she swore his eyes were watering. 'You okay big guy?'

Tim smiled and nonchalantly wiped his eyes with the back of a finger. 'This is all a bit much.' He sniffed, 'What are the chances?'

•••••

Manfred Schrader had arrived at his hotel just after 7.00pm after his flight from Timisoara to Milan, and a four hour train journey from there to Montreux.

Two hours later, anxiety ate at him and he couldn't settle.

He called DeLuca. 'Any news?'

'Everything's sorted Manfred, relax.'

'Relax! Relax!' The pitch of Schrader's voice an octave. 'You haven't spent two years planning this, you haven't put up with Archer all this time. You're not here, you're not taking any risks. How dare you tell me to relax.'

'Look, I've just spoken to Decebal, he's told me the two women have been taken care of. They didn't get to Archer, nobody has warned him.' Despite his frustration with the scientist, DeLuca managed to remain calm and reassuring.

'I won't be happy until they get here and I won't relax until I know Archer has suffered.'

'I understand Manfred.' said DeLuca. 'My boys will be with you by eight. I'll give you a call if there's any problem.'

Schrader ended the call and consulted the room service menu. Maybe a meal would help him sleep.

••●••

In the chalet, Susie, Tim, Anna and Natalya enjoyed the hastily prepared concoction of soup and pasta, and for a contented few minutes, no-one spoke. The only sounds, a variety of slurping noises and the crackling of the fire.

Tim put his spoon down and reverted to his original question. 'So, now that I've told you how we found you, are you going to tell us what the hell you're doing here?'

Susie gave Natalya a questioning look, as if seeking permission to recount their tale. She took the response of a small shrug of a shoulder to indicate she should continue.

Susie paused between mouthfuls and waved her spoon in the air. 'Let's just say someone is trying to stop us from getting to Montreux.'

Tim stared at Susie, then turned to Anna. 'We were right.'

Anna nodded. 'We found the message you tried to send me and put two and two together.'

Susie looked confused. 'How? I never sent it. I lost my phone.'

Anna looked over at Tim and gave him an encouraging nod.

'You mean this one?' With a flourish he reached into his bag and produced the phone they'd retrieved from under the car in Timisoara. He laid it with reverence on his palm and presented it to her.

Susie stared at the phone and shook her head in amazement. She reached out, took it from Tim and held it as though it were a piece of rare priceless jewellery. 'Bloody hell, I thought I'd never see it again.' Her gaze moved from the phone to Tim, then Anna, then back to the phone. 'It must have fallen out last night when we were both attacked.'

'Attacked?' Anna sat forward, a look of alarm on her face.

'It's a long story, but we were both caught, captured, kidnapped.' She flapped her hand in frustration. 'I don't know what you'd call it, but we went to Natalya's place to get her passport and they grabbed her.'

'We found it underneath a parked car.' Anna said, confused.

Susie shut her eyes as the memory of the previous evening replayed in her mind. 'Yeah, that would follow. I ended up on the road after chasing the man who'd taken Natalya.'

'What man?' Tim asked.

Susie inhaled and glanced again at Natalya.

Natalya made an apologetic face. 'You tell them, you know more about it than me.'

Susie nodded slowly in agreement. Her eyes returned to the flames. 'We discovered there's some sort of plot to poison Natalya's boss at a conference in Montreux. We tried to get to him in Vienna, but we missed him. We have to get to Montreux before tomorrow morning.'

Tim listened intently. His mind pieced together what he and Anna had deduced, along with what Susie said. 'That's got to be the conference Nick's working at.'

Susie froze, her mouth opened and her eyebrows shot up. 'What?' As though in a trance, she placed her soup bowl on the floor.

'Didn't I tell you, your boss asked him to go there and get shots of all the pharma big wigs? He told me about it. Said there was someone from the UK getting an award.'

'Oh Jesus. Archer told me he was being presented with a gong. It has to be the same event.' Susie's hand came up to her mouth as the full reality of the situation grasped her.

It was Natalya's turn to look confused. 'Who's Nick?'

'Susie's husband.' Anna whispered in Natalya's ear when she saw the look of panic on Susie's face.

Susie jumped to her feet. 'We need to go. We need to warn Nick.' She turned left and right, unsure of what to do next. Her heart raced and her breath quickened. She clenched and unclenched her fists and glanced at the other three in turn.

Tim stood up and placed a reassuring hand on Susie's shoulders. He forced her to meet his gaze. 'OK. Just breathe. In a minute, we'll get going. We've got plenty of time. We can ring Nick when we've got a signal and we can ring the venue and warn them.'

Susie struggled free of Tim's hand and backed away slowly. She took more deep breaths and nodded. 'Can't we do anything now?'

'We could finish eating and you could get changed into something dry.' Anna suggested.

'We've got your bag in the car, I'll get it.' Tim said. He turned and went outside.

Unable to settle, Susie retrieved her bowl of soup and stood in front of the fire to finish it. 'We'd have been totally screwed if you and Tim hadn't been able to find us.' She looked down at Anna and Natalya, who sat side by side on the sofa. They both nodded in agreement.

Tim returned with Susie's bag, and she went into the bedroom to change.

She emerged five minutes later. She had cleaned up and tied her hair into a loose ponytail. She'd changed into jeans, a pale blue shirt and her trainers. Her breathing had returned to normal, but she still looked anxious. She spotted Tim leant over the kitchen worktop, pen in hand. 'What gives?'

Tim glanced over at Susie with a serious expression. 'I'm leaving a note for the owners of this place.'

'Seriously? How's anyone going to trace us?'

Tim waved a hand around the chalet. 'That's not the point. Look at the damage we've done. Breaking and entering, lighting a fire, burning their candles, eating their food, using their facilities.'

'Don't forget the boat we sunk.' Natalya chipped in.

Tim did a quick double-take, unable to understand the remark. He shook his head, then continued. 'I'm just apologising and leaving them my contact details. For all we know, this place could have cameras hidden or someone might have seen us driving up the track.'

Susie watched Tim and shook her head. She couldn't help but smile. 'What can I say? Do you always do the right thing?'

Tim considered the question for a moment, his lips pursed. 'I'd like to think so.'

Anna had tidied up the remains of their impromptu meal and gathered together all their things while Susie changed. 'Come on then, time to hit the road. You can fill us in with the details while we drive.'

Tim placed a fireguard in front of the dying flames and, one by one, extinguished the candles. Under the light from his phone, he pulled the front door back into place as best he could and the four of them headed for the car.

CHAPTER 26

The hotel near Gletsch was perfect for his needs; functional, comfortable and not too expensive. Nick felt happy with his choice. He just needed to be in the right place at the right time, with somewhere to sleep and somewhere to get some food. Anything would be better than sleeping in a tent. The road from Interlaken to the hotel, especially the Grimsel Pass, had proven to be every bit as thrilling as promised. Part of him would have liked to go back sixty kilometres and do it all again, just for the hell of it, but he'd set himself a goal and he was determined to see the sun set over the Eiger and capture the moment. He had planned the shoot carefully and worked out it would take about an hour to hike the two miles to the summit of the Sidelhorn to get the view he wanted.

According to his research, the sun would set just before eight, and he intended to be in place an hour before that to set up and take in the view. He allowed another hour after sunset, the golden hour; that period of glorious light and long shadows, which meant it would be almost ten when he returned. With a full moon, there would be enough light to help him on his way back to the hotel. He checked his head torch, worked, just in case, and added it to the contents of the camera bag. A cloudless night had been forecast with a gentle northerly breeze, but it would be cold at almost three thousand metres, and he packed ski gloves, a thermal hat and a microfibre quilt jacket, which he folded and jammed into one of the side pockets. He secured his tripod to the outside of the bag, loosened off the straps that converted the bag into a rucksack and slung the whole assembly onto his shoulders. He stuffed his phone into the back pocket of his jeans, took a quick check round the room to make sure he'd left nothing he might need, and headed out the door.

Outside, the setting sun was still warm and bright, it shone directly into Nick's eyes as he set off up the trail and he flipped his Oakleys from forehead to face. He tucked his thumbs into the shoulder straps of the bag, inhaled the clear fresh air and strode with purpose towards the distant mountain top.

———————— ••●●• ————————

Once they had returned to the southbound Autobahn and got up to speed in the gathering gloom, Anna insisted Susie bring her and Tim up to speed with the events of the previous two days.

Settled into the warmth and comfort of the Merc's back seats, Natalya made no attempt to stay awake and curled up in the corner. She'd brought the picnic blanket with her from the chalet and within minutes was sleeping soundly.

Susie struggled to stay awake, but with Anna's prompting she recounted what Archer had said in the interview, what Natalya had told her when they met up in the bar and how they had been captured and held in the security office back at the Azllomed factory.

Anna listened with a mixture of amazement, shock, and awe. When Susie described the two men who had captured her and Natalya, Anna made a strange 'Aha.' noise that stopped Susie mid-sentence.

'What's wrong?'

'Nothing. It's just that when I got back to the hotel and got the lift to our room, there were two guys waiting to get into the lift on our floor. The way you've just described them, they'd have to be the same two. I remember thinking at the time they looked out of place. That was before I got to the room and found it trashed.'

Susie considered this for a moment. 'That would make sense. They must have found my keycard when they captured us, so they would have known which room to go to. Bastards!'

Anna unbuckled her seat belt and turned to kneel in her seat to face Susie. She nodded in agreement with her friend's assessment of the two men.

Tim concentrated on driving. His eyes never left the road, while his ears tuned into Susie's telling of the tale. 'So, they left you tied up in the security office?' He encouraged Susie to continue.

'Tied up and gagged.' Susie added, in case the full extent of their peril might be diminished.

'OK,' Tim said. 'What were they going to do with you both? I mean, not being funny or anything, but why didn't they just finish you off?'

'I've been thinking about that ever since. Natalya reckoned someone wanted to find out who we'd spoken to, and she thought whoever it was would be coming to find out.'

Anna held on to the back of her seat. Her gaze switched from Susie to Tim and back again. 'How did you get out of there?'

Susie couldn't resist a self-satisfied smirk. 'A little initiative and a bit of brute force.'

Tim looked in the rear-view mirror and caught Susie's expression. She moved into the middle of the back seat in an effort to stave off the temptation to snooze. He could see the fierce determination in her eyes. 'Save the details for another time.'

'So go on.' Anna said.

Susie told them about the van and chasing the train to Arad, then getting from there to Vienna. She told them about the scene in the hotel and their escape in the laundry van. Anna and Tim interjected from time to time when their own story overlapped.

'We must have been so close to you in Vienna.' Anna mused, and looked at Tim for confirmation.

Tim nodded, but said nothing.

After another hour, Susie had brought them up to the chase through the forest and their confrontation in the rowing boat. 'When I saw your headlights, I was sure the guy had gone back for his van and was coming to finish us off. You've no idea what a welcome sight you were.'

Anna's knees had cried enough was enough, as a result of the position she'd adopted, facing backwards, gripped by Susie's story. She twisted back, fell into her seat and winced at the pins and needles as circulation returned. 'Bloody hell, if you didn't have a story before, you've got one now.'

Tim said nothing for a minute. The other two watched him and waited for a reaction. 'The guy who chased you through the forest. He's the same guy your friend Natalya saw with the camera and the gas cylinder?'

'Absolutely positive.'

'So you're pretty sure he's on his way to Montreux for the conference?'

'That's the only thing that makes sense. Archer told me he was going there to make a speech and Natalya overhead them talking about Montreux. It has to be.'

'OK.' Tim said to himself as his mind raced ahead. He checked the satnav screen he'd programmed with their destination. 'We've got a few hundred miles to go, but we should make it in time to warn them.'

'Nick's still not answering his phone.' Susie said, she had charged her phone and had been trying to call him ever since the device had acquired a signal.

'No surprise there,' Tim gave a half laugh. 'You know what he's like. He's either left it on silent or he's forgotten to charge it.'

'Or, he could be sound asleep.' Anna suggested. 'It is after midnight and he's got a big day tomorrow.'

'Possible.' Agreed Susie. 'He's slept through thunderstorms and car alarms before now.'

'Any joy with the venue?' Tim asked Anna.

'No, it just goes to a machine, reasonable enough at this time of night,' she replied. 'We could call the police?'

'And say what? You suspect someone is going to release poison gas at a conference?' Susie scoffed. 'They'd dismiss you as just another nutter.'

Tim rallied to Anna's defence. 'It's not a bad idea. They might do something, send someone to take a look, call the venue and warn them. Trouble is, at this time of night, you're not going to get the A-team.'

Anna sat in silence. She crossed her arms and slumped down in her seat. She briefly glanced back to gauge Susie's reaction.

In the dim, reflected blue light from the dashboard, Susie frowned. 'I guess you're right. I just wish Nick would answer his phone. I'd be happier if I could just get a message to him. He's bloody hopeless.'

'We'll be there soon enough.' Tim consoled her. 'Try and get some sleep. You must be knackered.'

Susie mumbled an incoherent reply and sank back into her seat.

Tim pressed on; the Merc sped past a sign for Bern, 190 kilometres.

●●●●●

Decebal's eyes closed momentarily and the shock of the rumble strip made him jump. The van veered to the left as he over corrected and then snapped back as he fought to retain control. The absence of any other traffic meant he got away with the erratic driving without hitting anything, but for a few seconds he felt his heart in his mouth and he shook his head to clear the fog of tiredness that no amount of energy drink could mask.

The sudden movement jolted Sergei from his slumber and his head thumped against the passenger window. The seat belt held him in place and as the van resumed normal progress, Sergei turned and stared at Decebal through narrowed eyes, his features contorted. He grunted in protest but said nothing.

The road climbed into the mountains, swooped over valleys on impressive feats of civil engineering, on bridges perched on concrete pillars hundreds of feet in the air, then plunged into tunnels bored through solid rock.

Decebal opened his window halfway, to allow fresh air to blow away the cobwebs. The chilly, high altitude air felt close to freezing at speed, and after less than a minute, he buzzed the window shut again. He turned the dial on the temperature control, as he had done repeatedly for the last couple of hours, to try to find a temperature that kept them warm, but cold enough to keep him awake.

Another thirty minutes passed and Decebal began felt woozy again. He reached down and adjusted the temperature down a little. It helped, but he struggled to keep the van between the white lines. His speed had dropped, but the empty road, the darkness and the rhythmic hum of the engine, played tricks on his brain and convinced him he was still cruising.

He blinked repeatedly and stared at the road ahead. It curved gently to the left and dropped slightly towards another tunnel. He spotted red taillights in the distance, a tanker in the slow lane, travelling fast, close to, if not above, the legal limit.

As if on autopilot, Decebal pulled out to pass as the tanker gained speed on the incline.

The two vehicles travelled side by side and only inches apart as they rushed into the mouth of the tunnel. For half a minute, Decebal focused on the gap between the tunnel wall on his left and the looming bulk of the tanker on his right. He accelerated to get ahead of the tanker. The intermittent lights in the tunnel roof made the road feel narrower, and he sensed the tanker move to the left, as if reacting to the optical illusion. It squeezed him closer to the wall.

Decebal pressed harder on the throttle and, with a silent cry of relief, moved ahead of the tanker. Thinking he was clear, he moved to his right to escape the clutches of the wall and, without thinking, allowed his speed to drop.

He didn't check his mirrors and didn't see the tanker brake suddenly to avoid running into the back of his van. The noise of the tyres shrieking was the first thing that caught Decebal's attention. It made him glance at his door mirror in time to see white smoke that poured from the tyres of the cab while the tanker body slewed sideways behind it.

In panic, Decebal stood on the brakes and watched in horror as the tanker closed on him. He realised his mistake and accelerated again, but too late to give the tanker a chance to regain control. He saw the driver fighting the steering wheel, he could see more tyre smoke and with a sickening crunch, heard the tanker body smash into the wall of the tunnel.

The rear wheels caught on the guardrail and the speed of the impact ripped the tyre from one of the wheels and the tanker crashed onto its side. Wires and cables ripped apart and sparks arced between them. With nothing to slow it down, the tanker continued to slide as metal ground against tarmac.

The sparks, like fireworks, up the tunnel.

Sweat dripped into his eyes as Decebal urged the van to get clear. His focus was on the tunnel exit, urging it to come sooner, but he glanced briefly in his mirror and saw the tanker come to a stop. He couldn't see the fuel that escaped from the ruptured tank, but he saw the blinding flash as it reached the shower of sparks. He heard the whoop and the crash as the vehicle body exploded.

He didn't dare look back, but he sensed the fireball chasing him out of the tunnel. There was nothing he could do. He kept going.

•••••

'Ready for a pit stop?' Tim asked Anna, 'I bet those two are,' he jerked a thumb in the direction of the two sleeping women on the back seat.

'Did somebody say pit stop?' Susie mumbled, her voice thick with sleep.

Tim glanced at the rear-view mirror and saw a ruffled Susie as she peered ahead through half-open eyes. 'I thought you were out of it.'

Anna turned in her seat. 'How you doing?'

'Been better. Could do with a waz, though.'

Tim chuckled. 'We passed a sign back there, said there's a stop in 20k. We should be there in about ten minutes. Can you hang on?'

'Yeah, it's not desperate.' Susie unfastened her seat belt and sat forward, a hand on each of the two front seats. She took in the road ahead and the scenery. 'How we doing for time?'

Tim pointed at the satnav screen. 'It's all there.'

Susie screwed up her eyes and squinted at the screen. She leant forward between the two seats to get closer.

Anna looked concerned. 'What's wrong?'

'Lost a contact lens in that bloody water back there.' Susie said, her face a mask of frustration.

'How much can you see?'

'Enough, they're just for close up. What's it say?'

Anna checked the screen. 'We've got 212 kilometres to go. ETA is 7.30.'

'So we've got an hour or two in hand if we want to stop?' Susie looked at Tim for confirmation.

Tim tore his eyes from the road. They were approaching a tunnel. 'Yeah, should be OK, so long as we don't get held up.'

'Not much chance of that,' Susie said and flapped a hand at the scene beyond the windscreen. 'There's sod all on the road.'

Tim turned and smiled at Susie. At the same time, the inside of the car lit up bright orange.

'Shit!' Tim turned in alarm to see a fireball rushing towards them from inside the tunnel. He stamped on the brake and gripped the wheel with both hands. He felt the judder of the ABS through the pedal as the car's inertia fought against the force of twin callipers and ventilated discs.

'Fuck, fuck, fuck,' Susie cursed as her arms twisted behind her and she lost her grip on the two seats. She slammed forward; her head crashed against the dashboard and her legs became pinned behind the front seats. 'What the hell?'

Natalya, flung forward like a rag doll, woke in alarm. The seat belt dug into her neck but kept her in place.

The Merc stopped a few yards short of the tunnel with as tongues of flames licked towards it. Without a pause, Tim hit reverse and floored the accelerator. The car shot backwards to escape the heat. Without looking back over his shoulder, he dipped his head to avoid the glare of the fire and concentrated on his door mirror. He didn't let up until they were safely 100 metres from the tunnel entrance.

'Everyone OK,' he asked as he stared at the inferno in front of them, horrified.

Susie pushed herself upright and rubbed her forehead where she'd made contact with the dash. 'Jesus, we could have been in that if you hadn't reacted so quickly.' She laid a hand on Tim's shoulder, partly in self reassurance and partly in gratitude. Her eyes, saucer-like, stared at the flames.

Anna sat transfixed, her hands over her mouth. 'What happened?'

Tim released his grip on the steering wheel and exhaled loudly. 'Dunno, but our route to Montreux has just been well and truly terminated.'

Part Eight

Resolution

CHAPTER 27

The flames died back after the initial explosion, but the inside of the tunnel glowed, and a hostile bright light flickered from deep within.

Tim got out of the car. The heat hit him like a hammer blow and he squinted against it.

The three women joined Tim and stood in awed silence, illuminated in angry shades of yellow, red, and orange. They could see no vehicles or people and could only guess what had caused the inferno.

The other bore for the northbound carriageway appeared unaffected by the explosion. With little traffic at two in the morning, a few cars emerged, unaware of what happened in the southbound tunnel. Any driver who glanced over their left shoulder would have been shocked by what they saw. None of them stopped.

Anna turned her back to the tunnel and watched as traffic headed north. She spotted headlights heading that approached in their direction. She didn't look back at her companions. 'We're not going to get out of this in a hurry.'

An unbroken metre high barrier ran down the centre of a wide grass strip that separated the two carriageways. Tim studied it. He looked for a way through and realised it effectively trapped them. He responded to Anna's remark as he pulled his phone from his jacket pocket. 'I need to make a call.' He stared at the screen and rolled his eyes in frustration. 'Typical, no bloody signal.'

Susie watched as HGVs, panel vans, and one or two cars slowed as they grew closer to the tunnel. They didn't need anybody or anything to tell them they could go no further. 'Bloody great, now we can't even go back.'

Tim walked toward the slowing vehicles. Drivers appeared. They exchanged glances with each other and stood, uncertain what to do, as the tunnel continued to burn.

Tim held his phone aloft and waved it around in the universally accepted manner of those trying to make contact with the world. He pointed at it with his other hand. 'Has anyone got a signal?' He hoped at least one of the other drivers either understood him or could make sense of his rudimentary sign language.

A single voice answered his prayers. 'Ja. I have signal'

Tim located the source of the voice and saw a man wearing a pair of baggy shorts, a crumpled white T-shirt, and trainers. He looked to be in his early twenties. He waved his phone in response to Tim.

Tim guessed from his accent the young man must be local. 'Can you call the police?'

It looked as if he understood and a few seconds later, Tim realised he'd got through to the emergency services and was busy explaining the situation.

The other drivers pulled out their phones. Some tried in vain to make calls, others started speaking to loved ones or employers, and others thought the occasion was too good to miss, and took pictures pictures of the burning tunnel.

Tim shook his head in disbelief and returned to the Merc. The three women sat in the car with the doors open, Anna in the front, Susie and Natalya in the back. They could only watch the flames and wait.

They chatted for ten minutes and watched as minute by minute more traffic arrived from the North and backed up behind them. Some drivers sat with engines running and lights on, while others switched off and walked to the front of the growing line of stranded vehicles to get a better look at the accident.

The Merc and its occupants, positioned at the front of the queue, assumed the role of information centre as the curious and the concerned, came forward to ask questions and offer to help.

Tim kept his cool, unable to understand. He relied on Natalya, who spoke a little German to answer as best she could while he gave a helpless shrug and wished something with flashing blue lights would appear, sooner rather than later.

●●●●●

The sunset shoot from the Sidelhorn had resulted in a bunch of images that Nick felt justified the late night. The fresh mountain air and more than twelve hours travelling meant he'd slept soundly for seven hours and woke when the receptionist duly called with his alarm. After a quick shower, he wriggled back into his leathers and packed his "conference kit", which consisted of black jeans, shirt and shoes, ready for a quick change when he got to Montreux. He made the most of the buffet breakfast, packed his gear into the panniers and was on the road just after 7.30am.

The road from Gletsch down to Brig did not seem as much fun as the Grimsel pass Nick had enjoyed so much the previous afternoon, but it made his pulse pump nonetheless. The pass dropped a thousand metres over the initial ten kilometres, with a tarmac track that twisted and roughly followed the course of a very young river Rhone with its pale green glacial meltwater that cascaded down waterfalls and through narrow gorges. Nick felt high on undiluted adrenalin as he raced down the hairpin switchbacks. Low morning sun hid loose gravel in the shadows, and caused the cold tyres to scrabble for grip. It added to the thrill and excitement. It was just what he needed to set himself up for the day.

Once down to the valley floor, the scenery changed from wooded hillsides to broad productive pastureland dotted with farms. The road continued in a straight line southwest through towns and villages, any one of which Nick would have been happy to stop in for coffee, but not today. He pushed on, passed Brig and on through the bigger commercial developments. The road transformed into the Autoroute de Rhone as it became busier and the morning traffic built up. The extra carriageway gave Nick the opportunity to open up the BMW, tuck in behind the screen, and cut through the traffic without having to slow down. At Martigny, the Autoroute turned sharp right and headed due north, which meant only another forty kilometres to Montreux. He'd be there before 9am.

———————•••••———————

Manfred Schrader saw the convention centre, two hundred metres from his hotel. He saw a constant stream of delegates that emerged from taxis, arrived from the train station or walked from their hotels elsewhere in the city. He checked his watch; the conference was due to start in twenty minutes and Decebal and Sergei were nowhere in sight.

Impatiently, he paced the modest reception area. He stopped and looked out onto the Avenue Claude Nobbs that ran past his hotel and the convention centre. The rush hour traffic moved slowly. It would be quicker to walk. He stepped outside in search of a small white van.

Nothing.

He checked his watch again. He pulled his phone from a jacket pocket and called DeLuca.

'Where are your men? The conference is starting. They were supposed to be here over an hour ago.' He wanted to shout, but didn't want to attract any attention.

DeLuca took great delight in Schrader's frustration. He was in charge and he enjoyed rubbing it in. 'It's all under control Manfred, Decebal called me five minutes ago, they were delayed on the autobahn. He said they'd turned off and were just entering the city, going as fast as they could through the traffic.'

Schrader didn't sound convinced. 'Don't they realise how important this is?'

DeLuca might have lost his temper with Decebal when he heard about his behaviour in the forest, but he would not apologise to the Austrian. 'Listen Schrader. They've driven through the night, over a thousand kilometres without stopping. They'll be with you any minute now. Have you got the paperwork ready?'

'Of course I have.' Schrader scanned the approaching traffic for any sign.

'Great. Oh, and by the way,' DeLuca paused, and he knew his next question would invoke some hostility. 'Can you get a change of clothes for Sergei? Apparently, they had a little excitement in Vienna and he looks a bit of a mess.'

Schrader forgot all about not attracting attention and his voice rose in volume. 'What? Now you tell me. What do you think I am, a gentleman's outfitter? They've had all night to sort something out. What can I do now? They're already late. There's no time to go shopping.'

DeLuca had to agree with Schrader, but he would not say so. 'You'll have to be inventive, raid the hotel staff room, beg borrow or steal something. He only needs a shirt.' DeLuca let that sink in for a moment, then added. 'And he'll need to clean up.'

Schrader cursed in his native tongue. 'Mein Gott. I thought your men were supposed to be reliable.'

'They are Manfred, you do your job and they'll do theirs. They'll be with you any second now. Just find him a shirt. I'm sure you can manage that.' Without waiting for a response, DeLuca clicked off.

Schrader cursed again, stared at the phone, cursed that too, then stuck it back in jacket. In the course of the conversation, he had walked a hundred metres up the road away from his hotel and now he turned and retraced his steps. Beads of sweat stood out on his forehead and his face flushed. He contemplated how he was going to find any clothing big enough to fit Sergei when the blast of a horn made him jump. Instinctively, he looked to his right and glimpsed a white van that had slowed almost to a stop.

Decebal had spotted him and tried to attract his attention. Schrader looked around as if he had committed a crime and was afraid someone might recognise him. He took a couple of short steps over to the van. 'What's taken you so long?'

Decebal gave a hopeless gesture through the open window. 'Traffic.'

With supreme effort, Schrader managed to contain his anger. He pointed down the road to his hotel, where a blue parking sign indicated the entrance to the small car park at the back. 'Go and park down there and wait for me.'

Decebal nodded and drove off.

Schrader quickened his steps and followed. He entered the hotel by the main entrance, headed for the back door and arrived in the car park just as Decebal got out of the van and stretched his tired limbs.

Schrader looked around. 'Where's Sergei?'

The passenger door opened, and Sergei climbed out slowly. He hung on to the side of the van for support. He looked dreadful.

Schrader gasped when he saw him. 'Bloody hell. I was told you were a mess, but nobody warned me you looked like death.' He appraised Sergei, grimaced and turned away as though he'd been forced to suffer a foul smell.

Decebal walked over to Schrader. 'I go clean him up.' He took Sergei by the arm and led him back to the hotel.

'Hang on.' Schrader stopped their progress. 'Where is the equipment?'

Decebal let go of Sergei and went to the back of the van.

Sergei staggered momentarily before he regained his balance.

Decebal opened the back doors, reached inside and reappeared with two boxes, but he looked puzzled. He handed the boxes to Schrader as though the slightest knock would cause them to explode and then went back into the van.

Schrader grew impatient. He went over to the van and peered over Decebal's shoulder to see what he was doing. 'What is it?'.

Decebal shook his head. 'The bag. It's not here.'

Schrader had no idea what he was talking about. 'What bag? There was no bag, just these boxes. Now come on, we're late already, go and get that cleaned up.' He pointed an accusing finger at Sergei.

Decebal's face furrowed; it seemed beyond his understanding. 'The woman's things we took from her. We put them in a bag. It's not there.'

Schrader wasn't interested. He had what he needed. He glanced at his watch again. 'Sheisse, we've got to move. Go and make him presentable, find him a clean shirt and meet me in the lobby. I'll get this primed.' He tapped one of the boxes and went to his room.

●●◆●●

At 8.50am, Julian Archer knocked on the door of the organiser's office, just off the main entrance foyer of the Montreux Music and Convention Centre, or 2M2C.

Simone Anderson, radio to her ear, opened it and greeted the new arrival with a smile, and made signs to apologise for the radio. She indicated she'd be with him in a moment and invited him into the office.

Archer glanced around while Anderson finished talking. There was only one other person in the office, a woman with short red hair, hunched over a laptop. She wore a headset and talked quietly into a built-in mic, oblivious to the outside world. Cardboard boxes had been piled in the corner and their contents–programmes, leaflets, newsletters and assorted forms–lay scattered on tables ready for distribution.

'Sorry about that.' Anderson ended her call and offered a hand. 'I'm Simone Anderson. How can I help?'

Archer shook hands. 'Julian Archer, I'm...'

'You're our star speaker,' interrupted Anderson. 'How do you do? Pleased to meet you.'

Archer looked taken aback by the recognition. 'Pleased to meet you, too. I was told to bring this to the organiser's office.' He held up a USB drive. 'I guess that's you?'

'It is. Your chairman Aleksi engaged us. He's been working with me for the last eighteen months.'

Archer nodded. 'Ahh, you must be the A in ACE.'

'You've got it. Anderson Conference and Events, has a nice ring to it, eh?'

Archer shook his head in apology. 'Absolutely. Sorry, I should have realised.'

'No problem, I guess that's your presentation?'

'Yes, I was told your tech guys need it.'

'They do. I'm guessing you got our instructions about formatting?'

'Yes, thank you, very helpful.'

'I'll get one of the team to load this up ready for you.' Anderson took the stick, then asked, 'Do you want me to show you to the Green

Room, speakers only, you can get a coffee and relax away from all the noise?'

'That's OK, I passed it on the way here. I might call in after I've caught up with a couple of members of the committee. Thank you anyway.' Archer glanced around the office and shook his head. 'I suppose this is your most hectic time?'

'It shouldn't be, if we've done our job right, but live events have a nasty habit of throwing curve balls at us.'

'Aleksi speaks very highly of you, I'm sure we're all in safe hands.'

'Well, if it's any consolation, I've been doing this for twenty years. I've seen it all before, done it, read the book, got the T-shirt. I leave nothing to chance.' Her radio squawked. She gave a helpless gesture, shook Archer's hand, wished him luck and pressed the receive key.

Archer left her to it.

Out in the foyer, the public address burst into life. 'Ladies and Gentlemen, welcome to the Conference of the European Clinical Governance Council. Please make your way to the Stravinsky auditorium, the Conference will open in 15 minutes.'

••◆••

Gregor Robinson had arranged with the organisers for Nick to have access to the service yard at 2M2C, since he needed somewhere safe to leave his BMW. They always denied cars access on the grounds of limited space, but almost without exception, venues appeared to have a separate rule for bikes. He secured his crash helmet and gloves and took out his working clothes from the panniers. He shouldered the equipment he needed and went in search of his base for the day.

He had downloaded a copy of the conference programme and knew where he needed to be and when. On the first floor, the windows of one side of the media centre overlooked Lake Geneva and, on the other side, it looked over the Stravinsky Auditorium. Six enormous TV screens placed around the room kept journalists up to date with a live feed from the many cameras situated around the centre. The room already bustled when Nick entered.

The pre-conference hubbub appeared in full flow as print and broadcast reporters set up their positions, secured online connections, made contact with their offices, studied the programme, grabbed coffee, and vied with each other to look furiously busy and desperately important' Nick smiled, he'd seen it a hundred times before, and it always amused him. He found a quiet corner, a table with a view of the auditorium, that suited him perfectly. He placed his bags on the table and unpacked.

A journalist at the next table watched Nick as he pulled camera bodies, lenses, a laptop and a notepad out of his big. She gave him a polite nod. Nick had yet to change and his leathers looked out of place among the sharp suits and designer-casual business attire.

He returned the acknowledgement and smiled. 'Bonjour.' His schoolboy French wouldn't stand up to any scrutiny and he hoped she didn't intend to start a conversation.

'Hi, it's OK, you don't need the French with me. I hardly speak a word of it meself.'

The accent, pure Irish West coast, disarmed Nick and he relaxed. 'That's a relief, I don't know much more than bonjour, si'vous plait, and merci.'

The woman chuckled and held out a hand, 'I'm Siobahn, Irish Times, how d'you do.'

Nick shook her hand. 'I'm Nick, freelance photographer.'

Siobhan nodded at the cameras. 'I'd never have guessed.'

Nick gave a shrug, 'Bit of a a giveaway eh. How did you know I was English anyway?

'An educated guess,' she pointed at Nick's notepad, 'And that. That's a giveaway.'

Nick glanced down at the notepad and saw it had no cover and he'd written messages on the first page in bold black ink. 'He rolled his eyes and shook his head in mock admonishment.' You got me.' He needed to change and had an idea. 'Siobhan, could you keep an eye on my gear, I can't work like this.'

'Oh, shame, I thought you'd got dressed up for the occasion. Might liven things up a bit.' She smiled. 'Sure, be off with you, I'm going nowhere.'

'Cheers, I'll just be a couple of minutes.' Nick picked up his bag and made for the rest rooms.

He returned five minutes later to find Siobahn engrossed in a call.

She took in his changed appearance and gave him the thumbs up without pause in her conversation.

The sight and sound of Siobahn prompted him to dig out his phone. He'd been in such a rush since he woke he hadn't picked it up. He tapped the screen to wake it, but nothing happened. Shit, he thought, forgot to put it on charge last night. He delved deeper into his bag, found the charger, and connected the phone. He grumbled quietly about battery life, but left it. He set up his laptop ready for the day's pictures and fitted lenses to camera bodies, formatted memory cards and ensured he had enough spare cards and batteries in antic-ipation of taking several hundred shots over the next few hours. His phone would be fully charged by the time he returned at the next break in proceedings.

He heard the announcement over the PA that the conference was due to start, loaded himself up with the equipment he needed, and went to work.

He used the service corridors to gain access to the back-stage area and was in place and out of sight of the audience to the right of the speaker's podium a few minutes before Aleksi Jarvinen stepped up and opened the conference.

The auditorium house lights dimmed, and a single spotlight mounted high at the back wall of the hall lit the podium. 'Ladies and Gentlemen, friends and colleagues, welcome to the tenth conference of the European Clinical Governance Council.'

CHAPTER 28

It had always been Manfred Schrader's intention to set up his device, prime it for action, send Decebal and Sergei on their way and leave the conference hall before anyone could point a finger of suspicion at him.

His plans were falling apart, and for a man obsessed with fine detail and precise timing, the effect made him even more anxious than usual. He made a conscious effort to stop shaking as he removed the metal tag on the gas cylinder and armed the solenoid that operated the valve. The thought of triggering the release terrified him and he stopped several times, closed his eyes and took long, deep breaths to calm himself. He never wanted to rush the job, and the late arrival of the two men had raised his heartbeat. The stress caused the sweat on his brow to run down his nose and drip onto the camera lens. He had practised the routine many times and felt confident of putting it all together in less than a minute. With time against him, it had taken three times that long. When the pale grey lens finally clicked in to place on the camera body, he exhaled and dabbed his brow with a paper towel.

Decebal and Sergei waited in the reception area of the convention centre as instructed. Decebal had discarded the shirt that Schrader brought, and liberated a black one from the laundry basket in the hotel wash room. It almost fitted Sergei. The buttons strained to contain his barrel chest and expansive waist and the sleeves stretched tight over his bulging arm muscles. The wound on the side of his head still looked raw, but Decebal had cleaned the blood from his hair, neck and the side of his face. However, Sergei still looked like a battle-hardened street fighter.

Schrader arrived with the camera in both hands as though he held a bomb. He stopped and considered Sergei. 'I suppose that will have to do.' He shook his head in despair. 'Don't go into the hall until the lights have dimmed. We don't want anyone getting a good look at you. No one will believe you're a press photographer.' He left them and walked over to the registration desk where he collected their passes. A few latecomers cast curious glances at the two men and at Schrader as he hurried back to them. 'You'll need these to get in.' He hung one lanyard round Sergei's neck and passed the other to Decebal.

Sergei twisted the pass in his hand and examined it. His name had been printed in bold caps and the pass stated he represented Jurnalul Naţional. The writing meant nothing to him, but he felt important all the same.

Decebal placed his hands on Sergei's shoulders, looked him square in the eye and spoke slowly and carefully to him with a last-minute pep talk and a quick re-cap to check he remembered his instructions.

Sergei nodded and repeated, 'Da, da, da.' He knew what he had to do.

Satisfied that the time had come and there was nothing else he could do, Schrader gingerly handed the camera over.

Sergei took it like a child who had received a much-anticipated present. He gazed at it and smiled. He had no idea of the havoc he was about to unleash, but knew it was important. His shoulders straightened, his chest puffed.

Decebal winced; the buttons on the shirt would never hold.

Sergei slipped the camera strap over his head and held the camera in one hand and the pass in the other as he headed for the main doors into the Stravinsky Auditorium. The security staff had been preoccupied with checking delegate passes and had not seen the three men together.

Sergei's appearance didn't concern them. When he stopped at the door, they checked his pass and the expensive camera, and waved him in. Schrader and Decebal watched the doors swish shut as Sergei disappeared from sight. There was nothing else they could do.

'You know where to go now?' Schrader asked. He looked at the doors and trusted that Sergei wouldn't suddenly re-appear.

Decebal reported to DeLuca. He didn't like the way Schrader had spoken to him. 'Sure I know.' He was almost a foot taller than Schrader and he glared down at the scientist with unmasked disdain. 'I take the van to service yard, I have pass, and wait at back of hall.' With that, he walked off to retrieve his transport and get into position.

Left alone, Schrader felt vulnerable. He wanted to get out of the building and as far away as possible. But he also wanted to make sure the plan worked. He wavered, took a couple of paces towards the exit, then stopped. His pass was valid, he could sit at the back of the hall and watch from a safe distance. He thought of all the planning and effort he'd gone through to get this far. Most of all, he thought about how much he hated Archer and he wanted to see him die.

He took a deep breath and strode towards the auditorium.

●●●●

The slip road off the A9 down into Montreux couldn't have come quick enough. The silver Mercedes indicated right, the revs dropped, the speed fell away, and Tim eased from the fast lane as though piloting an airliner on final approach. He had driven at high speed for more hours than he could remember, negotiated a raging tunnel fire, and survived on snacks and takeaway drinks.

It had taken an hour for the police and the fire services to remove a section of the metal barrier, set up a contra-flow system and direct the Southbound traffic through the Northbound tunnel. The emergency services had tackled the fire in the tunnel from the other end and by the time Tim and his crew resumed their journey, an acrid black smoke remained the only sign of the devastation.

Tim knew they'd been lucky to get through the tunnel. He felt sure the autobahn would be closed for some time to come as soon as the police cleared the backlog of traffic.

Susie had swapped places with Anna when they stopped for fuel. She felt revived after sleeping for a few hours and was happy to sit up front with Tim. She checked the map and monitored their progress.

In the back seats, Anna and Natalya talked non-stop about their lives and compared notes, and at times, they had been reduced to tears. Several times, Susie couldn't help but turn to see how they were doing.

'Here we go,' Tim announced. 'Please return to your seats, put your tray tables in the upright position and fasten your safety belts.' He braked hard and hit the slip road.

Susie chuckled. 'Thank you, Captain Tim.' She checked the satnav, but didn't look up from the screen. 'Only a couple of miles to go.'

'Are you sure the service yard is the best place to go?' Anna asked from the back seat.

For the last couple of hours, the four of them had discussed options and what they should do when they eventually arrived in Montreux. Nick had told Tim that they had given him a parking permit for the service yard and Tim argued they could park nowhere else. They planned for Susie and Natalya to aim for the organiser's office and warn them about a plot to attack the conference.

Susie's primary concern was Nick's safety. She had tried to call him repeatedly, but as Tim had predicted, she received no response. 'I just wish he'd answer his phone. I don't even know if he's in there.'

'I keep telling you, Nick can look after himself. He's no soft touch.' Tim didn't ease up on the speed and tyres squealed as he swung the Mercedes through a roundabout. 'I know what he's like when things kick off. Don't let his laid-back attitude fool you. He doesn't miss a thing. If there's any trouble. Well....' He paused, and looked for the right thing to say.

'I know, just wish he was capable enough to answer his bloody phone,' Susie said.

Anna leaned forward and laid a reassuring hand on Susie's shoulder. 'Tim's told me stories about their time in the army. Even allowing for the usual macho exaggeration, I wouldn't like to get on the wrong side of him.'

'There it is.' Tim pointed ahead as they slowed for a red light. The convention centre was two hundred metres away.

Natalya perched on the edge of her seat and peered through the windscreen. 'Where's the entrance?'

The lights changed, and Tim strained to make sense of the signs and arrows in front of them. He nodded to his right. 'Main entrance. I'll pull in. If you two jump out, we'll go around to the service yard and park up. We'll see you inside.'

Susie turned to Natalya. 'Are you ready?'

'I hope so.' Natalya clung to the back of Susie's seat as Tim swerved out of the traffic.

The entrance was a pull-in and drop-off, designed for taxis. There was nowhere to park. Tim stopped outside the main door behind a black mini bus. He could go no further. Susie and Natalya slowly climbed out. Both felt stiff after hours in the car.

Two members of the organiser's staff who'd nipped out for a sneaky smoke stood by the door and raised eyebrows at the unconventional dress code, but smiled warmly and stood aside as the automatic doors slid open for Susie and Natalya.

They had both managed to register online for the conference once they'd acquired a 4G signal but despite repeated attempts neither could get through to the venue to raise the alarm. As the entered the foyer, Susie spotted one of the large screen monitors and saw that the event had begun. She urged Natalya'. Quick, we need to get in and warn them.'

———————•●●•———————

After thirty minutes, the chairman, Aleksi Jarvinen approached the end of his opening address. He welcomed delegates, brought them up to date with the current strategy of the executive committee, and outlined the aims of the conference over the next two days. Even without notes, he appeared animated and engaged the audience.

From Nick's point of view, he behaved like the perfect subject, an expressive face, plenty of arm movements, lots of pointing, smiling and, the icing on the cake, he didn't need to look down at his laptop or turn his back on the audience to point at the big screen behind him. Nick managed some great shots and, aware that the chairman was about to end his speech, he realised it was time to move into the

Auditorium for the front-on shots of the keynote speaker. He gingerly picked his way through the cables and found his way through the backstage corridors to the side entrance of the main hall.

They had given Dr Julian Archer a lavish and lengthy introduction. He made the short walk to the podium, accompanied by heartfelt applause.

Nick slipped into the auditorium. He waited by the door as the delegates settled and his eyes adjusted to the light. He looked around and took stock of the layout, the doors, and the location of the audience. Almost all the delegates had elected to sit in the front half of the auditorium, which left the rear empty apart from a handful who seemed preoccupied with their various electronic devices, heads down, oblivious to events on the stage. Nick counted three video cameras that provided live pictures to the mixer desk he'd spotted on the far side of the stage. All three focused on Julian Archer. His face filled the large rear screen at the back of the stage as he looked up, smiled, and launched into his presentation.

Nick moved down towards the front of the stage and spotted two other photographers crouched between the stage and the first row of seats. He joined them. They glanced briefly at the new arrival, a brief nod, then continued watching the speaker through their viewfinders, trigger fingers poised as they waited for the shot. The stage was a convenient height for Nick to lean on. He supported his weight on his elbows and held the camera steady, then shuffled sideways to get the angle he wanted. He had been so focused on the subject that he didn't hear or see a new arrival to the group.

It was the smell that hit him.

He took his eye away from the viewfinder without moving the camera and turned his head slightly to identify the source of the smell. He blinked and looked again and couldn't believe what he saw.

In an instant, Nick recognised the expensive camera as the professional choice for the job, but the huge 400mm lens seemed totally wrong for such close work. He turned his attention to the man that held the camera. It looked like he had just emerged from a bar-room brawl that hadn't gone in his favour. Nick noticed numerous scars and bruises on the man's neck, and a livid, bloodied gash that ran from behind his left ear to the collar. He also spotted a serpent tattooed on his forearm which extended to the back of his hand. The man's black shirt looked several sizes too small and his biceps struggled to escape the constraint. He'd swung his pass onto his shoulder and Nick could read the name, Sergei.

Sergei shifted his position to mimic Nick; the move released another wave of stale sweat and unwashed clothes.

Nick's nose curled involuntarily. Despite the smell, he couldn't take his eyes off Sergei. There was something about him that didn't add up. In fact, there was a lot about him that didn't add up. He just didn't look like a photographer, even though he had some expensive kit. The way he held it gave Nick the impression that he didn't understand what any of the dials, buttons, or switches were for. He didn't look through the viewfinder, but instead held the camera a few inches away from his face and looked down the lens as though it were a rifle barrel which he lined up with the speaker.

A cable led from a hole drilled into the lens to the little finger on Sergei's right hand.

Strange, why would anyone drill a hole in a lens?

But there was something else that niggled him. He just didn't know what it was.

••●••

At the back of the hall, the rear doors opened and Susie and Natalya slipped in as quietly as possible. The house lights had been dimmed and barring the emergency exit lights near the doors, the seating area of the auditorium was almost totally black. A few people near the doors turned and looked. Susie spotted Nick. She held Natalya's arm and pulled her close. 'He's down there.' She pointed at the figures at the foot of the stage.

'Which one? There's four of them.'

'The one on the left.'

Natalya squinted at the dark figures. 'How can you tell? They all look the same to me.'

'Believe me, that's Nick, I'd recognise him anywhere.'

'Can we get down there and warn him?'

Susie nodded and indicated the aisle that ran down the side of the auditorium. 'You wait here. I'll go down that way.' She headed for the aisle and never took her eyes off Nick.

She didn't see the large figure hidden in the shadows.

Decebal had seen the two women enter the auditorium, and he stood, hidden in the shadows, ready for a quick getaway. His brief had been to get Sergei out of the hall as fast as possible. The two women's appearance threatened that. He had to stop them from warning Archer.

Susie inched forward and squinted through the umbra, but without warning, something large filled her vision, clamped across her mouth and pulled her back.

Breath stuck in her throat, and she had no time to cry out. Instead, she felt enveloped by powerful arms that lifted her from the ground.

She kicked out, but it had no effect and in only a few seconds, she'd vanished through the exit door without so much as a sound.

CHAPTER 29

Anna climbed from the back seat into the front as she watched the other two disappear inside. 'Do you think I should go with them?'

'I'm sure you'd like to, but they've both got a reason to be there, Susie's got her journalist hat on and Natalya works for one of the key speakers. Besides, I want you near me. Who else will look after me?' He leant over and hugged Anna.

The people carrier moved off. Tim followed it and re-joined the traffic. The service yard was located at the end of a road that ran down the side of the Convention Centre. Large signs prohibited unauthorised vehicles. Tim ignored them and sped down the gentle incline.

'When I stop, get out and head inside, see if you can find someone to alert the police. Leave the rest to me.' Tim drove towards the gate, with hazards flashing and headlights on full beam.

Two security guards in hi-viz jackets stood either side of the closed gate. They were both big men, they looked to Tim as though they could moonlight as nightclub doormen. One moved to the centre of the gate and held up his hand to stop Tim, the other approached the driver's door and made a winding motion with his finger. Tim got the message and buzzed his window down.

Tim spoke before the guard made a sound. 'You need to call the police, there's a terrorist attack underway inside.' He pointed at the building.

The guard gave Tim a quizzical look, either he didn't understand English or he didn't believe what he heard. 'Pardon'

Anna leaned over from the passenger seat. 'Appelez la police, dites-leur qu'il y a deux dangereux criminels qui vont attaquer la conférence.'

The second guard understood Anna's message and joined his colleague at Tim's window. 'Comment savez-vous cela, pourquoi devrions-nous vous croire?'

Tim looked from the guards to Anna and back again. His language skills were basic at best. 'It is an emergency.' He ennuciated each word with deliberate care.

The two guards exchanged glances, unsure how to proceed.

Tim turned back to Anna. 'You didn't tell me you were fluent.'

She shrugged. 'You never asked.'

'Can you get them to understand, get them to call the police and let us in.' He nodded at the service yard beyond the gate.

Anna got out of the car and walked around to the two men, her smile appeared to melt their stern demeanour.

Tim watched as she spoke. He made out the odd word but the rest was lost in a rush of gallic to and fro. She pointed at the building, pointed at Tim, did a passable mime of someone taking a picture, and tapped on the radio one of the men had clipped to his jacket. Her efforts had the desired effect and after thirty seconds, one of the guards gave a reluctant shake of the head and spoke into his handset.

She turned to Tim and gave him the thumbs-up.

The second guard walked to a panel in the wall and pressed a button. Tim watched the gate slide to one side on its wheels, then drove into the yard. He got out and scanned the yard. He spotted Nick's bike parked in one corner, a couple of fork lift trucks, stacks of pallets and packing cases and a white van. He walked back to join Anna and the two security guards.

Anna took his arm and turned him away. 'They've called the police but I don't know if they're convinced or...' She spotted the van and stopped mid sentence. 'That looks very familiar.'

Tim nodded. 'I thought so too.'

They walked towards the van, Anna held tight to Tim's arm but kept half a step behind him. They slowed as they got close.

The van had been parked facing towards the gate as though ready for a quick exit. There was no sign of life in the van and, emboldened, Anna approached to examine a sticker on the windscreen. 'It's an official pass to park in here.' She stood back and studied the registration plate. Her expression darkened.

'What is it?' Tim recognised her concern.

She pointed, 'That's a Romanian plate, it's the same one we saw in Vienna.'

'You sure?'

'Hundred percent. Call me sad or whatever, but my brain seems to remember such things.'

Tim glanced around the yard again on the lookout for the van's occupants. 'Those two we saw in Vienna must be inside.'

Anna shuddered. 'God, I just hope the police have got the message and get here soon.'

••●••

It suddenly dawned on Nick.

The thumb.

The thumb on the Sergei's left hand was missing. He supported the lens in the palm of his left hand and where his thumb should have been, there wasn't one.

And the tattoo.

Nick recalled the footage from Susie's GoPro and made the connection.

He had to act.

Julian Archer was well into his presentation. The screen behind showed a chart illustrating the figures he quoted. The attention of the audience remained on Archer and the screen.

Nick slowly lowered his camera onto the stage.

Sergei leaned forward; he looked as if he was building himself up to do whatever he had come to do. The cable attached to the lens tensed as he took up the slack.

In one fast fluid movement, Nick turned to his right, snapped out his left hand and grabbed the front of the 400mm lens. He braced himself against the front of the stage with his right hand and smashed the camera into Sergei's face with all his strength. He heard the crack as his nose broke under the impact.

Sergei grunted in pain and released the camera as his hands came up to his face. The cable slipped from his little finger and the camera and lens crashed to the floor.

Nick instantly dropped to one knee and retrieved the camera. He held it by the lens and swung it like a club at the bloodied gash on the side of Sergei's head. As a professional photographer with an appreciation for expensive equipment, he almost hesitated to use it as a weapon. The camera body, built around a magnesium-alloy frame, had been designed for hard work. It made a fiendish weapon. Nick channelled all his fury into the blow.

Sergei bent forward, hands over his face, and hadn't seen what had hit him. But he'd felt it and his legs wobbled. He hit the floor in a crumpled heap.

Nick breathed hard, oblivious to the hundreds of eyes that watched in horror, and he gazed at the man on the ground to make sure he didn't get back up. He glanced at the lens in his hand. He held it by the hood that extended from its front; there should have been a reflection. But there was no glass in the lens.

Nick looked closer. He removed the hood and looked again. Where the front glass element should have been, he noticed a brass valve attached to a slim blue cylinder enclosed in bubble wrap that ran the length of the lens. The cable attached to the valve, a trigger.

Nick's eyes narrowed, and realisation hit him. He blinked and looked around. Barely fifteen seconds had passed.

Julian Archer stopped speaking and looked at Nick, baffled and shocked by the action a few feet in front of him.

Whispers and gasps rippled around the audience.

Natalya stood at the back of the hall, stunned what by she's seen. She quickly looked for Susie, but couldn't see her. Then she looked at Archer on the stage. Someone had to warn him.

Without hesitation, she ran down the central aisle towards the stage.

Archer stared down at Nick. 'What on earth is going on?'

Nick held up the camera so that Archer could see the cylinder. 'I'm not sure who or what he is, but he's no photographer. This is seriously dodgy. Looks like a gas cylinder.'

'Good God.' Archer came closer to study the lens.

'Dr Archer, don't touch it!'

Nick and Archer looked up and watched as Natalya raced towards them.

'Keep away from it. Dr Schrader made it. He's trying to kill you.' She said, breathless. Her face looked full of fear.

Nick made a quick assessment of Natalya and decided he had to trust her. 'I need to get this outside, can you look after my gear.' He didn't wait for a response and jumped over the body on the floor then ran to the exit with the camera.

●●●●●

Tim paced back and forth in danger of wearing a path in the concrete service yard. Impatience gnawed at him. He wanted to be inside, or at least help. He knew if he sat down, tiredness would catch up with him. He resisted the temptation. He wanted to know where Susie and Natalya had gone. He'd sent Anna around to the main entrance to ramp up the alarm with the organisers. He promised her he'd stay in the yard in case anyone came out the back way.

The two security guards eyed him with suspicion and curiosity, but they maintained station at the gate awaiting the arrival of the police.

Tim paused beside the Merc and leant on the roof. His phone pinged, and he glanced at the screen to see Anna had responded to his previous text.

"No sign of Susie, organisers ringing the police."

He was about to reply when he heard the swing doors from the auditorium open with a crash. At first, he couldn't make out what he saw, then it became clear.

Susie.

She was in the grip of a tall man, the one he and Anna had seen getting into the van in Vienna and driving off at speed. He held Susie off the ground with one arm firmly wrapped around her waist and the other around her chest, with his hand over her face. She writhed and kicked her legs furiously, but the man appeared impervious to her efforts.

'Susie!' Tim shouted, more as an instinctive reaction than any meaningful course of action.

The tall man turned at the sound of Tim's voice and sneered at him. He removed the hand covering Susie's mouth and reached into his back pocket. His hand whipped back into view; clenched around a short black handle.

Tim could make out the chrome fittings and instantly knew what it was.

'Stop him, Tim.' Susie shrieked.

The man pressed a button on the side of the handle and a thin, double-sided blade flicked out. He brought it up to Susie's neck and held its point tight against her jugular so tight that it dug into her flesh and drew blood.

She snarled in defiance and re-doubled her efforts to break free. She twisted and worked an arm loose, but the tall man caught it and pinned it between his body and hers.

Alerted by the commotion, the two security guards rushed towards Susie.

Her captor brandished the knife at them. 'Stay back.' He returned the knife to the neck of his hostage.

The guards stopped in their tracks alongside Tim. All three stood helpless as the man holding Susie backed towards the white van.

Tim shifted position to bring himself between the two guards. With a combination of eye movements and subtle hand gestures he got them to move outwards, a flanking manoeuvre to make it difficult for the man to watch all three at once.

Susie recognised Tim's tactics and responded. She brought her knees up to her chest, then, with her legs still bent, drove her heel backwards, aiming for the man's balls.

She missed by a fraction but the blow to his upper thigh made him flinch and he drew the blade across her throat, deep enough to open an inch long cut. Blood ran over his hand and down Susie's chest.

Tim and the two security guards felt powerless and watched as the man retreated to the door of the van. They knew their chance would come when he tried to get in. They prepared to act.

The man's eyes flicked between the three men who confronted him as he reached his vehicle. He pinned Susie between himself and the van in order to release the hand that held her. He kept the knife pressed into her neck.

Squashed against the side of the van, Susie found it impossible to move, but at the moment the door opened, the pressure against her back eased for a second and again she drew her knees up. With her feet level with the door handle, she kicked out with all her strength.

Her captor, caught off guard, stumbled back a step and tripped on a protruding drain cover. The hand holding the knife windmilled in an effort to retain his balance. He tried to recover but his hostage had too much momentum. His weight transferred to the leg that still felt weak from the vicious kick to the side of the knee Susie had inflicted just before he captured her. It couldn't support him and buckled under the strain. He released the knife in an effort to save himself and fell backwards. He sprawled, winded on the floor.

Released from his grip, Susie spun and dived for the knife. She pounced on the man, her knees landed full force in his stomach and drove the remaining air from his lungs. She stabbed the knife into his throat and would have pushed it all the way in but for Tim's intervention.

He grabbed the hand that held the knife. 'Hold it Susie.'

The two security guards jumped on the man's arms to stop them flailing as he fought for breath. They held him down.

'This is the bastard that ran me off the road.' Susie spoke through gritted teeth. 'Him and his little fat mate.'

She still had hold of the knife, but Tim's hand restrained her. 'I get it, but you don't want to go down for murder, not when these guys are watching every move.'

She handed the knife to one of the security guards and climbed to her feet. She heard the doors from the auditorium open and Nick appeared.

•••••

Julian Archer watched Nick go, then turned to Natalya. 'What's going on? How on earth did you get here?'

'I'll tell you later; we need to get the police or someone.' She pointed to the man on the floor. 'This one is dangerous.'

Two stewards arrived and looked concerned at the crumpled heap that lay at their feet.

Sergei stirred, he emitted a low growl like a bear waking from hibernation.

'Que s'est-il passé ici?' One of the stewards asked.

Natalya took control, 'He's not a photographer, he's a terrorist, he came here to kill Dr Archer.'

The stewards looked at each other and back at Natalya. They responded in English. 'Who are you?'

'I work for Dr Archer. I came here to warn him.'

The waking bear groaned again. They ignored him.

Archer intervened. 'I can vouch for her. She works for me. If she says it's dangerous, you'd better believe it. You're going to have to evacuate the building.'

Both stewards recoiled and stepped back, and one of them said, 'We need to call the Police.'

Natalya turned when she heard a commotion at the back of the auditorium. Two uniformed gendarmes rushed in. 'Looks like someone already has.'

The stewards shuffled nervously. They were both in their fifties and unfit, their role did not include confrontation with determined killers. Neither of them looked capable of putting up any sort of resistance. The relief on their faces spoke volumes.

Natalya was about to speak when Sergei groaned again and staggered to his feet. He held onto the edge of the stage, unsteady on his feet.

The stewards backed off even further. Natalya couldn't blame them. He looked menacing.

Sergei looked around. He rubbed his hand over face and blinked to clear his vision. The wound on the side of his head had reopened and his action smeared the blood into a ghoulish mask.

The two gendarmes arrived and for a second they looked startled by Sergei's appearance. One of them held up a hand to pacify the man but the gesture had zero effect.

Sergei bellowed. It sounded like a cold mix of anger and pain. He wanted a way out.

The three video camera operators realised they had something more exciting than Archer and zoomed in on the bloodied man. His image filled the large screen at the back of the stage.

The audience gasped. People rose from their seats and made for the exit.

Sergei spotted the illuminated emergency exit sign. He snorted and started to move.

The other gendarme whipped a small black and yellow device from his utility belt. He aimed at Sergei's chest and ordered him to stop.

Sergei ignored him.

The flash from the taser stood out in the darkness of the auditorium. The crackle of the electrical charge could be heard above the horrified screams from delegates in the hall.

As if he'd hit an invisible wall, Sergei's forward momentum ceased immediately. He jerked as the two fine wires hit him with a 50,000 volt charge. Already dazed and weak from the blows to the head he'd received in the past 24 hours, the taser instantly exhausted his last ounces of resistance. He crashed to the floor and spasmed for a couple of seconds, then lay still.

Both gendarmes, jumped on his inert body. They checked his condition, then handcuffed his hands behind his back.

Natalya tore her eyes away from Sergei and looked up at her boss who still stood on the stage. 'Are you all right Dr Archer?'

'I'm absolutely fine, Natalya. I haven't got a clue what's going on, but I'm fine.'

••●●•

Nick couldn't be sure, but he suspected the camera had lethal potential and he worried that its use as a club might set something off. He held it at arm's length. He had to get it out of the building as fast as he could, but he couldn't risk tripping or colliding with anything that might prove catastrophic.

He headed down the corridor which led to the service yard, at a pace between a fast walk and a slow run. He breathed fast and his heart raced as sweat glistened on his forehead. He turned his back to the doors to push them open and emerged into the yard.

It took a moment for his eyes to adjust to the daylight and at first he struggled to make out the scene that greeted him.

He spotted Tim, he couldn't miss him, but what was he doing here? Then Susie stood up.

Relief washed over him. Relief then confusion. What were Susie and Tim doing here in the service yard? What were they doing in Switzerland? He suppressed an overwhelming urge to rush to his wife and put the camera down in a gap between two stacks of pallets.

He walked towards Susie, arms spread wide, a puzzled but delighted look on his face. 'Hello my love, fancy meeting you here.'

'Thank God you're safe.' Susie rushed to him and threw her arms around his neck.

Nick wrapped her in his arms and hugged her tight. 'What the hell's going on?' What you doing here?' He spoke with his face buried in her hair.

Susie lifted her face from Nick's chest and studied him with concerned eyes. 'Are you okay? We've been so worried, we tried to warn you.'

'Warn me? You knew about the guy with the camera?'

'It's a long story, I'll tell your later. I'm just glad you're okay.'

'Yeah, I'm okay, there's been a bit of excitement in the hall but I think it's sorted now. What are you and Tim doing out here?'

'Later, we've had a bit of excitement here too.' She stood back and nodded towards Tim.

Nick gasped as he saw for the first time, the blood that had spread across her shoulder and down the front of her T-shirt. 'Jeez, love you're covered in blood, what've you done?'

Susie lifted her chin and exposed the cut to her neck, she winced. 'Guy with a knife. I don't think he likes me.'

Nick glanced left and right, he could only see Tim. 'Which guy?'

Susie turned and led Nick to the three men on the ground. Tim stood over them as if keeping vigil.

Nick slapped Tim on the shoulder. 'Bloody hell, Ace, looks like you've been having some fun.'

Tim grinned. 'Good to see you're okay mate, we've raced half way across Europe for this.'

Nick nodded at the two security guards and the man they held down. He shook his head slowly. 'Is this guy connected to the one inside?'

Susie looked up at him. 'Short, stocky thug with no neck?'

'That's the fella.'

'What's happened to him?'

'Last time I looked he was lying in a heap on the floor with a sore head.'

'Your handiwork by any chance?' Tim raised an eyebrow.

'Can't take all the credit, he looked like he'd already been hit with a sledgehammer.'

Susie gave a satisfied chuckle.

Nick peered at her. 'Don't tell me.'

'The dynamic duo, they've been a pain in the butt for a while. They got what was coming to them.'

CHAPTER 30

Manfred Schrader sat at the back of the auditorium unable to believe what he saw. His scheme, his ambition, his revenge; everything he'd worked for over the last two years. He could see it all falling apart in front of his eyes. He ground his teeth in frustration and thumped his fists against the arms of the chair.

He'd watched in eager anticipation as Sergei had taken up his position a few feet in front of Archer.

He'd watched in abject horror as one of the other photographers launched a unprovoked attack on Sergei.

He'd watched in unadulterated fury as the photographer who'd attacked Sergei picked up the camera and carried it out of one of the side doors.

He knew he had to get the camera back. If the police got hold of it they would trace it back to him. He'd be finished.

As delegates escaped the unfolding drama and headed for the exits, Schrader slipped into the aisle and joined them. Some made for the main doors at the back of the auditorium and some for the emergency exits. He kept his head down and pushed through the bodies towards the doors he'd seen the photographer leave by.

Two chairs to one side of the doors had been provided as a base for the security guards and he approached he noticed a hi-viz vest draped over the back of one of the chairs with a peaked cap hung on one corner.

As he drew level with the chair he paused briefly, He had an idea.

———————— ••●●•• ————————

Susie, Nick and Tim turned as one when they heard the double doors from the auditorium open and a trickle of people emerged. They saw stewards and security staff shepherding them into the yard and away from the building.

As the only one who hadn't been inside, Tim could only guess where they had come from or why they were being escorted outside. 'What's going on?' He looked to his two companions for explanation.

Nick watched with interest. Some of the delegates appeared frightened and keen to get away. Others looked angry and in no particular hurry. 'Looks like someone's made a decision to evacuate the place.' He rolled his eyes and shrugged. 'Not the smartest move when the danger has been removed.' His last remark aimed at the stewards, even though they were well out of earshot.

Tim looked at him with a questioning look. 'I don't follow.'

'Susie's mate,' he winked at his wife and nudged her with his elbow, 'had a camera with a gas cylinder in the lens.'

'Yeah, Natalya told us she'd seen them putting it together. We assumed it must had been some sort of poison or nerve agent.'

'Probably. I didn't stop to find out when I'd relieved him of it. I brought it outside, it's on the ground between two stacks of pallets.'

Susie tugged Nick's sleeve and nodded at the pallets. 'Those ones?'

'Yeah why?'

Suddenly alert, Susie straightened, she dropped the paper towel one of the security guards had given her to wipe the blood from her neck. 'One of the staff looks like he's taken in interest in something.'

All three watched the man, he was smaller than the other stewards and he appeared uninterested in the evacuation process. His cap sat low on his head and made it impossible for them to recognise his features.. He reached the pallets and bent down. As he stretched for the camera, the cap tipped forward and fell to the ground.

Susie reacted in an instant. 'It's fucking Schrader.' Her shout reverberated around the yard.

'Who's Sch...' Nick started.

'He's the sociopathic little bastard behind this.' Susie butted in before he could question her further and grabbed him by the elbow. 'Come on, we need to stop him.' She set off and dragged a reluctant Nick with her.

Nick saw Schrader flinch when he heard Susie call his name. He saw him snatch the camera and rush back through the double doors against the flow of people still leaving the hall.

'He's there, going up the side of the corridor.' Susie pointed at the fleeing figure and urged Nick to hurry. Hampered by the increasing number of people squashed into the corridor, their progress slowed. Susie could see Schrader getting further away from them.

Nick's height gave him an advantage over Susie. He could see over the heads of the crowd and saw Schrader dive through a doorway on the side of the corridor. He tugged her sleeve. 'He's gone left.'

Hemmed in by bodies all around her, Susie turned and looked back at Nick to check on direction. She barged in front of a group of delegates and saw the door. It had a no-entry sign and a pictogram to indicate a staircase. She pushed it open. The stairwell beyond, had flights going up and down.

They closed the door behind them and stood in silence in the hope of hearing footsteps. 'Up or down?' Nick squeezed his eyes shut and bowed his head as though it would improve his hearing. Neither of them could hear a sound above the noise of crowd on the other side of the door.

'You go down, I'll go up.' Decisive as ever, Susie tackled the flight in front of her, taking the steps two at a time. 'If he's not down there, come and find me.' She disappeared from Nick's view before had could protest.

She rushed the steps, two flights of eight to the next level. She opened the door on the landing and peered left and right along the corridor. No sound and no sight of Schrader. She refused to believe he could out-pace her and charged at the next flight of stairs driven by a burning urge for vengeance. She blamed him for everything.

At the next level, she opened the door. She could only go left. The corridor ended at the stairwell. She swore she heard footsteps retreating out of sight. It had to be Schrader and she sprinted after him.

The corridor curved to the right as it followed the rear curve of the auditorium. She passed doorways which she guessed gave access to corporate boxes. He could be in any one of them. She slowed to a stop and held her breath for a second. The retreating footsteps continued.

She rushed ahead and kept close to the left wall of the corridor to extend her view. She caught a fleeting glimpse of the hi-viz vest and sped up. Schrader came into view, he had slowed to no more than a laboured jog. He still carried the camera.

Her shoes made little noise on the resin floor, but enough to alert him.

He looked back over his shoulder. The shock on his face made it clear he hadn't heard Susie until then.

At the site of her approach he pushed open the nearest door and disappeared through it. Susie reached it seconds later. She grabbed the handle and pushed. The designers of the building had ensured the door would be soundproof. It took an effort and she felt resistance. It opened it a fraction, and she squinted through the gap. It looked like one of the corporate boxes, lit only by the light from the auditorium below. Working on the basis that Schrader had hidden behind the door, she stood back, placed her foot just below the handle and pushed with all her strength. It swung through ninety degrees and stopped when it hit something solid. If Schrader had stood behind the door, he would have been knocked flat. She stepped forward and leaned into the room. In the half light she could see the small room had been set up for a meeting, a table and eight chairs, notepads, pens and a carafe of water. Double-glazed windows formed the front of the box and sliding glass doors led out onto a sitting area high above the auditorium. The box was sealed tight. She couldn't see Schrader.

She took another small step and heard a noise. It came from the darkest corner of the box at the far end of the table. The muffled sounded of rapid gasping breaths. Without taking her eyes off the source of the noise, she reached behind her for a switch beside the doorframe and with a subdued click, bright overhead spots flooded the room. Schrader crouched on the floor. He had the hi-viz vest held over his mouth like a mask. His reddened face dripped with sweat and his eyes glared with undisguised hate.

When the lights came on, he dropped his mask and picked up the camera, his right hand supported the long grey lens. His left hand held the cable that ran from the it. He pointed it in Susie's direction.

She looked into the lens and saw, for the first time, the gas cylinder that Natalya had described. Her blood ran cold.

She stood stock still, one hand frozen in mid air, the other gripped the edge of the table.

•••••

Nick's concern for Susie left him lacking the enthusiasm to search the basement area of the building. His gut instinct told him that Schrader had gone up, not down. That, and the almost certain knowledge that Susie thought the same, hence her rush to go up before they'd agreed anything.

He opened a few doors, checked a couple of rooms, but his heart wasn't in it. The basement had nowhere to go. If he was on the run, he'd go for the roof, or at least the top floor. He doubled-back to the stairwell and climbed.

•••••

Susie tore her gaze away from the gas cylinder, and fixed Schrader with what she hoped was look of defiance. 'Cornered, like a stinking little whimpering rat.' She spoke to herself, it came out in little more than a whisper, but in the quiet of the room, Schrader could hear every syllable. 'What are you going to do now, creep.' She goaded him.

'Stay back...if you move... I'll pull this.' He gasped the words out between strained breaths. He nodded at the cable as he spoke.

Susie's chin jutted. 'Go on then, I can be out of this door in a second, you'll be stuck behind this table.' She nudged it an inch towards him to make her point.

'You'll...not get...away...in time...the gas...will hit you...like a bul-let.'

'I'll take my chances.' Susie gave the table another push.

Schrader leaned forward and placed his elbows on the table, partly to prevent her pushing it any closer and partly to allow him to aim the camera. His erratic breathing made it impossible to hold it steady. 'I've...got nothing...to lose...how...about you?'

'Suit yourself.' Susie grabbed the edge of the table with both hands.

Convinced he was going to be pushed back to the wall, Schrader threw himself against the table.

Susie timed her move to perfection. She took a deep breath and instead of pushing as expected, she pulled the table towards her in an extended jerk that left Schrader floundering. His left hand abandoned its grip of the camera body and shot out to cushion his fall. The weight of the falling camera body caused the lens to twist in his right hand and end up in his face. In the process he pulled the cable. She didn't stop to see the effect of her actions, the last thing she heard before she dived back into the corridor was a quiet click then a strangled scream. She jumped to her feet and slammed the heavy door closed.

She turned away from the door and almost collided with Nick.

'You find him?' he panted as he pulled up and looked around.

Susie took his arm and steered him away from the door, an urgency in her actions. 'Keep going, he's in there.'

'Why you leaving him?' Nick looked back as Susie speeded up.

'Best we don't go in there, he's just had a close encounter with the contents of that gas cylinder.'

It took Nick a second to realise what Susie meant. A look of panic spread across his face. 'Were you there when it happened?'

'No, it went off in his face, I was out of there before it hit him.'

The pair of them jogged to the stairwell, neither looked back.

••●••

Anna waited in the foyer next to the door to the organisers office. She'd waited while they called the police and witnessed the impressive speed of their response. She resisted the temptation to go into the auditorium to find Susie and Natalya. Within minutes delegates started to emerge. One of the venue staff came out of the office and told her the conference had been suspended and they were evacuating the hall.

She stood to one side and scanned the sea of faces in search of her friend and her sister. Her sister. She still found it hard to believe.

The sea of faces thinned to a trickle then dried up completely. Concerned, she poked her head through the doors to the auditorium and found it deserted. She turned back to the foyer and saw beyond it, out on the terrace, delegates congregated in small groups. She wondered if Susie and Natalya had left by another door. She decided to go in search of them.

Some of the delegates had found seats or benches, others stood in the shade of parasols or trees. Anna weaved her way through them. She cast about, but saw nobody she recognised until she reached the far end of the terrace. Natalya stood with her back to her, she appeared to be talking to a distinguished looking man, a gentleman Anna thought.

Natalya spun around when Anna tapped her on the shoulder. She jumped to her feet and hugged her. 'Where have you been? We've been looking for you.'

'I was waiting outside the hall, I didn't see you come out.'

'Oh, sorry. We came out the side entrance, it was quicker.' Natalya turned to the man she'd been speaking to. 'Dr Archer, this is my little sister, Anna.'

Julian Archer said nothing. Not at first. Then, 'Did you say, sister?'

Natalya saw Archer's expression; the way his features changed, the way his eyes dilated for a moment. 'Yes... I found out last night...'

Anna gazed up at him. 'It's amazing, we can't believe it.'

Archer's eyes smiled; warm and reflective, and he shook his head as though to himself, as the realisation dawned like the light of a new day. His voice fell to a whisper. 'I don't believe it. The chances...'

'I know, it's incredible.' Anna held out her hand. 'I'm very pleased to meet you, Dr Archer. Natalya has told me so much about you.'

Archer reached out and took her hand in both of his. 'Anna. Little baby Anna.' His eyes seemed to cloud.

Natalya's brow furrowed as she tried to make sense of Dr Archer's reaction. 'Do you know Anna? I'm confused.'

Archer released Anna. 'Sorry. That must seem really creepy.'

Anna regained her composure. 'Well. Yes, a little bit.'

'Please forgive me, this is a shock.' He took in a long breath. 'The last time I saw you, you were three months old.'

Anna looked at Natalya, who looked equally confused, then at Archer. She hadn't understood what he had said.

'You're adopted, right?'

Anna nodded, still unsure of Archer.

'And do you know where you were born?'

'As of two days ago. I learned more about my family when I was in Timisoara. That's how Natalya and I discovered we were sisters.'

Archer struggled for the right words. 'Have you ever wondered how you came to be in the UK?'

She hesitated. 'Are you going to tell me you had something to do with it?'

'You're half right. I was working in Timisoara for the UNHCR and came across you in one of those dreadful orphanages.' He squeezed his eyes shut and shook his head as though trying to block out the memory. 'I couldn't leave you. I had two young children of my own and seeing the conditions they kept you in, I had to do something.'

Anna turned slowly and looked at Natalya as Archer spoke. 'Did you know about this?'

Natalya stared at her boss. Disbelief and shock filled her head.

'No, I've never told her,' Archer said.

'Why didn't you take us both? Why did you leave Natalya?' Anna's voice trembled.

'I wish I could have.' The painful memory and the anguish he felt transformed his face. 'I didn't know you had a sister until a few weeks later and by then the authorities had clamped down.'

Anna wanted more detail. 'What did you do?'

They found a table and chairs under a parasol and sat down. 'I tried everything I could, but they made it impossible. There were a few of us who got babies out. You were small enough to hide, but...' He turned and looked helplessly at Natalya. 'I couldn't get you out. I ended up resigning in frustration. I thought I could do more if I wasn't bound by their rules.'

'Is that why you set up Azllomed in Timisoara?' Natalya asked.

Archer nodded. 'I felt I could do more to help if I had a base there.'

Natalya absorbed this information. She said nothing and stared at the ground as she pieced together what she had heard.

'So how did you help Natalya?' Anna asked.

'I did what I could. I found someone who would care for her properly. I kept an eye on her and helped out where I could.'

Natalya looked up. 'Was is you who paid for my school?'

'I couldn't live with myself for not being able to get you out. If I couldn't be there for you, I wanted you to have opportunities and access to a better education...' He tailed off and gave a helpless shrug. 'What else could I do?'

'And University?' Natalya asked.

Archer nodded.

She shifted in her seat and buried her head in her hands.

Anna sat down next to her sister. 'Are you all right?'

'It's a bit of a shock, but it makes sense. I always wondered how Uncle Gheorghe paid for it.'

'Uncle Gheorghe?' Anna repeated.

Natalya smiled and looked at Anna, then she looked at Archer. 'He wasn't really my uncle, was he?'

'He was a good man. He loved you like you were his own. But no, he wasn't your uncle. I met him when I was working for the UN and knew how much he and Cristina wanted a family. I knew they would love you and look after you.'

'You said he was a good man. What happened?' Anna said.

Natalya bit her bottom lip. 'He died; cancer, when I was 18.'

'And Cristina died a year after that in a car accident. It was tragic.' Archer said, eyes closed.

Anna studied Archer's frozen face, then Natalya's, and she realised how painful the memory was to both of them. 'Let's go for a walk and get away from the crowd. It's a lot to take in.' She squeezed Natalya's hand and stood up.

Archer remained seated, unsure if the two women wanted him to join them.

'You too Dr Archer, you can fill us in on some of the details.'

Archer smiled and nodded. He said nothing and followed the two women down the stairs the led to the lakeside promenade.

CHAPTER 31

S usie and Nick retraced their steps down the stairwell and emerged into the service yard. The situation had changed and the chaos they'd left behind had been replaced by a semblance of order. The evacuated delegates had been directed around to the front of the convention centre and police vehicles had parked at random angles inside the yard and on the road outside.

Nick spotted Tim. 'He's over there.' He nudged Susie and nodded towards what he took to be an incident van. A dozen uniformed police stood around chatting, they appeared relaxed.

Tim looked to be in conversation with a woman in a dark blue trouser suit. She had a serious demeanour and made notes as they talked. He looked up when he saw the couple walk over. 'You get your man?'

They glanced sideways at each other as though to agree a pre-determined script. 'You tell him.' said Nick.

The woman who had been talking to Tim, turned to Susie. 'Tell me what?' She spoke English with a trace of an Italian accent, her vowels slightly extended.

'Sorry, I should have said,' Tim interrupted, 'this is Captain Russo, she's in charge.'

'Your friend told me you went back into the building. Why was that?

'Did Tim tell you about the camera?'

Russo looked at Tim for clarification, he shook his head.

Susie responded. 'The man behind this attack had designed a camera with a gas cylinder built into the lens, he came here to kill one of the speakers.'

Russo frowned. 'Where is this man and this camera?'

'That's who we went after, he took the camera back inside after my husband removed it from the Auditorium.' She indicated Nick with a tip of her head.

The Captain's eyes flicked between Susie and Nick, she held her hands out. 'So where is he?'

Nick grimaced. 'Can you get an NBC team here? He activated the gas cylinder in one of the corporate boxes.'

'Number seventeen.' Susie butted in.

'Is he still there?'

'We assume so. We didn't hang around to find out.'

Russo reacted. She called one of the uniforms and spoke rapidly to him. She called two others over and gave them orders. They rushed away to secure the doors from the hall. She turned back to Susie and Nick. 'Were you there when he activated the gas?'

'No, I got out just before, and Nick arrived after I closed the door.'

'Okay, that's good. One of my officers is calling the biological weapons facility in Lausanne but it'll take them an hour to get here. In the meantime, we'll have to keep the place locked down and I need to get statements from all three of you.'

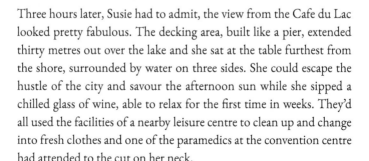

Three hours later, Susie had to admit, the view from the Cafe du Lac looked pretty fabulous. The decking area, built like a pier, extended thirty metres out over the lake and she sat at the table furthest from the shore, surrounded by water on three sides. She could escape the hustle of the city and savour the afternoon sun while she sipped a chilled glass of wine, able to relax for the first time in weeks. They'd all used the facilities of a nearby leisure centre to clean up and change into fresh clothes and one of the paramedics at the convention centre had attended to the cut on her neck.

Nick sat opposite her with his back to the sun. He reclined in his chair, feet stretched out in front, and held a long, slender glass of local beer in both hands. He gazed at his wife.

Susie caught Nick's stare in her peripheral vision. 'What?'

He narrowed his eyes as she met his gaze. 'Just trying to read what your expression is saying. Smug? Content? Relieved? Happy?'

Susie considered the question for a moment. She looked at Nick, pursed her lips and turned slowly to take in their surroundings. Her focus settled on the convention centre three hundred metres away and she contemplated it for a little longer. Finally, she turned back to Nick, her voice full with conviction. 'Validated.'

Nick tipped his head left and right, weighed up the judgement. He nodded. 'Yeah, OK, I get that. Is that another way of saying I told you so?'

'A bit. You were right about my impulsiveness. I know I get carried away at times, but I see it more about having a goal and not being put off when things get a little sticky.' She stopped and waited to see if he disagreed. He said nothing, but watched her closely. 'When I pitched the idea to Greg, I thought there'd be a story there, but never thought I'd open such a can of worms.'

Nick smiled. 'Well, you've certainly got a story love. When this comes out, you're going to have the Nationals all over you.'

'Possibly. Depends what the police say.' She shrugged. 'Captain Russo didn't seem to think we were in any trouble as far as she was concerned but I may have committed a few minor offences in the last couple of days. All totally justified, of course.'

'Well, after giving that interview to the local TV crew, you're going to be easy enough to track down.'

'I don't know, who takes any notice? Just another talking head on the daily news.' She stirred in her seat and looked around. 'Where have those three got to? They said they were popping to the shops for a few essentials. What's the time?' She waved her empty wrist at Nick. 'Bastards took my watch.'

'Just gone two, they've been gone over an hour.'

'I wish they'd hurry up, I'm starving.'

'No surprise there, you must have worked up a bit of an appetite.'

'True, we've survived on junk for the last forty eight hours.'

Nick stood up. 'I'll get some menus, they can't be much longer.'

Susie watched him go, and as she followed his progress, she caught sight of Tim, Anna and Natalya approaching along the lakeside promenade. 'They're here.' She called after Nick.

Nick greeted the new arrivals, who each carried at least one shopping bag. He shook his head in mock disbelief. 'I thought you were just going to get a few essentials.'

Anna grinned at him and held up a bag with a name on it Nick had never seen before 'These are essentials.' She said, her tone defensive.

Tim rolled his eyes at Nick.

Nick chuckled. 'Come one, we've got at table over there.' He indicated Susie, who waved back. 'I've just picked up some menus.'

They picked up drinks and all five mulled over the choice of food for a few minutes then Nick went back to the bar and placed their order. He returned to the table, sat next to Tim and put a hand on his shoulder.

'What's up?' Tim asked, he looked puzzled.

'I haven't had a chance to thank you. Susie told me everything you've done. You've still got it, Ace.'

Tim shook his head. 'I did bugger all, she's pretty fearsome when the red mist descends, I wouldn't like to mess with her.'

Susie caught the end of Tim's remark.

'Just remind Nick every now and then.' She winked at Tim.

'Whatever. Just so you know. I appreciate it.'

Tim raised his beer bottle in acknowledgement. 'You're welcome.'

'What are they doing with those two guys who've been after you?' Anna asked.

Tim shrugged. 'They've taken them away. One of them's pretty badly beaten up and I don't think the taser did much to improve his condition.'

Nick retrieved his beer and took a long pull on it. 'So...' He began, and paused to wipe his mouth and ensure he had the attention of the others. They all turned to look at him. 'So, if those two are the ones who ran Susie off the road...'

Susie nodded. 'And they're the same two that tried to mug me in Reading.'

Nick did a double-take. 'What? You never said anything about being mugged.'

'I wasn't, I never gave it much thought at the time, I thought they were just a couple of local crims.'

'Jeez.' Nick rolled his eyes. 'So they must have been following you.'

Susie shrugged. 'Guess so.'

'So someone must have tipped them off and someone must have told them about your Wednesday morning bike ride. How else would they have know which way you went?'

Susie studied her husband, he'd made a profound statement.

'And.' Nick said, struck by another thought, 'That note someone pushed through the letterbox. How did they know where you lived?'

'I thought...' Susie started, then shook her head. 'It would have to be someone at work.'

Tim listened to the exchange and asked. 'Who did you tell you were going to Slough?'

'Just Greg.'

Anna took a sudden sharp intake of breath, the noise caused the others to turn. 'I've just remembered something.'

Susie, Nick, Tim and Natalya waited for her to say more.

'That kid we tracked down, the one sending the emails.' She looked at Susie.

'What about him.'

'When we left him you said you were going to tell Greg.'

'Uhuh.' Susie frowned, 'But...hang on a minute.' She smacked her palm against her forehead. 'Greg wasn't there. I told Lee to pass the message on.'

'And the next day, the kid had gone.' Anna said.

'Who's Lee?' Tim asked.

'Lee Longmuir, the European ed...' Susie stopped as though hit by a terrible truth, she tipped her head back, stared at the clear blue sky and slowly shook her head.

Nick sat forward. 'What about him?'

'He was in Greg's office when I told him about going to Slough and I've got a map of my bike route pinned up beside my desk. He could have taken a picture of it any time.'

'So...' Nick started again, his eyebrows knitted together. 'So are you saying he's the one giving orders to those two goons?'

Susie snorted at the idea. 'Get real. Those two wouldn't give him the time of day. He must have been talking to someone with money, or power, or influence. Or all three.'

Tim considered this and asked. 'Who does he deal with, day to day.'

'He's back and forth to Brussels a lot, he speaks to MEPs, bureaucrats, hangers-on. You know the sort, nosing round for a story or some insider gossip.'

'Has he ever mentioned anyone in particular?'

'No, he hasn't, but now you mention it, Greg once told me his uncle's an MEP, I think that's how he got the gig.'

Nick appeared to have a moment of insight at this news. He held his bottle of beer to his lips and absentmindedly blew across it's open top making a musical noise like a small friendly fog horn. 'What's his name?'

'Who, the MEP?'

'Yeah.'

Susie screwed her face up as she tried to recall a conversation that took place over a year ago. 'He was a Knight of the Realm.' She pondered a moment longer and tapped the side of her head. 'Sir somebody Lawrence.' She announced as though she provided the winning answer in the local pub quiz.

Nick sat up at this. 'Not, Sir Giles Lawrence?'

'That's him, why?'

'Don't you remember me telling you about him when I came back from that job in Birmingham. He was getting an award from the PM.'

Susie shrugged and looked sheepish. 'Sorry babe, I remember you said something about the PM but I must have zoned out and didn't hear the rest.'

'You Googled him, remember? Big bloke, you commented on his...size.'

'Oh yeah, him.' She held a finger to her chin and looked suitably contrite. 'I never made the connection between him and Lee.'

'Well.' Said Tim, 'He's going to have money and power and influence, isn't he?'

'True. But, if he was being awarded for campaigning against junk email, surely he's one of the good guys.' Anna chipped in.

Nick was more sceptical. 'Sounds like a perfect cover story if you ask me.'

Tim agreed. 'Who would suspect an honest upstanding politician?' The cynicism in his voice accompanied a look of mock outrage.

Susie appeared dubious. 'Even if Lee did blab to his uncle, it doesn't explain who our two friends worked for.'

Natalya had listened to the exchange in silence, but commented. 'They didn't work for Dr Schrader, I'd never seen them before.'

Susie responded, 'No, according to the police Captain, they both had Albanian passports, they were operating in the UK, so it can't have been him.'

'You're forgetting that kid.' Anna said. 'He was scared stiff of someone.'

Susie nodded as she remembered the conversation. 'There's also the small matter of distribution. I ordered and received a packet of those diet pills in the post. Someone organised that, and a website, and all the PR, and the social media, and of course all the emails they were sending out.'

All five sat in silence for a moment as they digested the facts. Susie's shoulders slumped and she exhaled loudly. 'We might have our suspicions but we've got no evidence to tie Lawrence to this. I can point the finger at Lee, but for all we know he was innocently passing on the latest goings on at the magazine to his uncle.'

Tim frowned 'So why would Lawrence be involved, what's in it for him?'

'The cynical answer is money.' Susie said. 'He's an MEP, thanks to Brexit he's going to be out of a job soon enough.'

'Obviously, but apart from being an MEP, does he have any other business?'

Nick had his phone out and appeared engrossed. He suddenly sat forward. 'Something's been bothering me and I've just made the connection.'

The others, shocked into silence, looked at him expectantly

'Remember when you looked him up on Google and you found he had a logistics business?' He spoke to Susie who gave a brief nod.

'Remember what it was called?'

She shook her head and shrugged.

'It was GPL.' Nick pointed at his screen as though the others could see it.

'Okay, is that meant to mean anything?'

'I thought it must be his initials, and it is, his middle name is Philip.'

'That makes sense, but so what?' Susie looked at Nick as if he was losing his marbles.

'Ahh, but...' Nick paused to drag out the tension and savour his find. 'GPL stands for Global Pharmaceutical Logistics. That's why he's involved.' He sat back with a self satisfied look on his face.

Tim gave Nick a playful thump on the arm. 'No shit, Sherlock.'

Something bothered Susie. 'There's a piece missing.' The other four looked at her. She marshalled her thoughts as she spoke. 'If Schrader produced the stuff, and the kid we tracked down was sending out the emails to sell it; are we saying Lawrence was behind the distribution?'

Nick realised what she meant. 'You think it wasn't Sir Giles and his logistics company?'

Susie shook her head slowly as she considered the problem. 'No, he'd never get his hands dirty. People like him never do. I doubt those two thugs ever knew he existed. They must have been getting their orders from someone and it wasn't Schrader.'

Tim sat impassively and listened to Susie's reasoning. 'The tall one, the one who had the knife to your throat.' He paused and saw Susie touch the bandage on her neck. 'When the police searched him, he had a phone on him. They'll be able to see who's been ringing him.'

'That would make sense,' Susie said and agreed. 'You think the Swiss police will follow it up?'

'Oh yes,' said Tim. 'You bet they will. Whoever the middle man was, he can't stay lucky forever.'

They were interrupted by a waiter who arrived with their food. Further discussion ceased as plates were shuffled around on the table until all five had what they'd ordered.

As they started eating, they heard the noise of a phone ringing. They looked at each other and at the collection of phones on the table. 'It's Greg.' said Susie, she tapped her screen to activate the speaker. 'Hi Greg.'

'Well, looks like congrats are in order.' He sounded excited.

They exchanged glances. 'Thanks Greg, but who's told you.' Susie looked at the other four who all shrugged.

'Nobody's told me a thing, I've been watching the news. You're making headlines.'

'Seriously?' She peered at her phone, unable to comprehend what she heard.

'Seriously. They're reporting a foiled terrorist attack and who should I see being interviewed but our very own investigative super-star.'

Susie looked up from the screen and glanced at Nick who beamed back at her. She looked at the other three and they all grinned. 'I thought they were just a local TV crew, I didn't think anyone would see it.'

'Well, you'd better prepare yourself for a shock. You're going to be in demand, you're the hero of the hour.'

'Bloody hell.'

'Now now, you're going to have watch your language if you're going to be on TV.'

Susie gave a little laugh. 'It'll all blow over in a couple of days, I'll have my fifteen minutes of fame then I can get back to work.'

'Don't be so sure, you'll be getting offers from the big boys, they'll tempt you away from me.'

'No chance, Greg, I like it where I am.'

'Hmmm,' Greg didn't sound convinced. 'Just take it easy, we can talk more when you're back. Well done Scoop, one hell of a story.' The line clicked off.

Tim raised his glass. 'I think a toast is in order. To Susie.'

Anna, Natalya and Nick echoed the sentiment and clinked glasses with him.

Susie looked suitably bashful. 'Thanks guys, but I think a more important toast is to you two.' She raised her glass towards Anna and Natalya. 'Whatever else has happened over the last few days, nothing means more than you two finding each other.'

EPILOGUE

Sir Giles Lawrence sat in his study. He sat in silence and stared at the mobile phone that sat by itself on a notepad in the middle of the desk. He reached forward and tapped the screen; it lit up to display the time:14:25.

Schrader still hadn't called.

He expected a call at least two hours ago.

He promised himself that he wouldn't worry. He promised he would remain calm and wait for Schrader to call. He swore he would not relent and make the call himself. Schrader could be busy; he didn't want to disturb him.

DeLuca had called just after nine and assured him that the Jones woman had been taken care of and his two boys had arrived with the equipment. DeLuca had told him not to worry. *Easy for Lucky Frank to say*, he thought, *he's expecting me to pay him when this all goes through*. He considered calling DeLuca but dismissed the idea, he didn't want to give him the impression he was desperate.

The ding-dong of the doorbell broke his reverie. Without moving from his chair, he shouted to his wife. 'Can you get that my dear, I'm expecting Lee.'

He heard a muttered acknowledgement from the kitchen, then footsteps across the hall and the door opening. More footsteps then a knock on the study door.

He counted slowly to ten, then called out. 'Come in.'

Lee Longmuir pushed the door open and took a tentative step into the room. 'Hi uncle Giles, how are you?'

Lawrence rose to greet his older sister's son. He'd proved very useful over the last few weeks and it was time to reward him. 'I'm well Lee, very well indeed.' It never occurred to him to ask after his visitor. 'I'm just waiting for a confirmation phone call then I'll be able to announce a brand new phase in the growth of GPL.'

Longmuir continued to stand in the centre of the room. He knew better than to take a seat without being asked to do so. 'That sounds very exciting uncle Giles, is that why you've asked me here?'

'Absolutely my boy, without knowing it, you've been a key part in the process.'

Lee gave his uncle a puzzled look. 'How do you mean?'

'The information you've provided has been invaluable.' Lawrence tapped the side of his nose.

The puzzled expression intensified. 'What information?'

Lawrence gave an expansive gesture. 'Let's have a drink to celebrate and I can tell you everything.' He turned to a decanter behind his desk while Longmuir stared at Sky news on the muted flat-screen TV.

The online banking screen refreshed, but the figures it displayed, remained the same. Gianfranco DeLuca scowled at it and stabbed at the keyboard to refresh it again. It made no difference. His account showed no payments had been received.

He didn't possess the restraint of Sir Giles Lawrence. He wanted to know. He last spoke to Schrader just before nine after he'd heard from Decebal. He'd called Lawrence and told him the job would be done by eleven. He'd told Schrader to call him as soon as his boys were out and clear.

They had agreed he'd be paid the moment confirmation of Archer's death had been received.

Eleven had been and gone and Schrader hadn't called.

DeLuca had no reason to doubt the job had gone as planned. What could go wrong. They had eliminated the journalist and Archer's assistant, Natalya. They could no longer get to Archer and he would have no warning. All Sergei had to do, was get into the right place and pull a wire.

So why hadn't Schrader called him?

He relented and called. He got no answer. He checked the number and called again. Not even a voicemail message. Schrader always answered the phone. Maybe the man was in a signal dead area. He gave it ten minutes and tried again. Same result, and concern began to gnaw at him.

He told himself to get a grip and wait ten more minutes. When Schrader still didn't answer, DeLuca allowed the concern to grow to worry and he called Decebal. He didn't want to, as he knew the man would be on the run, but he had no choice if he wanted a situation report.

DeLuca waited and counted the rings. He'd reached nine and was about to give up when the phone was answered. He waited for the usual 'yes boss' but there was silence. The silence continued, DeLuca said nothing, he listened intently, he could hear muffled noises but nothing else. Maybe the phone was in Decebal's pocket, and he'd answered without realising? He didn't think it was likely, or even possible, but the notion made him speak. 'Hello.'

A female voice responded and took DeLuca by surprise. 'Hello, who is calling?'

'Shit!' DeLuca killed the call and dropped the handset as though it had suddenly gone nuclear. He glared at it in horror, then with a shame-faced shake of the head, he relaxed remembering it was a burner, nobody could trace the call back to him.

He picked it up again and called his paymaster.

••●••

Lee Longmuir turned from the silent television and watched his uncle pour generous measures of malt whiskey into two tumblers. He enjoyed the occasional drink but had never developed a taste for the hard stuff and certainly never indulged mid-afternoon. He didn't want to appear ungrateful and assumed the occasion must be worthy of a special celebration.

When Lawrence handed him the drink and cheersed him, Longmuir's thanks were effusive he and made a show of savouring the smoky aroma and holding the glass to his lips, even though he inwardly recoiled at the smell and the taste.

'Well Lee, I suppose you're wondering what it is you've done to help?'

Longmuir nodded but thought it best to say nothing.

'You recall telling me about one of the people at your magazine and her investigation into a new weight loss medication?'

Longmuir frowned, 'You mean Susie Jones.'

'That's the one. Well...' Lawrence paused, took a deep breath and squared his shoulders in preparation for his big announcement. 'I've been working with a research chemist in Europe to develop it and today we're ready to launch it to the world. It's test results are amazing, it's going to be worth a fortune.'

'I'm confused, I'm sure I heard her tell Greg, the editor, it was illegal. That's why she was investigating it.'

Lawrence dismissed the notion with a wave of his hand. 'No, she had it all wrong, it was all under wraps, we had to keep it secret until today.'

'What's so special about today then?'

'Today..' Lawrence began before being distracted by something. He stopped speaking and stared over his nephew's shoulder.

Longmuir turned to see what had caught his eye.

The TV showed two presenters discussing the ongoing political and economic fallout from Brexit but a banner along the bottom of the screen, announced a terrorist attack in Montreux.

'Turn it up.' Lawrence's voice sounded suddenly strained. 'The remote's on my desk.' Without taking his eyes off the screen, he jerked his thumb behind him.

Longmuir did as instructed and they heard the presenter finish the discussion and turn to address the camera. 'We go over now to Pierre Bianchi in Montreux.'

The picture switched to a stern-faced reporter in his mid-twenties, who faced the camera, microphone in hand. 'Earlier today a conference of the European Clinical Governance Council was brought to a halt by a suspected terrorist attack that could have left many dead.'

Longmuir's curiosity rose and he shifted uneasily, a feeling of dread crept up his spine.

The reporter continued. 'The attack appears to have been foiled by the actions of a UK journalist, Susan Jones.' The reporter turned to his side and the camera pulled back to show Susie standing next to him.

Susie's words were drowned out by a thump and crash as the heavy lead crystal tumbler fell from Lawrence's hand and smashed the glass-topped coffee table in front of them.

Longmuir jumped at the noise and looked sideways at his uncle, to see his hand thinking it still held the whiskey. The colour had drained from his face. His mouth gaped open and his eyes looked as though they would burst from their sockets.

'Uncle Giles.' Confusion and concern swirled around Longmuir's brain.

Lawrence staggered and grabbed at Longmuir's shoulder for support. He took a step backwards and sank into the armchair behind him, his eyes still glued to the screen.

Longmuir's attention was diverted by movement outside. He glanced up and saw a police car heading up the drive.

Lawrence breathed rapidly, he clutched a hand to his chest and squeezed his eyes tight shut. He appeared to be in extreme pain.

Then his phone rang. He'd left it on his desk. 'Get that for me Lee.' He ordered between laboured breaths.

Longmuir passed the phone to his uncle, while watching the police car roll to a stop at the front door. He didn't want to add to the older man's stress by saying anything, but his curiosity jumped another notch.

Lawrence's phone continued to ring, he stared at the screen. It wasn't the call he had been waiting for, it was DeLuca. He accepted the call and activated the speaker function. 'Have you seen the news?' The other man's voice sounded tense.

Lawrence was about to answer when he heard the doorbell, followed by familiar footsteps in the hall.

'Did you hear me?' Have you seen what's happened?' DeLuca's voice increased in volume.

'Yes.' Lawrence snapped. The monosyllabic response was all he could manage, as he tried to hear the conversation at the front door.

'This changes nothing you still owe me, I've done everything we agreed.'

The study door opened, and Lawrence turned to see his wife stand back while two policemen walked in.

The Author

The inspiration for Sharp Focus came from years the author spent working as a pro photographer and specialising in event work, conferences and exhibitions and seeing how freely he was able to move around and how close he was to people who would normally be protected by many layers of security. Duncan has been a keen triathlete for almost 40 years and apart from competing, he's organised events, ran the governing body and started the magazine 220, which is still going today.

Duncan lives in rural Derbyshire with his wife Frances and a collection of four-legged friends.

For more information and news about forthcoming books, join *Team Susie*, at duncanrobbauthor.com or follow duncanrobbauthor on Facebook

The next book in the Susie Jones series - Four Meals From Anarchy – comes out in the Spring of 2023 – you can read the first 1,000 words of the prologue at the end of this book.

If you've enjoyed Sharp Focus, this author woud really appreciate an honest review on Amazon (or wherever else you've read it) it makes a huge difference and means a great deal.

Acknowledgments

It would be impossible to write a book of any description without the help and support of others.

Over the (many) years it's taken to bring Sharp Focus to you the reader, friends and family have been a constant source of encouragement and I am grateful to them all. In particular my darling wife Frances who not only has a sharp eye for detail but is an invaluable sounding board, able to come up with suggestions and alternatives when I back my characters into a corner or leave a plot hole wide enough for an elephant. I'm sure I have tested her patience and tolerance to the limit but she never fails to pull something out the bag.

Thanks also to A J Humpage whose coaching and editorial advice has sharpened up the narrative and corrected some truly horrible literary howlers. She writes an excellent blog – All Write, which I can't recommend enough.

Book Two - Prologue

Due to be released in the early Spring of 2023.
Four Meals From Anarchy
The second Susie Jones book.

Prologue

The cable writhed and twisted like an evil serpent in its death throes. The inner metal wires curled in on each other, different materials expanded and contracted at different rates, the copper pushing out, the zinc alloy pulling in. Some elements fused together, others pushed apart. Sparks jumped between the strands of wire, the heat grew intense, the metal braiding glowed red hot, the outer pvc casing slowly melted, dissolving into a muddy liquid then evaporating as an acrid black smoke.

Viktor Volkov and Dmitry Egorichev watched in ghoulish fascination from behind the half inch thick glass screen. They couldn't smell the smoke or hear the popping of wires as the heat eventually caused them to crumble. All they could do was watch. For a full five minutes they said nothing, eyes wide, mouths gaping as the scene played out. From the moment Viktor pressed the activation button to the last whisper of smoke being sucked out by the extractor fan, it had only taken five minutes for six feet of data cable to be reduced to a black stain on the white resin floor of the chamber. After months of experiments, after trying hundreds of radical algorithms, after one failure following another, it had worked. They had developed a virus that would not only render software useless but physically destroy the hardware, the wiring, the logic boards, the microchips and anything attached to them. They turned to each other and high-fived, grinning like a pair of naughty schoolboys.

They were a little older than schoolboys, Viktor 29, Dmitry 28, but they behaved as if they were ten years younger. They'd been hacking into computer systems for over ten years and creating viruses for most of that time, viruses that had already caused damage conservatively estimated in the tens of millions of US dollars. Their notoriety had brought them to the attention, firstly of organised crime leaders, then the SVR who discovered them while breaking up the gang the two geeks had found themselves working for. Initially the SVR dismissed Viktor and Dmitry as a couple of computer nerds, clever, but ultimately harmless. It was only when the intelligence agency delved deeper into the activities of the two young men that their true genius was realised and they were put to work on behalf of the State.

To Mecheslav Medvedev, the head of the computer infiltration programme, they were his prize possession and he guarded them jealously. He handled them like a protective uncle, giving them anything they wanted, denying them nothing and attending to their every need.

Not that the required much; nether drank, smoked or took drugs, they ate little and showed no enthusiasm for the women he supplied. He arranged adjoining apartments for them in a brand new luxury development in the Arbat district, a popular area for government employees. They were chauffeured to the office every day as neither of them drove and they rarely went out. They had little contact with their families, their choice, and were content, or even thrilled to spend long days in front of a computer screen or experimenting with specialist equipment, experimental systems and sophisticated instruments. Medvedev was astonished at the speed they acquired new skills The office he assigned to them was more like a laboratory and provided they had a regular supply of fresh coffee, the two of them would work late into the night or the small hours of the next day, making few demands on him or his staff other than a hunger for new challenges or a fresh target. Their brief was simple; develop new ways to attack Western intelligence and create maximum infrastructure damage, with particular emphasis on computer systems and commercial operations.

Dmitry was the first to identify the possibility of the creating a computer virus that could do physical damage. Along with Viktor, he had devoted his efforts to software programmes that could be delivered by email to personal computers or direct injection into servers. They had proved highly effective and caused considerable embarrassment to government departments, utility companies and multi-national companies. But Dmitry wanted more. Their victims were fighting back, security systems more and more difficult to infiltrate, and to make matters worse they were starting to trace the source of the viruses back to Russia. What really concentrated Dmitry's mind was the fact that however much damage he did, however much data his victims lost, they had developed back up systems and could restore the software within a few days. Reputations might suffer and the Western press loved to highlight the failings of big business to protect the data it held, but ultimately everything was back to normal after a week.

Dmitry wanted more, he wanted to create lasting damage. He and Viktor had been the outstanding students in their class, leagues ahead of the others, they'd seen the disruption that a virus could do and got a vicarious satisfaction from seeing the headlines. It frustrated Dmitry that it was short lived, and he knew he could do better. The pair recognised the weakness in most viruses. They relied on their victims taking some sort of action for the damage to be done. They needed to find a way to target specific devices at a time of their choosing and then deliver their virus, surgically inject it, in such a way that their victim would know nothing about it, until it was activated. A sleeping bug, awaiting the command of its master. It was Viktor who came up with a name for it, it had to have a memorable name, and seeing it come back to life after lying dormant for a six month trial he called it Aurora, the sleeping beauty, if the name was good enough for Tchaikovsky it was good enough for him. He conveniently ignored the connection to Disney.

They watched a moment longer as the chamber cleared, three feet long, eighteen inches high and 12 inches deep, it had an hermetically sealed lid with a single outlet at the back connected to a 4 inch wide flexible rubber pipe that sucked the poisonous fumes through a series of filters, before venting them to the outside world. Viktor released the catches on the lid, opening it cautiously before prodding the remains of the cable with a steel ruler. 'We need to call Dracula and let him see this.'

Dmitry was still grinning at the effects of the virus. 'It might even put a smile on his face.' Medvedev rarely smiled, his dour demeanour and dark features made the nickname the two referred to him by, almost inevitable.

...if you want advanced notice of the publication of Four Meals From Anarchy, sign up with Team Susie here.

Printed in Great Britain
by Amazon